Large Print Book Program

Donated and Funded Equally by

**Rhode Island Lions
Sight Foundation, Inc.**

**Lions Clubs
International Foundation**

1986

**District
42**

R.I.

*North Smithfield
Lions Club*

ADVENTURE IN ROMANCE

To Crystal Stevens, Cornwall seems a romantic county, and in accepting a post there as companion to the bedridden Mrs. Tregarth she feels that she is striking out for herself, and leaving behind the commonplace routine she has known before. But Crystal little realises the nature of the situation in which she finds herself, nor what frightening experiences she will be called upon to undergo before she is through with her adventure. This is the exciting story of Crystal's sojourn at the sinister and mysterious mill-house, and of how she wins through to true love and the hope of happiness.

ADVENTURE IN ROMANCE

URSULA BLOOM
as Sheila Burns

A Lythway Book

CHIVERS PRESS
BATH

37140

First published 1955
by
Hutchinson & Co (Publishers) Ltd
This Large Print edition published by
Chivers Press
by arrangement with
the author's estate
1986

ISBN 0 7451 0259 X

Revised edition 1986

British Library Cataloguing in Publication Data

Bloom, Ursula
   Adventure in romance.—Large print ed.,
  Rev. ed.—(A Lythway book)
  I. Title   II. Burns, Sheila, *1895–1984*
  823′.912[F]   PR6003.L58

  ISBN 0–7451–0259–X

ADVENTURE IN ROMANCE

CHAPTER ONE

I

The adventure in romance began that afternoon in spring when the light was bright on the trees in the park, and the pigeons in the city cooed to one another in sentimental ecstasy.

The city office was one of those aggravating ones that opened until twelve on a Saturday morning, when all the others had discreetly closed. Crystal had accepted the job, and she had never thought of asking about this; it was one of those things that no self-respecting girl would expect from an office, and she had taken it for granted that they did not open during the week-end. Nobody else did, so why should they?

Afterwards, it was too late. Any mistakes were always too late when working for a stout and earnest gentleman like Mr. Hellston, who himself apparently never made mistakes, and prided himself on this! Besides, she had been so scared of not getting the job that, even if she had known about this, it is doubtful if she would have refused it.

Everything had depended on her acceptance of the post.

It would have been a very different thing if Crystal had been a member of a large family

1

with countless benign uncles and aunts to take her in; with fond parents, and with a large comfortable home where she was ever welcome. She had no one to whom she could turn, and none who would say, 'If you get on the rocks, dear, come along to us, and at least we shall be able to pop some butter on your bread.' She had hardly any relatives. There was her great-aunt Victoria, it is true, but Great-Aunt Victoria lived an extremely dull existence in the north of London, and nursed the lamentable opinion that all modern young men were cads, and all modern young women were sirens. There was really no hope of getting any comfort out of Great-Aunt Victoria, and they had met perhaps three times in their lives, quite plainly hating each other on sight.

Crystal was the product of a romantic young couple who had fallen desperately in love and had run away. They had been so happy with each other and had nursed the belief that if they loved sufficiently, the fates would be kind to them. In each other they had the greatest gift that life could offer to them, and they were rich in happiness. Following a star, they had gone hand in hand along the road to their own enchanting adventure.

Crystal's father had been an artist, who painted pictures of the sea that he adored. Her mother had gone in for music. She had done this against the wishes of her family, who thought that there was no future in chamber concerts, and a grand piano; they felt that the only wise thing for a girl to do in life was to have a sound secretarial training and abide by it, with the idea of ultimately marrying the managing director.

The young couple had gone off and had married in a state of utter bliss. They had travelled about the Continent, her father painting seascapes in all the loveliest places: Malta, where the eye and ear watched over the Grand Harbour, and the flowers smelt so sweetly in the Barracca gardens. Capri, with the bluest sea in the world. Algiers, with the Voice summoning the faithful to prayer, the tinkle of bells, and the sea, always tranquil and amiable, caressing the shore with its tideless waves.

Her mother got occasional engagements in local restaurants, and played on into the early mornings when the dawn flushed the east with rose and amber. It was, of course, not the career for which she had studied, but at the same time, it *was* music. The people of these countries listened tenderly to Schumann, and Beethoven, and Liszt. They loved it. They recognized the great masters, and that was something of a triumph to the young girl.

Of course money was close; there were times when they had to be content with a roll of bread, and a little fruit. They laughed about it, for had they not got love? And was not love the most tender happiness ever?

Crystal was born in Hamburg on a spring afternoon when the Alster was coming to life after a long winter which had been bitterly cold. She was born in their humble lodging, unexpectedly soon; it was one of those tall, thin houses, in a little crooked street behind Brahms's house, where the doves cooed, and the green vine climbed pleasantly and opened vigorous new leaves to the sunlight. Soon the honeysuckle would be in flower in festoons of pale pink and bright yellow.

They called the child Crystal because they felt that crystal was always so beautiful. It shone for ever, and still crazily in love with each other they believed that this child would go far, and do great things. Was she not the daughter of their love? And they felt it to be the greatest love the world had ever know.

The child's early memories had been of a vague, nomad life, when nobody had any money and often very little to eat. They wandered from town to town with no abiding place. The little girl spoke fragments of so many languages that it is doubtful if she ever knew one of them coherently, but that did not matter. She could ask for bread, and sometimes that was the most important thing of all. Her people laughed a lot, and worked very hard, believing that one day a ship would come in, bringing gifts most rare.

'That will be the day!' her mother would say, and clap her hands.

'That will be the day,' her father had echoed gaily.

Some days are destined never to be born. Her father had become grievously sick. His lungs had been threatening a break-down for some time. At first they treated it casually, they could not believe that life would be unkind to them, for fate was a charming person. Had she not helped them so much already?

But there came the time when landladies did not like the sound of her father's cough, when doctors shook their heads; finally that dreadful day when he was committed to the hospital. Crystal never remembered when she last saw him, or even when he actually died, for by that time her mother had left her with the kind nuns in a small convent school just outside Paris.

Then the war came.

In the end it was her mother who took Crystal away, for she became unduly nervous in the early days of the war. She had a premonition that hostilities would stretch across France, and before the victory came too much would be lost. She had tired of France, and for the first time she took Crystal back home to England. When they had established themselves in lodgings together, she launched out into the routine of concerts for the Forces, and was prepared to work herself to death for this end. The child went to a convent in the Midlands, very different from the amiable and pretty

5

surroundings of the one just outside Paris, of course, but a kind place.

She grew to love the white-washed chapel with the statues, and the nuns who walked with their rosaries chinking slightly, and the quietly friendly Mother Superior who always saw after the girls, and loved them all.

In 1942, a bomb killed her mother.

The child knew that it was bad news when she went into the Reverend Mother's little room, with the first snowdrops in a Benares bowl on the table, and the distant scent of incense blown in from the chapel. The curious thing was that she did not find herself crying, and she could not fill herself with a vivid remorse, because when she came to think more closely about it all, she knew that she had never really known her mother.

Through the years she had been just a waif child, a shadow at the heels of her father and mother deeply and passionately in love with each other. The picture faded. Dying was the memory of the little restaurants where *Maman* worked, restaurants with the smell of spiced food, of omelettes and of coffee with the pale blue percolators that had always struck her as being so pretty. The trips they had taken into Italy, into Austria with the little houses with their curved roofs, and the window-boxes spilling bevies of petunias in imperial colours. The hyacinth mountains, rising in silver points, and the waterfalls crashing down them.

She had been nothing but a leaf in the storm that had suddenly risen to blow so defiantly across shattered Europe. It seemed to her as she stood in the Reverend Mother's study, with the first snowdrops in their Benares bowl, that this mother was far nearer to her, and they knew each other better than she had ever known the woman who had given her life.

She had inherited the reddish-brown hair that her mother had possessed, and the hazel eyes with flecks of jade in them, framed with the long black lashes which she had once admired in her handsome father's face. She had a peach-like Scandinavian skin, warm and beautiful, and a figure that was *svelte* and willowy. She was going to be very pretty, but as she grew up more and more, there came to her the knowledge that she was wretchedly and bitterly alone. The convent was always kind to her, and had accepted her as one of the liabilities that war brings to distressed countries. Once the Reverend Mother had written to Great-Aunt Victoria in Hampstead, and had made inquiries as to whether there were any other living relatives who could share some of the expenses which, with the years, mounted up. She asked only the most modest remuneration for all the sympathetic care and expenditure that had been made on the child's behalf.

Perhaps it was only to be expected that she

had met with the most singular defeat.

Great-Aunt Victoria was a spinster lady who prided herself that she had never spent a farthing awry, and was most certainly not going to start doing it now that she was in the seventies! She told the Reverend Mother just what she thought about the letter. She had strongly disapproved of the marriage of which Crystal was the outcome. She insisted that her dead mother and father had been two crazy young people who instead of taking proper employment and earning their daily bread in the accepted manner, had deliberately committed themselves to the silly arts, and in consequence had suffered for their nonsensical ideas.

She sat back contentedly after having despatched her letter to the convent. If some silly old Reverend Mother was thinking that Great-Aunt Victoria would part with a farthing for a great-niece who could not help herself, then, wrote Great-Aunt Victoria, the Reverend Mother had better think again. Because she wouldn't. Never, never, never, each one of them heavily underlined.

She never gave the matter another thought.

The convent did not despair; they completed their job of giving the child the best education that was possible for her. She wasn't clever. She found lessons trying, even though she did work hard, and examinations were a positive nightmare, for she did not pass a single one of them. She painted pleasantly, but not with the talent that had most certainly flowed through her father's fingers. She played the piano well, but not well enough for a world in which there was always a very vigorous competition. She would not make her living that way.

The nuns were continually telling her so, and if a girl had to earn her daily bread and put a little butter on it, not to mention succeeding it with a nice piece of cake, then she had to take home a thing called a pay packet every Friday night, and it had to be a large one.

'If you went through a secretarial course, it would mean that whatever happened you would have knowledge to fall back on,' suggested the Reverend Mother quietly.

They had been so nice to her that she did not see how she could refrain from following their good advice. She couldn't. She played for safety, and did what she was told, with the result that she became a secretary.

II

She found the course at the secretarial college extremely trying and was alarmed lest in the long run she would not be able to pass. She did pass, however, and worked first of all for a solicitor in a dull little midland town, lodging at a hostel. The work was not inspiring, and she had not realized when she had embarked on it, that it could be so distressingly difficult. There

9

were so many words in the language of a solicitor that had never come inside the convent. She hated the hostel where there was no privacy, and everything seemed to be frayed, shabby, and general property.

But she stayed for two years with the solicitor, because the Reverend Mother (her only real friend) had pointed out the major importance of getting a good reference. During that time, again acting on the Reverend Mother's advice, she had gone to a night school in a frantic attempt to perfect herself in another language. After all, as a tiny child she had had a conversational smattering of at least four of them, so that when she came to think of it, they couldn't be so difficult.

But they were difficult; and the old trouble of the examination room cropped up again. She did not do well, becoming over-nervous, so that she knew it was most unlikely that she would ever pass. In the end she gave up the idea.

She came to London acting on a sudden impulse, and took a job in the suburbs, working in a dull office on the north side of a street in Sheen. It seemed to her that none of the people she met in that office were really alive, and they never would live, she was sure. The salary was skimping, for she found it far more expensive to live even in the cheapest digs in London than it had been in the provincial hostel.

The salary in Sheen hardly went round, and

dedicated her to intolerable bun lunches for ever. She searched madly for other employment and spent a lot of her money on stamps which brought no replies. It had been a year ago, when, by the grace of God, she had found Messrs. Hellston, Wargrave and Rogers, who had replied to her inquiry, and to Messrs. Hellston, Wargrave and Rogers she had gone immediately for an interview.

She got the job.

The firm paid well, if not extravagantly, because they believed in getting the best. Her particular work was for Mr. Hellston himself, a large blond gentleman in the fifties, with a roving eye, and a great deal of conceit and pomp, which at times were more than trying. He liked to paint his own portrait as a sophisticated *roué*; he liked to talk of dark mink ties, and blue mink wraps, of solitaire diamonds, and holidays in the warmest part of the Riviera. He was surprised that Crystal knew the Riviera, though hardly in the way he did, but she knew it.

She came to the conclusion that there are men who in the middle years go in for that sort of conversation in a suggestive manner, hoping to give the impression of having been gay dogs. Mr. Hellston had never been a gay dog. That was obvious.

The other girls sympathized with her.

'Oh, he's just seeing how the land lies; he is

always doing that.'

It did not sound encouraging.

Mr. Hellston went on seeing how the land lay, and talking roguishly of the holidays which friends could take together, and looking at her out of the corners of his eyes. She didn't like it, but she had got to keep the job. Whatever happened she wanted to stay here, because a great deal depended on it. It was the first decent job she had had, though when she started to think more closely about Mr. Hellston, she wasn't so sure that it *was* a decent job!

In the self-service café at the corner, where one scrambled through cheap lunches in record time, she often met Tony Thorpe. He was a clerk in Timpkins's, a spruce little office down the street. He hated the work there and was continually dreaming of better times when he could get other and more suitable employment, but like her own, this had been the only job that had offered itself.

He was now hoping to win one of the really big football prizes, and like thousands of other young men lived for the day. He worked hard with it. It would have to be none of those trumpery little wins, he told Crystal as they ate in the self-service, none of those two-pound-ten touches (he had had two of them already, and if it hadn't been for the worst possible bad luck, the last time would have entailed a seven-thousand-pound win). But one of these days a telegram would come, and he would know that he was in the money. That would take him out along the high road to adventure, and he awaited it.

'Money makes all the difference in the world to the sort of life that one can live,' he told Crystal over welsh rarebit and baked beans.

'I know that, but I have never been able to try it myself.'

He sighed heavily.

'It always seems to be such a shame that only the old get rich. When money is all the good in the world to you, you don't have a bob to spare! You have to be fifty before you find the way, and when you are fifty you might just as well be dead, you're almost that, anyway.'

'I suppose you are.'

He said, 'Have you ever taken a peep inside the Daimlers and the Rolls-Royces? The cars that really matter? If you have, then you have only seen old faces looking back at you. It's a fact.'

His own young face was powdered with light brown freckles, and he had eyes like cornflowers. He made a little grimace of dismay.

'Maybe,' said Crystal comfortingly, 'you will win one of the enormous prizes in the pools, years and years before you're fifty?'

'If I don't, I'll drown myself. I have all sorts of good ideas of what to do with it. I want to go down the Grand Canal in Venice, and hear the

13

gondoliers singing as they go along. I'd adore to see the Austrian Tyrol, and the Steppes.'

'The Steppes? You really do want to see some of the most extraordinary things, and I doubt if you would be frightfully keen on the Steppes if you really saw them. There are lots of more exciting things. The *Langelinie* in Copenhagen, Hamburg, where I was born, Capri, the Kasbah. Lots of things.'

He became suddenly serious, looking at her with the cornflower-blue eyes that were so provocative. 'You'd be the most wonderful companion to travel with. What a sickening shame it is we have not got the money to marry, and go round the world to see all the adventurous places we want so much to visit, and to go together!'

'I shall never marry.'

'But of course you will, you know you will.'

'Most certainly I shall not.'

He said, 'You're beautiful, don't tell me you did not know it? You have the queerest lights in those hazel eyes of yours. I'd marry you and adore to do it, but I'm in the same position as the little old church mouse, who eats the bellows of the church organ, because there isn't the wherewithal to buy anything else. I'd want to give you pearls to wear, and those long-stemmed roses in winter; the sort of flat that film stars live in, with white fur rugs everywhere; and then we'd travel. We'd go everywhere.'

The woman who ran the self-service looked in their direction.

'We'll have to go,' said Crystal.

They got up and went back to work in dismal offices where nothing exciting ever happened, and where the work mounted up and very often the powers-that-be were in a temper.

Tony was a pet! Crystal liked him, she knew, and she agreed that it was a shame that he hadn't a bob, like thousands of other young men of his age, but that was the way that life worked out. That night when she went back to her digs, she thought again, and perhaps more vividly, of her own daringly romantic parents, who had just gone off and had got married on nothing! It had been singularly courageous! They had starved and feasted across Europe on the most romantic adventure of all, and even if at times they were utterly miserable, and often very hungry, they had been ideally happy at other times, and always content with their lot.

But it made rather a mess of my life for me! she thought.

The joy of the new job with the decent pay packet every Friday night, the sort of pay packet that could allow for a few extras (provided one used caution), had enabled her to move to bigger digs.

The house was an old one overlooking the park, and once upon a time a highly respectable middle-class family had lived in it, where today

15

it was split into the occupation of three large flats. The clean windows looked out upon the profuse park, where the plane trees tossed their leaves in summer, and the flowers blossomed pleasantly. Mrs. Biggins was clean and busy, but her major trouble was that she was what is known as over-respectable. She belonged to a religious sect that disliked dancing and playing cards, and eschewed gentlemen friends. On the occasions when Crystal and Tony went to a cinema, they had to part at the far end of the Albert Bridge Road, for if Mrs. Biggins had seen him, she would have dismissed Crystal as her tenant for ever.

Mrs. Biggins meant well, too well probably. She was a Rechabite, a T.T., and a strong supporter of the proper ritual intended for a seventh day of rest. No cooking that day. No fuss. Nobody had ever managed to talk her down, not even Mr. Biggins, and one evening when she was feeling slightly low-spirited after a violent attack of influenza she confided the real truth about Mr. Biggins, who had never been seen. He wasn't really dead as all the world imagined, and on which score she had managed to get a lot of comforting sympathy. Mr. Biggins had been one of those perverse men who had gone his own way. He had been most unkind, for ever sneering at the uprightness of Mrs. Biggins, and the rather horrifying cleanliness of the home. He had slid about on small mats, and

16

had got into trouble through marking this and that.

One day he had walked out of the house with never a word, and when the evening came, Mr. Biggins had not returned. It was an unfortunate thing that the weekly pay packet went with him, and it was natural that his wife was a good deal more concerned about that than she could possible have been about the lost love and admiration of the man who had led her to the altar, and had given her his name.

She had spent a mint of money on trying to pursue him, for her sense of virtue had raged against his atrocious behaviour. For some time nobody had been able to help her, in spite of all she had spent, and then he was discovered in Ealing, which he apparently thought was a safe distance away. He was engaged in a pleasant little greengrocer's business there, had a cart of his own, so that what was left over from Saturdays, could be sold in the streets on Sundays when Mr. Biggins in person became something of a spiv!

All that was bad, and had worried Mrs. Biggins considerably, but there was worse to come, for the wretched man now declared that he had remarried, believing he had turned his back on all the previous life, and he had produced what his wife could only call 'a black-haired piece!' It was bigamy!

The first and only legal Mrs. Biggins was not

the kind of woman who could submit to treatment of this sort, and give way to a spurious wife, and say nothing about it. She sought the comfort of the police, and Mr. Biggins went to prison.

'It was what he deserved,' said she, not in the least regretful for him.

When he finished his sentence, he did not leave prison chastened and repentant. Instead he left it breathing fire and fury about having lost his love, to whom he promptly returned, and they went on living exactly as they had done before. He never gave a penny to his real wife, or, as she called herself, 'the woman who had suffered for him', with the result that she had to let lodgings to keep the wolf from the door.

During the few months that Crystal had already spent in Mrs. Biggins's house, she had gathered that without a doubt this was not the kind of landlady with whom one could play tricks. Mrs. Biggins would do anything for her, there was in fact no limit to her kindness, but it all had to be done her own way; any other way would never do.

The bed-sitter was large and charming. Well furnished, it had the merit of great cleanliness and always looked fresh and beautiful. It was lovely to look out on the trees of the park, to wake in the morning to hear the birds singing as though one was in the country, and the voices of children playing on the green. The food that was

18

brought her was well cooked, and pleasantly served, and for all this one could put up with a self-righteous, stout little woman who nursed a resentment against life, and thought that she had been 'hard done by'.

Crystal hoped that Mrs. Biggins's amiable *ménage* would last for ever.

It didn't!

III

It was a Saturday in the spring.

Already there were serious signs of disturbance in Battersea Park, for the boats had all been brought out of winter quarters, cleaned up and launched on to the lake for the summer. The trees were thickly budded, primroses and crocuses spattered the grass profusely. By the Old English garden the flowers were quite abundant, and gave the impression that the sweet of the year was coming in. The almonds had cast pale pink tears on the cold earth, the prunus still showered blossoms; soon there would be the roses, and all the vivid beauty of the summer time.

Recently Mr. Hellston had been very trying.

He had discovered soon after Christmas that he was considerably overweight, and had gone into a home, where he had undergone a most difficult cure. His temper had never been the same since. He must have had a very ill-advised doctor, Crystal and Tony thought, for this

19

doctor had encouraged Mr. Hellston with all sorts of fancy stories about his returned youth.

When Mr. Hellston reappeared at the office, he looked coy, and he talked still more whimsically of blue mink and diamond bracelets. Spring had gone to his head.

Today he had come up from the country for some very special work, he had warned Crystal of this only last night, and he wanted some special attention for it. Somehow, when she rose and looked out across the new green of Battersea Park, Crystal had known that this was going to be difficult. Then she made a big mistake. She put on the big new grey coat that she had bought in a fit of wild extravagance, and on the principle of 'Anyway, what does tomorrow matter? I may be dead before it comes'. The coat had been purchased at the new little shop in the King's Road, Chelsea, posing flatteringly in the window, and as it went so well with her soft grey frock, the one she only wore on high days and holidays, Crystal had gone inside, and although it was much more than she could afford, she had bought it.

Today there were those bright clear skies that signify later trouble. Looking out you would have thought that summer had come already, for you could almost see the leaves bursting on the trees. There was the acrid scent of flowering currants, of spring flowers, and blots of pale pink blossom all along the drive in the park. It would be just the day for the new spring hat, the wicked little hat that she should never have bought, but had done so to go with her coat. She popped it on to her reddy-brown hair, a grey, twirling little hat with a bunch of veiling, and because she now was in the mood that cannot say no to a good idea, she tucked a bunch of violets into her coat.

She knew that she looked like a million dollars.

She walked to the bus in the King's Road, and went along to the city by a devious route. It did not matter. Usually on a Saturday morning Mr. Hellston was late.

She was set down by St. Paul's, rising in a great memorial over a city strangely empty at this time of the week. She walked down the familiar street, with the too-tall offices on either side of it, so that the real daylight never penetrated to the pavement itself, and the sunshine never spattered it. On a Saturday morning the city had the week-end atmosphere, and grew sleepy. Somehow Crystal had never got over the habit of resenting the fact that she had to come here on such days, when in both of the other offices where she had worked, there had been no suggestion whatsoever of Saturday mornings. The pay might be good, most certainly it was, and she had been able to afford all manner of small private extravagances like the new grey coat, the dove dress, and the absurd little hat; the work was easy and she did manage to get away earlier than most; but the week-end penalty stuck in the throat.

She climbed up the stairs with their peeling lino, and the funny pieces of broken flooring. The offices of her firm were on the second floor, and she opened the lift door, closing it as a precautionary measure behind her, for Mr. Hellston had a nasty habit of listening for this, and bounding out if it was omitted.

Crystal went inside.

She supposed that as offices went this was a pleasant one. The typists' outer room was commodious, and had that detestable fluorescent lighting which the firm thought was wonderful, but which Crystal disliked. The desks were the right height, the chairs comfortable, and the machines entirely modern. The cloak-room for the girls had a clean mirror, good basins, and decent soap. It was not the frowsty little dark hole most ladies' cloaks became, and some proper attention was paid to it. It was a nice office, but absurd as it might be, everybody was always complaining about it.

Crystal tidied herself, took up her papers and pen, and then went down the passage to Mr. Hellston's own room.

Crystal tapped at the door.

'Come in,' he commanded.

The moment that she went inside she realized that it was one of those mornings! It had been absurd to arrive here in her dove–grey frock with the bunch of violets. A coincidence, of course, that Mr. Hellston was wearing his new spring suit, and that he had a primrose in his buttonhole. She didn't know why the sight of the primrose irritated her, but it did. The air of the office was not Saturday morningish, it was piquant, it was flirtatious, and Mr. Hellston was smiling with a slightly overdone amiability, and rubbing his large fat hands together. In spite of the cure that he had undergone, and his devout attention to the demands of a non-starch diet, he was still very stout. He had a melon-shaped face, pale and flabby, and had been born with mouse colouring. Everything about him was non-committal and pale, eyes, hair, and mouth. One really hardly noticed if he had eyelashes and brows, for most certainly they, too, were pale!

'Ah, here we are!' said Mr. Hellston, apparently bursting with the joys of spring and smiling benignly.

She shut the door behind her, and went over to the chair specially prepared for her on Mr. Hellston's right-hand side. He was now prepared to deal with the post, for the letters were strewn before him and the tortoise-shell paper-knife ready to rip them open.

'A pleasant day,' said Mr. Hellston affably; and then, 'You are looking very charming, if I may say so. But I should have said that you needed a nice little dark mink tie to go with that enchanting shade of grey. They are most becoming.'

Crystal had heard that one before! She made no answer, for she realized that it would be only asking for trouble, and experience had taught her it never worked out well. Whatever happened she had *got* to keep this job.

'Going out somewhere nice?' he asked her, in that silliest mood of his, all sparkle and smiles.

'I *was* going out. It's nothing much, only the pictures this afternoon with a friend.'

'A boy friend?'

'Well, yes, it *is* a boy friend,' she admitted, knowing that he wanted to know everything about it, and that she was not prepared to tell him.

'Now that's a pity, for I had intended asking you out to lunch with me.' He prinked the primrose with a fat finger. 'Hence this! It is the day for lunching out, and something perhaps of a royal command.'

'I'm awfully sorry, but I am meeting Tony outside the tube station at a quarter to one.'

This was a mistake, and she recognized it as being one the moment she had said it, for the large bland face wilted noticeably. He pulled himself up just a shade in his chair, an uneasy movement that she knew well, and was quick to recognize its significance. 'I'm sorry. I thought you would be delighted to lunch with me, and I have already booked a table for us at the Caprice.'

'If—if I—I had only known last night, Mr. Hellston, I could have arranged this. I could have put Tony off, but it is a little late now.'

'But not *too* late!' To her horror he reached out a large fat hand and touched hers. It was one of those slightly moist hands, the kind she liked least. 'It is high time that we had a talk, my dear. I have been thinking about you quite a lot, a remarkable lot, I should have said. I expect that you are aware of it?'

Nervously she glanced at the pile of letters (more than usual), and if he was going to carry on like this, they would never get through them in time. Besides, it was dangerous ground, very dangerous indeed!

'We must keep our pretty eyes wider open, my dear. I have thought about you, and I have made plans for our future. Yours and mine.'

There are moments in life when one becomes only too well aware of the fact that fate has run off, and one is heading for disaster. She saw it ahead of her now! Whatever proposition Mr. Hellston was about to put up to her, it would be the wrong one, and she would do far better not to listen to it.

'Let's get on with the letters,' she besought him, and her voice had taken on a desperate tone.

'Not at all. They can wait. There is nothing of

the slightest importance here, nothing as important as what I would suggest for ourselves. For you and me, m'dear. And we will most certainly discuss it right now.'

If she could have stopped him going further, she would have done so, but she knew too well that when our Mr. Hellston got the bit between his teeth, off he galloped at speed.

He looked at her with an amiable placidity that was most agitating. 'I want to marry you,' he said.

Crystal hadn't expected that.

She was so completely horrified that she turned round sharply and stared at him. The colour rose to her cheeks, she could feel it. All through this depressing interview she had been trying to avoid catching his eye, but now she faced him. She was twenty-one. Had he not contributed towards the small gift that the office had given her on her birthday? So without a doubt he knew. He himself was well over fifty, she had never actually found out his exact age, for Mr. Hellston had a womanish dislike of permitting that news to leak out. Most certainly he was past fifty-five, and might be well near to sixty.

'I couldn't,' she said.

It did not move that bland smile. 'Ah, naturally you are bewildered by what I suggest. You never thought of my desiring it?'

'Of course I didn't.'

26

'I like innocence. I admire the *ingénue*. I always thought that you were a thoroughly charming girl, and after some years of being a bachelor, I have now made up my mind to marry and live happily ever after.'

'I dare say, but I am not the right girl for you.' She prayed that the horror of the thought would not run away with her and she would commit herself into a spate of words which rose tremulously and would most certainly lose her the job.

He still smiled! 'I intend to marry you,' he said. 'I realize your surprise. But good fortune comes to some,' and he waved a waggish finger.

She would have to be plain-spoken; she would have to try to put it in such a way that the meaning was quite clear, and of course this way was the way he would dislike it most of all! My job, she thought, I have *got* to keep my job.

'Please, don't let's talk of it,' she began. 'I have my life to live in my own way, and no wish to marry. I am completely happy as I am, I like my job, and my digs are very comfortable.'

He went a trifle pink, in fact pinker than she had ever seen him, for she herself had privately thought that it must be years since Mr. Hellston had blushed.

'I am offering you marriage, m'dear,' he said, 'the sort of marriage that most girls would jump at with outstretched hands. They would thank God that they had the opportunity. I have a

27

magnificent home in Wimbledon, and a small bungalow in the New Forest. I will sell both if you wish to live somewhere else. I will settle a sum on you for clothes (they used to call it pin money, when I was a boy!). I will be generous and you will be most envied by my friends and your own.'

'I'm deeply grateful, and I realize that of course this *is* the chance of a lifetime, and I—I'm being silly. But I feel that marriage isn't like that. You have to love a person deeply—you have to be in love.'

'Oh, nonsense!' said Mr. Hellston; 'that is sheer foolishness. You've read a lot of silly books.'

'Yes, I may be foolish, but that is just the way I feel. I would not marry a man with whom I wasn't passionately in love; that is what I really mean.'

'And you're not in love with me?'

He had cornered her now, and the smile had become glassy. She tried to avoid an answer but he was determined to have one.

'I—I, oh dear, how dreadful this is!' she said, 'you are asking too much. I never dreamt of this happening, it would have—horrified me if I had. Do let's forget it all, go on with the work, and think no more about it, please?'

'Certainly not. I could never forget it. I have my personal feelings, and of course my pride. How do you suppose, Miss Stevens, that I could

keep you on in my employ knowing that you—
that you had turned me down?'

This is the red light! said her heart, look out!
This is where trouble is popping round the next
corner. 'You're making it very difficult.'

'Then change your mind, and be sensible.'

There is a moment in the life of every man
when destiny overtakes him. She rose. She
tucked her note-book into her bag, and slipped
the top back on to her Biro pen. Although she
knew quite well the result of the action she took,
she could not stay herself from turning on him.
'I shall never change my mind. Nothing in this
world would make me do that. Anyway, I don't
think I can carry on with the work today, and
must ask you to forgive me.'

He looked at her again and she thought how
fishy were those eyes! That had been perhaps
the first thing that she had noticed on the day
when she had come here for the interview.
Those cold, cold eyes in that large pale face! The
thought of marrying him was something beyond
human belief.

'But,' said Mr. Hellston primly, 'there are the
letters to answer. We have to do the work of
today, *and* today, not tomorrow. Most certainly
we have to go through with the letters.'

'I can't.'

'Perhaps you do not realize that I personally
am in no mood to go through with the work, but
I am not a shirker. I have never yet shrunk from

29

a task, because in all circumstances one does one's work.'

She knew that it was intended as a telling reproof and that it did nothing. The pomposity of it was horrifying. That for a husband! was all she thought.

'I'm sorry. I'm afraid I cannot do it today.'

'If that is how you feel, Miss Stevens, then there is no more to be said. I would remind you that I have paid you the greatest compliment that a man can pay to a woman. I have asked you to marry me, and you have refused.' He waited, but she said nothing. 'Apparently you are entirely adamant. I had been sure that this was to be the happiest day of my life, and find that it is nothing of the sort.'

'It isn't the happiest day of my life, either.'

'Very well. There is no more to say, and of course your employment here terminates. You would wish it to be that way, I understand. I will send your salary and your cards to you on Monday morning, and you will not return.'

If she had wanted to argue there were no words left to her, nothing that she could say, for it was plain that she could not stay on here after this. How she hated him! The trouble was that the pay was so good, and the hours fairly comfortable, and she *had* thought that she was lucky. Luck had gone! It had taken unto itself wings and had flitted out of the window.

'Thank you,' was all that she could say.

She went to the door, and out of it, without looking back. She closed it quietly, remembering that the Reverend Mother had always said that dignity was an attribute. She thought that she heard him make a funny little noise, but was so scared lest he should call her back, that she pretended not to have heard it. She went to the cloaks and slipped on the big grey coat which most certainly she ought never to have afforded, and which now would leave her broke for months. She pulled on the hat, aware that her hands were trembling, for it had not been a happy experience.

Thinking about it as she powdered her face, she realized that Mr. Hellston was not the sort of man to give her a reference. In a panic she knew that she would have to start from scratch again, and now it might be exceedingly difficult. Wherever she went now it would mean forfeiting her summer holiday, for it was well into spring, and nobody would want her if she was going to ask for her fortnight as soon as she got there. Without a reference, she would be in a dilemma.

Crystal went down the stairs holding her head high. It was the last time that she would descend, and she thought of the thousands of feet that had climbed up and down. They had got people nowhere, just as they had got her. She heard the throb of the buses, and the general whirr of the street beyond, and she came

31

out into the yellowness of the spring sunshine, aware that she was crying.

She walked down the street towards the tube, and all the time she was remembering that ridiculous spring-time urge that had made her buy a coat she could have done without, and an absurd little hat, too. The grey frock as well. All of these things had been a big dip into her savings, and now she would probably be calling on those savings more than she had done for a long, long time. The shabby little post office book stood at about eleven pounds, she supposed, and Mrs. Biggins would need payment, for she didn't believe in allowing people to run into debt.

Crystal walked along the street in something of a daze, for she had no idea of what to do next. The more she thought about the event of the morning, the more agitated she became, yet there had been nothing else that she could have done. Once Mr. Hellston had committed himself so far, she had either to refuse him and leave, or accept him and live unhappily ever after. There had been nothing for it but to say no, get her hat and coat and come right away.

On and on she went, the street comparatively clear, for at this time on a Saturday morning the city is never busy.

She started to cross the road, and would have walked under an approaching car, save that a hand shot out and a kindly man's voice said:

32

'Here, half a tick! You're a bit young to die, don't you think?'

Her heart jerked as she turned a somewhat surprised face to a young man who had stopped her, and only just in time. She realized that he would be very little older than she was, pale with very flaxen, fair hair, and sea-blue eyes. Of middle height, and smiling, she realized instantly that he was kind, that he was the sort of friend who stayed in your life for ever, and that she liked him.

'How good of you! Thank you so much.'

'Not at all! I don't like to see the young and pretty take risks. Look before you leap next time, and then don't leap at all.'

'I'll look.' Because she could recognize something different about him, something unlike any man she had met before, she said, 'You're not a Londoner? You don't look like one, anyway.'

'Of course I'm not a Londoner. Who'd want to be that? Too noisy, too stuffy, and too dirty. Indeed no, I come from a small Cornish village where we never see a stranger's car even in these enlightened days. If we want thrills and excitement we go into Penzance or St. Ives, and we don't go there very often.' He smiled at her. 'Maybe we'll meet there one day, you never know, it's a small world. Good morning.'

He turned and walked away, his shoulders a trifle hunched, and without looking back. In

33

one way, a ridiculous way, Crystal was disappointed. She did not know why she stood there looking after him, and thinking of a part of England which she herself had never visited, but which, when she came to think about it, must be the loveliest part of all. She got a sudden dream picture of anemone fields, of sandy beaches with palm trees, like the ones she had seen in the south of France, so long ago that she hardly dare think of it. She thought of the black cliffs, rugged against the sky, and the huge gulls, whose wide wings spread out like the sails of boats.

Then she turned, and looking carefully first to right and then to left, she crossed to the tube station.

IV

She didn't tell Tony about it all until they were having their lunch, because somehow she felt that if she confided in him too soon, she would say too much.

Tony listened to the story and she knew that he wasn't at all happy about any of it. He said at last that Mr. Hellston's offer of marriage was 'like his cheek,' but he realized that whatever she had done or said it would have put 'paid' to the job. It might, he agreed, be difficult getting somewhere else just now, but of course, he would run his eye over the advertisement columns—and if he heard of anything he would

34

let her know at once.

'I dare say it will be heavy going at first, Crystal, but I've got a hunch it'll be all right.'

'I have a hunch that something'll happen. I'd almost like to go right away and leave London for the summer. It would be wonderful if I could work in a seaside hotel, or something of that kind, though I should think that sort of job is snapped up pretty quickly.'

He said, 'Yes, and what is more I bet there are several girls with the same idea, all bursting to go and work at seaside hotels the moment the summer comes. I'd stick to the job you know, you might have luck this time. I never believe in changing your horses in mid-stream. After all, you are a secretary and you'd better go on as one.'

Crystal knew that he was trying to hide his real anxiety from her, and this lunch was not one of their most successful. She had started it in the wrong mood. She had received her first proposal, something that she had always thought would turn out to be something of a red letter day, instead of which it was not a red letter day at all. She had got the sack, and she had nearly got herself run over into the bargain! She was thinking of the young man with the startling fair hair, who had come from Cornwall. Perhaps Tony was giving her the right advice when he warned her to forget it and enjoy the week-end. That was theirs, anyway! There was nothing that she could do about a new job before Monday, so why spoil Saturday and Sunday on that account?

They went to the pictures, but it was a poor film, one of the depressing kind, the last thing to see on a day that had started so badly. By strange coincidence the depressing film was followed by an educational film on Cornwall.

The Cornish picture had the added attraction of being in colour. There was Polperro with its funny little streets and quaint waterways, the sort of town one never believed could be in England. Penzance on a sunny morning with the flower-boat from the Scillies arriving across a pale blue sea. Land's End, rugged, with every wave wearing a white frill. St. Ives, a perched little city of crooked streets, innumerable steps and a beach where occasionally the seals played contentedly. There were flower-markets, and the north coast with its coves, St. Agnes with a sea the colour of zircons, Boscastle, Padstow, and Bude, with miles of silverish sands.

'It must be quite the loveliest part of the world,' said Crystal when the picture ended, and the last gull flapped its way across the screen. 'I met a man who came from Cornwall today, he had the lightest, most flaxen-coloured hair that I have ever seen on a man, and I thought they were all very dark in that part of the world?'

'I believe they are. But they are mostly

36

immigrants, and maybe this was someone from somewhere else. Anyhow, what were you doing picking up with a strange Cornishman on the very morning your boss makes love to you? It looks to me as if you've been having a busy day, my girl!'

'A bit too busy.'

'Don't lose heart.' He had his arm in hers as they went out into the street, pleasant with the early evening of spring-time. 'You mustn't let it get you down. Maybe it is all for the best, and from this moment your whole life changes. You never know.'

'It looks to me as if I should never get as good a salary again.'

'Oh yes you will, maybe better. Maybe the star turn of jobs. Don't fret, take it in your stride and thank the Lord that you have got away from that nasty old man.'

They said good-bye at the far end of the Albert Bridge, so that if one of Mrs. Biggins's innumerable friends saw them together, it didn't matter really.

As she walked back, Crystal thought about Tony. He was the heavy-steady of her life, she supposed, the sort of worthy and quite charming young man that every girl has up her sleeve, and always feels that she ought to love passionately yet never does.

How different it would have been if Mr. Hellston had been young and handsome, the sort of romantic hero that most girls would love and admire, then the upshot of today would indeed have been very, very different.

Battersea Park was merry with voices, and it seemed quite a shame to end the day at this early hour and go indoors where she would feel thoroughly miserable. But what else could she do?

She let herself in; there was Mrs. Biggins standing in the hall, almost as though she was waiting for Crystal, and suspicious. There was always the faint smell of one of those reliable soaps about Mrs. Biggins. Her hair was dragged back, and pinned with a superfluity of hairpins of plain silverish steel, all of them sticking out in points. Mrs. Biggins did not seem to be aware of the fact that the little bun of hair was thinning considerably and needed far less to skewer it in place. An apron stretched itself about her bulging waist, and the stomach rose in a ridge just under the waistline, while above it a spare tyre curled itself into a comfortable coil.

'Oh, so you're back early?' said Mrs. Biggins.

'It's lovely out, but I have some mending to do,' said Crystal. She had made up her mind not to tell Mrs. Biggins what had happened; not yet, anyway.

The next remark took her aback.

'A gentleman's been here to see you,' said Mrs. Biggins slowly. 'It made me wonder what's been going on at your office this morning? He was a well-dressed gentleman, said he was Mr. Hellston himself, and I think he looked like it. The fat kind, but pasty-faced with it. Shouldn't think he was really healthy. He came here in a big car.'

'Yes, it must have been Mr. Hellston.'

'I don't like rich gentlemen calling on my young ladies,' said Mrs. Biggins severely, and her prim little mouth was set like a trap, for she had been waiting for this. 'It leads to no good, it don't. If you'd been in, that'd have been a nice thing. And you living in a bed-sitter, think what ideas it would have given him! No, I won't have gentlemen cross the threshold, it isn't right nor proper, and I'm not having it in my house.'

'I expect he only brought my salary.'

That surprised Mrs. Biggins who flattered herself that she was one of the women who know everything, and here was something that she hadn't suspected. 'But you gets paid on a Friday. You know that.'

Unpleasant as it might be, now there was nothing for it but the truth. 'I'm sorry, but this morning Mr. Hellston dismissed me.'

Mrs. Biggins stared at Crystal, through steel-rimmed glasses that were bound round the bridge with wisps of cotton wool that had felted. 'Oh, my stars!' said Mrs. Biggins, not liking it at all. 'That's torn it! And now what'll I do about me rent?'

'I've paid it up to date.'

'Yes, I know, but what about the next time? There's always another Friday.'

'I imagine Mr. Hellston left a small envelope for me?'

With obvious reluctance, Mrs. Biggins produced an envelope, well and truly sealed, for Mr. Hellston had also been born with a suspicious nature, and thought that every man he met was an incipient thief, and that went for the women also.

Crystal knew that Mrs. Biggins watched her as she mounted the stairs, with the glossy lino shining more than it had done even on the day when it was bought, and the brass of the stair-rods glittering whitely. Mrs. Biggins wore herself to a frazzle cleaning the place to this state of solid perfection, and then took it out of everybody else because the fatigue had made her snappy.

The bed-sitter smelt stuffy; in Crystal's absence that wretched Mrs. Biggins was for ever sneaking into it and shutting the windows in case dust got inside. Crystal opened them and sat down on the comfortable chair. She opened the packet. Perhaps she still had some faint hope that, if Mr. Hellston had really cared for her, he would have been decent about the cheque and have made it out for a couple of weeks, seeing that it was entirely his fault she was leaving the firm.

She had made a mistake if she expected that

he had a latent kind heart. He had never been that sort of man. The cheque covered merely the sum which was her right, the amount for which she could ask, and he had enclosed with it one of the printed visiting cards of the firm's, and scrawled across the corner in his own pompous handwriting were two word: 'With comps'.

Perhaps it was the card that brought her to herself more vigorously than anything else. If he had been here, she would have thrown the thing at him. He could keep his 'comps'.

The affair was over and done with now. It had ended abruptly, of course, but the best thing that she could do was to pull up her socks, straighten her shoulders and face the future resolutely. Maybe fate would give her the next chance? Maybe fate would lend her a hand.

Fate did!

V

It began almost immediately, when Crystal took up the magazine which lay on the side table. It was a woman's magazine, popular with Mrs. Biggins who thought that it published 'ever such nice stories'. It had also a large column of holiday addresses, of people who wished to dispose of puppies and kittens, who sold garden produce, and agitated folks who could not get domestic assistance in the home for love or money.

She sat back with a cup of coffee, and read

41

down the columns, taking her time. They offered all the usual things which she would have expected. Mothers' helps galore were wanted; there seemed to be endless jobs going for girls who would help unfortunate mothers ('somebody in for the rough'); teachers with the highest qualifications; school matrons who had had previous experience; and references were always wanted. Then quite suddenly Crystal came upon the advertisement which seemed to be the real proof that the fates were taking a hand in it.

The little paragraph was headed CORNWALL.

CORNWALL.—No previous experience necessary. Handsome remuneration offered to a young lady capable of running a home, with very light housework, for invalid lady. Own suite. Good resident maid. Charming surroundings and own car if desired for shopping. Must be quiet, reliable, active, and not a gossip.—Apply: SMUGGLER'S MILL, Trelanlyn.

It was a very different advertisement from the others, and it definitely said something. She liked the sound of the address, and instantly her imagination went on ahead of her, dwelling in a leisurely fashion on the Smuggler's Mill. It would be sweetly old, with perhaps a field of flowers around it, and the sea not too far away. The more she thought about it the more it fitted into the picture that she had seen this very afternoon with Tony.

Acting on a sudden whim, she rushed round to the post office in Battersea Park Road, and got a telegram off to Smuggler's Mill, just before the office closed.

It was the maddest thing that she had ever done.

She realized that next day when she lay in bed late listening to all the familiar sounds of the Albert Bridge Road, and knowing that she had done something completely idiotic. To Crystal, who had lived in various lodgings most of her life, and whose childhood had been that nomadic existence across Europe with no real home, the thought of Smuggler's Mill was a magnet. But she expected nothing from her telegram. She thought of it now as having been a wild extravagance, and blamed herself for wasting money.

On the Monday morning, so early that she could hardly have believed that it was possible, she got the reply, and it was the longest telegram that she had ever seen. Apparently the name of the family was Tregarth. Mr. and Mrs. Tregarth (she was the invalid wife, the trouble being arthritis), and the son Luke Tregarth, who had dispatched this rambling telegram to her. The message explained that no actual nursing was required, but a certain amount of companionship; there would be shopping, household supervision, and the task of making herself generally agreeable. The salary offered somewhat took her breath away.

Until she began to read the telegram, Crystal had been only playing with the idea, probably because she had seen the film of Cornwall so recently, and also because of the fair-haired young man who had prevented her from being run over in the city on Saturday morning. Now everything changed. She read it through and through, and from it she gathered that she had been about the only suitable person who had applied for the post, which seemed strange, seeing that they had so much to offer. They wondered when she would be free. An express letter followed it up.

'Luke Tregarth!' she thought, and then to herself, 'It's an interesting name, very different from the more general ones, and he sounds as if he would be a charming man.' She was attracted. Maybe a dream called to her; if it did, she had the feeling that it would be a delightful dream. She wired back, for the stamps had been enclosed for this, and she said that she could come this very week if required, and would like it.

It was after the telegram had gone that she became perturbed over her sudden action, all of which had happened, it would seem, out of the

44

blue. A chance advertisement, her telegram, and then the wire back. Cornwall now seemed to be a long way from Battersea on this bright morning when the spring was so vigorous in the bursting trees. It was quite warm and summery, and she went out and sat by the lake watching people boating, and wondering what was the right thing to do.

Her own mother had once said that it paid in life to take chances! That had not been the Reverend Mother's idea, for she did not hold with too many chances. She would walk through the cloisters of the convent, her ebony rosary chattering as it dangled from her knotted belt, and she looked the epitome of a woman who has never taken a chance in her life. Perhaps, thought Crystal who was in that mood, the chances one regretted were the ones one didn't take?

The letter when it came was encouraging and gave her all the details. The Smuggler's Mill was apparently a little isolated, standing well away from the village itself, in a small valley, with the sea fairly close to it. The family lived well, she gathered, and they had a resident maid who had been with them for some time, and who did all the cooking, though she had a woman in to help her with the housework.

Crystal imagined that the lack of neighbours was something typically Cornish, so much so that it did not worry them, though Luke, who

45

apparently wrote all the letters for his family, explained that Penzance was a charming spot and within range; there they could shop, and there were all kinds of entertainments. They kept a large car, his own, and a small runabout, which perhaps she would like for herself?

Crystal thought of driving a car, of the joys of going into Penzance, and perhaps to St. Ives. Perhaps it would be possible to go over to the Scillies some time, and see the fields of narcissi which perfume all the islands with their heady scent. She could not stop herself from thinking about this with enthusiasm. It was the sort of dream job that any girl would want, and time after time the name kept coming into her mind. Luke Tregarth! It was an unreal name, a name that went for something, a name that made her anxious to see the man.

His next letter enclosed a first-class ticket to Penzance, and some money to be spent on the journey, called 'train expenses'. The die was cast!

When Crystal told Mrs. Biggins, the little old woman stared aghast through those steel-rimmed glasses with the felty cotton wool bridging.

'Oh, but how could you go? Not knowing who you was going with, and such awful things happening?' she said.

'I'm sure it's all right.'

'Oh no, you shouldn't do that. What about

the clergyman? You could write to the clergyman and he'd tell you. It isn't right for a pretty young girl to be going off like that, and a young man there, too. It seems funny his mum don't write, maybe there isn't a mum, and that was just the red herring on the trail.'

'She has arthritis.'

'Oh! All the same she ought to write. I see trouble here if you asks me, it's sticking out a mile! But of course all the modern young people are that obstinate, and you'll probably go, then regret it all your life.'

Crystal knew quite well that if ever there was a first-class trouble-seeker it was Mrs. Biggins, and nothing that her lodger did or said would ever convince her that everything would be all right. Worse happened when she went out to sup with Tony in the little Chelsea café.

It was small and homely, and burnished wooden table-tops had no covering cloths, only mats, and red candles standing in twisted wooden sconces, to give a very pleasant light.

She told Tony of the project for the first time. He had known that she had 'something in view', but not what it actually was. She had received another letter from Luke, with a photograph of the mill in springtime. The daffodils grew wild about it, and there were thick bunches of cream blossom on the trees. If she had had any further doubts about going, all of them were in the melting-pot by the time that she received the

47

photograph. Tony listened to everything she told him, and turned the picture over and over in his hand. He did not seem to think the way that she did.

'I don't like it, Crystal.'

'But you must like it! It'll be such a change for me. No letters to take down, and Mr. Hellston going too fast for me. No bullying. Just a life of my own, and my idea is to stay there all the summer anyway, then perhaps return to the secretarial life in London when autumn comes.'

He wasn't happy. 'All the same it's a pretty big risk to be going off there alone without any information as to what sort of people they are. Why don't you get a reference of some sort, or write to the vicar, or something?'

'Mrs. Biggins thought of that. She *would*! I don't suppose that there is a vicar, for this is just an outlandish old mill, and I doubt if there are any neighbours.'

'Worse and worse! You can see that you might be letting yourself in for a stay with a pack of murderers.'

'What will you think of next?'

'Anyway, all houses are in parishes, and parishes are in the charge of vicars of some sort or another. I'll find someone to tell me about it. I've got some Penzance friends, and they would know.'

'It'll be a bit late in the day, Tony, for I am taking the plunge on Friday. It's going to be the big journey of my life, the most exciting ever.'

'And I hate the idea! Never mind, I'll find out who the vicar is, and I shall write to him.'

'I wish you wouldn't. After all, this is my own life, surely I can do what I like with it?'

'Not throw it away.'

'I'm not throwing it away. I'm doing exactly what I want to do, and all I ask is that you leave me alone.'

It would be dreadful if it did go wrong, and the hour came when she had to eat her words, but for the moment all that would be a long way ahead.

They sat in a gloomy silence until the coffee came, and then she tried to talk, remembering that is part of the good behaviour necessary for guests.

Undoubtedly the main trouble was that Tony loathed the thought of parting with her, not that he really thought that this journey was a dangerous one.

'Don't be silly about me, dear,' she urged.

'I wouldn't be if I didn't love you.'

'It isn't love, it's just friendship.'

They went up the Albert Bridge Road, hand in hand.

VI

In the next two days Crystal bought a few clothes that she would need, for Luke Tregarth had sent her a small cheque to cover any

49

outgoing expenses that she might think to be necessary. He termed it airily a small cheque, but to her it seemed to be generous.

She bought good, stout country shoes on his suggestion, he seemed to be a very practical young man, and she had discovered by now that he was twenty-eight. She bought a divine pair of nut-brown slacks, with a jumper that brought every glowing light into her hair. She did not suppose that she would need lots of woollies, for anyway Cornwall would be warmer than London, and maybe it would make the smart grey coat look a little odd.

On the Friday morning everything was packed, and Tony called for her bright and early in a taxi. He said that there would be lots to do at Paddington; the seat to be found, sandwiches bought, magazines, and the luggage arranged. When Mrs. Biggins saw what she was pleased to term 'a gent' waiting in the taxi, her cheeks were flooded with magenta, and she shipped a face of the greatest disapproval.

'Of course, if I'd known that this was going on,' she muttered to herself, 'if I'd known. . . .'

There was nothing that she could do now, for Tony was at the front door, and both he and Crystal could afford to be considerably amused that she should make such a scene. Crystal swept down the steps into the taxi, not caring a fig what Mrs. Biggins thought or said. They drove away.

'Well, that's that!' she told Tony.

'It's not that at all! You can't possibly make this journey, because something surprising has happened. I wrote to the vicar. I found that he lives about two miles away in some fantastic little village where there are only fishermen, poppies, and fat gulls. Oh yes, and some odd chap who goes in for bird–watching has built himself a special place on the beach for it; it was Sally Richards who told me.'

'I wish Sally Richards—whoever she is— would leave me out of this and go away and drown herself.'

'She was born there and she knows more about it than most people. Anyway, she was the one who gave me the vicar's name. It's a Mr. Ingram, not married, and he lives there with his ma in a big gaunt vicarage where they take P.G.s because his stipend is so rotten.'

'He doesn't sound awfully nice to me.'

'She said that, too. I wrote to him immediately, and asked if he could tell me privately anything about the Tregarths and Smuggler's Mill, where they live. I pretended that you were my sister, because I thought that made everything seem a bit easier, and I said that I was rather worried about your going off into the blue with complete strangers.'

'Oh, Tony, why ever did you do that? When I get there and my surname is Stevens and yours is Thorpe, Mr. Ingram is bound to think there is

51

something funny about us.'

'Yes, but what else could I do? If I had said that you were merely a girl friend, I should never have got a thing out of him. That was plain. Apparently he thought rather seriously about it, for he did not wait to write. I suppose he realized that it would be too late, because I had explained that you were starting today. I got this telegram first thing this morning.'

He brought it out of his pocket and handed it to her. The taxi was jogging towards Hyde Park as she read it. It was brief.

Project regrettable. Advise you cancel. Charles Ingram.

CHAPTER TWO

I

For a moment, Crystal did not know what to do, nor how she really felt about this, as she handed the telegram back to Tony without a word. It was, of course, far too late to stop the whole thing even if Mr. Ingram did think that it was regrettable, and this attitude had probably only come about because the Tregarths were not C. of E. or did not contribute to his rummage sales, and church fêtes.

'I don't believe a word of it,' she said at last.

She didn't want to believe it.

'Don't go off to Cornwall, Crystal. I do beg you not to go.'

'But I've fixed everything up now, and even spent some of the money they sent. I've made all arrangements, and I am abiding by this. What's more, I'm going to like it. I've got a hunch about it, it's going to be the biggest adventure of my life.'

'But Cornwall is a queer part of the world, even the commentator at the cinema said that. I also have got a hunch about this, and beg you, dear, please don't go.'

'But I *am* going.'

The conversation lagged; she saw him looking at her with reproachful eyes, and knew that she had hurt him, yet there was no way out of it. It was far too late to change her mind; the Tregarths expected to see her this evening, and this evening she would be there, whatever else happened.

They drove gloomily across the park and came eventually to the greater gloom of Paddington Station, with swirls of grey smoke under its roof.

Still hardly speaking to each other, probably because now there seemed to be no words left to say, Tony got a porter to collect the luggage. Crystal realized that she felt singularly depressed. Everything was dim, just when she had thought that she would be at her happiest, and it wasn't made easier in that she herself had been secretly appalled when she had read Mr. Ingram's telegram. She wasn't going to like him, that was plain!

With overdone politeness, Tony helped her buy sandwiches and chocolates, contributed the magazines he knew she liked best, and was very nice, but all the time he looked like a hungry dog who speaks with his eyes because he cannot speak with his mouth.

Impulsively, she said, 'Tony, I'm so sorry to go away like this and know you are angry with me, but don't you see it isn't ending? I just have to go away, have this adventure, and enjoy it, but I'll come back.'

'Of course it isn't ending, I know that. For you it is only just beginning, but I don't like the sound of any of it and am worried to death. I bet you're going to be darned sorry that you ever started out on this dam-fool journey, if you want to know the truth, and I wish to goodness you'd see how right I am and not go down there.'

She said nothing. She just got into the train. The carriage was empty, with a reserved place opposite to her. Tony stacked in the luggage, arranging it over-carefully, then he turned to her, one hand still on the hat-rack.

'Crystal, I do care for you so. I know we are neither of us madly in love, but that's the sort of thing that only happens in books. You and I could be so awfully happy, it would be the sort of happiness that lasts, yet here you are hopping off to the other end of England on a wild goose chase. It may be awful.'

'It may be such fun. If Mr. Hellston had never wanted to marry me, I should have been sitting for ever in his office taking down his pompous letters. I've been lucky. I may be making a mistake, but it isn't everybody who gets the chance of some adventure, and it has come to me.'

'All the same . . .'

'Oh, Tony, don't! It's no good. Don't you see that it really is no good at all? I'm sick to death of being hard up in London, at least I shall have tried something different, and if it fails, back I'll come and for ever.'

The other passenger arrived, a middle-aged woman with an expensive fur coat, and lots of off-white luggage.

At last the guard was standing ready and the porters were closing the doors. No longer was Tony inside the carriage with her, but he was framed in the window looking at her with those still reproachful eyes, and the grin that she had come to love.

'If ever I win one of the big prizes in the pools I'll charter a plane and come right down to fetch you away.'

'I know.'

'One of these days I've got a hunch that I shall win one of the big prizes.'

'Who's got silly hunches now?'

Slowly the train began moving, almost imperceptibly at first with Tony running by the side, then he fell back, and became a mere dot in the distance, but still waving frantically to her; the parting was over, and gratefully she sank back into her corner of the carriage.

Ahead of her lay a long, happy journey into the sunshine, and the part of England where the new spring was already established. Ahead of her lay adventure, perhaps a romantic one, opportunity, something that she was really going to enjoy.

London seemed to stretch on for miles in rows of little houses, gradually growing into vistas of gardens, and it was Reading before they came to the pastoral country that she loved. The willows were sprouting along the sides of flooding streams, and the marsh marigolds were vividly yellow. In the woods she saw children gathering wild flowers, and dozed a little, tiring of the magazines. When she woke again they were in the west country.

Devonshire was lifting its undulating lands, and there were lush woods, greener than the trees in Battersea Park, and groups of woolly old ewes with their lambs.

She ate her sandwiches and dozed again; when she woke, the sea was the other side of the window, and ahead of her were the rosy cliffs of Dawlish against which the gulls flapped their glittering wings. She was glad now that she had followed the hunch. Glad that she had come here. It pays to take life by the forelock and make the most of opportunities.

From Plymouth on the train lost speed. Now they had left the Tamar behind them, and the great ships that throng Devonport. Cornwall itself appeared, looking disappointingly derelict. Crystal came to the conclusion that she actively disliked the drab houses with their slate roofs, and it was something of a shock after the warm verdure of Devonshire to find a county that she did not think she liked.

It was raining, too; the sky overhead was darkly grey, and there was a film of silver in the air.

'Are you going to Penzance, or Falmouth?' asked the woman opposite her.

'Penzance.'

'Oh, then you change at Truro. The Penzance train comes in just behind this, it is really the second part of this one. This part goes to St. Ives.'

'But the porter said . . .'

'Oh, they always make mistakes! None of them know Cornwall properly. I was born at St. Agnes, and I ought to know.'

She started to talk about St. Agnes, which had, she said, the bluest cove anywhere round the coast, with Mullion a far distant second. She had lived in St. Ives ever since her marriage, and

57

apparently she thought nothing of Penzance, but said that it was just a seaside town like thousands of others round Britain and most of them over-trippery and vile.

It was interesting hearing her talk, and the stories she had to tell were enthralling. She spoke of the piskies on the moor (the last hold of the piskies in England, so she said), of the mermaid of Zennor who came to church on rare Sundays. This was, she explained, a county of legend and of history, and King Arthur had been here. It was good to its own folks, but could be cruelly hard on strangers who came, and she looked dubiously at Crystal who had foolishly admitted that this was her first visit to it.

'I shall love it. I know that I shall love it,' she said, and looked out of the window, disliking the fact that she would have to get all her luggage out at Truro. Too bad of the porters at Paddington; at least they should know that much!

The afternoon had darkened. The sunshine, which had been so vivid over the beautiful pasture lands of Devon, had flickered away altogether, and now the first light rain had thickened, and it was coming down in a steady stream. When they came at last to Truro, which was a huddle of grey houses, it was pouring.

'Here we part,' said the woman. 'Maybe I'll see you later. That is if the delights of Penzance ever let you free!'

'I want to see everything that I can of Cornwall whilst I am here.'

The woman looked at her with significance. 'I have the feeling that you won't be here for very long,' she said.

The station was cold.

Somehow Crystal had been so sure that it would be very much warmer, but the rain that was falling had a sleety tang about it, and the greyness made it seem as though the night had already descended on them. The first train went out, and she stood there with the luggage around her, waiting. At last a porter came up to her, a little wizened man, with a game leg. He looked at her and asked if he could help.

'I'm waiting for the Penzance train,' she said.

'It's gone, miss. That last one was it. It come in from London, and went out a little way back. I thought as how you'd got out of it.'

'I did. The woman in the carriage told me that I had to change at Truro. She said that that part of the train went to St. Ives, and another part came in after it, and picked up the passengers for Penzance.'

He looked at her vaguely, lifted a hand with a crooked finger, and pushed his cap back scratching at a grey-streaked forelock. 'Must have been St. Ives Martha,' he said, 'expensive-looking lady, good furs, and jewels, and things. She's the mad one about these parts, always doing things like this. Prophesying storms what won't come, seeing queer things, and telling folks all kinds of odd stories. In the old days they'd have burnt her for a witch, and if you asks me, a good thing too. She wasn't born in these parts, though she tells everyone that she comes from St. Agnes, but she was born in Wales, and I always says the Welsh are queer 'uns. So she was at it again, was she?'

Feeling chilly, and for the first time very worried, Crystal said, 'When is the next train?'

'Not for a fair time yet, and you've missed the bus, too. There was a bus, but that's gone now.'

Crystal could have wept. She said, 'The people to whom I'm going were to have met the train at Penzance, and I've come here to a new job, now what'll I do?'

'I reckon they'll guess what's happened, and come along and meet the next train if they've got any sense,' he suggested. He was a pleasant man, sparsely built, with a mahogany-coloured skin, and thick dark hair streaked with grey. 'You go and get yourself a good cup of tea and some Cornish splits, there's lots of time for it, and maybe you'll feel better after. I'll mind the luggage for you.'

She went into the refreshment room and ordered herself a cup of tea. It was thick, dark tea, over-strong, and served in a clumsy cup that was chipped at the edge. They had no Cornish splits, the girl said, but a nice cake, true

60

Cornish. It was made of saffron, something to which she was entirely unused, and did not know whether she liked it or not. Probably not! She drank the tea and listened despondently to the rain; now it seemed that the time would never pass.

It was almost dark when the train arrived, quite dark when she got to Penzance, and the rain was pouring down worse than ever. She got out of the train with the dreadful feeling that maybe everyone had been right about this. Cornwall did not like strangers. The weather had turned against her. Everything had gone wrong. Now she was remembering what Mr. Charles Ingram had said in his telegram:

Project regrettable. Advise you cancel.

II

After all Penzance offered a brighter prospect, and about the station there was a certain liveliness. The woman in the train, who had obviously been as mad as a hatter, might have condemned the place for not possessing the true spirit of Cornwall, and being like every other seaside place, but it was at least alive.

Crystal got out of the train and peered uneasily amongst the people who had come to meet it. Surely Luke Tregarth would be here?

She saw that a young man was coming out on to the station platform, shaking the rain from the heavy old army mackintosh that he wore. He had no hat, yet his hair, drenched as it was, was golden fair, a colour which radiated in the lamplight. He walked with squelching gum-boots, and as he came, suddenly Crystal saw that undoubtedly this was the young man who had stopped her from being run over, that dreadful last Saturday morning when she had lost her job! It was the man who had said, 'Half a tick! You're too young to die.' They were the words that she would never forget. She acted before she could stop herself, running eagerly towards him, holding out her hands; her eyes were excited, and her voice urgent.

'Oh please, please ... I know you don't remember me, but do help me!'

He stopped. 'By jingo!' he said and grinned. Then again, 'By jingo! It's a small world, isn't it? You're the little girl in London who tried to walk out under a car. What in the name of fortune are you doing here on a wet night?'

She could have wept with sheer pleasure at seeing someone whom she knew, or practically! She explained in a sudden spate of conversation. 'I came here to a new job, and made a fearful mistake, for there was a mad lady in the train who told me that I had to change at Truro. I did, with the result that I am three hours late. I thought maybe the people would realize what had happened, and come to meet me, but there isn't anybody here for me.'

'Well, I'm here now, and I've got a car outside. We'll wait a bit and see if anyone turns up, then I'll take you along wherever it is you want to go.'

'The address is Smuggler's Mill, I believe it is rather a sweet old place, certainly the photographs of it are quite lovely. The people's name is Tregarth, and she is an invalid with arthritis, wanting someone to run the house until she is better. The son wrote to me.'

'Oh, he did, did he?'

There was something about his tone of voice that made Crystal halt, and stare again at him, for suddenly she realized that this man knew the people and detested them. Here was someone else who did not like the prospect for her, someone who actually knew the Tregarths.

'Is anything wrong? Do you know something about it?'

'I thought I knew everything, save this. I had no idea that they had arranged to get you down to keep house for them. There's a father, the most odd man you've ever met, and a son, of the good-looking sort. The mother has been ill for ages, it is true, stuck in bed I believe, for nobody has caught sight of her for a very long time. They keep themselves to themselves because they are that sort of people. What do you know of them?'

'Only that the vicar doesn't like them!' It seemed fantastic to be standing in the station

63

with the rain beating down, and discussing an entirely strange family, to whom now she would have to go, whatever she discovered.

'Charles Ingram? I bet he doesn't like them! I don't live too far away myself. My name is Mervyn Peters, what's yours?'

'Crystal Stevens.'

'It's a pretty name. I have a little bungalow on the beach, or almost, for I go in for bird-watching, and write books about them.'

'I've heard of you.'

He grinned at that, then he looked at her luggage standing there bundled in a little group. 'Well, as there isn't a sign of Luke Tregarth, I'd better take you along there in my car, we'll get this luggage into it, and make a move.'

She followed him because there was nothing else that she could do. He called up a porter and between them they packed everything into the back of his car which was just outside the ticket office door. The rain seemed to have increased, and the night to have grown very dark. The wind blew in off the sea, and she could see the bay away from the myriad lights of Penzance blinking along the front, and the farther lights of Marazion beyond. She wished that she had arrived to a more friendly welcome, for this was a cold night, and she felt that she was soaked through already.

She got into the car beside Mervyn.

'You'll be right as rain,' he told her, 'maybe I

worried you unduly, and that's not fair. The old lady's family have lived in that mill for generations, and it came to her. People say that her husband wants her to hand it over to him and she won't do it, because she is obstinate about some things, but in this part of the world people do talk.'

'What do the Tregarths do?'

'I've no idea. Something to do with the Customs and Excise, I did hear, but they keep pretty quiet about it. They're a set of clams. If you get into any trouble there, you'll have to send for me and I'll get you out of it. I love Cornwall, but I must say that I am very far from predisposed in favour of the Tregarths of Smuggler's Mill.'

The car climbed a hill out of the town, when a sudden gust of wind caught it, and a squall of rain came pelting down on to it. It sounded like hailstones.

'Not a very propitious night,' he said.

'Anything but.'

Then the car gained speed.

III

The wind was rising, blowing in sturdy blasts across the country-side. The rain beat down on them, and when they passed under the avenues of trees which here and there lined the road, the noise was like that of urgent drumming.

Crystal waited for a short time, then after they

had gone some way, she said, 'You know, you've worried me a bit about these people! I wish you'd tell me the truth. I have the feeling you are keeping something back from me. What is it that you really know about the Tregarths?'

'I don't know much, certainly nothing personally. I speak to Luke, I've never spoken to his old man, or the mother, because she has been so ill, but I've heard people talking about them, and the whole neighbourhood dislikes them.'

'Perhaps because they aren't Cornish?' she suggested, feeling the spirit of loyalty which made her want to take their side.

'That's where you're wrong, because they are Cornish, both sides of the house. The mother's people have lived for about a couple of hundred years in that old Smuggler's Mill, and some time before that at Land's End, so I'm told. The Tregarths come from Mullion. There is no excuse for disliking them because they are not Cornish folk, they *are* Cornish folk, every man jack of them. No, it isn't that.'

The depressing rain still fell, spattering on to the car, and before them the road stretched, gleaming white and silver and with water beside it in the gutters. Now through the dark clouds overhead came the prying eye of a jaundiced moon.

It was dismally depressing to find it so completely different from everything that she

66

had expected of it. About this journey there was something grim; the place had become eerie! It might be the way that the moon looked at her, peering through the clouds, it might be that already she had come to dread the idea of arriving at Smuggler's Mill, which in the photograph had looked so bright and gay, and tonight, in this weather, could obviously be nothing of the kind.

'What—what'll I do if I just hate it all, and find it unbearable?' she asked falteringly, returning to the subject uppermost in her mind.

'You'll have to let me know. I'll do anything I can to put things right. I dare say it won't be as bad as all that. They're human anyway, all but the old man. He is inexplicable. Oh, I expect you'll settle down, and maybe the neighbourhood has got the wrong impression, and they are charming people at heart. By the bye, I have always been told that old Mrs. Tregarth is a pet, if you ever get the chance to see her.'

'Who nurses her?'

'Oh, the district nurse pops in and out; I believe she does not need a resident nurse with her, and they have a maid, a rum little piece, but a darned good cook, I'm told, her name is Karin.'

'A foreigner?'

'No, I don't think so.' Again Crystal got the impression that he was avoiding an issue,

67

accepting questions, then shying away from the answers. Was he hiding something from her? Something that he did not wish her to know?

'I shall keep you to your word,' she said, 'and if I do get into difficulties, most certainly I shall get hold of you to help me.'

They drove on for another mile, with the wind shrieking like a banshee, and now she could hear the sound of the sea pounding the cliffs somewhere near by.

'Is it much farther?'

'Only about a mile, then just round the corner. We are coming to the village itself.'

The moon had risen more, and she could see more clearly in consequence. It was a typical Cornish village, with the plain houses and the slate roofs shining wetly. In an inn the lights were lit and streamed out in a flood on to the road. A mission room stood a little apart from the other buildings; there was a Baptist chapel, and around it a yard of growing nettles quivering in the wind, with rakish tombstones, like decaying old teeth swung to curious angles.

The trail of houses ended in a few straggling ones, and the church itself. Now there was an occasional old farm or so, the screeching of night birds, and the lowing of cattle in byres. The road dropped with an abrupt suddenness, plunging down to a small bridge, with white-painted fences on either side of it, and she could hear the sound of a river gulching through the

68

bricked hoops of arches.

'It's just ahead,' said Mervyn.

She stared through the wind-screen with a keen desire to catch the first sight of her new home! She saw the mill, recognizing it only by the hump of the roof, and in a single instant she realized that the photograph which she had been sent had been no true picture of it at all. It was gaunt and rugged, not flowerily romantic as she had thought it would be. The car jolted to a standstill by the entrance.

Somehow she had thought that one would enter it through a wrought-iron gate which would be open on to a garden full of spring flowers; instead of this she saw that the gate had been torn from its hinges years ago, and where it had once stood, two dismal rotting posts were stuck like ghost sentries. One leant back with an eerie absurdity, whilst the other was foreshortened, where time had decayed it to pieces.

She looked out on them dismayed.

The garden had received no proper attention for a considerable time and had become a positive wilderness. Even though none of its details were plain at the moment, there was sufficient to make her realize what when the light of morning came to it, it would be a tangle of sow thistles, flamboyant dandelions, and nettles. The place was almost derelict, and it had a most grisly appearance.

'I'm afraid I daren't take the car in through the gateway,' said Mervyn, 'there's a walloping great pool of water there, it always happens if we get a storm, and the whole place is all pot-holes. My springs are not too hot, and I daren't risk this. I suggest you go inside, and tell Luke to bring a barrow out for your luggage.'

Crystal did not like the idea at all; also she did not want to part with Mervyn at this moment. Suddenly it seemed that when he went, all direct association with the civilized world went too, and as she opened the door of the car and stepped out, another scud of rain beat down on her.

'Oh, I do hate this! Now I'm beginning to wish that I had never come. I loathe saying good-bye.'

'It isn't to be good-bye. Of course we shall be meeting again. Don't you think that I shall allow Smuggler's Mill to swallow you up, because I shall do nothing of the sort, so you mustn't worry about it. You nip inside before you get soaked to the skin, and ruin that nice coat of yours. Send Luke out here for the goods.'

Crystal did not say another word.

She passed between the almost derelict gate-posts, feeling that she was going into some stark prison. She squelched along the gravel that had once been a drive, and as Mervyn had said she did indeed find it full of fantastic pot-holes, so that she stumbled.

Ahead of her she saw the shape of the house itself more clearly, with here or there the small yellow eyes of a lighted window. From beside it came a sound of moaning. The noise increased; it was a dreadful creaking noise, like phantom oars in rowlocks, or the sound of swan's wings against an August sky, when the swans change their homes. After a moment she found that it was the mill-wheel regurgitating as it went round and round, splashing the water back into the river beneath it, but the noise that it made was gruesome.

Crystal had at last reached the door with its one wide step, and she groped for the place where she supposed the bell must be. Her fingers found nothing. Perhaps she had become unreasonably afraid, possibly more so than she had ever been before in her life, because everything had mounted up against her.

Her chilly hands went on searching for the bell-push that she did not find, and passing on to the middle of the door, on a level with her own face, she found a small iron grille, of the kind that one sees only in very ancient houses.

She beat her hands on the door itself, and it seemed to her that they made a strangely hollow sound, something that she had never heard knocking make before; there was no reply. She waited and beat again. Then she called out.

After a short while, she heard the sound of a man's feet coming across a stone-paved floor,

71

the echoes ringing, as he approached the door outside which she stood. The fact that he was not hurrying himself was irritating, and now the rain seemed to have become worse than it had ever been before, literally teeming down. She would have done anything to escape the mechanical monotony of that grinding mill-wheel, the howl of the wind, and the cold gradually numbing her.

The man was still not hurrying.

He must have come to the other side of the door, outside which she stood waiting, yet nothing happened. Nothing at all! Then, quite suddenly, a shutter of wood shot back behind the little iron grille, and a strong yellow light came out and shone blindingly into her face, making her blink and start back by very reason of its unexpectedness. A man was standing the other side of the door, staring out at her, but he had all the advantage, for the light being behind him, his face was in the shadow. She could only see his eyes and knew that they were very dark, with whites that were luminous and gleaming. It was a man who never said a single word, but just stood there, staring out at her through the eerie little grille.

'Please, please let me in! It's pouring with rain out here, and I'm soaked through,' she began.

'Who are you?' and he made no effort to admit her.

'I'm Crystal Stevens. You were to have met me at Penzance, but something went wrong, and I missed the connection at Truro.'

'I did meet you. The trouble was that you were not on the train,' he said curtly.

'No, but I am here now, and please let me in. I'm wet through.'

He must be the most extraordinary man, she thought, for he still hesitated, and she felt that if she had to wait any longer, she would turn and make her way back to the waiting car where she would implore Mervyn to take her away from here for ever. Even if it meant admitting defeat, she could not stand much more of it.

However, the young man the other side of the grille must have thought better of it, for there was the rasping sound of a heavy iron bolt being shot back, and the door opened. She slipped inside.

IV

The man shut the door after her, and elaborately shot the bolt into place as though it were of major importance; then he turned to survey her. He wore breeches and riding-boots, no coat. She saw that his shirt was crumpled, that he had no tie, but that his throat was beautifully moulded like that of an Olympic athlete. His hair was thick and black, but a little long, falling forward on to his face, and he peered through it at her. Yet he must be young, in the late twenties she

73

would suppose, and her heart said, 'So this is Luke!' She stood there, the drops falling from her wet coat and spotting the paved floor. She could hear them.

'Well!' she said at last. 'I must say that I don't call this much of a welcome!'

'I came to Penzance to fetch you. What more could I do? You mucked it all up!'

'I tell you I missed the connection at Truro.'

'There is no connection at Truro. There was no reason for you to get out of the train that had brought you all the way from Paddington, and I don't see how any of this happened.' All the time those dark, searching eyes were fixed on her face, as though he hoped to detect her in telling him some lie. It made her very angry.

'The woman who was travelling with me told me that the train split into two at Truro, and I had to get out to catch the second part. She was mad, I know now.'

'Of course she was mad.'

Crystal lost her patience a little. 'Good heavens!' she said, 'aren't you going to ask me in? A friend brought me here in his car, and he is outside the gate with all my luggage, waiting to get away. Aren't you going to do anything about that?'

'A friend? What friend? I understood that you knew nothing and no one in Cornwall. That you had never been in this part of the world before?'

'That's perfectly true, but I just happened to

have met Mervyn Peters and he brought me here.' She knew that the look in his eyes changed, and immediately sensed that he did not like the idea, though he said nothing. 'Now, either I go away at once or you take me in to the fire, but this can't go on,' she insisted.

'Sorry. You'd better come with me, then I'll go out and see about the luggage. You're pretty wet, aren't you? It's the devil of a night.' Then quietly, looking at her as though the thought had struck him for the first time, 'And you're a pretty girl, too! Red hair is the world's best, isn't it?'

Without waiting for her reply, he led the way across the stone hall and away to the far end. She saw that the whole place was practically empty of furniture. A huge grandfather clock stood in one corner, towering over-high, like a corpse that is heightened by death, and sewn into a shroud. She had no idea why she kept thinking of such dreadful things, but she had grown morbid and could not stop herself. There were no pictures and no rugs. The Welsh dresser at the far end was completely devoid of decoration, save for a man's riding-whip that had been flung down on to it. Luke opened the door beyond, and for the first time she saw the living-room of the old mill.

It was an L-shaped room, and she could not see what lay beyond the corner. In the part where she stood, she was again aware of an

75

almost complete lack of furniture, nothing save an over-long refectory table half set for a meal, the other half cluttered with a pile of odd papers, a broken-down typewriter, and a big pewter ink-well. The ingle occupied half the wall, a giant ingle of venerable red bricks, with seats at its corners, and cushions flung down before it. Amongst the cushions and half on a rag mat lay a lurcher dog. It stared at Crystal with baleful eyes, lifting its lip slightly, to show the glittering shine of teeth. There was something ominous about the dog.

'Hey, Pixie,' commanded Luke, and at the sound of his voice, she dropped her lip and laid her head the other way, becoming motionless, her eyes averted.

The room was destitute of any real attraction, and Crystal glanced round it apprehensively. Yet a good fire burnt in the ingle, and the logs made a pleasant sound, though out of the distance there still came the noise of the mill-wheel. Then, as she stood there, her eyes fell on the solitary picture that hung beside the ingle. It was a great picture of a garden full of modernistic flowers in blobs of paint. There was a tangle of love-in-a-mist, of crimson poppies, and a welter of cornflowers and of rye. A Man walked through the garden, a Man in white raiment with His eyes full of joy, and looking at it Crystal realized instantly that it was a masterpiece. The eyes of the Man were full of a loving emotion, for they were speaking eyes. Compassionate and tender, they seemed to smile at her, so that suddenly she had the feeling that she had not come here in vain; that she need not be afraid, and had made no mistake. In this dismal house the picture spoke of some quality of good which now she believed that she would find.

She went over to the hearth, and looked down at the tattered old rag mat, of the kind that she had always thought only lay in the kitchens of very poor people. The room was furnished with a brick floor, and here and there an occasional rush mat lay, but it gave the impression of something frugal and poverty-stricken, or of people who had no real interest in their home. Perhaps the truth of the matter was that it was not a home, but just a house. All the time, Pixie watched her.

Luke said, 'I'm sorry if I sounded a bit gruff just now when I looked through the grille. I suppose that I got fed up going to Penzance, then not finding you there. I thought you had chucked in your hand, and were not coming after all, or that you heard something, and had changed your mind.'

'Heard something? What could I have heard?'

'I don't know. I just don't know.' It seemed that his tone was evasive, and he was going to say no more; realizing that it would be a mistake to pursue the subject, she changed it.

'That is one of the most beautiful pictures that I have ever seen. Who painted it?'

'I did.'

She could not believe it, and wheeled round sharply to face him. 'You did? But it is a masterpiece. You must be a very great artist!'

'No. I just paint to amuse myself sometimes. I have not done any of it for a very long time now.'

She glanced down at his hands, and saw suddenly that although his body might be that of a rather rough man of the sea, his hands were those of an artist. She knew that she was attracted to him, the man with the gruff voice, with the indifference to the clothes that he wore, with the dark eyes under lowering brows, and the rough hair, but the sensitive hands of a man who paints beautifully! His voice, too, how husky it was, yet it could change suddenly, and become almost tender!

He looked at her and smiled. 'Get warm,' he said.

'I think it would be better if I could go up to my room and get out of my wet clothes.'

'I'm sorry. I'll ring for the maid to take you whilst I go out and see about the luggage. Then we'll have a bite down here.' He rang an old-fashioned bell, a question-mark in white porcelain on the wall beside the ingle. As he did it, Crystal could hear the clanging sound of it echoing a long way off. They waited. Out of the distance there came the sound of quick feet in slippers that did not fit accurately and therefore shuffled.

He said, 'Karin may seem queer to you, but she's a good girl, and has been wonderful with my mother. She never jibs at work, and when you get used to her I am sure that you will like her.'

'I know I'll like her,' yet Crystal was remembering the way Mervyn had become silent when he had talked of her.

There was a tap at the door, and it opened. A woman the size of a child entered, her body rocking as she walked, her funny little arms jerking.

'You rang?' she squeaked.

For Karin was a midget.

V

Karin took Crystal upstairs to the bedroom that had been allotted to her. There was no carpet on the stairs, and their footsteps made a strangely hollow sound that was gloomy. They went along a winding passage, lit only by small church-like oil lamps that were stuck on the wall, giving a gleamy light through their stove-pipe globes, whilst the reflectors behind them were smeary.

Karin prattled gaily as she went on ahead, her funny little body swinging to and fro, running in places so that she should not delay her, and obviously delighted to meet a new face. She

79

wore a stiffish print frock, which bunched, for she was a very extraordinary figure; her hair had been permed into an outrageous display of curls, and a miniature apron, the size of a man's pocket handkerchief, was tied around the middle of her; one could hardly call it a waist.

'This is the room, miss,' she said, and opened the door.

The door opened on to a beautiful room, which was exquisitely furnished. She stepped from the barren landing with its worm-eaten floor, on to a velvet pile carpet of peach colour. The tiny half-tester bed was hung with a matching chintz on which a lovely design of gardenias trailed amongst their glossy leaves. The same material curtained a big bay window. The fire blazed in the grate, and the room gave the comfortable feeling of luxury. In the corner was an oak tallboy, and another door half-open, beyond which she could see that there was a bath-room equipped with pale pink which matched the curtains. The whole place would have taken any girl's breath away, but appearing in this house it was unbelievable.

'You have a nice bath, and get really warm again, miss,' Karin suggested, 'then I'll get the supper ready.'

Crystal was going to like Karin, just as Luke had said, and she felt herself attracted to the midget already. She was recovering from the first unpleasant impression that Smuggler's Mill had made on her, and everything was getting better. Then she realized as she went into the room, that it must be situated very close to the river, for there came the creaking, grinding sound of the mill-wheel turning round, and the water dripping back. Its proximity was almost irksome.

'The mill-wheel is very close, surely?' she said.

Karin nodded. 'Oh yes, miss,' she agreed, 'it's just below this room. The other lady—Miss Stella—didn't like that.' Hurriedly she put a finger to her lips as though she had said too much. 'Oh dear, I wasn't supposed to talk! That's my trouble. I chatter, but it is so nice to find someone to chatter to. You'll get used to the mill-wheel, miss. Everybody gets used to it in time.'

'It is such a beautiful room. Somehow I never thought of finding anything quite as lovely here.'

For a moment Karin peered at her, her bland little brows knitted together in perplexity. Then she quirked her fingers, the fingers of a child of six years old, and beckoned Crystal closer. She climbed on to the ottoman sofa, decorated in the same soft peach chintz, and scrambling on to it, by standing on tiptoe Karin could just reach Crystal's ear.

'Mr. Luke had this room done. He meant to get married, and they got this room ready. It's beautiful. It had to be, for everything must be of the best. There's a little sitting-room through that door, and that's pretty too. Just before the marriage she came here—the bride, I mean—and something went wrong. I don't know what happened to her, Miss Stella was her name, but she went out of the door and she never came back.' She nodded to emphasize her remarks. 'Now I'll go back to see about the supper.'

She climbed laboriously off the ottoman and scrambled to the floor, going shuffling to the door, where she ran into Luke bringing in a couple of suitcases. He came into the room and put the cases down.

'I'll bring up the trunk.'

'Not just yet. I'm going to have a bath. I've got chilled to the marrow, and I do get such awful colds. It would be a bad start. I don't want to stay in these damp things a moment longer than I can help. When I'm ready, I'll find my way down. Will that be all right?'

'Of course. Your coat *is* wet. And don't start off with a bad cold. That would indeed be a bad beginning.'

He went again. Her first idea of him had been wrong; through the grille she had gathered quite an outrageous impression, and regretted it. He had charm. He had the sort of attraction that she had never met in a man before, an attraction which made her glad to have come here. She had done the right thing.

She locked the door, and slipped out of her wet clothes, hanging them up before the cinder fire. She went into the bath-room and had the best bath of her life. The towels matched the soft pink *décor*; there was exquisite soap, and bath crystals in a large pink bowl. As she warmed, she felt that the whole of this unreal world slipped into a better perspective. She saw it no longer as a nightmare, which until this moment was what it had threatened to become; it had changed into a romantic adventure.

She dressed again slowly, feeling relaxed, and almost happy. A sense of excitement was within her heart as she put on the little silk frock which she had thought would never look right for Cornwall, but which now looked lovely. Made of tender powder blue, it clung to her, and she swathed a dull tangerine sash round her waist, a colour that gave new lights to her hair. She had the feeling that tonight she must look her best. There was a purpose in it.

She coaxed the damp hair into shape, then she opened the door of the beautiful bedroom, and went down the passage, back to the living-room.

'May I come in?' she asked as she opened the door.

On the ugly rag mat, Pixie snarled at her.

'Shut up, Pixie,' said Luke as he rose from the shabby old typewriter on the far end of the table. He stood there in the breeches and the tired shirt, but she noticed that he had brushed his hair, which was raked back from his head, and it disclosed eyes which could read the soul and which were dark as peat. He had rare good looks, and was even better looking than she thought when they had met, but that had been in such difficult circumstances that it was best to forget it.

'I'm sorry if I'm late.'

'You're not, and I believe there is some supper ready. I apologize for work being here,' and he indicated the typewriter, its tin cover battered and chipped, so that pale spots of cheap metal showed through the japanned lid. 'When you've had your supper, you must come and see my mother who is waiting to see you. Meanwhile there is lots to explain. I'm sorry my father is out, but our job takes us out and about a lot.'

'What is your job?'

'We deal with Customs and Excise.'

'But surely there are no Customs and Excise needs in this part of the world? There is no major port close at hand, is there?'

'There are Customs and Excise people all over the country, you know,' and he smiled at her a little quizzically. When he smiled he had great charm. 'We never disclose what we do. There is always a lot of hostility to me in this sort of job in this kind of place. They say the policeman has no friends, maybe that applies to us also! We're unpopular always.'

84

So this explained what Mervyn had said. She nodded. They sat down at the table, and he took the lid off the delicious-smelling tureen of soup that Karin had brought.

The soup was excellent, followed by a chicken that was beautifully browned, and served with roast potatoes and a pineapple salad, the sort of food that Crystal would never have expected to receive in this eerie little mill house, which had appeared to be so ill-furnished and so gloomy. When the chicken was finished, Karin returned to bring in a great pottery dish of glistening baked apples that had been stuffed with cloves and served with a clear ginger sauce.

They sat over it.

'She *can* cook,' she said; 'after self-service cafés, cheap baked beans on toast, and frizzling a bloater over a gas-ring in the bed-sit., this is sheer heaven!'

Luke told her a little of the life in this Cornish village where his forebears had lived before him, and of the work that she would be expected to do for them.

His mother had been stricken with arthritis some years ago, and for the past three years had been more or less confined to bed. She had tried every kind of treatment of which they had heard, and she had been to London under all the specialists, and there had been no improvement. In their desperation they turned elsewhere and now they had got in touch with a French doctor who came across to attend her. He came over occasionally by boat from one of the islands in the Channel, and his cure was a revolutionary one, entirely different from anything else that had so far been devised for the malady.

Most certainly she was better than she had been for some time, because she could turn over in bed, clumsily, he admitted, but it was no longer an impossibility, and although she grew very despondent, she had brighter moments. The French doctor had warned them that she would be depressed, for one of the points on which he insisted was that she should get a great deal of sleep. For this purpose she was given a nightly sleeping draught which had a depressing effect, but this could not be avoided.

'What does the local man say?' asked Crystal.

It seemed that the Tregarths had quarrelled with him, for he was a most unpleasant creature, would not come when sent for, and was horribly difficult. They had quarrelled with the vicar, also.

'Mr. Ingram?'

Luke turned his eyes to her, they were smouldering now like incipient fires under the thick dark brows. His mouth had become a saw, and he scowled. When he spoke, it was through clenched teeth which changed his whole tone.

'I thought you said that you knew nobody in this part of the world. I asked you when I wrote to you, and most certainly that was what you wrote back. But you know Mervyn Peters, and

86

now it seems that you know the vicar also.'

'No I don't. I have only heard of him. His name is Charles Ingram?'

'Yes, it is. You've not met him?'

'No.'

'You've missed nothing.' She did not like the suggestion of a sneer in his voice, and the dark fire that continued to glower in those eyes. 'He is the eternal proof of the fool of the family going into the Church. A nit-wit; and an interfering one, which makes it so devilishly awkward. We owe most of the hostility towards us in this village to the fact that he would interfere in what was not his own business.'

Then he lapsed into silence, sitting there clicking his fingers together with the nervous tension of one who is uneasy and wants to hide it. Crystal waited for a few minutes, then discreetly changed the subject once again.

'Isn't it difficult having a doctor who is on a far-off island, or is it close in?'

'Forty miles out.' She got the impression that he was still angry with her. 'There is not likely to be any sudden change with Mother, just a gradual improvement all the time. She is—she is a very darling person, proud in a way; the house belongs to her, and to her people before her, and you'll love her, everybody does.'

There was the sound of Karin coming shuffling down the stone passage beyond the door, and she came in with a great jug of steaming hot coffee. She set the tray before Luke, then waited a moment, tittering a little, her funny little hands fluttering at the pockets of an absurd baby apron.

'Something the matter, Karin?' Luke asked.

'Just a message. Only a message. Mrs. Tregarth says you won't be too long, will you?'

'No, tell her we are both coming up to her the moment we have finished the coffee.'

He was composed now, and he smiled again. The dark fires died out of his eyes, and the set saw-like line from the mouth. He seemed to have no association with the man who had peered at Crystal so grimly through that grille or the one who had sat there, hunched and glowering because he learnt that she had friends in the neighbourhood, and suspected her of deceiving him. He poured out the coffee, helping her to clotted cream from a full bowl, going on talking all the time. Once the mill had been so charming, he remembered it when he was young, and his mother kept the garden beautiful, and the house glorious. He had sent Crystal a photograph of it as it had been, because like that, he had loved it so much.

'It was a little misleading,' she told him.

'Oh well, the days for fancy work are over and done with, I suppose. Money doesn't go as far as it once did, and people haven't the time to fiddle about with flowers. You can't expect it, can you?'

'I don't know.'

He had a strange knack of asking questions, letting them fly almost as if they were barbs which he hoped would draw blood. He was, she felt, inquiring about her and trying to make her admit to opinions, desires, and ambitions, so that he could assess her from them. She withdrew into her shell a trifle bewildered, yet she knew that he attracted her. He had something that other men she had met had never got. His handsomeness was appealing, his way of flying straight to a point, and of changing. He was a weathercock man, a vane veering in the wind, and for the moment she did not understand him, but she would.

Given time (now she was determined to have the time) she would understand him completely.

There would be a lot to write back to Tony in the first letter which only this morning she had promised him should be posted as soon as possible after she got here. She would tell him everything, of Luke's broken romance of which Karin had whispered, of the beautiful suite with the soft pink bath-room which she dare not believe was her own.

She finished her coffee.

'Now let us go up and see your mother,' she suggested, gently.

VI

The crux of this whole situation lay in what sort

of a woman Mrs. Tregarth really was. Already Crystal had the hunch that she was going to like her; maybe she was misled by Luke's admiration for her, by the fact that when she was about the place flowers had blossomed in the garden and the house had been well furnished and beautiful.

They went out of the room, the dog watching them with never a movement. Her eyes were the colour of water, and the strangely twitching upper lip was still raised in the half-snarl that defied the world. Luke looked back at her.

'She's a strange creature, that dog! I often wonder what dogs think of, and if they think;' for a second his eyes challenged Crystal's. They were beautiful eyes; they had the power to flash fire, to tell secrets, to use words that the lips would never dare to use. They had command in them. For a moment she found herself wondering about Stella. Had this girl lost something or gained something, when so near her wedding-day she had backed out of the affair because of the mill-wheel that went round and round and whose noise disturbed her? Now Crystal knew that this man, who on first meeting had frightened her considerably, had the power to provoke emotion. He could unleash in her feelings that she had not thought could be. He realized it, also. He saw the look cross her face, and smiled a moment, then impulsively he reached out a beautifully modelled hand and laid it on her arm, encouragingly, sympathetically, almost as though there passed from him to her some inner and beautiful expression of human emotion.

'Maybe I'm not as bad as I seem to be?' he suggested, and smiled.

'I—I never thought you were too bad.'

She felt the blood surge to her face, and then she made no other remark but followed him up the bare staircase which echoed hollowly to their footfalls, and along the uncarpeted landing which lay above it.

She disliked the lack of decoration everywhere, and longed for pictures and ornaments, for flowers in bowls, yet there was nothing. The noise of the mill-wheel, which seemed to turn for ever, had slipped into the distance and had become almost a whisper, something of no importance to them.

Just outside the massive door, Luke paused and turned to her. In a low voice he said, 'My mother is a very sick woman. She fosters strange creatures of the imagination, as sick people do when they are confined so long to one room. Bear with her, remember that a long illness is very hard to bear. Please be kind to her.'

'But, of course. That is why I have come, isn't it? I am quite sure that your poor mother needs all the kindness that she can get. Oh, I do so hope that I will have brought luck to this house, that everything will change, and this will be the beginning of her getting really better.'

For a second she caught his eyes. He gave her a look, one that had no association with the glare with which he had greeted her through the grille. It was the look of a man who seeks friendship in a desperate but hopeless search for happiness. A soul lost in a desert which he believes will destroy him, and from which he feels there can be no escape.

Yet all he said was, 'Thank you,' in a subdued voice.

He opened the door.

The room beyond was long and low, with dark oak rafters striping the ancient ceiling. It had little likeness to the beautiful bedroom that Crystal now occupied, for the tiled floor had only a few rugs on it, no velvet pile carpet, and it conformed to no set colour scheme. The curtains were obviously old and worn, the colouring had faded out of all knowledge, but the log fire burnt pleasantly in the wide brick ingle, and the bed was drawn close to it. It was a big double bed, of the kind which had been so popular at the beginning of the century, made of brass and iron in a stereotyped pattern.

Lying there was the sick woman. Mervyn had said that she was Junoesque, a compelling person, large and handsome, and he had given the impression that at times her manner could be overpowering. Now it would seem that she must have shrunk to practically nothing, for she was a small woman, wizened with her illness. The face that peered up at Crystal was strangely lined, and looked almost like a walnut against the bright linen of the embroidered pillows. If she had had beauty she had lost it with the stature that the illness had taken from her. Her body seemed to be lost between the hillocks of feather overlay, and was covered with an eiderdown quilt, once a bright pink, now faded in common with everything else in this tired old room. The eyes, dark and languid, stared helplessly at Crystal, and the girl knew that here was someone sick with the longing for a friend.

She went closer to the bed, and saw that the coverlet peeping from under the eiderdown was of old pink wool, in holes, and a corner of it sadly moth-eaten. None of this was quite what she had expected after the luxury of the quarters that had been allotted to her; the completely modern bath-room with its pale pink bath, the fitments, and untarnishable silver taps; the hot towel-rail which would be an eternal joy; the bedroom itself, spacious and up to date, with the tiny sitting-room which probably had been originally intended for Luke's dressing-room and which now had an escritoire in it, a comfortable chair and a Knowle sofa.

'I've come to help you, and try to get you well again,' said Crystal, quite tenderly.

The woman did not speak, but still stared at

her, the eyes utterly pathetic in the rutted face which once had been beautiful but now had lost everything. Even hope! Crystal realized that she was so worn out with her illness that she had no power left to fight for her own life.

'You'll hate this place,' said Mrs Tregarth at last, 'it's unhealthy. Unwholesome, too! You'll hate it.'

'I won't. I haven't come here to hate it, but to love it, and I don't find it unhealthy or unwholesome, anyway not yet. I have come here to get you well again.'

'Oh, if you only could!'

'I can, and I will.'

'Is that a promise?'

She still stood there looking down at the poor invalid; she reached for her hand and took it into her own, a hand gnarled like some willow tree which, growing ancient in the river mist, has become twisted out of all knowledge. At that moment she realized that Mrs. Tregarth was looking beyond her to her son, almost as though she was asking Luke if it really was a promise.

'I *will* make you better,' said Crystal.

'Thank you, dear.'

The eyes that the woman turned to her for a moment, changed. She swallowed down unshed tears, then she said, 'I've been alone. So terribly alone,' and, with a furtive glance at Luke, 'Ask him to go away for a moment so that we can talk. Do ask him to go away.'

It was difficult to do that, and not the sort of task that Crystal would have chosen for her first one for this poor sick creature, but there was no means of avoiding it. She glanced up, the subdued light from beside the bed finding new and vivid red in her hair, lighting her eyes until the jade darts came into their warm, sherry colour.

'Your mother wants to be alone with me.'

Luke stared at her, he could not believe what she had said, and she knew that now his eyes had the same look in them as they had had when they had glared at her through the grille in the front door, such a little while previously. Without uttering a word, he turned, and walking out of the room, closed the door behind him so that it did not make a sound. His mother listened for the echo of his receding steps along the bare boards of the landing, but it never came. There was just the distant rustling sound of the mill turning and turning, but none other. The sick woman moved herself with a grotesque difficulty towards the girl, levering her body up, much as some crab, lost to the tide, levers himself ponderously out of a rock-pool.

'You'll stay with me? I've been so bewildered by everything that is going on and so frightened. I need help. Something is happening in this house, something that neither Luke nor my husband want me to know. They won't tell me anything and now I have had to give up asking them. I want it to be you and me together in this. Oh God, that it should have to come to this!'

'Maybe it isn't as bad as you think. Don't you realize that staying in this one room, being ill and alone, lying here hour after hour, may have jaundiced your feelings so that now you don't know what is happening? I don't suppose that anything is really amiss, you know.'

'It is! It is very much amiss.' She dropped her voice to a whisper. 'They want me to hand over the mill to my husband, to transfer the deeds into their combined names, his and Luke's. I won't do it. This mill belonged to my people for over two hundred years, and nothing will make me give it up. You see, I know what would happen to me if I did. I know, and that is what they are trying to keep from me.'

The poor creature was obviously suffering from dreadful delusions. Crystal made a frantic effort to try to help her. 'I shouldn't worry about any of that just now. It's all going to be very different, for you have got me.'

'Yes, I've got you. It is an immense relief to see the sort of girl you are. I thought—I did think that my husband might have got somebody old, and hard, and grave. I could not have borne that! Then they had difficulties in getting anybody; some would see this place first, and they did not want to be isolated and lonely. They—they did not like the sound of the mill-

96

wheel going round and round. It had to be someone from far away, someone from London.'

'I'm from London.'

'I know, I know. You see it could not be anyone local, for the local people dislike us. It's come to that. I don't know quite what has happened but it *has* come to that. We'll have to fight this together, my dear.'

'Of course we will. Now don't get yourself too worked up, because if you do you'll never sleep, and I am sure that the doctor wants you to get lots of sleep.'

'That doctor!' For a moment there was a look in her eyes reminiscent of Luke's when he had peered out from behind the grille. 'That doctor! They give me things to sleep and it means that every morning I hardly know what I am doing. Then my husband comes in and asks me about making the new deeds for the mill. One of these days I shall give way, because I shall be so fuddled by that wretched sleeping draught that I have not got the ghost of an idea as to what I am doing. That will be too horrible!'

'It isn't going to happen. I am here to stop all that.'

'Bless you, dear child. You and I will get on awfully well together,' and taking Crystal's hand closer, she put her lips to it, and kissed it again and again.

That was when the door opened quite

suddenly, almost as if the moment had been deliberately chosen.

'Finished?' asked Luke, as he entered.

'I'm only tiring your mother, and if we talk too much she will have a wakeful night. It is time we left her now.'

'It won't mean a wakeful night!' Luke's voice was quite determined. 'Mother will have one of her tablets. Dr. Fénon insists that she should have them every night to make sure that she sleeps well. It is imperative to the cure.'

'But, Luke, they make me feel so ill next day.' Mrs. Tregarth's voice was pathetically protesting from the bed. 'I don't need them, and I don't want to have them; a little natural sleep is worth all that they can do to me.'

But Luke ignored what she said and had gone to the side, picking up a small flat box, its white lid ringed with black, and on the centre-piece the spidery writing of a Frenchman.

'Here you are, Mother.'

'Please, Luke, I don't want to take it. I know that they are bad for me, for they make me feel so awful when I wake, and that does not go off for hours.'

'You must take it. Dr. Fénon says that you are to take them.'

'Sometimes I wonder if that man really is a doctor, I mean a doctor as we know them here in England.'

'Of course he's a doctor. What else do you

98

suppose he is? Of course he is a doctor, and doing his very best for you. If anybody in this world can make you better he is the man. Now drink this down.'

He stood over her until she drank it.

VII

When they were sitting together later, talking in the L-shaped living-room with the fire purring like the sea, and Pixie asleep on the shabby rag mat, Luke was quite a different man.

He was charming, this Cornishman with the jetty black hair and the mahogany skin, against which his eyes flashed from time to time. She shrank from the fact that he had a particular attraction, and that there was something he could rouse in her which surprised her. It was a response which had remained silent to the arts of Mr. Hellston murmuring of little dark mink ties and blue mink tippets, of Tony, and even the golden-haired gay charm of Mervyn Peters.

They talked for a while, the clock going on, and when it was nearly midnight she went up to bed. Now she was quite uncertain of how she really felt about this place. Was it mysterious, or was this her imagination? She knew that she was already fond of the poor sick woman, a prisoner in that shabby room, but it was highly possible that she imagined much. She was also deeply attracted to the young man, who might be devil or might be angel, in some mysterious manner

99

of his own. For an angel had painted the exquisite picture of the Man in the garden, and most certainly a devil had given his mother the sleeping tablet!

Crystal wondered what sort of man the French doctor was; all she knew was that his name was Dr. Fénon, and that he came from an island forty miles out to sea. Now she found herself far from sleepy, and she was wondering what the head of the house was like. He had put in no appearance, and somehow she found that she was beginning to think about him. Karin had told her that he would not be back until very late. Already she had found that queer, bunched-up little Karin was an amiable personality, the kind on whom she could rely. If there was anything wrong in this household, Karin knew nothing of it and went on her own way, getting on with the work of the place. Crystal and she were going to be friends, which was an excellent thing, seeing that much of the development of the house depended on the two of them.

She undressed by the low fire, more awake than she had thought would be possible. Beside the big bay window the mill-wheel seemed to be increasing its speed, and groaning more than ever. She realized that it had several speeds, which might be influenced by the tides, by the height of the river, or maybe by a mill-leat flowing past the house itself. The sound of the

100

water churning its way back into the river was irksome; she did not know why it irritated her, as it continued slowly but insistently, for a mill-wheel is seldom still.

She finished her unpacking, arranging everything in the drawers freshly papered and prepared for her. Then she heard a clock striking midnight somewhere in the hall.

At that moment she heard another sound beside that of the mill-wheel, gyrating and pounding. It was the noise of a car coming down the lane, stopping a moment, then turning in at the gate itself. Instinct told her to go to the window, and she stood there, lifting the curtain very cautiously indeed, for suddenly fear directed her.

It would never do to be caught peeping!

The dark hulk of a big car had come to a standstill just a little way up the drive, and was now standing where she had an excellent view of it. Two men got out. The first man was smally made, he had rather rapid, jerky movements, and was very active. She saw him turn to say something to his companion, and realized that he was like a puppet dancing on a string, moving quickly this way and that, talking jerkily also. He gesticulated with over-busy hands as he spoke.

The other man was a much older person, and instantly she knew that for the first time she was looking at Mr. Tregarth himself. He was a big man, not a man who had grown stout with the accumulation of the years, but one who had always been too big. Too tall also, and too wide. He did not carry himself well, for he stooped a good deal, his clumsy head poked forward, and sunk down in between two bulwarks of shoulders. Crystal could not see his face, for his cap was peaked, with a peak that caught the lights from the house and gave the impression of glistening as if made of glass, and this peak came down and hid his features. But she felt that they were solid, just as instinctively she knew that he was a very dark man, that his cheeks were pouched and sagging, and that she was not going to like him.

Yet she watched from behind the safe covering of the curtain. Two men, one so agile and one so heavy, coming towards the house. She heard the sound of the door opening, and then slammed to. She waited for the next sound. There was none at all! Only the mill-wheel turning round and round in its ceaseless creaking duties.

No more.

CHAPTER THREE

I

After the curious adventures of a mysterious

evening which she could not hope to get into its proper perspective, the strange thing was that Crystal slept quite well. She had thought that she was bound to lie awake, listening to the creaking turns of that mill-wheel, but instead it acted as something of a lullaby, and she fell asleep, not waking until the next morning. Then it was the brightness of the sunshine streaming into the room that awakened her.

She sat up in bed, staring round unable to believe that this was not Mrs. Biggins's, with Battersea Park lying just beyond the window in all the vivid greenness of the fresh spring day.

She remembered what had happened, and getting up, drew the blinds to see what manner of view lay beyond her window. It was even better than she had thought possible.

The green pasture land went to the cliff-edge, and she realized for the first time how close the mill must be to the Channel. On the horizon she could see the blue zircon sparkle of its waters, and every wave was fluted with a white frill which caught the light. She saw it with the hunger of someone who has been a prisoner in a London office for long hours, and who sometimes has longed for a sight of the sea.

In the garden immediately below the window itself she saw a very contrasting scene compared to the drive with the pot-holes, the nettles, and the groundsels, and the sow thistles with their yellow flowers. Here there was a brick walk, which, even if weedy, still retained some of its original beauty. The Dutch flower-beds which once had been meticulous (if she could judge from the couple of topiaried box bushes which had kept much of their inspiration) were full of weeds with their flowers, but now showed a brave array of crown imperials, yellow and russet red, of Solomon's seals, and wild forget-me-nots growing in a raggle-taggle of vividly blue blossoms. The weeds had been unable to choke the profusion of these flowers. Beyond the river was an orchard gone wild, and here amongst the grass was cow's parsley in a cobwebby lace, and pheasant-eyed narcissi, their heady scent coming across the water into her room.

A may tree, the first that Crystal had seen out this year, was already budding into soft pink, as the wind which had sunk into a light breeze played with the leaves. It was a peaceful and countrified scene, one about which one could have no doubts.

Why had she been suspicious last night? She had the best living-quarters that she had ever had, far, far better than any others in this house, the salary was excellent, the best she had ever been offered, and she ought to realize that she was the luckiest girl in the world.

Also, there was Luke!

He *was* attractive; he could rouse in her an emotion which had stayed quiet with every other man she met. If last night she had ever thought about throwing up the job, most certainly this morning she knew that it would be madness. Whatever might be going on in Smuggler's Mill was not her business, and as long as it did not affect her, she had no right to query it. She had come here to keep house, to see after the sick woman and make the home happier for her presence. This was what she would now set out to do.

Karin brought in some tea.

The new day held promise in it. It was a spring-like world, dressed for the occasion, with narcissi in the grass, and the crown imperials in the border. She dressed slowly, for Karin had already told her that there was lots of time, and she went downstairs in a house that was dead quiet.

The mill-wheel had stopped.

Somehow she would have expected it to go on and on, right through the day, and only cease, if it ever did cease, when night came. Now the silence that filled the house had a strange quality about it by reason of the vigour of its contrast. The hall was still. She went into the living-room where Pixie the dog lay sprawled on the rag mat, which gave the impression that she had not yet left it. The light of the sun came in and made it a golden room, and the long picture that Luke had painted so surprisingly well had a vivid beauty about it.

She went to it, and stood there looking at the unreal garden and the Man who walked in it, with the morning light glistening on the simple gown. She could not understand how a young man like Luke had ever done it. About him there must be something that as yet she did not understand, but something that she would discover, for she stood on the threshold of romantic adventure, and before her lay everything.

Pixie watched her with expressionless eyes the colour of water. Her upper lip was no longer snarling, but Crystal felt that so far they had not reached the moment when they made real friends of each other. It would come. She had now made up her mind that whatever else happened, she would make friends here.

She turned to the table.

A green and white gingham cloth was spread across it, and in the centre an enormous blue bowl was filled with golden-trumpeted King Alfred daffodils. The food was delicious. On a large, unpolished wooden board, scrubbed snowy clean, there were a couple of newly-baked loaves, and by them a pound roll of yellow country butter, the kind that she had not seen in London for years. The cut-glass bowl of freshly-stewed rhubarb had with it a jug of clotted cream, there was one of those plump Victorian egg-stands in silver, and half a dozen boiled brown eggs standing in it.

On the side there was a ham, and it wore a pert little frill about it, and was covered with light brown bread-crumbs, looking most attractive. Crystal did not have to ask, for instinctively she knew that it would be home-cured.

Luke came into the room.

This morning he wore a canary yellow sweater with a polo collar that came right up to his dark face. Somehow he looked different from the way he had appeared last night. His cord breeches were off-white, his hair lustrous from recent brushing, and she realized in the light of this new day that he was a strikingly good-looking young man. If he was at times something of a termagant, did it not make him more attractive? It seemed odd to be having breakfast alone with him, yet here they were sitting down at the table, her heart making curious noises as she poured out from the stout silver tea-pot.

He said, 'Slept well? That's right. My father won't be long, usually he is the first here to a meal, but he was up late last night, and he is getting older these days. Life tires him more. He is a Cornishman as we all are, and to some people he may appear to be abrupt. Don't be misled in that way. He doesn't mean it.'

'Of course not, and by the way, I saw him from my bedroom window last night. He did come in very late and he had a friend with him.'

Luke shot her a quick look, for a moment his

brow knitted, then he shook his head. 'Oh no, my father did not bring anybody here with him. You must have dreamt that. He came in very late indeed in the car, but quite alone.'

'But I saw him. The other man, I mean. He was small, the dapper kind, and he got out of the car first, your father afterwards. Leastways, I thought that it must be your father, he was a big man who stooped a little, and very tall indeed. I am sure that I saw two people.'

Luke had been cutting one of the freshly-baked loaves, and he stopped to look at her. About his eyes at this moment there was something similar to that look which she had noticed when he came to the grille last night, and she had been waiting outside in the rain.

'Before we go any further in this, let me advise you, don't start spying on us! Spying will take you nowhere, and may send you a long way back. We are simple folks, country folks, and our work is our own as are our lives! We have had too much of this sort of thing already, and we don't like it. We want no eavesdroppers here. You came down to see after my mother, to run the house, and for no other purpose. Maybe the less you look out of your window the better it will be for everyone. You understand that, don't you?'

Crystal knew that suddenly she was dismayed that he should have so entirely misinterpreted the meaning. The tears smarted into her eyes, and she felt herself flush.

How smouldering were those eyes, how tanned the high cheek-bones, and how stern his jaw! She knew that Luke would have made a name for himself on the films, for he had beauty, he had personality, and the power to rouse in a girl a tremendous realization of his personal attraction. She swallowed down the tears.

'It's just that I am new here, and everything is so strange. I'll get used to it, of course, if you'll bear with me; I'll do my best. I wasn't spying, please don't think that of me!'

As she said it she had the strange feeling that she was being watched. It is a knowledge that comes suddenly, and for no reason. She turned sharply, prompted by her own instincts, and then she saw that behind her the door had opened silently, or perhaps they had been so much occupied with each other at the moment, that they had not been aware of it. The man she had seen descending from the car last night was standing there, stooping a little, over-tall, over-broad, and staring at the pair of them. Under beetling dark brows that straggled like gorse bushes across his face, he looked at her with the compelling eyes that had a strong likeness to his son's. Save that in the older man's eyes there was no tenderness, no involuntary melting, for he was not a kind man. The way he stood there silently staring, had in itself something that was both repellent and alarming.

'Oh!' she said swiftly.

Luke turned and saw what had happened. 'It's my father,' he said, and all the joy had faded out of his voice. The timbre changed; now it was the schoolboy who sees the master coming sloping in at the door, and knows that it is the end of play! Then he pulled himself together. 'This is Crystal, who has come to run the house, do the shopping and keep an eye on Mother,' he said.

The big man made no sound. He came across the room to the table, holding out a hand that seemed to be gigantic. Yet when Crystal looked down at the great palm which enclosed her own hand, she saw that the fingers were long and almond-shaped like an artist's. They were beautiful fingers, capable of painting as Luke had done, and she wondered if she had made a mistake about all this, and really she had come into the home of great artists, and this gift was something that they did not intend to disclose.

Mr. Tregarth did not greet her; he merely shook hands in complete silence, then went to the arm-chair at the head of the table and opened the newspaper.

The meal was eaten in silence that was a strain, and the moment she had finished she excused herself, saying that she would have to go to see Mrs. Tregarth.

As she entered the room with the strange

brass-knobbed bed, she saw that Karin had already opened the windows and the fresh air was coming in. Undoubtedly she had been quite right when she had told herself that it would be warmer here than in London, and the scent from the narcissi was delicious. Yet on the bed the breakfast-tray had hardly been touched. The tea was half drunk, only the top taken off the egg, and the toast lying crumbling. Crystal stared at it.

'You don't feel like breakfast today?'

'It's the sleeping tablets. It's always the same when I have them, I feel quite dreadful later. I'd rather lie awake all night than fight these appalling mornings. They are so terrible.' Then in a half-whisper, 'That man was here again last night. He came in the middle of the night and then they woke me.'

'Which man?'

'Dr. Fénon. It's strange how he comes and goes and they never seem to be aware of when he is coming, or why. It always gives me the shivers too, because I can't like him. Even if he is the only man in the world with a cure for my present condition, I shall never like him.'

'I suppose he was the little man who got out of the car. I saw them come up and looked out because I had not yet gone to sleep.'

Mrs. Tregarth moved restlessly in the bed, with the uneasiness of a woman restless from long hours of drugged sleep. 'I was dead off

111

when I saw him as if I was in a dream. My husband was with him, and they stood at the end of the bed and would not go away.'

'Did he know you had had the sleeping tablet and ought to be asleep?'

'I don't know. I never know with him.' She began to cry a little. 'My husband wants to get the mill into his own name. He says it would save death duties, but I am not dying yet, and I think it is cruel that such a thing should be suggested to me. I am old and useless, and I know that I shall never be any better, and that he wants to be rid of me. But I won't give him the mill. If I signed that deed, then I should have nothing left to live for, I know.'

It was a helpless position, and although Crystal took the woman into her arms in a desperate attempt to help her, she knew that she could give her no real comfort.

She stopped crying. 'Luke is a good boy. Do remember, whatever you see or hear about this place, that at heart Luke *is* a good boy. He was such a dear before he got under this baleful influence. He paints beautiful pictures, and I wanted him to get right away and go in for painting, because I always hoped he would be a great artist.'

'He will be one, I'm sure. I think the picture in the living-room is quite wonderful. It was the first thing I noticed there.'

His mother was comforted. It was obvious

112

that she was devoted to her child, but that something had come between them, something had upset the whole running of the household and she was afraid of that something. Was it that French doctor who had come unseen by any save herself, and now seemed to have disappeared again? No, thought Crystal, it was the father. Even last night when she had peered through the curtain at her bedroom window, she had disliked him on sight, feeling that about him there was something of the vulture; the way that he had stood in the drive had left a lasting picture in her mind, the shoulders hunched up like the great bones of giant wings. Vultures wait for someone to die, and she had the feeling that there was much in what this poor thing said. She was in danger and that danger came not only from the dapper little doctor, but from the stocky husband also.

There was a rap at the door and the district nurse came in. She was a plump woman in a starched print frock with a navy blue coat over it. She had greying hair and may blossom complexion, and pleasant eyes.

'Ah, this is the new help,' she said, and set her bag down on the ottoman. 'Well, and what do you think of Cornwall? You started off on a nasty enough night.'

'Yes, it did rain, but today is fair enough.'

'Yes, today is beautiful.'

Crystal went to the door. She said, 'Now I'll

see what wants doing in the house, and leave you two together. Karin will tell me about any particular likes and dislikes for lunch, won't she?'

She went down the stairs, the household duties absorbing her, and perhaps that was what she most wanted. The dour master of the house seemed to have disappeared, but Karin was ready for her with a list of shopping that she wanted to be done before lunch-time.

'Mr. Luke's going into Penzance, or maybe St. Ives, he'd give you a lift,' said Karin, 'and then you could do my shopping.'

'Of course. Can I borrow a basket?'

'You'll want two baskets,' and Karin chuckled with delight as she went off to get them.

Crystal took them into the hall almost coinciding with the sound of the car coming into the drive driven by Luke. He had gone down to the village for petrol. She looked round the bleak hall with some trepidation, anxious above all else to give it something in the way of a welcoming quality which was now sadly missing from it. Surely new curtains could be bought to replace these very shabby ones? There seemed to be no lack of money in some things, yet so much in others. A few bright rugs on the floor, some horse brasses on the Welsh dresser, and a big bowl of flowers on the central table would make all the difference in the world to the place.

114

Luke came bursting in. 'Ready to come over to St. Ives with me?'

'Ready and waiting.'

The coupé car was almost new. It was painted in a soft shade of beige, and on the bonnet a silver fish mascot speared up into the sunlight. Luke turned with the deftness of an experienced driver, and they went out through the gap that had once been a gateway, where the cock-eyed posts stood so drunkenly awry. The lane beyond had trees in it, very different from the usual Cornish scenery, and a hill rising up from the river.

'Why don't you get a few things mended in your home?' Crystal asked him. 'The mill is a sweet old place, and with a little spent on it could be quite lovely. Surely it couldn't be madly expensive to buy a gate, or fix new posts there? Last night those two wretched things looked so macabre and eerie that they gave me the jitters.'

'I know.' He stared ahead of him, but she realized by his tone of voice that he was very well aware of her. 'The place does look neglected.'

'It gives people a very wrong idea.'

'My father doesn't care about those things. When Mother got so ill that she was tied to her room, he didn't care any more. She was the driving force at the mill; well, anyway, it is her house.' She wondered if she detected

115

resentment in his tone, and could not be sure. He went on after a moment. 'Mother loved pretty things, and she was the one who designed the room you've got.'

'It's beautiful.'

'It was for me. I don't know if anyone has told you, but I—well, I was going to be married.'

Crystal did not know if his voice invited confidences, if he wanted questions to be asked, or whether it was wiser to give silent condolences. She chose the latter. Anyway, she was not going to reveal the fact that Karin had already told her about the broken engagement. As she said nothing, Luke continued:

'Stella was quite the loveliest thing I'd ever seen, so lovely that these days she models for the artists in St. Ives, and they are pretty good choosers, I can tell you. I suppose it was that her beauty fairly knocked me backwards, for that's just the way things happen. Love at first sight. Have you ever met it?'

'No,' and even as she said it her heart turned over, for now she could no longer be sure. It had not been Mr. Hellston, nor Tony, nor Mervyn, but she could not be so sure that there had not been something about Luke. Last night the whole of her personality seemed to have changed, when they had talked in that strange living-room with Pixie snarling on that hideous rag mat, and the glorious picture on the wall of the Man in the garden.

116

'Well, it can happen. I thought Stella loved me too; anyway, it seemed like it. The date was fixed, everything arranged and Mother delighted; she always wanted me to marry. Then, a week before the actual day of the wedding, the whole thing bust up.'

'Don't tell me about it if you'd rather not. Sometimes it is rather painful talking about this kind of thing, even if it does help in the long run.'

But he still wanted to talk.

He began a little abruptly. Stella had been a glorious creature, and meeting her on holiday in Penzance he had immediately fallen in love with her. The idea had been that they would continue to live on at the Mill after their marriage, and a week before the day itself, she had come to tea. She had made excuses. The awful part was that he recognized them as excuses, and he knew that somebody had been talking to her. It was the village, he felt, the village that disliked him and his family so much and were like a solid force against them. Stella had put it down to the noise that the mill-wheel made. She hated the noise of it crushing against the water and did not think that she could entertain the idea of living on with that noise going all the time.

She had broken off the engagement.

At first he could not believe it, and had thought that he would break down; then he had gone on because people do go on, they have to.

Stella had bought herself a small cottage in St. Ives, and said that she intended living there for the rest of her life.

'If only she had gone away!' he said.

'Yes, but—but if you feel like that why are we shopping in St. Ives now, when Karin says we can get it equally well in Penzance? It does not make sense to me. If you feel so badly about it, why do you run the risk of meeting her again?'

'Because I don't feel badly about it any more. I've got over it. Leastways, I think I've got over it. Stella goes round with every rich artist in the place. The poor chaps are no good to her, I know that by this time, and in a way it helps. Besides, it is all very well of Karin saying we can buy the same things in Penzance. I have to go to St. Ives now because my father has something special that he wants fetched.'

'Why doesn't he fetch it himself? He must know that you run this risk and that it is hateful for you!'

'You don't know my father.'

'You mean he doesn't know?'

'I mean that it is never possible to persuade him to do anything like that. He goes his own way. He walks on his lone.'

'I see.'

They passed through Hayle and came now to the tidal stretch of water, with the Old Quay House on the right, and the road turning sharply and climbing a little into Lelant.

118

Rising to the top of the hill she saw the sea, turquoise blue, coming into Carbis Bay, lit scintillatingly by that sharp, definite light which is so essentially St. Ives. The trawlers were on the face of the water, and she saw the black rocks, and the great gulls swooping to and fro. On the road itself they came to the anemone gardens, vivid in the glory of the spring sunshine, with rivulets of violet and prune, with claret and petunia, and that deep rich rose-red.

'I—I always knew that St. Ives would be utterly beautiful,' said Crystal, suddenly sinking back amongst the comfortable cushions of the little car.

'It is. It's an incredible place and I hope to show you every inch of it some time, when we have the whole day to ourselves. That isn't today.'

'No,' she said softly, 'it isn't today.'

II

Luke was very charming, and about him on this drive there seemed to be little of the strange man who had peered through the grille at her last night. They came at last into the little crooked streets of St. Ives; it seemed that all the events of last night had travelled a very long way off. She would forget it. She had been tired, she had been frightened and had magnified everything outside its ordinary perspective, but this was a new day and it had every promise of

119

happiness in it.

They dropped down on to the sea front, with the fisherman's beach on the right. The trawlers were in and their baskets of silver fish gleamed in the brilliant sunlight, whilst the gulls screeched and circled about them. Luke brought the car to a standstill near the life-boat, and he got out. A couple of tabby cats sunned themselves complacently, and looking into the myriad tiny alleyways, some with their flights of steps, and all rising, Crystal saw that the place abounded in cats; they streaked through the shadows, this way and that, and some of them were themselves shadows.

'Where do they come from, Luke?'

'Have you never heard the old nursery rhyme:

As I was going to St. Ives,
I met a man with seven wives,
Each wife had seven cats,
Each cat had seven kits . . . ?

Well, that is what happens in St. Ives. Surely you knew?'

'I never took the rhyme seriously. I thought it was just a piece of fun.'

'Well, there was a bit more to it than that really. In the very old days the mice gnawed the nets as they hung to dry in the fishermen's lofts. One wretched little mouse could easily do a hundred pounds' worth of harm to a net and something had to be done about it. So they invested in cats. It's a tradition in St. Ives that you never get rid of a cat, for they owe their salvation to them. There must be literally thousands of them roaming about every street in the place.'

He took her down to the Porthmeor beach away from the strong smell of the fish and the shrieking gulls. She saw the surfing waves coming in, and the black Headland in the distance. The sands were soft and silverish, and near the water itself the gulls had patterned it as with the delicate fronds of ferns as they walked about the shore. They sat down under the rocks, and smoked a cigarette.

'It's lovely sand,' she said thoughtfully.

'It cleans everything. Even the marks off a suit will go if you sit here. After you've come to know St. Ives a little better, you will find that your skin goes soft as velvet from contact with the water here and the sand. London people get rough skins for the water in which they wash is so hard, but here in St. Ives the water is very different. They say this part of the country is crazy because we have our piskies and our little people. Maybe that's true, maybe it isn't, but it's a fine part of the world.'

'Of course it is.'

'Another cigarette?'

'Thank you.'

He lit it for her, and as he did so for a single

second his eyes caught hers. Was it her imagination that there was admiration in his? That for a moment he almost said something which, after all, he did not say? It was certainly not her imagination that her hand began to tremble and that she could hear her pulse quickening and feel her colour rising. It seemed to be a hundred years since yesterday when she had come out of Mrs. Biggins's house and had driven to Paddington with Tony, and they had discussed Charles Ingram's telegram. She had forgotten the journey with the worsening weather and her own sense of catastrophe, and then the horror of being marooned at Truro. Now none of that mattered at all. Yesterday had changed everything in her life. Not only had an entirely new set of circumstances entered her world, but she had met a man who was completely different from anyone she had ever met before. A man who was two men in one. One man who scared her, the other—and now she had to confess to the truth—a man with whom she could fall in love.

At last Luke looked at her. 'Well, this won't do the work of the day. I have to fetch my father's parcel or there will be a row when we get home again; you have to do the shopping. I'll show you the best shopping streets, and leave the rest to you. Then pick you up again in the car, and maybe we shall have time for a cup of coffee at the Copper Kettle, before we start back home. Would you like that?'

'I'd like it very much.'

They got up, shaking the sand from their clothes, and they went through the little broken alleyway, up Back Lane towards the Island. As they walked away, the music of the tide running in still came to them like the frail echoes of some flute, then died out. Crystal knew that the place had great charm and that at this moment she was perhaps happier than she had ever been before. The man who last night had frightened her so considerably, now had the power to give her this complete happiness. He was not unreal or sinister. They could be friends.

He took her to the street where the shops were, and showed her the way back, and she went alone to begin her shopping there whilst he fetched the parcel.

Crystal bought meat from the butcher at the corner, and fresh fish from the far shop where a black-haired black-eyed boy spoke in the broadest Cornish and told her fairy stories of the beaches and the mermaid of Zennor who went to church where they had a special choir stall for her.

It was happy shopping, friendly shopping amongst a friendly people, and the result of it was that she was a little late in returning to the car, for not only did she find that everyone wanted to talk to her, but all the streets looked much alike and as yet she was a stranger to them and continually lost her way. Besides, she had remembered that Karin particularly wanted two new pudding basins, being very exact about the sizes, and she had overlooked these, having to return again to the shops when she had almost reached the car.

At last she had finished.

'Good heavens, I had come to the conclusion that you were lost!' said Luke.

'I thought I might be, for all these alleys are very similar, but I caught sight of the sea and that is always a landmark.'

'Right! I think there is still time for a coffee at the Copper Kettle.'

'Lovely.'

The Copper Kettle was the café on the front with the beach sprawling before it, the gulls still screaming and the trawlers still selling their catches. It was approached by an outside stairway which rose to the first floor, and once inside that door Crystal saw that the walls were hung with pictures of all kinds, though most of them were marine paintings. In the little café, as in every other in St. Ives, all manner of pictures were displayed in the hope that at some time or another a sale would be effected. For the artists lived this way.

Crystal and Luke sat down on an old oak settle with cushions of flowered chintz, and beside them a ship's lantern hung, chinking a little when the breeze from the open window caught it and swung it to and fro. Beyond lay the shore, and the turquoise of the sea with its rising tide, and farther out the French crabbers circling round, and the Island itself against the sky line.

A girl took the order for coffee and cakes, and went off to fetch them. Luke lit another cigarette, his long, slim fingers caressing it, the hyper-sensitive fingers of an artist. She noticed them again.

'You ought to have been a St. Ives artist, you have the right hands for it. That was the first thing I noticed about you, your hands.'

'Now I thought it was my eyes when I had the audacity to look through the grille at you.'

'That was a very nasty thing to do. It came at the end of a filthy journey and scared me stiff. I wish you hadn't done it.'

'So do I—now. I'm always doing things I wish I didn't do. Something comes over me. Do you know ...' for a moment he stared at her and there was appeal in his eyes. They became the beseeching eyes of a spaniel, and then the lids lowered again. 'No, I can't tell you. All that will be for another time, but not now.'

'I saw your eyes first, your hands next, and I still think you should have been an artist.'

'I came here for a time. I suppose I believe that anyone can be what he wants to be, provided that he wants it sufficiently. I suppose I didn't want it sufficiently. Anyway, there was too much in between me and being an artist and it didn't work.'

'Meaning?'

'Meaning that you want to know too much. I've warned you that me and mine don't like being spied on, and you'll make a shocking mistake if you start that sort of thing. I'm not an artist; I never shall be one now. Ask no questions and you'll be told no lies; I learnt that when I was one of those Nosey Parker little boys for ever asking questions. In our home you'll find that the wise person asks no questions; she just accepts.'

'I'm sorry. I thought it was only natural when one got into new surroundings to want to know a little about them. Also I was interested because I believe that the world has lost a great artist.'

'I'm not as clever as you think, but thank you for the compliment.' She was looking fully into those handsome eyes that could go into slots and reveal nothing, yet at another moment could be sympathetically understanding, tender, and kind. He had the power to stir a deep emotion within her. Did he know it? she wondered. Was this her secret to be for ever kept from him, or was he already aware of it?

'I still think that your picture at Smuggler's Mill is quite wonderful. The man who could paint that could indeed paint everything.'

'Could he?'

For a single second his hand brushed hers and lingered, almost as though he liked the feeling that there was contact between them. In that very second a girl with a blonde head peered round the corner of the oak settle and gave a little affected laugh.

'Well, well, well!' she said in a voice that was half-bantering and yet half-questioning. 'Wonders will never cease! What d'you know about that?'

III

The girl was Stella Thayle!

Somehow from the first moment that Luke had told her about this girl, Crystal had had the instinctive feeling that this would happen. She looked at the girl. Stella was far more beautiful than Crystal had thought she could possibly be. She had one of those extremely fine skins which are like porcelain, with a colour that was a warm coral, and a dimple which danced outrageously in one cheek. Her hair was gold, and although Crystal realized by the first look that a certain amount of help had been given to it from a bottle, it was the sort of hair that you could only admire.

It had been cut by someone who knew everything about such work, with a heavy bunch of boyish curls artlessly sloping forward on to the forehead, and tight up at the sides. The back was cropped like a young lad's, and

127

although the curls were the reward of some expensive perm, they gave the appearance of being Nature's own private gift to the girl. Her eyes were dark blue, and the surround was of black lashes and brows, which had been wooed by mascara, but done so cleverly that no one challenged them.

The effect was languorously exquisite, and admirably fitted in with the clothes she wore, for Stella's great-stock-in-trade was a dress sense. She wore nigger brown slacks made rather tightly, but she had lovely legs and superbly slight hips. The trousers clung in all the right places, and if she needed them to be kind to her, then they were kind, meeting a honey-gold sweater which was clipped into the hand-span waist with a wide webbing belt the same nutty brown as the trousers. It had no clasp but was caught together by a unique pair of lobsters. There was something ridiculously fascinating about the belt, and the fact that similar but far tinier lobsters were dangling from her ears.

There was no doubt about it that Stella as a model would go a very long way, and the artists knew quite well the best when they saw it.

'Well, well, well!' she said again. Half-derisive, half-annoyed.

Instinctively Crystal realized that this was probably the last meeting that Luke would want. The warmth died out of his eyes, the

128

friendliness ebbed, and no longer was he relaxed and at ease, but strained and tense.

'Hello, Stella!'

'What have we here?'

Even though she must have been aware of the atmosphere she had caused, and the fact that she was not wanted, Stella caught hold of a small chair and gave it a swift turn so that she brought it into position beside the table. There was something studied about the casual way in which she sat down on it. Something that called for attention. Luke steeled himself for the occasion.

'This is Crystal Stevens. She has come down from London to look after the house, and help with Mother. She arrived last night.'

'I see,' the beautiful but remorseless blue eyes looked at Crystal as though they could read right through her, and did not like the message that they read. 'You came last night?'

'Yes, in the pouring rain.'

'And what do you think of Smuggler's Mill?'

Stella leant forward a little, her lovely eyes glistening. She had great beauty, this girl, a very dazzling kind of beauty, something that Crystal had not expected to meet.

'I like it. I have never been to Cornwall before, and I just had no idea that there was anything quite as charming in England. It is the most wonderful spot.'

'Like the people in it.' Stella gave Luke a

129

quick look, it might even have been an accusation. Then she said, 'What about the mill itself? Haven't you found out anything peculiar about that wretched wheel that goes on creaking and groaning all the time?'

'I have found it noisy, of course, but I shall get used to it. One can get used to anything.'

'I wonder if that's true. Well, you know your own business best, and I'll leave everything to you. Good luck to the mill,' and she shrugged her shoulders, dismissing the whole thing.

The little maid now returned with a big japanned tray on which was freshly-made coffee, a great bowl of sugar and some cream, and a delicious-looking plate of cakes.

'You might ask me to join you?' said Stella.

'Of course!' Yet even as Luke said it, Crystal realized that he resented this. 'What shall I order you?'

'Nothing too fattening, please. Something that doesn't put on weight, because a good girl can't be too careful, can she? Order me oodles of black coffee and no sugar at all. Certainly no cream. Oh, what cream can do to the hips!' and again she shrugged her shoulders. She turned once more to Crystal. 'So you think that you'll like your new job, and the place it's in?'

'Yes, I think I'll like it.'

Luke had been sitting there scowling. His face had darkened considerably as he watched the two of them, and now he interposed rather abruptly. 'You are asking too much, Stella. Crystal has not had time to look around her yet, how can she know a thing about it? She was soaked through when she arrived last night, and I thought she would have caught the cold of her life. Talk about a little drowned rat!' and he gave a nervous laugh. Crystal realized that he was not happy.

Stella wasn't listening. She was helping herself to a cigarette from a bronze case that she had opened rather clumsily. She was one of those people who have developed the disconcerting habit of never taking their eyes off the other person. She watched her all the time, and whatever else she did she did not look at it, but went on staring.

'How lucky for you, Luke, that she looks like anything but a drowned rat this morning! I should have said that you were in luck's way, but then you are one of those men who are always fortunate with your women.'

'Don't be so idiotic! My women indeed, as though I never knew another man!'

His tone had an edge to it. He showed that he was chafing against her banter which was so honey-sweet that somehow Crystal suspected the sickle behind it.

'She knows about us, I suppose? You and me, I mean, but then of course she does. Naturally you would have made sure of that before you brought her into St. Ives.' Her gaze shifted from his glowering face to Crystal's. 'I am the girl that Luke didn't marry. I suppose there is always a girl like me in every man's life if only he admitted the truth. If Luke hasn't told you, then I'm telling you now. I would have married him, but I simply could not stand the mill. It has something in it. His father's influence probably, I felt that all the time. Then there was that French doctor . . .'

'Look here, Stella, there's no need to go over the ground again. You hated the place and you hated my people. It's the world's oldest story. Crystal is new to this part of the country, and she isn't interested in our house, in my father, or the doctor. What's happened to your own boy friend, Stella? The one you got rid of me for? I heard that he had gone off with an American girl, who was down here a little while back. Was that just one of the stories that was going the rounds?'

Stella stubbed out the cigarette without any sign of emotion at all. It was noticeable that she remained without irritation. 'Darling, he went with the rounds, and with the wind. The American girl with him.'

Stella was a strange creature, she would never confess to the fact that once she had loved Luke Tregarth deeply, and had come to Smuggler's Mill with the idea of marrying him. He would inherit much, she had thought, and then the barrenness of the place had seared into her

132

heart. There was his father too, that big man with the hunched shoulders and eyes that reminded her of a game-cock. He insisted that when Luke married they would have to continue to live on at the mill, for their work entailed this. What was their work? Stella had asked, and she had never discovered the answer to that question.

Most certainly they were not entirely Customs and Excise as they said, even if their expeditions were connected with it. The village talked, she knew that. Anyone who lived in the place for very long was bound to find that out. She had become madly suspicious, but got no nearer to the right answer, and then just before the wedding there had been that crashing row.

She remembered it as she stubbed yet another scarce-smoked cigarette into a beaten-copper tray, and watched Luke and Crystal talking together over coffee and creamy cakes.

It had been the miserable creaking of the mill-wheel as it turned round and round that had disturbed her so much. She hated the continuous noise of it thrashing the water. She had implored Luke to have the wretched thing stopped, leastways whilst she was here, what did they want with a mill-wheel anyway? They did not use the water as the more usual mill does, and it could quite easily stay leashed, in fact there were times when it did. But to have the thing eternally turning round with all that

133

creaking and groaning, the wheezing and the heavy splash of the frenzied water, was more than she could bear.

Perhaps already both of them had had pre-nuptial jitters, and both were in the wrong mood to argue? Luke had gone very quiet at first, his face darkening, his mouth set again like a saw. Then he had refused. In the end she had not been able to control herself any longer, but worked herself up into a most furious temper. She had declared that she would go right away, even at this last moment, unless the wheel was stopped for her, and he, growing obstinate, had turned chalky white and had refused.

She would never forget the way he had said it.

'I can't do it, Stella. It's just that you don't understand, but I can't do it!'

The row broke.

It had gone from bad to worse, as she should have known it was bound to do. She had been forced to keep her word, and carry out her threat. And she had turned and gone home. The wedding had been cancelled.

Luke could still attract her; he could make her heart thump louder, and the colour rise in her cheeks. She detested the idea of his sitting there with Crystal, and knowing that they would drive back to the mill together. She disliked Crystal's brownish-red hair, and the sherry-coloured eyes. She was good-looking. It might have been so much easier if she had been dead plain.

Stella had only just started on her own strong black coffee when Luke looked at Crystal with irritation in his voice, something that he tried to hide, yet did not succeed in doing.

'We mustn't be too long, Crystal.'

'I have practically finished.'

Stella leant forward and looked at Crystal as though she could read right into her very heart. 'Next time you visit St. Ives, you must come to see my cottage, because I think that you would like it. The fisherman's loft is rather a lovely one, and it looks right out to the Head. From it you can see the most wonderful sunsets. Every night I sit there on a pile of cushions and watch the French crabbers coming in. It is a sweet place, and if you want to see a real Cornish interior, then come and visit my little cot.'

'I'd like to,' promised Crystal, and knew that this was something that she would do. She had the premonition that this friendship was not going to end here, it would go a great deal further.

Luke rose, a little impatiently. 'It's high time that we went.'

They came down the staircase into the air that smelt so pleasantly of ozone. The gulls still screamed, and the fishermen's boats were still unloading.

Luke said, 'I'm glad that's over. I suppose you had to meet Stella, and maybe now is as good as any other time, but it was a bit of a strain.'

'And done now.'

'Yes, done now.'

They had come into the street, and it was then that Crystal saw a face that she knew. The sun was shining on Mervyn's fair hair, as he stood hatless on the pavement edge. He wore old grey flannels, and the sort of shabbyish tweed jacket which every countryman keeps as a prize possession. He turned and recognized her.

'It's you!' she said.

He grinned, and she knew that he was delighted to see her, for he had a schoolboy expression that betrayed all his innermost thoughts.

'Hello, this is great! How did you get on last night?' Then for the first time he noticed her companion, and in a changed voice spoke to him. 'Hello, Luke! Shopping, too?'

IV

Crystal got the impression that the men disliked each other, and could not think how it was she had not thought of this before. Luke's voice, too, changed his tone. When he spoke it was almost lifeless, and certainly uninterested.

'Hello!'

Mervyn turned back to Crystal, his yellow hair catching the sunlight, his eyes bright and his nose crinkling as he laughed.

136

'So you've come out shopping! St. Ives is everything I said it was, don't you think?'

Crystal was aware that Stella had come out of the café; she stood now on the top step of all, standing there and staring down at them. 'Hello!' she said.

Mervyn grinned. 'So you're here as well! I might have guessed it!' Then he ignored her, turning back to Crystal. 'You like this place?'

'It's beautiful. I did not know that there were places like this in England. It looks as if it ought to be somewhere abroad. Why do people go and stay at Margate, and Southend and Great Yarmouth, and all those trippery places, when there are wonder-spots like this?'

'I'll tell you, because this is a great deal farther away for most of them, and people loathe long journeys. Thank goodness St. Ives is never trippery, and remains the loveliest spot we have got.'

'Of course.'

Luke tapped her arm. Looking at him she realized that he disliked Mervyn, for that glowering look had returned to his eyes, and his mouth was set. 'Look here, we can't stay too long. I've got the parcel I came to fetch, and you have finished your shopping. It's high time we were on our way back, because there is lots to be done at home, both for you and for me.'

'I'm sorry.'

She got into the car beside Luke, and neither

of them looked back. Still the trawlers were selling their fish and the gulls were screaming, and the few guests who were staying in St. Ives leaned over the taffrails of the esplanade and watched the fishermen's market. A fisherman strode past them, his boots making a squelching sound as he walked, and the tin ear-rings jangling in his ears, whilst his old-fashioned stockinged cap dangled in the breeze. Everything about St. Ives was picturesque, Crystal felt, as she sat back in the car.

They started ascending through the multitudinous perplexing streets, climbing up and up, and coming again to the anemone field with its brilliant flood of colour, and to Lelant, with the road down to Carbis Bay. They went down the hill to the estuary. The tide had come in considerably whilst they had been in St. Ives, and many of the sedges which had been so valiantly waving when they came this way earlier in the morning, were now submerged. The water lapped close to the roadway, singing a whispering song to it, and across the centre of it a little skiff with a brown sail that was patched with scarlet, jerked to and fro.

Still Luke had not spoken a word, but sat there almost as though he were alone, with his mouth set, and looking ahead of him. Crystal had already learnt that when his mouth was set like a saw, and the nostrils dilating, he was in one of those moods. He was, it seemed, two men: the pleasant, amiable one with infinite charm, and the one who rebelled against life in general.

At last she spoke. They could not go on this way much longer. 'Why are you so annoyed with me?'

'I'm not annoyed. I just wondered how many more people I should find you knew in the neighbourhood. It's a bit surprising to go there and find you meeting someone.'

'But as Mervyn Peters brought me to your place last night in the rain, of course you knew that I had met him.'

'Where did you meet him?'

'I told you. It was in London. I was stepping off the kerb into the road and should have gone under a car if he had not put out of hand to save me.'

'What on earth made you do a silly thing like that?'

'I don't know. I'd just lost my job and was a bit dazed, I suppose. Last night when I was stranded at Penzance I don't really know what I should have done if he had not given me that lift. He is the only person I know round here, so I honestly don't see why it is worrying you.'

'It isn't worrying me. With my mother as ill as she is, we have to be unsociable people. The neighbourhood can hardly expect us to entertain, I should think, whilst we are so worried about her state of health. Then there is our work. The very nature of that work keeps us on our own.'

'What work do you do?'

He did not reply. She looked at him to see why he was so quiet, and instantly knew that this was not the man who had painted that beautiful picture of the Man in the garden, this was a stranger. It was the man that she did not like. He must have become aware that she was looking at him, for he began to speak rather tersely.

'I told you all our work is to do with Customs and Excise.'

'I see.'

'It means that we are out all hours of the day, and have no regular times, but are here today and gone tomorrow. We want no questions, no comments, and no prying. In particular no prying. Our job is our own business, and we take it very unkindly when people want to know too much about us.'

She thought that he relaxed a shade as the road climbed, and now they were passing through pastoral country where gorse bushes flamed profusely, and rabbits scuttled to and fro in the great wide fields.

'I'm sorry. Maybe the reason why I get annoyed is because the village is so hostile to us. It is beastly living in a place with neighbours that don't really like you, because I have never done a willing thing to annoy them, yet I know

140

they are all talking about me and if they can say anything nasty, they do.'

'But how did it begin? Maybe I am asking more questions, and that will make you mad again, but this sort of thing does not start for no reason at all. What was it?'

He was silent again, but he slowed the car down and she realized that he did it so that he could talk. After a moment he told her. 'I meant to be a painter. It was something that lay deep down inside me, something that I wanted more than anything else in the world, and would have given up everything to be. As a kid I used to study with a chap in St. Ives, he was one of the strangest kind with a ginger beard and wore bedroom slippers all day and sometimes a smock. But he could paint. He inspired the best in me. We got on well and I think he would have made a great painter of me, then—well—for no reason at all I chucked it. I was so crazy on it that it was life itself, but I threw it up.'

'Why, if you loved it?'

He brought the car into the side of the road, where a belt of fir trees grew. They had a sweet resinous scent about their olive-green branches, and afforded a kindly shelter. He waited a moment, bringing out a cigarette and lighting it slowly. Crystal saw that his hand shook.

'I did love it. I suppose it is the work which I have always wanted to do and for which I would give up everything else in the world, but I shall never do it again. My father hated it. I suppose I have got to confess that you won't have been with us much longer before you realize that he is a very strange man. To me he is a stranger, but perhaps lots of children feel that way about their parents at times. He just told me to give it up, and I gave it up even though it was the thing that I wanted most in all the world.'

She watched him, fascinated.

'But why? You are an individual and have your own life to live and your own way to cut through to the light. Why did you give it up?'

He went on smoking, almost as if he had not heard her, and the blue haze half hid his dark face.

'Yes, I'm an individual as far as any of us are individuals when somebody else has control over us. When you are a member of a large family, I imagine that everything is very different, but I was the only child and maybe I was a bit spoilt. Mother is the spoiling sort, of course. All my life my father had wanted me to come in with him, and he said he would make me. I said he wouldn't. Well, he won!'

'But you could go back?'

'No, I couldn't. That's the extraordinary thing, I couldn't.'

A wave of compassion filled her. She felt that this man had not been allowed to pursue the career he most wanted above all others, and that the sense of frustration had soured him. Perhaps

142

he became aware that the wave of pity stirred her, for, as the firs sighed together and the branches rocked with the creaking noise of a wooden ship at sea, he put out his hand very gently, and took hold of hers.

'You're a nice girl, and we're awfully lucky to have found you, but maybe you have not been so lucky in the finding of us. You must think that we are a queer set-up. Maybe we are; maybe we aren't. I'm sorry about that, but it is one of those things that just can't be helped.'

He sat there for a moment and she got the impression that he longed to tell her more, and was at one time just about to do so. Apparently he decided against it, for he came to with a jerk.

'This won't get us home, will it? We'd better be on our way, or all kinds of questions will be asked.'

They finished the journey hardly talking.

Was it her imagination that told Crystal that the sun had gone in, and that now the valley was in the shadow? As they dropped down into it, it seemed to be ominously gloomy, with something that alarmed her. They turned through the gate with the futile posts sagging on either side, and as they came to a standstill, she heard the dismal creaking of the wheel once more. It was the deep sound of the thrashing water, and the groan of the machinery as the thing moved.

'Oh, that noise!' she exclaimed involuntarily,

143

before she could stop herself.

'Then you don't like it either?'

'What do you mean by "either"?'

'Stella loathed it. I suppose that infernal wheel was the beginning of all the trouble between us.' He choked a little, then in a low voice he spoke hurriedly, almost as if this was something which he had to say and finish with, something from which there was no escape. 'Sometimes I, too, wish that I had never heard the wretched thing. I hate the sound of it creaking and groaning as though someone were tormenting it. If you ask me, someone *is* tormenting it, the rest of us too! That is the answer to the whole thing. Somebody *is* tormenting us.'

The car came to a standstill before the door and Pixie trotted out to meet them.

Still the mill-wheel turned, and Crystal got out of the car, realizing that her limbs seemed to have stiffened. She looked back at Luke, aware that he had a great power of attraction, something which was irresistible and which was growing on her, something which drew her closer to him all the time, yet when they came really near to each other, dropped an iron curtain between them.

She had the strange feeling of complete frustration.

V

Crystal went to her room, brushed her hair and got herself ready for lunch, then went downstairs where Mrs. Tregarth's tray was prepared for her and standing on the side.

'I'll take it up for you,' she told Karin.

She went to the invalid's room to find Mrs. Tregarth lying back amongst the crumpled pillows, and now it seemed that her eyes were full of a great weariness that dismayed Crystal. They had once been such beautiful eyes, for she bore traces of that almost unreal beauty that had been hers as a young woman. As Crystal entered, Mrs. Tregarth turned to her and smiled.

'It's good to see you, dear. I must say that today has been a bad day.'

'I hoped you would have got over that wretched sleeping-draught by this time.'

'Not yet. It seems to hang about me for half the day. I wish I had the strength of mind to be really firm about it and say no, and make it no; but everyone is so certain that they are right for me, even Luke, and when everyone is so insistent, it really is very difficult to hold out, isn't it?'

'If they make you feel so ill they cannot be doing you much good, even if it is necessary for you to sleep.'

'I know. Sleep from those tablets gives me the most dreadful feeling of depression. I lie bemused for hours after waking and feel as though I had been through some horrible ordeal which I cannot quite remember, but which still has the power to frighten me, and does.'

'I'll speak to the doctor when I see him.'

'*When* you see him!' The invalid looked at Crystal with despairing eyes. 'They won't let you see him, my dear.'

'But of course they will! If I am here to see after you, I shall want to talk about you to the doctor.'

Wearily the older woman tried to push her deformed body into a more comfortable position in the bed, and she shook her head.

'He comes at such strange hours. Nobody ever tells me when he is coming, and sometimes I don't think they even know. There is something sinister about him.' She beckoned with a crooked finger, the joints in great knots, and Crystal came nearer to the bed. In a much lower voice Mrs. Tregarth said, 'They'll tell you that all this is just the whim of an invalid who does not know what she thinks, or what she is to do. Because of that, it means nothing. But that is not really so! I know a great deal more than any of them think. It's my husband.'

'Don't tell me if it hurts you.'

'You're a dear girl, and bless you for trying to help me. Luke is hard at times, but again that is not his fault, it is my husband's influence, and I realize it! You see, he always wanted this mill for his own so that he could do what he liked

146

with it. I have refused to hand it over to him. I sign no deeds, because it is my own mill, as it was my forebears' before me.' She was working herself up a little, perhaps because this spate of emotion had been dammed for so long. 'This mill would not have come to me at all, if my people had had a son to carry on. But it did come, and I have a son and the mill will go to him. That is what I want most. That is why I am so deeply worried. Oh, my dear, don't let me die before all this is settled up.'

'You're not going to die, whatever gave you that idea? You are going to get lots better. They do such wonderful things these days, and with all the research work they are doing, I am certain that a cure will be found, I am . . .'

She stopped, aware that the door had opened and someone was coming into the room without making a sound. Both women turned their heads simultaneously, and Crystal realized that it was Mr. Tregarth himself. He walked ponderously, and very slowly, always with the head slightly lowered so that it sunk in between the gaunt hillocks of his shoulders, and rested there, giving the impression that the neck was immovable. But the sharp eyes under those beetling brows which had reminded her of gorse bushes virulent in spring (and were as thorny), burnt with the deadly fire that saw everything.

He came to the end of the old-fashioned bed, and lifting his big horny hands, laid them on the

147

knobs at either end of the foot-piece.

He stood there staring.

If only he said something it would have been so much easier, but no word came at all. He just looked at them and the eyes accused them of a secret, even though his mouth was entirely still.

The silence was terrible.

Suddenly Crystal, unable to bear it a moment longer, turned to him and in a husky voice spoke to him. 'Mrs. Tregarth is just going to have her lunch.'

She lifted the tray into position, and, unfolding the napkin from its silver ring, placed it carefully before the sick woman.

The man stood supporting himself with the rail at the end of the bed, watching Crystal as she cut the chicken into small pieces, and mashed the vegetables. She knew that her hands trembled unnecessarily, and also was convinced that he had realized it too, but he made her scared. He made Mrs. Tregarth hideously nervous as well, and she chafed restlessly, yet there was nothing that either of them could do.

When the time came, Crystal removed the meat plate, regretting that the poor woman had been unable to eat more, but obviously the presence of her husband agitated her, and now she was in no mood to eat at all. Crystal went to bring the pudding from the side, a frothy lemon sponge, with a couple of delicious wafer biscuits beside it, but Mrs. Tregarth waved it away with one of her poor, twisted hands.

'No more, I don't want any more! I tell you, after I have taken one of those dreadful sleeping-draughts, I cannot eat anything. I don't want anything. I know that they are quite wrong for me, or they would never make me feel so terrible.'

'Would you like some coffee?'

'Yes, yes, I would like some coffee, thank you so much.'

'I'll fetch it for you.'

To save Karin the extra work, Crystal piled everything on to the one big tray and carried it to the door, weighed down by it. The big man made no attempt to open the door for her, even though he must have seen how laden she was. She contrived to open it herself with considerable difficulty, and slipped out into the passage. Only when she got into the gloominess that lay in the centre of this eerie house, a dimness that even the spring sunshine could not penetrate, did she realize that the big man had come out of the sick room, too! The realization that he was just behind her made her turn quite faint.

He put out a hand and laid it compellingly on her shoulder.

'Look at me, Miss Stevens.'

She wanted to refuse. She couldn't. Turning, she found herself staring into a pair of the most fantastic eyes that she had ever seen, eyes that pierced her through and through, eyes that were inescapable.

'What has my wife told you, Miss Stevens?'

'She has told me nothing, nothing at all. Only that the sleeping-draughts worry her considerably and that she would rather not have them.'

'You are not speaking the truth. When you speak to me, you must always tell me the truth, for that is something on which I insist. You understand that, don't you?'

'Yes,' she said, hating herself for admitting it.

'It is quite untrue about the sleeping-draughts. She must have them. Her only chance of full recovery from this malady of hers, lies in very long hours of sleep. Deprive her of those, and she will die. I hold you responsible for this and insist that you will give them to her.'

'They make her feel dreadfully ill.'

'All that is invalid fancy. My wife is imagining the whole thing. She desires to be ill, and a malady born of the spirit exhibits itself in the body. She wishes to ail, and she does ail.'

'I feel that she desperately wants to be well. I do not think that she wishes to be ill.'

He looked at her, and his eyes seemed to fill with fire. They were assuredly the strangest eyes that she had ever seen, and they completely mesmerized her.

He said, 'You are not here to think but to obey orders. Understand that, you are to obey!

What happens may seem to be harsh to you, but I am master of this house and the man who is employing you, and here my word is law.'

Already she recognized him as being a power!

She knew that he was sinister, but struggled to pull herself together and hide what her inner feelings were. If she was to help Mrs. Tregarth at all, and that was what she most wanted to do, then she must appear to obey him.

'I will always do my best,' she said in a low voice, her eyes averted.

'If you deceive me I shall know. I always know. I do not keep people to cheat me, and once I have been deceived I never give anyone a second chance. You understand that, also?'

'Yes,' she replied, 'yes, I understand.'

There was a long pause, then the clutch was released on her arm, and he let his hand drop. For a moment she could not move, even if he had released her, then she made a tremendous effort, and went down the passage knowing that all the time he watched her with those deep-set eyes of his. The mere fact that he could do this without speaking a word, frightened her considerably. All she hoped was that he did not realize that she had been aware of it.

She felt very sick as she went downstairs.

CHAPTER FOUR

I

It seemed that after that very little happened.

The master of the house now ignored her, certainly he showed no more lively interest, and his eyes for ever avoided her. She came to the conclusion that she had been tensed up and had imagined the whole thing.

There came letters from London.

Mrs. Biggins had been worried and wanted to know how the job was going, and if Cornishmen were as wild and as dangerous as she had always thought they must be. She had not re-let the bed-sitter, for she was convinced that sooner or later Crystal would be coming back to her. Then she announced that the gent in the big car had called again. He seemed 'dreadful upset' when he learnt that Crystal had gone down to Cornwall, and had said he would send a letter for Mrs. Biggins to forward. Enclosed was the letter.

Somehow Crystal had never expected to see Mr. Hellston's writing again and was considerably surprised at the sight of it. He wrote pompously. He had come to the conclusion that they had both acted on impulse and had done very wrongly. She had been wrong in refusing his proposal of marriage, which after all was the highest compliment that a man could pay a girl, and perhaps he had been a little hasty in dismissing her.

He was willing to reconsider what had happened, and again he asked her to be his wife.

The thought was almost ludicrous. As she laid the letter down, she compared Mr. Hellston with Luke. A great deal had happened to her, almost too much. When she had refused Mr. Hellston, she had not even met Luke and had not become so poignantly aware of the fact that there is such a thing as love at first sight. Now she realized how hopeless it would have been to contemplate a marriage of this nature.

She tore the letter up.

There was another letter from Tony, full of news. Suddenly life had turned out lucky. The job that he never expected had materialized, and to his great surprise he was going into it at the end of the week. Promotion was in the bag! In the brief space of but a few minutes, his salary had been doubled, and he was, as he put it, sitting pretty.

As everything was now so entirely different, he intended coming down to fetch her home on the first available opportunity, that was if she did not do what he felt sure she would do, pack her bags and come rollicking back to London. They would have a June wedding. They would go to Venice for their honeymoon, and make it the most wonderful trip of their lives. He had everything planned.

He had taken against the employment offered by the Smuggler's Mill from the very beginning, and he mentioned it again. The fact that he was so sure, made it that nothing would ever induce Crystal to admit what was happening here. Not that she actually knew. Mrs. Tregarth was a pet, Luke was attractive, the old man revolting. But there was more to it than all that, something sinister, alarming, and always there. One thing she had now decided, she intended to go through right to the bitter end. Mystified as she still was, at times most nervously frightened, she meant to continue until she saw what ultimately happened!

She never replied to Mr. Hellston's letter and it gave her an amused comfort to think of him raging in the office where he had so often deliberately outdistanced her in dictation. To Tony she wrote congratulations, but she put it quite plainly that she was not going back. Marriage meant more than a good job, and a honeymoon in Venice. It needed something that neither of those things could give her, and she was waiting until she fell really in love.

She paused at the escritoire where she wrote her letters in the tiny room where Luke had planned to dress when he was married to Stella.

Had she already fallen in love? A little, said her heart. And was it madness? A little, said her heart again.

She posted the letter.

Her original qualms began to die down. Mr. Tregarth came and went without question, following no schedule, and applying himself to no domestic rules. Sometimes he returned so late that the dawn was almost breaking, and often Luke was with him.

Some of the things that Mr. Tregarth had said about his wife's illness were true. She did complain, and had the tendency to foster strange ideas in the loneliness of her room that had become little short of a prison.

Perhaps it was only natural that she should become inhibited, losing all touch with the world in which they lived. She was a creature of vague whims, the fancies of the sick. She was apt to believe that others were against her, even Luke, but she had taken to Crystal, and was happier and brighter for seeing her passing in and out of her room.

Dr. Fénon did not visit her.

'I want to see that doctor,' she told Luke.

'You never will.'

'I have done once.'

'You thought you did. That was all it was.'

He was nicer to her these days, glowering less, and gradually it dawned on her that everything she had felt for him on their first meeting had been grievously wrong. He could be uncouth and rude, but there was far more good in him than bad. He was gauche with

155

strangers, probably shy, suspecting them on sight, for he had been born with a highly suspicious nature, and rebelled against all save those whom he knew really well.

He had immense attraction.

Never had she met a man who was so astonishingly handsome in a rugged way, and who could change with the facade of his moods. She adored the glossy black of his hair, and the deep caverns of his dark eyes which could light with pure gold fire when he was roused. She loved that skin which was weather-toned, and the crimson of his mouth, against which his teeth were so white when he laughed. Most of all, perhaps, she admired the gentleness of hands that had been destined to paint pictures, and had never been allowed to follow the heart's desire.

'I wonder why you decided to come here?' he said, and playfully laid his hands on her shoulder.

'Because my boss at the office asked me to marry him, and as I had refused, I lost my job! I suppose that was the real reason.'

'You seem popular, don't you?'

'It was the first and last proposal I am ever likely to receive,' she warned him, a little piqued.

'First maybe; but probably only because you have kept yourself aloof. You are not very approachable, you know! The last it won't be,

156

and surely there has been more than one?'

'I don't count Tony.'

The eyes staring so closely into her own, fired somewhat. 'And pray, who was Tony?'

'The heavy-steady in my life. I am not the sort of person who believes in second bests, and it would have to be all or nothing for me.'

'I feel the same.'

Before she could stay herself, she said, 'You had Stella. Surely that was falling in love?'

'I wonder? Love goes even deeper than mere passionate attachment, and these days I have every reason to believe that was only passionate attachment. Perhaps ahead of me there is something more? Some time when I shall feel deeper, the great time when life is kind to me, and turning the next corner, I meet the girl whom I was born to adore.'

The moment had suddenly become tense, and Crystal realized that Luke's hands were tightening a little as they clasped her shoulder, and in doing this, becoming something of a weight. Something that she could hardly bear! She found her eyes drawn in his direction, so that she stood there staring into those dark ones of his, whilst her colour rose in a high tide on to her cheeks. If only she could have done something to prevent herself from blushing! But she could do nothing.

'You're a sweet kid!' he said at last, and released his hold, turning his head away.

No more!

She went from him, because she felt that she would burst into tears if she stayed longer, and did not wish to risk that. Whatever happens I must not love him, she told herself as she crossed the hall. This place is too full of mystery ... I must not love him!

II

It was from Karin that she learnt most. Karin had been lonely here, and was delighted to have someone to run the home. She had been deeply disappointed when the wedding did not materialize, and gradually Crystal got the story of it out of her.

The young couple had been in love; the suite had been changed from derelict and seldom used rooms, where, as a little boy, Luke had spent his childhood, and which had never been used since.

The rooms were finished, the suite ready. Everything was finally arranged, then it had happened on a June day, when the lawn was being mowed by the men preparatory to the raising of the marquee for the wedding reception. Already the L-shaped living-room had been full of gifts, their white labels tied on to them with ribbon, and every time the postman came to the house he brought still more.

It had been that very afternoon that the bride-
158

to-be came to put her final touches, and when she entered the house, it occurred to Karin she was not in her usual gay good mood. She had gone up to see the finished suite, with the lovely soft pink hangings, and the brand-new bathroom, in shell pink, too. While she was up there planning and making those last arrangements, the mill-wheel started stirring. Coming out of the silence, for it had not been working when she had arrived, had made its groaning additionally noisy, and it had gone round creaking and crushing the water beneath it. Karin had heard a little sharp scream in the room upstairs, then the two of them talking, Stella and Luke. They had come downstairs together, she expostulating, he rather silent, and she begged him to have the mill-wheel stopped, saying that she could not bear it another moment, and he had said it was something that she would have to get used to.

'I just didn't know what the trouble really was,' said Karin; 'just the mill-wheel, so she said, but it seemed to me that it wasn't only just the mill-wheel. She had heard it lots of times, and if she came to live here, she would hear it lots of times more. But she didn't come to live here.'

Karin had gone on with her work in the kitchen that day, and after a while she heard the front door slam, and thought they had both gone out. But they hadn't! When Karin went into the living-room, with all those wedding presents spread about it, it was to find Luke standing there staring ahead of him, almost as if he did not know what he was looking for, nor why. He had turned to Karin in an odd way.

'Miss Stella isn't coming back,' he had said, 'she won't marry me, after all. It's all off! Tell the men not to go on with the lawn, for none of that matters now. It doesn't mean a thing.'

Then he had walked past her out of the house, just as he was, in his shirt-sleeves and with no coat, and he had not come back for a week.

The affair had been a nine-days' wonder, with all the village talking about it and everybody conjecturing what had happened. Most of them decided that there had been another man in it, one of the richer artists at St. Ives probably, and sooner or later Stella would marry him.

Or maybe Stella had found that Luke was dependent on that sick woman in the bed upstairs, or worse, on the man who said little, and had those strange eyes that looked through people, and read the very secrets of their hearts. Whatever it may have been, the truth had never been disclosed, and nobody would ever know why they had split so surprisingly suddenly within a few hours of their wedding.

The affair had ended.

But even though Karin dismissed it as finished, for Crystal it had not ended. It seemed surprising to her that Mrs. Tregarth who had gone to so much effort to get that suite made perfect for them, never mentioned the affair. She talked more of herself, of her illness and the hopelessness of it. She associated the sleeping draught with death, and rebelled against it every night, loathing taking it, for she suspected it.

'We will pretend,' said Crystal. 'You can always accept it, drop the tablet into the bed, and say you have taken it; then nobody save myself will ever know.'

'You are on my side, Crystal?'

'Of course I am on your side! You know that. What is more, I am with you in this for ever. You and I are going to be great friends.'

With a pathetic gesture the older woman caught her young hand in her own twisted one, and laid her face caressingly against it.

'I need a real friend more than anything else in the world,' she whimpered; 'oh, my dear, if you only realized how much, how desperately much, I need a real friend!'

III

The days passed rapidly. There was no further communication from Mr. Hellston, but several from Tony, who seemed unreasonably distressed that Crystal was satisfied to stay on. He had secretly hoped that she would find it depressing, and return.

He had underestimated the power of the country now rapidly waking to warmer days,

161

and to the beauties of springtime. She liked shopping in Penzance and in St. Ives, and on occasions she met Mervyn.

There was the afternoon when he asked her to visit his own bungalow built on the beach, and close to the wild-bird life that interested him so much.

'I think you'd like it,' he said.

'Like it? I'd love it. I've never seen anything of the sort before.'

'Tomorrow afternoon?'

'Tomorrow afternoon as ever is,' she told him.

It was one of those days when both of the men had gone out in the motor-boat and Mrs Tregarth was asleep. Mervyn came round in the car in which they had made that original journey here, and they started off together.

He said, 'The bungalow is the sort of place you would never find on your own. It had to be something of an outpost of empire if I was to have the opportunity to see the birds as I wanted to see them. Now it seems that I am almost part of them. They're absorbing. I just can't begin to understand people who are not interested in birds.'

'Of course not, I am most anxious to see it.'

They drove over the moor, with little farmsteads here and there, through the village and then on a broken road which descended to the sea. The beach below them was rocky and wild, the cliffs rising sheer at the sides, and Crystal became aware of the thousands of birds who nested there.

The broken road came to the shore itself, ceasing to be. The tide was far out, and there was an even strand of sand where it never came, along which she could see the mark of the tyres. Slowly they went along it to the bungalow. It was built of red bricks, a vigorous contrast to a country where there are few red bricks, for nearly every house was of stone and slate-roofed. Mervyn stopped the car by it, and they crossed the veranda to go inside. One entered into an enormous living-room which appeared to take three sides of the bungalow and look out on all of them. It was furnished with comfortable hide chairs, and there was a look-out arranged in the corner window, from which one could watch nesting birds. Obviously everything had been selected by Mervyn who did not attach great importance to the background of his life. There were no flowers and few ornaments, for the house was dedicated to his life with the birds, and bore the hall-mark of this everywhere.

'I'm afraid it's pretty ordinary,' he said, 'but when men live alone like I do, they get absorbed in their jobs and don't bother too much. Perhaps every man ought to be married and live happily ever after, if the truth were to be known. But then not all of us are fortunate enough to play Prince Charming to Cinderella at the ball.'

He turned from her to the window. 'This is the most wonderful spot for birds. Every kind of gull seems to come here. I've got a special room for it where I'll take you later, it shows the cliffs and the gull nurseries. There are hundreds of them there. They are not pretty babes; I would say that this bird has the ugliest young of any living thing. But then I think the young are always ugly.' He stopped a moment and grinned in that infectious manner of his. 'I once saw a young nephew who was a few hours old, and at the time I thought he was the ugliest thing I have ever seen, but a bird at an hour old is even worse that that.'

'I've never seen one.'

He told Crystal something of his own personal life. She had already become interested in him, interested as one would be in a brother, someone in whom one has complete confidence and on whom one can rely.

He had been one of the school misfits, he said, for he had never passed an exam in his life, and he and his school-masters had come to the conclusion that he never would.

Today, when examinations are so very important and the whole quality of a man's learning is judged only on the certificates he wins in the examination rooms, he felt hopeless. He saw the future in a dark shroud.

He had bought a box-camera, the best that he could afford, and had gone away for his holidays, spending them with a doting godmother who lived in the heart of the country, and who had encouraged him to photograph wild birds.

'I was a bit hard on my parents,' he said, with another of those giggles that crinkled his nose so attractively, 'and my father being something of a scholar, you can imagine that I was not at all the sort of son that he wanted. No parson's stipend is made of elastic, as everybody knows, and I was ashamed of myself, but in the end luck came my way.'

He filled the tea-pot and brought it to the table, then sat watching her whilst she poured it out for him, before he went on with the story.

When he had failed hopelessly in an exam which the average boy or girl takes at school with almost no effort, he was at his wits' end. It was that very week when the garden was lush with may and the guelder roses dropping to scatter a powder of greenish snow on the grass that life changed. A car broke down in the lane outside the quiet country rectory where usually nothing ever happened. It was one of those expensive-looking cars that one associates with rich folks, and Mervyn went out to see if the trouble was serious and if he could help them at all.

A largely-made man, who wore casual clothes

extremely casually, mopped his brow, and cursed. He was one of the kind that know nothing about the inside of cars, and that was only too apparent when one watched his pathetic endeavours to put the thing to rights.

He had brought the man into the rectory to eat one of the frugal cold lamb and tapioca lunches, on which it always seemed they had to feed. But there were fresh green lettuces from the back garden, rosy little radishes and the first cucumbers, even if it was a poor man's lunch. They got talking. Hamilton West came from the West Country, and was in a fury at being stopped on his way to Norfolk. Already Mervyn's attention had been attracted by the contents of the car, for although there was only one very small suitcase (excused by the fact that Mr West never travelled with much luggage, not caring what he wore), there was a handsome camera, a cine-camera also, and a whole pile of books on birds.

He was a naturalist.

He knew that in Norfolk there was a corncrake's nest and he was now on his way to visit this. The corncrake was gradually dying out, which he deplored, and he wanted to get photographs of it. When he heard of Mervyn's interest and noted the way that he handled the books, and then saw some of the photographs that the boy took, Mr. West had been forthright.

'You'd better come to Norfolk with me. You'd be a grand help on a job like this and we could cope with it together.'

From that moment Mervyn had never looked back again. The corncrake's nest in the lush ditch of a Norfolk farmstead was the beginning of his whole career. If Mr. West's car had not broken down outside the gate he would never have had this miraculous opportunity. He had been the luckiest man alive.

He had discovered after a time that his real *métier* lay in water birds, in particular the marine ones. He dedicated his whole life to the study of them, and had been remarkably fortunate in the first book that he had published. On the proceeds of that book the bungalow had been built.

He was writing a book now on the gulls and a publication date had been fixed, but he had got behind with the last few chapters because the nesting had been tricky this year. A bad storm had spoilt his best photographs, and he had to get others. The weather had set out to be thoroughly awkward and distress him, and he knew that he was running time close in getting what he wanted.

'But it's easy to work hard when you love your job,' he said.

He helped himself to plum cake and chocolate biscuits, eating both together with a schoolboy carelessness.

'Now tell me how things go at Smuggler's Mill!' he asked.

'You don't like Luke Tregarth, do you?'

'Oh, I think he's all right, but I admit to distrusting both him and his family.'

'I don't see how anyone could distrust Mrs. Tregarth, she is so sweet. Her illness has got on the top of her, and you can't really wonder at that, but she *is* a nice woman.'

'Oh yes, she's all right. A bit pompous . . .'

'You're wrong there, for she certainly isn't pompous. She isn't big as you said, but wizened up. It is this wretched arthritis, I suppose. I feel desperately sorry for her lying there and having this odd little doctor, whom nobody ever sees, attending her. I got a glimpse of him that first night, because I peeped through the curtains, but that didn't go for much. It was about two in the morning anyway, and certainly not the time for a doctor to pay a visit, I should have said. Besides, he comes from an island said to be forty miles out.'

'Good heavens!'

She said, 'Nobody knows much about him. He is a Frenchman purporting to have some miracle cure for arthritis.'

'There isn't such a thing.'

'I suppose it is only natural that everyone wants her to try this cure; she has tried everything else.'

Mervyn nodded, but there was something like

derision in the movement. 'I told you that I didn't trust the family a yard, and I don't. If any doctor had a cure for arthritis, whatever nationality and however unusual, he would not be living forty miles out plumb in the middle of the Channel; he would be making a packet at some great hospital.'

She agreed. 'Maybe he is in the experimental stage, and needs guinea-pigs!'

'If that is so, then he ought not to be experimenting on patients like this. I don't like the sound of it at all. May I have some more tea?' and he handed her his cup. 'When I last saw Mrs. Tregarth, she was one of those Junoesque women, bigly made. I think she was what you would call a fine figure of a woman.'

'She has shrunk to almost nothing now.'

'I imagine not much can be done to help her, because of the others. The old man has the face of a criminal and some of us think that is what he is. As to the son, if he had any *nous*, he'd break clear and start again. I can't think why he doesn't do that. No *nous*, I suppose.'

'Once he almost married, you know.'

'Indeed I know, and *did* the village talk! I wondered if you knew about it, but you do. If you ask me, Stella had a near squeak, but, mind you, she was always the kind that knew which side her bread was buttered, and she seems to be doing remarkably well at St. Ives now.'

He paused a moment, sipping his tea. Crystal

169

realized that he liked neither Stella nor Luke, and cherished a wholesale dislike of the Tregarth family, save for Mrs Tregarth. She did not share this opinion, knowing that she cared for Luke, and admired Mrs. Tregarth, feeling that the only one to dislike was the husband. There was something about the silent, looming figure of this man, who always hunched between giant shoulders, giving a particularly forbidding impression.

But Luke was not forbidding.

He might be two men, the one who had stared at her through the grille the very first night that she had arrived, and the other man, charming and sympathetic, who had driven her into St. Ives next day, showing her crooked streets, old houses, and the French crabbers coming round the Head, with real delight.

He was attractive. Perhaps dangerously so! Dare she confess, even to herself, the truth that a tide, greater than she could command, was rising within her, and the man who was so kind could command her, whereas she admitted fear of the man who had glared through the grille? She said nothing.

'Don't go falling in love with Luke,' Mervyn warned her, almost as if he had read her thoughts.

'Of course not! I am not the sort of girl who goes about falling in love—I hope,' she said, and laughed. She prayed that he would not notice how uneasy was her tone. Then she changed the subject. 'I must not stay too long or I shall get into trouble when I return to Smuggler's Mill. Let me see your work-room, may I?—and the gull nurseries?'

'Of course. It's a proper bachelor's den, you must not mind that. It is one of those places that never get dusted, but to me it's good fun.'

He went on ahead, and opening a door they both entered a small room which ran along the far side of the bungalow. The whole of one wall was fitted with spacious windows. On the table before it lay the field-glasses, and picking them up, Mervyn handed them to her. She saw now that she was staring up the side of a gigantic black cliff, and that thousands of gulls were nesting there. Never had she seen a more wonderful sight, for here they were away from human eyes, and completely in their natural state. It was the enormous nursery of the cliff.

'I could never have believed it,' she said.

He looked at them tenderly, and in his eyes was the fondness that a man gives to his own children. 'I know. Birds are very wonderful things.' About him was a certain sentiment as if each one of those gulls was of his personal family.

He went to the book-case and brought out an enormous book, opening it to show her photographs that he had taken from this same window. They were excellent. She turned over

171

the pages, not realizing how fast the time was passing, for the subject was absorbing. He explained the difference between the kind of gulls; there was so much to learn, and everything of the greatest interest.

Suddenly she looked up startled, and seeing the little clock on the side, realized that she had been expected back at Smuggler's Mill an hour ago.

'Good heavens, Mervyn, look at the time! I am supposed to be home again and helping to get the supper ready. Whatever will they think?'

'I don't suppose Karin will be too worried. She is the queerest little thing, but an awfully good sort. I'll take you back in the car, it is farther than it seems.'

'I daren't stay a moment longer.'

'So you're afraid of them too? I thought you would be! It's that old man. There is something repellent about him, the village says he can mesmerize with those eyes, and has the look of the Evil One. They would!'

'It isn't true, of course. I know the place is gruesome in some ways, it is both eerie and fantastic, but that is just the way it is made. I don't feel that Mr. Tregarth can do anything really to harm one.'

'I shouldn't be too sure. I've heard stories,' and there was something about the way he said it that was disturbing. She wanted to ask more but dare not. Maybe the answers would be the ones that she did not want to hear, and anyway time was on the wing, and there was no time to wait.

She got into the car beside him.

They went along the beach on to the narrow little track road that climbed the cliff. The sea was hyacinth, and all the white frills seemed to have left it, now it was just a gentle placid water. The sky hung over it like a light blue canopy, one shade darker than the water.

Mervyn said nothing as he drove up the difficult zigzag road and turned on to the cliff itself, descending into the scattered village beyond.

They dropped down to the gate of the mill, which had given her such a turn on the night of her arrival.

'This darned place looks grim,' he said as he stopped and she got out; 'it is grim, mark you. I shan't come in and up that wretched drive, for the springs of my car are not of the best anyway, and I'm not risking trouble with them which might easily happen here.'

'Thank you for having me.'

He smiled at her in the bright sunshine, his hair that purest gold, his eyes larkspur blue.

'It was lovely seeing you. I—I have few friends and value those who come to visit me. It's nice to meet somebody after my own heart, so come and see me again, remembering that you are always very welcome.'

'I won't forget.'

She turned and walked along the rubbly drive to the old house with the grille in its door. She knew that if she had stayed talking longer she might have said something foolish, asking for his guidance, his aid, his advice.

For she also needed a friend.

IV

As she opened the hall door which wheezed like an old man with acute asthma, she saw that Mr Tregarth himself was standing in the hall.

It was most unusual to see him indoors, for he was one of those men always conspicuous by their absence. She was so surprised to see him there that she gave a little exclamation, and as she did so, there came to her the dreadful intuition that Mervyn had been absolutely right in everything that he had said about Smuggler's Mill. Secretly, deep down and entirely within herself, she *was* afraid!

Mr Tregarth looked at her. 'Where have you been?' he asked her.

Somehow his very voice could alarm her. She did not think he had ever spoken to her so directly before. 'I went to tea with Mr. Peters. I had mentioned it and they did not expect me back too soon. I—I'm sorry that I am late.'

He stood there staring at her with those somnolent eyes of his, that searched down into the soul.

'You were due back here some time ago.'

'I'm sorry.' Her own voice sounded quite unlike herself, and she flushed uneasily.

'Please come here,' he directed her.

She wanted to refuse. The strange thing was that she couldn't do it when he looked at her like that, almost as if he detested her.

'Very well,' and it was not herself who agreed to this.

Mr Tregarth opened the door on the far side of the hall, a door she had hardly noticed before, and had thought probably went down to the cellar. The door led into an office.

It was very cold, for it was on the north side of the mill, and no fire had been lit in the grate for days, for it was piled with dead ash, the output of old pipes, and with spills like driftwood in its dirty grate.

The place smelt of enclosure, of stale mist, of coarse tobacco and of must; it was detestable. She saw that it must be the oldest part of the mill, for the raftered ceiling came low, and to her horror Crystal realized that the spiders had set grey lace curtains beneath the dark beams, and that no one had done anything to remove them for many months.

The pair of small windows were made of a glass that had gone smeary, and dead flies lay along the grit-rutted sills, where again the venomous spiders had done their worst.

Crystal realized that the stained and faded

cushions in the chairs had not been shaken for a long, long while, but sank in clumps of congested stuffing into the corners of sagging tapestries. A desk was piled high before the window, and on it there was a tired ink-pot, with the ink dried up into a dark grime of its own. The plain wooden arm-chair was shaped in a circular manner, and fitted with more cushions faded out of belief. There were no pictures, and the hair-cord carpet had been laid on the floor for years, and was already trodden into thready holes, through which the 'weeping stones' of the cold floor protruded clammily. It was a hateful place.

'Sit down,' ordered Mr. Tregarth, and he indicated a rush-seated chair, similar to the kind that one sees in old churches.

The rush seat was coming undone, and the pieces stuck out like the straws in the hair of a madman. She sat down cautiously, because the power to deny him seemed to have left her, and she felt that the chair would probably collapse. However, it remained unexpectedly firm.

'Young lady,' said Mr. Tregarth, sitting in the round wooden chair, his arms along the rails so that his shoulders became more hunched than ever, 'I consider that it is high time that you and I came to a proper arrangement.'

'I thought we had one? I came here to superintend the house, to see after your wife, and I thought that I was doing everything in my power to fulfil my duties?'

'Yes, you are doing your duty by those items. I have no fault to find with that, but there are other things. Most definitely there are other things.'

He did not look at her, but opening a drawer that smelt outrageously of stale tobacco, he brought out an old pipe, the bowl blackened with use, and accompanying it a jingling tin box which jarred noisily against the stem. He opened the box and produced from it a coarse-cut shag, moulding it with his fingers already so stained that he might have been of negroid descent, and he began to ram it into the discordantly stinking bowl of the pipe itself.

She had gone deathly still.

At last the pipe was filled to Mr. Tregarth's satisfaction, and he brought out a box of matches from his pocket, shook it several times, listening to it as though it had been a watch that he had suspected of stopping, then, selecting a match he lit the pipe. A great bonfire of smoke came from it, almost hiding him. It started her choking.

At last he spoke again.

'The point is this. I know what has been happening, because, much as it surprises you, I have friends in this place, and I realize that you have been talking about me and mine. You want to discover a lot of the things that I have not told you, and do not intend to tell you.'

She looked at him aghast.

Had she done this? She raced through her mind, and felt that there had been nobody she had asked. She had mentioned it to Mervyn, of course, only this very afternoon, but Mervyn disliked the family so much himself that he would have repeated nothing. She dismissed all thought of the news travelling from that direction.

She had asked Luke, his own son, but that had only been in the course of casual conversation, the sort of questions that you do not call questions, for any newcomer would ask them. But surely Luke had not said anything? What could he have said?

Karin? She thought of Karin again, but the little midget creature was impersonal. It was doubtful if she had ever repeated a thing in her life, and her whole angle on Smuggler's Mill had been that it did not matter what other people did, and anyway whatever went on was no business of hers.

There had, of course, been Mrs. Tregarth.

Crystal thought of the moments when Mrs. Tregarth had sobbed on her shoulder, and to her indeed she *had* confessed some of her own doubts and apprehensions. The invalid woman was utterly wretched; she herself was frightened, and surely she would never have repeated anything to the husband of whom she appeared to be so utterly terrified? Crystal could

178

think of no one else, for she had been careful in all her dealing with the trades-people, with the farmers, and the chatterbox who ran the post office, and who always tried to lure people into talking with her.

Who was it had told on her?

She replied, 'Most certainly I have not been going round to different people asking questions. The truth of the matter is that I know very few different people.'

'You know some of them, anyway.'

'Well, who could it be?'

He still stared at her with those eyes that never flickered. 'You know some of them as I have said. Today you have taken tea with a man who lives in the village. This Mr. Peters, who under the guise of watching gulls about which he writes books, has been spying on the neighbourhood for years.'

'Spying?' She felt bewildered beyond all knowledge. What on earth could he mean?

'Exactly.'

'But he does write books, and for them it is obvious that he has to watch bird life.'

'Indeed!' The voice was as cold as this room with the low-raftered ceiling, and the smell of dust and disuse which seemed to be part of it. 'If you are to stay here, Miss Stevens, you must ask no more questions. You have to learn to leave me and mine alone. Your work here is to attend to the house and wait on my wife. You are to do nothing outside that.'

'If I am to attend to your wife, I think that it is only fair that I should know something of her case. I am worried for her. She hates and resents these sleeping-tablets which she is forced to take, and which made her feel so ill in the morning that I cannot see that they are doing her any real good.'

He was silent for a moment, then took the pipe from his mouth and laid it down on the desk, where it glowed a little and lit up the dark scars where it had lain a dozen times before, to leave these marks behind it.

'So that's it, is it? That is what is worrying you? I imagine you have never seen a bad case of arthritis before, or you would understand. Have you so little knowledge of life that you do not realize that this is an incurable disease, and that Harley Street is full of people who go there for cures, and find none?'

When he spoke, he did so very slowly; he knew perhaps how irritating were the long pauses, and how she chafed against them. His eyes watched her, they never flickered for a moment, and she had the strange impression that they were coming closer.

The man still sat there in his wooden chair with the circular back, and the sagging cushions. Yet his eyes seemed to come forward towards her, and although she tried not to look at them in some unbelievable way they forced her to gaze.

If only she could stay herself from looking at him, but the unflickering eyes impelled her!

He went on talking. 'I admit that I had become desperate about my wife's condition, we tried everything and she was getting worse all the time. Then I heard of Dr. Fénon. He was the only man who was achieving actual cures in this disease. Was it not natural that we should clutch at straws? Admit that?'

'Of course.'

A moment ago she had felt that it was utterly wrong, yet those eyes commanded her admittance to his remarks. She had to agree with him because he was deliberately forcing her to accept his view, even if it were wrong. She could feel herself weakening. She was no longer able to fight him any more.

'I myself went to see Dr. Fénon and brought him here. He believes, as he has always done, that he *can* effect a permanent cure for her, but from the first he told us that the treatment would be a rigorous one. He mentioned the sleeping-tablets. Sleep, he said, was essential. During sleep you know that the body rehabilitates itself. You did know it?'

'Yes, of course.'

She had the unpleasant feeling that this was not herself who was talking any more, but someone entirely under his power, and remote from her personality. Even her voice seemed to have dulled, to have lost its vigour, and to be unnaturally calm, whilst within herself she felt turbulent and desperately frightened.

'I have committed myself to this cure for my wife. We discussed it, and she has agreed. We understand that it was her only chance. You have to understand it, also! I have heard all sorts of people discuss this man's work. Just as you have heard people discuss my work.' He paused, but she made no move of dissent or assent, so that he rapped the table before him with a sudden little commanding gesture. 'You heard what I said? You *have* listened to people discussing my work?'

'Yes, yes, I have.'

'I work for the Customs and Excise authorities.'

'You are a Customs officer?'

'No, I am higher than that.'

'You are higher than that.' She was repeating what he said, because now there was nothing that she could do to resist him.

'The Customs have a secret service of their own. A body of men who go out and about, to see that the Customs officers adhere to their duties. These men have to be watched. Their faults have to be corrected. I am one of those men who go unseen, unexpected and uninvited. For that reason my work is completely secret.'

'Your work is completely secret.'

'If you ever divulge this, I shall know. If I do

182

know, I shall have to take means to stop you. Both I and my son work for this end. You understand what I mean?'

She said, 'I understand what you mean,' in the mechanical voice which had no tone, and was not really her own. She did not understand what was happening.

'Now are there any more questions? Have you anything else about which you seek information? It is the last opportunity that I shall give you, for I don't agree with all this prying. What you want to know you ask *me*, you understand? Say it after me.'

Wretchedly she said. 'What I want to know I ask you.'

'If you do not abide by this, you leave. Luke will take you in the car to Penzance, and leave you there to catch the first train back to London.'

'But—but how could I?'

'That is of no interest to me. It is what will happen to you if I hear any more of this prying round the village. You ask no questions and you are told no lies. You ask me, no other. Say it after me.'

She heard the dull, mechanical voice saying it after him, and did not know why she did it. The eyes had never left her face, they had come nearer and nearer. They looked searchingly into her own.

'And when I want you, you come here to me.

When I tell you to go, you go. When I ask you to stay, you stay; and you stay *silent*. Say that after me, too.'

She must be dreaming this, as she heard her voice dully repeat the words, 'I will stay, and I will stay silent.'

Mr Tregarth pushed the smoky pipe from him, and lifting his hands clapped them together with a sudden abruptness that was singularly disturbing. It was as though a gun had been fired in the low room with the close ceiling; as though Crystal had been struck suddenly in the face and she did not know whether it was real pain, or the sudden shock, or what had made her so amazed. Now the eyes had gone farther away, they had receded back into that austere face, which stared at her, but somehow not in the same way. Her head ached. She could feel a little tic starting to throb in her temple, and all the time she looked at those eyes which had retreated back under their strange palisade of eyebrows, which fell in long spikes like the wild bushes on a common.

'All right?' he asked.

'Yes, I'm all right.'

'You're feeling queerish, aren't you? You turned a little faint, but you'll be better in a moment. Remember that you just turned faint.'

She knew that it was a lie, but the mechanical side of her was ready to accept anything that he suggested to her. She knew that he had power over her, a power that she could not challenge.

'You had better go out into the air,' he said.

She did not reply, but drew herself up; for the moment her very movements were not her own, for she was stiff. It must be clammy down here and the very spirit of the place had got into her bones. She jerked a trifle, as if she were a marionette dancing on a string that was governed by an unseen hand.

It was a dreadful feeling.

At last she was able to escape from that piercing gaze of the sullen eyes, and she went out into the hall which she had always detested, but at this moment it no longer seemed to be gloomy. After the darkness, and the macabre horror of that sour-smelling study, anywhere would have been delightful!

She went up the stairs, the jerk leaving her limbs, the stiffness fading. The pain in her head was clearing too, just as Mr. Tregarth had said it would, and she wondered if she had been suspicious or whether she had really fainted.

Fear made people do silly things! It made them hypersensitive. It made them foolish. She had experienced the unbearable feeling that in some way this man had compelled her, that he had a power over her, something against which she could not fight.

The world was bewildering.

V

On the landing, she saw Luke watching her. He had come out of his mother's room, and along the corridor to the head of the stairs. Now he stood there watching her closely, his mouth pursed, and on his face a look that she had not seen there before.

'You're not well?' he said.

The sound of his voice was a comfort, and she knew that she could tell him what had happened.

'Your father was annoyed with me for staying out later than I should have done. He called me into that dreadful study.'

Luke put out a hand and touched hers.

'You're icy cold, you poor kid! Come quickly into the sunshine, it's streaming into your room, and will do you all the good in the world.'

He had hold of her arm and drew her into her own room.

The very sight of warm sunshine and of pastoral country lying beyond the window made her feel better. She lifted her hand and wiped away a tear, whilst Luke watched her sympathetically.

'It was dreadful in there. I really don't know what I had done that he should have been so extraordinary in his behaviour.'

'What did he do, Crystal? Tell me what he did. It is very important that I should know.'

'I don't really know. That is one of the strange parts of it, I don't really know. He just

186

looked at me, and all the time I got the impression that his eyes were coming nearer and nearer, even though his face remained far away. It was the strangest feeling. Just those eyes, and coming nearer all the time.'

He sat down beside her and both his arms went round her. This must be the strangest afternoon of her life; first that detestable experience in the study, now Luke beside her in the sunny room. He had taken her into his arms. Tenderly those beautifully shaped hands caressed her, soothing her as if she were some little child who was afraid of the dark.

'You must go away from here, Crystal, right away, and as soon as you possibly can! It isn't safe for you to stay here a moment longer.'

'But I can't go away.'

'You have got to go. I want you to believe what I am saying to you, my sweet, because— oh, I don't suppose you have noticed it, but you are very sweet to me.'

'Oh, Luke!'

'I love you, Crystal, I knew it the first evening that you came here. I suppose it was knowing it that made me so abrupt, so gauche, so utterly beastly. But I do love you and for that very reason I recognize your danger all the more strongly. You have got to go right away, and never see any of us again.'

She began to cry weakly like a young child, and the arms about her tightened. He stroked

187

her face.

'You mustn't cry, darling, that won't help any of us really. The one important person is yourself, and we have got to take care of you. My sweet, I love you so much.'

'Why did this have to happen?' she whispered.

'Because you are you, and I am I. Because we were made for one another, but there are barriers between us that are impossible to destroy. That's why.'

It seemed unbelievable that this could be the man of whom she had once been afraid!

'You have got to trust me, darling. You have got to lean on me in this and let me guide you through. Anything might happen if—well, if you don't. I will take you to Penzance tomorrow morning, and you shall catch the London train.'

'I won't go,' she told him.

She lifted her arms and laid them about his neck, triumphant that at last all barriers were down, and even it there were things that she did not understand, she could be tremendously happy with him. He laid his hands on either side of her face and kissed her vehemently again and again. It seemed that in this moment he suffused her with a new and vigorous life, then as he released her, she heard the mill-wheel beginning to turn, creaking and complaining as it went. With it came the steady drip of water, the splash as it returned where it belonged, and the increasing whine of a wheel grown husky.

'Oh, that hateful thing!' she whispered.

'You hate it too? Shall I tell you the truth? I have always loathed it. That is since it became a sign of something—something that I detested. It has to be there, there is no escape from it, but the noise of it drives me mad.'

'We'll forget it.'

'We can't forget it, because it is an important part of life here. Tomorrow, whatever happens, I have to take you into Penzance, and you will catch the Riviera Express.'

'I won't go.'

'But you must go. It is for your own dear sake, and because I love you so much that I refuse to see harm coming to you. Crystal, my sweet, I have to protect you from what is here, and for that reason must send you away.'

She shook her head. 'I won't go, darling!'

'But why do you want to stay? My sweet, my own, own sweet, why do you want to stay?'

He released her, and getting up, stood before her, his eyes bewildered, his hands now sunk into the deep pockets of his breeches, whilst all the time the mill-wheel gained speed, churning and slashing through the water, groaning wretchedly as with the sound of a soul in torment.

'I don't understand you, Crystal. In your heart you are scared. I can feel that. Yet you are determined to stay on here, whatever I say.'

189

She rose, also. At this moment she had an exhilarating sense of pride as her arms closed about him, and she drew his face down to her own.

'Perhaps I want to stay because I love you,' she admitted.

CHAPTER FIVE

I

Now she knew that she did love him, and once the big emotion had begun in her heart there was nothing that she could do to stay it. In a way perhaps she had known that this was love, even in the first horrifying moment when she had seen him looking at her through the grille, a love mixed with fear, yet a pleasurable fear, that had the power to torment her to tears, yet send her into sheer ecstasies of joy!

Crystal knew that she would rather stay here and suffer with Luke, whatever was destined to happen to them, than go back into a safe world, to work in a city office with safe people, and in the end to marry some stout city gentleman for security purposes. Or Tony! But now, in the last few minutes, she had experienced for the first time in her life, the greatest of the human emotions, the kind of love that she had always known existed, but had never actually met. It was hers!

'Crystal, how brave you are! I guessed you were brave but never knew that you were like this. Only you can't do it, my darling, it's a risk that I won't let you take.'

'But I shall take it. This has happened to us. We were meant for each other and we are staying together.'

'He won't let it be that way, darling.'

'He?'

Gently he released her. 'There is too much involved in all this, far more than you can imagine or even think of. I have got to put you right out of my life.'

'You mean that you don't love me?'

'On the contrary, I adore you.'

They clung together again, and whilst he held her to his heart, she forgot the horrors of the interview earlier in the evening.

At last he released her.

'It would be a crime to let you stay.'

'All the same, I'm staying.'

'Stella didn't.'

'Let's forget Stella! Anyway, I don't think that I am like her in any way. I am made of entirely different calibre.'

'My dearest!'

Downstairs the dinner-bell rang, it was the bell that poor little Karin had to climb on to a chair to strike. Everything about this strange house was extraordinary and unbelievable. It was imbued with all the fantastic qualities, and both Crystal and Luke knew it.

He looked at her, his mouth twitching. 'This will be very difficult, you know. My father is one of those men who are quick to notice an atmosphere, and this is something that we have got to try to conceal from him. I suggest that I go down first and say that you are with my mother; then you come along afterwards.'

'All right.'

Before she went downstairs to join the men for this dinner which she felt sure would be decisive, she slipped into Mrs. Tregarth's room to see how she was. A tray had already been brought up, but apparently the poor woman had little appetite for foods and she had hardly touched it. She turned her head wearily towards the girl, her voice fretful.

'You've been away such a long time, and my husband has been sitting here with me. He stares and stares! After a while it seems that his eyes are coming nearer and nearer, I don't know why, it just happens that way! Oh my dear, I have had such a dreadful afternoon.'

'But it's all right now.'

She saw that the tears had trickled through Mrs. Tregarth's closed lids, and were rolling down her cheeks in glazed roadways. 'It has been so horrible. Never leave me again, Crystal dear. You will stay here always, dear? You *will* stay?'

'Of course I'll stay. I am here to get you better, and get you better I will.'

'Sometimes I believe that isn't possible.'

'But of course it's possible. I promise we will manage it between us. Now I have to go down to my dinner, or I shall only be making further trouble.'

Crystal kissed her.

'The moment dinner is done, I will come back and read to you. I promise that, and we will have a wonderful evening together.'

As she went downstairs, somewhat slowly, in spite of the fact that she knew she was late, she felt that something stranger even than she had thought was going on in this house. Its mystery soaked into her like damp through walls. It seeped. Now she had come to the conclusion that she had imagined much of her talk with Mr. Tregarth; she had fainted, which was the explanation for the feeling of general confusion which had come over her.

It was absurd to feel that there was something uncanny about the big, hunched man; he had been worried that she was late, and had shown it in a blunt, rather abrupt way. No more.

As she entered the long L-shaped living-room, she knew that already Mr. Tregarth must have spoken to Luke about it, for Luke's manner had changed. Slipping into her seat, Crystal looked across apprehensively at Luke, but he avoided her eyes. It seemed to be always the same thing when his father was there, he was ill at ease, and the other man, the stranger who had peered at her through the grille, was obvious.

She could not have believed that this was the same man who, but a short while ago, had held her in his arms vowing that he loved her.

She tried to make casual conversation; she had gone into the invalid's room, she said, to see how she felt tonight, and finding her both poorly and very depressed, had decided that when they had finished the meal she would go back and spend the rest of the evening with her.

The men said nothing. Then Luke made a casual remark, but there was no reply from the older man, and they sat through the rest of the silent dinner, until Crystal was so embarrassed that she hardly knew what she was doing. When Karin brought in the coffee, she rose.

'I'll go back to Mrs. Tregarth now.'

The older man looked at her from under his beetling brows with the unflickering eyes that were so sinister.

'I am going over to the islands, and the motor-boat will be awaiting me in the creek. You need not expect me back until dawn.' He paused, one of those pauses at which he was so proficient. 'I may bring the doctor with me.'

Crystal flushed. She said, 'I should so have liked to meet him and learn what he really feels about the case. I am worried for Mrs. Tregarth.'

The room seemed to thrill as though an electric current had shot through it. Electricity filled it. There was another of those emphasized silences that were so hard to bear, then Mr Tregarth spoke in a voice that rumbled as with thunder. He was furiously angry, she knew.

'You will not see Dr. Fénon. You will never see him. Remember that I tell you it is impossible for you to see him.'

His tone turned both of them to statues. Crystal could feel the strange, confused apprehension running through her, the feeling she had had when she had seen those eyes coming closer, and looking at her, commanding her.

A moment later there came the noise of the mill-wheel starting again. It gave that heaving belch which was always the beginning, then slowly rotated, gaining speed, yet groaning as though appalled at the enormity of the task before it. At the end of the table, the older man was staring at Crystal with those darkly-sullen eyes that seemed to hold all the resentment in the world.

'You will not see the doctor,' he said, stressing every word. 'Remember that! You can never see him.'

Summoning all the strength left in limbs that seemed to be absurdly weak, Crystal went to the door, surprised that she had the strength to do this. It was then that she determined that, whatever happened, she would see Dr. Fénon if he ever came to the house again. She would wait up all night, for her faith to Mrs. Tregarth was pledged, and she would stay loyal to that faith.

As she went up the bleak stairs, through the gloom of this impenetrable house, she knew that now was the moment to act. She must do what she could before the old man controlled her as he controlled Luke, making two men of him. For the man who had looked at her through the grille that first night had been the one under his father's influence, and the other man was the man she loved. If she was to help him break away from all this, then she must act now.

Those eyes could come considerably nearer.

Whatever happened, that must not be.

II

Late that evening the weather changed.

The wind rose and began to howl as it came in from the sea, screaming to itself, and she could hear the waves pounding on the foot of the great black cliffs. Mrs Tregarth had talked; then, whilst Crystal was reading to her, she had fallen asleep fairly early, confident that she was safe whilst this girl stayed with her.

It must have been eleven o'clock when Crystal saw the big car come quietly out of the garage in the drive, and realized that old Mr. Tregarth himself must be driving it, crouching over the wheel. The car came to the front door, and

196

stopped there. She saw the bright light streaming out as that door opened, and then realized that Luke had come out of the house, and got into the car beside the driver.

He wore oilskins, and a peaked cap. It hurt Crystal that he had not warned her that he, too, was going, for she had understood from the unpleasant scene at supper that the older man intended going alone; now she knew that both of them were on their way to the creek where the motor-boat rode at anchor.

Why was it Luke acted this way?

Already she knew that he did not care for his father, from odd fragments that he had let drop now and again. He was afraid of him, and no wonder, for Mr. Tregarth was awe-inspiring even for the fact that he said nothing, but sat watching with those furtive eyes that never let one be. He could influence his son and together they worked on this overseeing of the Customs and Excise.

This work took them out at all hours of the night, for undoubtedly if smuggling was afoot, it was in the dark that it took place. It was useless trying to understand what had happened and to put a name to it, because she would never discover it and it was best forgotten, for she had no part in this strange, silent life that went on in the mill. She loved Luke, that was her only excuse for wanting to know more.

As the car drove off up the lane, the mill-wheel slowed down and stopped.

Crystal glanced at the invalid, wondering whether the silence coming after the noise would disturb her, but Mrs. Tregarth was too well accustomed to the noises of this house, and she slept on peacefully. She had never heard the car depart.

Watching her, Crystal felt that it was quite inexplicable that the French doctor should order sleeping-tablets for a woman who quite obviously slept easily, and required nothing of the kind. She settled herself more comfortably in the chair, aware that this was going to be a long wait, for she had made up her mind she would stay here until the men returned.

The clock crept round lethargically, and still the woman in the bed slept without a sound. Occasionally, when Crystal woke, for her neck stiffened and the position became uncomfortable, she looked hurriedly across at the bed, but the invalid was always the same.

It must have been well after three when she became a great deal more wakeful, for the heavy rain had stopped, and had changed to a fall of silverish threads against a background of confused stars. The east was already beginning to lighten for the new day.

Then she heard the far-off sound of a car coming up the lane. Instantly she was on the alert. She went to the window and hid herself against the curtain alongside, so that she could look out yet not be seen, for the sense of self-preservation was suddenly strong within her. She could see the side lights of the car through the thickening hedgerows, heard them hesitate for a moment at the entrance, then turn slowly in at the gateway. For a single second the whole room was illuminated by the vivid lights, then they turned away as the car began its jolting progress over the pot-holes in the drive.

The car halted outside the garage with hardly a sound. It was obvious that the driver was purposely being very quiet. The engine had stopped throbbing, and the lights were switched off.

Watching intently, Crystal saw that Luke had got out of the car, and that the light of the dawn glistened on his oilskins. Then Mr. Tregarth himself got out; she could always recognize him even when the light was not very clear, for he reminded her of a vulture awaiting death, perched on the arm of some derelict tree, the great wings hunched, and the hungry, avaricious eyes staring.

Out of the car there came that dapper little man, the one that Crystal had seen here on the night of her arrival. He was a twitchy little man, with a gnat-like personality. He carried a small case in his hand, and with the other pulled the collar about his throat to protect him from the thickening rain.

The pert little doctor skipped over the

puddles, and walked fast; Mr. Tregarth was slow, for apparently his limbs had stiffened with the journey so that he lumbered. She did not hear the door open, nor close behind them. Yet she knew that by now they would be inside the house and would probably come straight upstairs, bringing the doctor to see the patient.

It would be dreadful to be caught. She wanted to see him, but not in the presence of the others. For the first time it struck her that she should not have stayed. She looked around her in doubt. 'You will not see Dr. Fénon. You will never see him. Remember that I tell you it is impossible for you to see him,' was what Mr. Tregarth had said only last night at supper, and hurriedly she knew that she wanted to put off the moment. She must not see him yet!

Desperately she looked round the room.

If she stayed here by the window, they would burst in on her, and seeing her there, know that she had kept watch.

She stared round, becoming more and more alarmed, and knowing that if she tried to escape along the landing, she would only run into them as they came upstairs. That would be almost worse than staying where she was!

Then she saw the tiny unused room on the right, which had once been a powder closet, at a time when Georgian gentlemen and their beautiful ladies powdered their young hair in the romantic travesty of age.

Crystal realized that her future, and Luke's too, depended on what she did at this precise moment and there was hardly a second to lose. She opened the door to slip inside, her heart making a horrible noise, and overcome with an agony of apprehension that she would faint.

As she shut the door softly, she smelt the warm scent of old dresses that have hung for a long time in a cupboard. An uncurtained window admitted some chance sweetness of the dawn, but the strange thing that first struck her was that the place was illuminated, for a light burnt in it. It was so entirely unexpected that she turned in some bewilderment to the wall whence the light came, and saw there a tiny statue of a blue Madonna, in a little niche. Her cloak was drawn around her, her hands crossed on her breast, and a thin gold halo lingered about her bent head. Just under her a tiny lamp burnt, but in partnership with the new dawn it gave an eerie contrasting beauty to the place.

The door fitted badly, for one of its panels was so split that the chink was wide enough for her to see through. She heard the main door to the room opening, Luke's step, then the other steps, and from the bed, the sudden, heavy sigh of a woman waking.

'Who is there?' came the frail voice of Mrs. Tregarth, awakened so suddenly that she did not realize what was going on.

The man who replied was her husband,

201

speaking gruffly, and using that compelling tone with which he rapped out orders, obviously expecting them to be obeyed.

'I have brought Dr. Fénon with me. It is high time that he saw you again, for if we let it go too long, the injections lose their power. Time is short, he could only come now.'

Mrs. Tregarth had now become aware of the fact that both men were in her room. The old bed creaked wretchedly as she moved the cumbersome body that was so twisted by the disease that afflicted her.

'But I was asleep! Beautifully and naturally asleep. I don't want any more of those beastly injections. You know that I am better without them and that they only confuse me.'

Mr. Tregarth's voice was commanding. Through the chink of the warped door, Crystal saw him standing at the far end of the bed, his large hands on the brass knobs.

'I tell you, you are too ill to make a decision, and you must leave this to the doctor to help you. The illness will kill you unless you do what you are told. You should hand everything over to those who want to do their best for you, only you are so perverse. The mill. Give me the deeds of the mill so that I can make the changes that will make us all rich. I demand the deeds.'

He sounded dynamic.

'I will never give them to you.' From the bed the sick woman's voice was insistent. It raked a

202

little, she sounded dreadfully ill, tired of the fight, and longing to sleep on, naturally and without drugs. On the brass knobs of the ugly bed, the old man's hands gripped harder until the knuckles became glazed.

The French doctor came forward. 'Madame must not alarm herself unnecessarily. Madame must make herself aware of the fact that those who try to cure her, desire much that she will become well.'

'You will kill me,' she said miserably, and there was a sob in her voice.

The doctor advanced to the side of the bed. He was a dapper little man with a face carved like some wooden nutcracker. Cadaverously his sunken eyes stared at her out of caverns.

'It is a sick fancy, madame, for indeed you do forget that the doctor lives by the needs of the patient. She grows tired, but he must go on. When the patient dies, the good doctor loses much money. When he loses much money, he cannot live. Madame, indeed that is the great sense, yes?'

Crystal heard the sound of water running from the tap, and the grating of the metal cap as the doctor unscrewed the lid of the hypodermic syringe. She felt rather sick and prayed Heaven that she was not going to faint, for that would make the position impossible.

If Luke was there he made no sound, and she came to the conclusion that he was absent. It

203

was Mr. Tregarth who did the talking.

'Look at me,' he was commanding, and his hands thumped the end of the bed in a desperate attempt to force the issue. 'Look at me. Look at me.'

She gave a wretched, forlorn little cry. 'It is so wrong to look at you. There is something quite terrible in your eyes and I am the one person who knows it. I refuse to look at you. I refuse to come under that influence.'

'You shall look at me.'

There came a long silence.

In the powder-closet Crystal had the feeling that this would last for ever, it was something that would never end, something that told her nothing of what was going on in the room. She now knew definitely that she had not imagined that those eye came closer and were compelling. Mrs. Tregarth called it 'the influence', and it came through that man's eyes. In the room a man moved quickly. She knew that Mrs. Tregarth had no longer resisted against that injection, but that whatever they had done, had been done under compulsion.

Then there was the sound of footsteps, of a door opening and closing. They had gone.

Crystal still stood there like a statue, with the light burning before the little Madonna in her blue gown and the sweetness of the dawn increasing. About the powder-closet there was something of peace and of great beauty, she got the impression that it was here that Luke had found the inspiration for his picture.

Cautiously she opened the door.

The room beyond appeared to be much as when she had left it, save that a hand-towel was flung down beside the wash-basin, and the woman had turned over in the bed. She lay there apparently in a deep sleep. Usually she rolled over on to her side, finding it easier to sleep this way, but now she was prostrate on her back, her eyes tightly closed, and her hair like a drift of seaweed in a grey shadow across the surface of the pillow.

Nobody else was in the room.

The moment that Crystal found she had it to herself she went over to the bed, but Mrs. Tregarth did not stir. It was no longer the peaceful, serene sleep that she had enjoyed throughout the night, but had an unreal quality about it. She was not herself, even if her breathing was easy and her face was composed; now there was nothing that could be done to help her. Her sleeveless night-dress revealed the dark stab of the needle on the upper part of her arm. Smaller than a mole, it asserted itself in vigorous contrast to the deep creaminess of her skin.

Crystal went over to the basin where one of the taps had been left dripping. In the waste-paper basket beside it was a scrap of paper, the label which had been torn from a box, and an ampoule snapped at the neck and marked only '1 c.c.'. There was no name to it. Crystal turned it over and over in her hand, then slipped it into her bag. She had the feeling that this was the only piece of evidence that she had yet collected, and even as she told herself this, she knew that she had no proof that it was really evidence.

She slipped back into the easy chair where she had spent the night, and she must have dozed off. When she woke morning was advanced, though the patient still lay drugged on the bed. She had the feeling now that the affairs of the night had been a bad dream, something that she must forget; that she was exaggerating the mysteries of Smuggler's Mill, and that the doctor had never been here at all. Yet in her bag lay the broken ampoule.

I must not ask too much, she told herself.

III

There was a letter from Tony that morning. He wanted to come down and see her, and was planning to make Penzance the centre spot for a summer holiday. As she read it she knew that she did not want Tony here now; he would ask too many questions; he would not be satisfied with the answers he got, and she would not be happy in having to lie to him.

What she felt for Luke was something so different from anything that she had ever felt for Tony that he would be bound to detect it, and

206

question her. She realized that very probably there could be no future for herself and Luke, for he was two men. She was almost certain that his father was responsible for the strange man who did what he was told, and whose face darkened, and whose eyes went somnolent, and whose whole expression glowered. Luke, who gave his mother the sleeping-tablets that she did not want to take; who, suspicious of strangers, had glared at Crystal through the grille; quite different from the one who had painted the exquisite picture, the only beauty in that L-shaped sitting-room. Alien to the charming person who drove her out to shop, who talked to her, and at times took her into his arms. The man who said 'I-love-you' with his mouth against her own.

She was tired this morning, and could not face the task of writing to Tony and putting him off. She would leave it. Last night she had seen a little—but not enough. She knew instinctively that there was more to come. There was now no trace of the little doctor, no sign of him, for he was apparently some ghost which at the first light of day would vanish. Luke had gone out in the car again, and did not appear till lunch-time, which was when Mrs Tregarth began to stir, waking from the enforced sleep. It was a dreadful awakening.

She complained of a violent headache and was sick. She could eat nothing, but lay there, crying forlornly to herself, and so depressed that it was difficult to rouse her. When Crystal tried to discover if she had any memory of what happened, she found that it was a blank.

'Something happened in the night,' was all that she could say. 'I don't remember what is was, I never do. The strange thing is that I never do know what has happened, only that it *has* happened. It makes it very difficult.'

She began to cry again.

'Don't let's talk about it until you feel better,' Crystal suggested; 'have a nice cuppa, curl up and get a natural sleep. That will help you more that anything else, I'm sure.'

She tucked Mrs. Tregarth in, and then towards evening went out for a walk towards the village, for she had a longing for fresh air.

She walked fast down the lane and beyond to where it widened out into the road itself, one way going to the cliff, the other into the sprawling, scattered little village. How ugly were the small houses, the chapel with its mushroom-coloured brickwork, and the church, its squarish belfry battlemented against a sky that was the colour of a robin's egg.

She went on to the shop with a feeling of general forlornness. She bought the bread, pushing it into the big basket she had brought with her, and she started on the way home, wishing that she felt happier.

Soon this part of the country would be bright

with rhododendrons, for already there were traces of the faint translucent mauve blossoms amongst the dark leaves. She had come to the country in the very sweet of the year, and every hour now more flowers came. But still the coast-line was rugged. Still the waves lashed cruelly, and the cliffs were gaunt. It had a sinister flavour which was hard to escape from. Already it seemed to be an eternity of time since she had worked in that city office with Mr. Hellston and he had offered to marry her. His melon-shaped face with all those chins, had receded into the distance. Then she had thought of Cornwall as being the dream county that she would never visit, now she had come here and had found it far more beautiful, yet far more gruelling, than she had ever anticipated it could be.

She was just about to cross the road, when she heard the warning hoot of a small car that was rapidly approaching. Crystal pulled herself out of the road and on to the verge with a gasp; she seemed to make a habit of trying to get under cars, and stood there shaking. Then she saw that the tiny car had come to a standstill before her, and that Stella was looking out of it.

'Hello, silly one!' said Stella.

'What are you doing here?'

'Maybe I have the prior right. Cornwall's mine as much as it is yours. Any old way I found it first.'

Stella leant over the little door of the car. 'If

you want to know the truth I came along here to see if Luke was anywhere about. Is he at home?'

'I'm not sure.'

'Or is it that you don't want to tell me?'

'Don't be absurd, why shouldn't I want to tell you?'

Stella folded her arms on the edge of the car door and rested her head on them. 'Because you are in love with Luke. Most women feel that way about him, he has charm, he has beauty, and he—if you get him as he really is—is a very, very delightful person. But he isn't always like that.'

Crystal said nothing even though Stella waited for her to drop a hint. Then, as there was no reply, she went on again.

'I'm still in love with Luke myself, even if I gave him up willingly because I found out things. Horrible things.'

'What did you find out?'

'If I tell you, you'll only go and tell him.'

'I don't think I shall.'

'Or the old man, which would be worse. Has that old man ever got you into that grim study of his, and looked and looked at you, and looked, with his eyes coming nearer all the time, until you could have sworn that they had left his head and were actually coming at you like lethal weapons?'

Crystal felt herself pale as she answered. 'Yes, he has,' she admitted.

'You knew what it meant, didn't you? It was the evil power behind that place. The old man has got Luke the same way, but the one person he can't get is the old lady. She won't go under, and he can't do anything to her whilst she stays that way. When I found that was going on I felt pretty awful about it. It wasn't only that, either. How much do you know?'

'Nothing at all,' said Crystal, 'save that this doctor comes in from the islands, and he does something to Mrs. Tregarth and makes her feel most dreadfully ill. She has sleeping-tablets which do much the same thing. Luke gives them to her, also; that is the one thing that I cannot understand.'

Stella stared at her. In this mood she had about her a new quality. It struck Crystal that she was a good girl at heart, and that she really wanted to help.

She said, 'Now look here. That old man is up to something, what it is I don't know, but it is certainly nothing to do with the Customs and Excise people like he says. The whole place hates him and distrusts him, but they can't do anything about it. On the face of it there is nothing against him, and he knows it.'

'But what could he be doing?'

'That's what I don't know. Luke is in it too, I realize that, but I think Luke is in it by compulsion, and hates the whole idea, but can't get out of it. I've always felt that. I don't think

211

his mother knows about it, but one thing she does know, which is that her husband wants to get possession of the mill. It's hers, you know, and she won't part.'

Crystal told Stella of what happened only last night; the conversation that she had overheard through the chink of the powder-closet, the strange visit of the men just before the dawn actually broke.

'Yes, well, there you are!' said Stella, 'that is what is happening. Then there is that mill-wheel, and if you ask me that has got something more to do with it than we think. It makes such a dreadful noise going round and round, and creaking and groaning. I tell you, it pretty well drove me crazy. I tried to get Luke to stop it, but no, he wouldn't. Said he couldn't. That was when we finally split. We had the most shocking row, and I suppose that I am well out of the whole thing, but Luke is one of those men a girl can't help loving. Funny how it gets you! But the trouble with him is that the old man has something which he holds over him. The village is not so far wrong when they say that he hypnotizes people. I am sure he tried to hypnotize me with those eyes of his coming nearer all the time. It was just after that that he told me about the mill. He says that unless the wheel goes round the house isn't the same value to him, and nothing would induce him to allow it to be stopped. What do you think he means by that?'

'I should think nothing at all.'

'Well, I think you are wrong. I believe there is a great deal more to this than we know. I—I wonder how far I can trust you. You're a nice kid. I should have said you weren't their sort, and have no vice in you.'

'You can trust me completely. I can keep a secret, you know.'

'Can you? There are a lot of secrets to be kept in this.' It seemed that Stella had lost that rather teasing, bantering manner which had been the first thing that had struck Crystal about her that day when she had gone to the Copper Kettle with Luke. Now she was worried.

She said, 'I don't believe the doctor is a doctor at all. I don't think Luke, the real Luke, has any share in this business, and he resents it horribly, but does not really know quite what is going on. Under his father's control he acts like an automaton. It is the old man who is to blame for everything. I shall never forget that final row we had. All the time I had the feeling that it wasn't Luke at all but his father to whom I was talking. Have you had that feeling? Perhaps I was lucky to get out of it, maybe you would be lucky to get out of it, too. Why don't you go away whilst you still can?'

'Because—well, because I don't want to.'

'Because you're in love with Luke?'

'Maybe.'

'Well, you're a braver girl than I am, and good luck to you. If you want a friend, send for me. I'd do anything I could, but I think the old man has got my number and would very soon have me out of it if he could. Once I thought that the Smuggler's Mill was a spooky spot, but that isn't true. There isn't the sign of a spook there, it is just that wretched old man. If somebody would push him over the cliff, it would be a boon. He'll kill that unfortunate wife of his, if he gets a chance.'

'But Luke loves her.'

'He won't be allowed to love her, if his father feels that way. You don't realize what is happening. I doubt if you have the hang of it all. I haven't much, but I've got something of it. Keep your eyes skinned, and maybe you will see things more clearly, for there are lots of things yet to find out, and I warn you, whether you are with me or against me, I am going to find them out. All of them.'

Without saying good-bye, she started the car and it shot off down the hill, leaving Crystal to stare helplessly after her.

She walked back, hoping that she might see Mervyn, for he at least was reliable, one of the people on whom she could lean. But she did not meet him. She turned back down the lane and in at the broken gate, her basket growing heavier as she went.

As she went up the drive, skirting the pot-

214

holes, Luke came out of the garage. He wore gum-boots, and a reefer coat with a peaked cap pulled down over his eyes, but he smiled at her, and she knew that he was no longer in the bad mood.

'Hello, Crystal! Let me take that basket.'

'Oh, Luke, it was such a dreadful night.'

Perhaps she should not have confessed to it, but somehow she had to tell him. He put his free arm round her.

'I know, I know. Try not to think about it. None of this can go on for ever. There has got to be a way out, and we will find it. Oh, how I wish you'd go away for a time! This is no place for a sweet girl like you.'

They entered the hall. 'Your father isn't in?' she said.

'No, and you realized it by my behaviour.'

'I know you are scared of him.'

'It's worse than being scared. It's more than that, it is a power that he has.'

They had come into the L-shaped living-room. Pixie lay on the mat, and flowers had brought a new meaning to the place. It gave an air of friendliness, which had not been present on the night of Crystal's arrival. It had charm, and the newly-washed curtains were at least clean, if faded.

'Darling,' he said, 'you have got to trust me.'

He closed the door behind him.

Luke was standing in the window, with his hands on hers, and he was looking down into her eyes. The wretched mill-wheel was silent, and in a way Crystal was glad about that, for had it started that noise again at this particular moment, she did not think that she could have borne it. Now there was the quality of spring about the room. Beyond them lay the garden, the pheasant-eyed narcissi withering, and the rhododendrons coming on in their big pink and pearl blossoms.

'I love you so much,' Luke was saying, and then, slowly, he leant forward and laid his mouth against her own. His lips were very warm, his eyes, close to her own, full of a deep emotion. She did not know how long that kiss lasted, but he released her very gradually.

'Luke!'

'You ought to go away, my dear; even if Mother wants you here, you still ought to go away.'

'I want to stay for ever. Only let me know more about it all. It is your father, isn't it? He does something, something strange, and I—I want to know what it is.'

'There is nothing more that I can tell you. My father was always a strange man, I agree, but what he does and what he is are nothing to do with anybody else. We go about our duties, he and I, and those are silent duties.'

216

'But your mother . . . ?'

'My sweet, this is no part of her, either. Don't let's talk of her.'

Crystal put her arms about his neck, and they stood looking into each other's eyes. 'I am laying all my cards on the table, Luke, because it is the only thing that I can do. I don't understand this strange doctor, I suppose he *is* a doctor, but I am sure that what he is giving your mother is wrong and that it is not helping her to get better.'

A little frown had come to Luke's brow; she watched his eyes as they stared at her with perplexity, almost as though she had spoken in some other language, one which he did not understand.

'That isn't true,' he said at last.

'She hates it all. Why can't it be stopped? It is doing no good.'

'But it is doing good. Six months ago she could not turn over in bed; she can now. Clumsily, I admit, but still it is something. You would not let us make her go back on that, would you? That would be impossible for her.'

'But *is* she better?'

'Yes, yes, she is better. She has got to get much better. Much better still.'

They heard the hall door opening. In a single instant he had changed. His lips brushed her cheek again, with the significance of farewell. The hands relaxed on her shoulder. Hurriedly

217

she whispered, 'I'll stick by you, Luke. Whatever happens in the future, do remember that you and I are together in this, and together we will sink or swim. I promise you that.'

She had just time to feel his hands grip her shoulders with an impulsive reciprocation, then the door of the room opened, and Mr. Tregarth came in.

V

It was Luke who brought Mervyn to tea that day.

Suddenly the heat broke. There had been a wet evening, and a stormy night with the clouds low, but at dawn it had cleared, and a hot sun had risen. It was from that morning that the heat-wave broke. There is something tempting about the first really hot days of the year, and the promise of the new summer. The sea was translucent and blue, and against the sky that matched it the gulls' wings seemed to have become unreally white.

In the afternoon she had some mending to do in the wild garden, where the flowers were coming out with the hot sun, almost as if a fairy had waved a wand over the place and had commanded it.

All the windows of the mill were open, and the wheel silent, which gave the place a leisurely atmosphere, which Crystal enjoyed. Karin had brought the tea out into the garden, just beyond the big windows of the sitting-room.

'It's always lots nicer in the summer out here,' she said, 'and this is the first bit of real summer we've had, isn't it?' Her small face, shaped like a pear, was shiny with the heat.

'Yes, it is the first bit of real summer.'

Karin stood there fingering a tray and smiling. 'It's a shame that poor thing upstairs can't come down and enjoy the garden a bit. Do you think she's been getting better since you got here? You ought to know. She don't seem so much better to me.'

'It's a long job, I fear.'

'Yes, miss, I know.'

Karin shifted again uneasily. She said, 'Something's wrong somewhere about this. All sorts of things go on here what you don't expect. They're going on all the time.'

For a moment Crystal wondered if Karin was trying to get something out of her. Was she helping the old man who had accused her of prying? She could not be too careful.

'Oh, I think it's a nice house. I don't think anything funny goes on here; it's awfully easy to imagine that sort of thing in an old house, and this *is* an old house, it's a very old house, isn't it?' and she smiled, she hoped casually. 'Get the rest of the tea, do, Karin,' and she returned to the mending.

She was not going to fall into any trap of that nature, yet judging by the rather pathetic look

219

the girl had given her, it was not a trap at all.

There came the sound of voices. Crystal could not believe that it was really Mervyn's voice, yet he preceded Luke coming out through the open french windows on to the tiny bricked terrace, where the tea was set. Neither of them had coats on, but wore tennis shirts and short sleeves; both were brown as berries.

'Why, Mervyn!'

'My car broke down in the lane. I was jiggling with it when Luke came along and suggested that I should come inside for tea. I thought it was a very good idea.'

'A grand idea.'

Mervyn stood before her in khaki shorts, his hands on the belt. He said, 'When it gets hot in this part of the world it gets too hot. How are you keeping up, Crystal? We shall have you bathing before long. I'll take you over to try a spot of surfing at St. Ives.'

'It would be wonderful,' she said.

'Then let's do it,' said Mervyn. 'I don't know what will happen to my car . . .'

'We'll get the garage to see to it.'

That was when Karin came staggering out with the heavy tray and the tea on it. She set it down, mopped her face with a man's handkerchief which seemed to be incongruously large for her size, giggled to them and went back indoors. She seemed to be enjoying the weather.

They sat over the tea talking of how long the

220

heat-wave would last. Discussing the promise of the tourist season, for already the great cars had appeared along the coast road. Mousehole was full. The beaches were beginning to show that the crowds were coming and going. It was the beginning of the season by which so many landladies lived.

'Everyone except ourselves lets rooms in this village, you know,' said Luke. 'Oh, Mervyn doesn't, I think, but all the others. People come round worrying you and saying they have nowhere to stay, and somehow you can't turn them from the door. Besides, it is a means of making a lot of money which the village folk like.'

'You would not have spare rooms in this place,' Mervyn said. 'The Smuggler's Mill looks large, but it isn't so really. In the old days they used to use the cellar as an extra room, what have you done with it?'

'Locked it up,' said Luke quite brusquely, 'and like the words of the old song, "My father has the key".'

'I believe it was rather a nice room, for although it calls itself a cellar, it is what house-agents call sub-basement, or ante-basement, or something like that. One half of it comes up for air, doesn't it?'

'I don't know.' Luke's voice was quite terse, almost as though he did not want to answer questions about it.

'It is actually shut up?'

'Absolutely. The floor wasn't steady or something; it would have cost the earth to get it put to rights, and in these hard times my father decided against it. Whatever you call it, it is only a cellar really, and that isn't quite good enough.'

'No.' Mervyn lit a cigarette and was guarded in his movements. Had he sensed something that was different? Crystal wondered. She got up.

'I'll go and get my things. I've got a bathing-dress somewhere but it may take me a minute or so to find it. I'll bring towels for all of us, shall I?'

'Yes, do,' but Luke's eyes still avoided her.

She went upstairs to get the things, and to say good-bye to Mrs. Tregarth. It had been one of her good days, and she said that weather made a difference to her, in the heat her bones always felt easier. She was sitting up in bed with a new book sent down from London for her, and very happy with it. She smiled when she heard where they were going.

'If you've never surfed before, you are going to love it,' she said, 'it really is the most enjoyable sport, and I used to do a lot of it before I got ill. Newquay has wonderful surfing, and I liked it near Tintagel. But St. Ives'll do for a start.'

She found the men smoking, and talking in a

casual manner of the tides, of the village back-chat, of everything that went on.

'Ready?' asked Luke.

The three of them packed into his car, and started off along the road to St. Ives. The tide was in on the estuary, the little waves lapping against the reeds, and boats sailing across towards the sea. They turned the corner to Lelant, and on down into St. Ives itself, going to the Porthmeor beach, leaving the car in a little back lane and walking down to the rocks.

Today, in the early evening, the beach was beautiful. The waves were coming in, tasselled with spray. One after another they rolled up and broke, a magnificent sight, on the beach itself. They went on to the rocks, each to a corner of his own. How hot it was, for the sun had streamed down on to them all day! Slowly Crystal undressed and drew on the green bathing-dress which she had bought for Ramsgate, and which she was now wearing in this romantic little town the other end of England. She sat waiting for the men, her hair pushed up under the matching cap, her arms hugging her knees. She saw the fishing-boats off the Head, and heard the sound of the waves as they broke to her left. Then a 'Halloo', from Luke.

'I'm coming,' she called.

She scrambled down on to the silverish sand. It was warm to her feet. The men had brought down the surfing-boards, and were waving to her; she went to them. She had thought that the water would be cold, yet when she pushed her feet into it, it was very pleasant. She plunged out into the waves, one—bigger than the rest—almost knocking her down. The men came in after her. They swam out with the boards, and turning, came in on the waves.

Crystal had never thought that anything could be so exhilarating or so delicious. Time and time again they went out, to come back riding in, and when tired out, they dragged the boards up the beach, then lay down on the hot sand to dry and smoke. In the distance a woman was singing in one of the studios. The gulls screamed at the water's edge, and Mervyn talked of them, of the photographs he had taken recently, and the new book, now nearing its finish.

At last Luke sat up almost dry, and lit a last cigarette.

'We ought to be thinking of getting home. Mother'll be wondering what has happened to us. What about it? Shall we get dressed again?'

They raced back to the rocks, but now they had become cold, for the sun was fast sinking. It seemed as though a little cloud was rising, a cloud that hid the sun. Crystal dressed slowly, for after the delight of surfing she found that she was more tired than she had thought, and lethargy suffused her. She dragged on her frock and buckled the belt. She picked up the little

Shetland cardigan and fastened it down the front. The heat had gone and she would be glad of something woolly after all.

She went back to the men who were waiting for her at the top of the alley-way. The sand was deep and loose impeding every step and dragging her back. Still the woman sang in one of the studios, and her voice sounded pleasant.

They drove home not talking very much, each of them tired after the exercise, and they dropped Mervyn half-way down his road.

He stood there waving them good-bye. This evening it seemed that he and Luke had got on quite well; there had been nothing of that spirit of dislike which had been so noticeable before.

'You enjoyed it?' Luke asked her, as they moved away.

'It was beautiful. I had no idea that anything could be quite so wonderful. The extraordinary sense of triumph as you come riding in.'

'Yes, it is good fun! One of these days we'll go up the coast. It's pretty good at Perranporth, we'll have a shot for it there. You'll love it.'

'Yes, I'll love it.'

He said, 'I wish all our evenings could be like this. Happy. Worried about nothing. Life just being kind to us, and as a result we being kind to life. That is how I would have chosen them to be if I could have done the choosing, but in this world men and women don't do the choosing. The gods do that for them, and sometimes the gods have very funny ideas.'

'What do you suppose the gods have for us?'

'I hope me for you and you for me!' he said, and then stopped the car. A great clump of fir trees was to the right of them, and they cast an agreeable shadow which enveloped them. He put his arms round her and drew her close to him. He still smelt of the sea, that faint tang of water which lingers, just as the whisper of the ocean stays with those shells brought inland yet still bearing with them the echo of the sea.

'I love you so much, my dear.'

'I love you, Luke.'

'That night you came to us, I have never told you about it. I had had a most dreadful time. My father had been difficult, everything had gone wrong, and I had the feeling of being alone. Alone for ever. I prayed that you would come and be nice, I kept on praying it, and when I went to Penzance and the train came in and you were not there, the disappointment was almost more than I could bear. I came home, and felt that I had left all hope behind me. There—at Penzance!'

'Then, after all, I came through the rain to you. Oh, Luke, you might have realized that I should have let you know if I had not been coming. I should have done something about it.'

He paused a moment, then said, 'It was not only that. You know Miss Mowser in the post office?'

'Dear old Chatterbox?'

'Dear old Chatterbox is just about right for her. She had taken in a telegram the night before, from Mr. Ingram. Of course she ought not to tell these things, but she has read every telegram she has ever had, and broadcast it, also. She broadcast this one. The telegram went to an address in London, warning someone to keep away. You were the only person I knew who was coming to this place, and I thought it went to you.'

'It didn't, you know. Tony was the person who had written down inquiring of the vicar because he was afraid of my coming to strangers. The awful part was that he pretended to be my brother, and he most certainly isn't my brother.'

'It seemed pretty awful to me. You had been warned off and you had kept away. I couldn't blame you, but that hurt. I came back from Penzance in one of those bitter moods that get me. I just can't help myself. I had a set-to with my father when I got back, and then he went out. After that—a long time after that—you just arrived.'

'And did not get the best welcome in the world!'

'Because I could not believe that it was you! I was pretty well sure that it wasn't. That was all.'

'You've got a very suspicious mind.'

'If you had had my life, you'd have a very

227

suspicious mind; it is something that is born in you, something that goes on, and now it is too late to cure it.'

She kissed him again and again. 'I'll cure it one day, Luke; I'll cure it, you know.'

'Is that a promise?'

'Yes, the best promise ever. Where there is love there must be trust, and we've got the one. Now the next thing is to get the other.'

He kissed her slowly.

'That is what we must now set out to find,' he said, 'perfect trust. And pray God we'll get it.'

'We will,' she promised him.

CHAPTER SIX

I

It was the Whit week that it happened. In life there are weeks of strange events, and this was one of them. It started when she was wanted on the telephone one morning, called away from the breakfast-table, although she could scarcely believe her ears.

'It can't be for me, really,' she told Karin, but she went, aware that those unpleasant eyes of Mr. Tregarth were following her.

The telephone was in the hall; she took it up, just as she heard the district nurse's little car stopping in the drive. The call came from

Tregenna Castle Hotel at St. Ives, and she was asked to wait. Then after a pause a man's voice spoke to her, a voice she knew only too well.

It was Mr. Hellston!

'I have come down to this part of the world to find out what is happening,' said Mr Hellston somewhat pompously. 'My offer still holds good. I have not had a decent secretary since you left, and am disliking the situation very much. I cannot think why you took yourself off like that, and what you are doing in Cornwall, I simply cannot imagine. You had no reference, you know.'

'That was your fault,' she snapped back.

She was quite surprised to hear the tone of her voice, but apparently not so astounded as was Mr. Hellston. He was not used to people snapping at him. He had, for years now, gone through life in a comfortable, sensible sort of a way as a little potentate in his own world. As a little potentate he intended to remain, and this was more than he could accept.

'How dare you!' he began.

She cut him short. Ever since she had been in his employ she had been longing to do what she now could do. Before, her hands had been tied. Now she was free. She said, 'If you think I would ever marry you, you are completely wrong. Your pomposity would drive me crazy! I was astounded that you had the audacity to ask me in the first place, and I am a great deal more

229

astounded to hear that you have followed me down here. Please leave me alone.'

There was a moment's silence and she knew exactly what he was looking like! His eyes went more pallid with indignation, she knew, his lower lip dropped and twitched, but it did not take him as long to recover as she had expected.

He said, 'I shall now make it my business to visit your employers and explain why you left me, and about this most unpleasant conversation between us. I have always been goodness itself to you, I have paid you the greatest compliment that a man can pay a woman, and all you do is lose your temper, and burst out with disgraceful remarks like this.'

She said, 'If you come here ...' but the receiver had been slammed down.

It was useless trying to convince herself that he did not know where she was, because undoubtedly he had discovered it somehow or other, even to the telephone number.

She went back into the sitting-room. Both Luke and his father stared at her, and she knew that look required an answer.

'It was my previous employer,' she said, 'he is staying at the Tregenna Castle, and he is, I believe, coming over here immediately to tell you what an awful person I am.'

Feeling weak at the knees, she sat down again in her chair, rather helplessly.

'So he is, is he?' asked Luke, the dark look

coming over his face. 'Well, he is in for something of a reception!'

Then Mr. Tregarth spoke. He said, 'Leave this to me. When the door-bell goes I will answer it.'

'Wouldn't it be better if no one answered it?' asked Crystal, still aware of the feeling of utter wretchedness and limpness.

'No.' The eyes would not let her go. 'No, most certainly not. This man has to be met and his visit ended. Leave this to me.'

Neither of them had words with which to refuse him; they sat there waiting for the sound of the car approaching, and it seemed to take a considerable time.

Then at last, when Karin was clearing away the breakfast things, and the district nurse had gone off again, they heard the sound of the Bentley outside. The bell rang imperiously. It was Mr. Tregarth who got up, and went to the door. Across the breakfast-table Crystal's eyes met those of Luke.

'Well?' she said.

'It'll be all right. My father is very good at this kind of thing. I'm rather sorry for your late employer, so don't be too upset.'

They heard the grille grind back, and Mr. Tregarth's voice, 'What do you want?'

The tone was a shot from a gun, it would have petrified both of them, and apparently it petrified the visitor also, for there was a moment's hesitation, then the voice, 'I wish to see the owner of the house.'

'I am the owner of this house. I don't like visitors, and never see them. Whatever you want, I would be glad if you would take yourself and your car off.'

Again the remark seemed to have upset Mr. Hellston considerably; usually he made the unpleasant remarks and prided himself that he could silence an unwelcome visitor with a few choice sallies; now he was the one silenced.

However, he rose to the occasion. 'I wished to speak to you of an ex-employee of mine who is here in your service, I believe, Miss Crystal Stevens.'

'I have never heard of her.'

Crystal turned amazed eyes to Luke, and he made a little *moue* of indifference with his lips. They were entirely in his father's hands, and whatever he said or did, they could not interfere. 'But,' said the amazed Mr. Hellston, 'I telephoned her at this address within the hour, and most certainly she spoke to me.'

'You imagined it.'

'Most certainly I did not imagine it.'

'Then you were drunk. You are probably drunk now, and not wanted here. I should be obliged if you would take yourself and your car out of my drive.'

With an indignant rattle the grille banged to, and there came the ponderous sound of Mr.

Tregarth returning to the living-room. He opened the door and his face was sheet white. He stared at the two sitting there, and he said, 'Never again! I will not permit visitors, I don't want them at this house, and if any more come, then that is the end. You go back to London, Miss Stevens, and by the next train, you understand.'

Nobody said anything. He sat down, finished a last cup of coffee (he always drank innumerable cups), then without a word he stalked out. She looked at Luke, but he avoided her eyes. The mood was coming over him; he mumbled something, she did not catch what it was, and went out after his father. A little while later, when she was arranging the flowers, she heard them taking the car slowly down the drive.

She went up to Mrs. Tregarth, who was looking a great deal better, and delighted that last night she had pretended over the sleeping-tablet, and had it concealed beneath her pillow.

'How happy you and I could be together!' she said, 'we think along the same wave-length, we understand one another. You and I, and Luke. Poor Luke! Under his father's influence he changes, I know. He is such a dear person really, and it is quite wrong that his father should influence him as he does. I wish that there was some escape. I wish ...'

She turned her head awkwardly towards the

window, and looked out of it to where the cliffs rose, and beyond them the blue sea danced with a myriad sequins thrown upon its blue cloak by the radiant sun.

'One day everything will be all right,' Crystal told her, and then, acting on impulse, she bent over her and kissed her. For a single moment the twisted hands clawed at her own, and pressed them and into the eyes welled a deep emotion.

'I love you, dear,' whispered the older woman.

II

Before she went out shopping, Crystal went round the house for a final tidy-up. In Cornwall there was little dust, but this house worried her, for she was always thirsting to rearrange it. It was too bleak and forlorn-looking, and although she had made some improvements, she had not finished.

Today the door into Mr Tregarth's study was open, a most unusual thing. Looking into it, she was appalled at the dust, the tobacco smell, and the general air of dilapidation. She took a duster inside and got rid of some of the innumerable spiders' webs that hung like dirty curtains before the window. She managed to open it a little, and the first inrush of clean sweet air was a joy to the place. She cleared up the grate, where the ash of numberless fires cluttered in a grey dust that was most unpleasant. She went back to Karin for a cobweb brush.

'It's the master's study, and I never saw such a mess,' she said.

Karin started with horror and put an agitated finger to her lips. 'Oh dear, you hadn't ought to be in there. He won't like it. He gets ever so angry if that is cleared up, and I've never dared go in. Wouldn't dare go in now, in case he caught me.'

'But the place is filthy. I shall just give it a lick and a promise before I go out, and maybe he won't be too angry.'

She went back with the cobweb brush, having warned Karin to let her know if there was any sound of the returning car. Karin thought they had gone down to the motor-boat, probably across to the islands, which would mean that they would not be back for a very long time. Inspired by this thought, Crystal worked on. She managed to make the place look far better. But the floor was paved with weeping stones, and when she looked out of the refreshed window, she saw that the trouble was that the lawn beyond came up to the sill. The study was sunk down almost as though it were half a cellar. She thought of what Mervyn had said about the cellar, and looked about her.

Then she saw the door.

The paint had long ago worn from it, and was so faded and dirty that one had no idea what its original colour had been. On a peg there hung a dirty old mackintosh, its pockets and cuffs frayed with unreal tassels of material. She went to it. The door was not opened by a handle as most doors, but by a latch, with something of the stable-door about it. She never knew why she did it. Perhaps she had not thought that it would open, for, if it held any secret, it would be locked. Yet it yielded to her touch. In an instant she looked into a room much smaller than the one in which she stood, smelling of wet stones, and of oil. It was lit by a strange little window which opened on to something approaching an area, and had a set of bars before it, rusted beyond recognition. It was small enough to be no larger than a cupboard, she realized, so that surely it could not be the cellar that Mervyn had mentioned. An old kitchen-table stood to the right, whilst before her was a strange piece of machinery reminding her of a mangle.

It must, she thought quickly, be something that was discarded from the home, yet it was beautifully clean, the cleanest object in the two rooms; the iron work was polished and oiled, the handle newly painted, just as the old kitchen-table had recently been scrubbed. A pile of clean paper lay upon it, weighted down by a heavy weight bound in old but clean linen. She could not understand it.

She stared at it helplessly.

At that moment she heard the swift patter of running feet, and knew that Karin was scampering up the hall, her small, peculiar body swaying from side to side, her funny little hands fluttering.

'They're coming back, miss, they're coming back,' she was screeching.

In the instant Crystal shut the door, but she had a picture photographed on her mind. She had seen something that she could not explain. She had looked into a tiny cellar, and there had been something all the more unexpected because it was completely clean and polished. Something cared for, in the annexe to an uncared-for room.

She ran out into the hall.

'They're coming back, miss.'

She just had the time to get into the living-room, her heart pounding, to collect her shopping basket and money and pretend she was off shopping, when Mr Tregarth walked into the house.

She passed him in the hall without a word. He stared at her from under the peaked cap that he wore when he was going to the motor-boat, and he looked at her with those eyes which she dared not tempt to come nearer. Soon he would discover that she had cleaned his study and be angry; she had forgotten to close the window, maybe that would infuriate him!

She wished that her legs did not tremble so,

and that she herself did not feel over-anxious, but there was nothing that she could do about it. She walked out into the drive.

It was hot with summer. The flower scent went with her into the lane, and she climbed up the hill to the village itself. There was very little shopping this morning, nothing necessitating a trip to Penzance, or to St. Ives, and in some ways she was sorry. Today she would have liked to go farther afield and not run the risk of perhaps running into Mr. Hellston. On second thoughts she reminded herself that St. Ives would be more dangerous than the village, but she would keep her eyes open.

She bought her bread, and fish from the tiny fish shop round the corner. The owner was a fisherman who often had delicious mackerel for sale.

She came out again into the village street and the summery sunshine could make even this bleak little spot look bright. It was busying itself for the fresh season. Then she saw that a man was approaching her, a man with smiling eyes and a long, loping walk. She had not run into Mr. Hellston.

She had run into Tony.

III

There were too many men in Crystal's life, she decided, in that first quick flash of recognition. Tony had never been anything more than the

238

best friend, and she had not wanted him here in the village, particularly now when everything was difficult.

'I had to come,' he said. 'What an awful village! I thought you said that Cornwall was lovely? I call it dreadful. All those splits; all those grey houses, and fat gulls. I call it beastly,'

She shook her head. 'Oh, Tony, why did you do this?'

'I wasn't happy about things. I felt that you had changed a lot since you got down here, and I wanted to know what was happening. Ever since I had that telegram from Mr. Ingram, I could not feel too happy.'

'It was a mistake that you told Mr. Ingram you were my brother.'

'What else could I do? Do you suppose he would have told me a thing if he had thought I was just the hanger-on?' He linked his arm affectionately in her own. It was more than she could bear.

'Now look here, Tony, I know I'm being awful, but this can't be. Mr. Hellston has come down to St. Ives, he came over to Smuggler's Mill this very morning and there has been a shocking row with Mr Tregarth about it. He hates visitors. He would hate to see me with you now, and there would be another awful row.'

'I'm not surprised to hear that he disliked Mr. Hellston; who wouldn't? But I'm different! I had to come down. I'm in the money now, and it is a new life that I can offer you. You can't just send me away. I want you to leave this beastly place. I've heard all sorts of things about Smuggler's Mill, and if you ask me "smugglers" is the operative word.'

'That's nonsense!'

'That's only because you don't know. Something funny is going on there. The general opinion is that Mrs. Tregarth will die pretty soon, and then heaven knows what will happen. The old man is a menace.'

'Well?'

'And the young man too.'

'You're saying nothing about Luke.'

'So that's the way the land lies, is it?'

'Yes, it is.'

'He's got round you, too. I thought something dreadful was happening, and the sooner you come away, the better. I was first in the field.'

She stopped dead. 'Tony, it was never the same field at all. I told you that caring for a person was insufficient, it had to be love or nothing, and what I feel for Luke *is* love. I adore him. I wouldn't care if he was the last man left in the world, I wouldn't care if he was the worst man left in the world. None of those things seem to matter, when you're in love.'

He stood there staring at her, his hands twitching a little, his eyes confused. 'Crystal, what has happened to you?'

240

'The thing I've wanted most in my whole life. To be in love, and nothing else matters.'

They stood facing each other now, and she heard the familiar toot of a car coming down the road. It slackened speed, and drew up beside them. Luke was driving it, his dark eyes surprised. How handsome he looked with the wind blowing his hair, and his shirt open, the collar blowing a little! For the first time she realized that the wind was freshening.

'Hello, Crystal. Want a lift home?' he asked.

It was Tony who turned in a fury, for some strange reason recognizing him as the cause of the trouble. 'You're Luke Tregarth?'

'I am.'

In a burst of indignation, Tony said. 'I've come down from London to see Crystal; we used to be each other's, but she has changed. Everything has altered and I want to know why. I just can't think what is going on in this place; it is something that oughtn't to be happening.'

Crystal laid her hand on the edge of the car, and she felt Luke's close over it. 'Were you two engaged?' he asked. She shook her head. 'How—how much does this fellow mean to you?'

She tried to speak, and the wind blew her hair across her face for a moment so that she could not see; when she could she saw only Luke's eyes demanding the truth of her. Somehow Tony did not matter any more! She said, 'We

241

were friends in London, never more than friends really. Now, feeling as I do for you, I realize how small that emotion was. I couldn't return to it.'

'You've got to choose,' said Luke gently. 'Take your time. You've just got to come to a decision.'

She stared at Tony, the colour rising to his cheeks as he stood there in the tweed coat, the sort of tweed coat Londoners wear and believe countrified, but which really are nothing of the kind. Then she turned to Luke. Come, my sweet! said his eyes. His red mouth broke into a smile, there was something completely irresistible about it.

She felt the tears misting her eyes, she knew that she could not hold out any longer. 'Luke, Luke darling, it's you,' she said.

He opened the door of the car and she got into it. For a moment she turned back to Tony.

'You can't possibly . . .'

'I can, and I will. Don't you see, Tony, there isn't anything else that I can do, nothing else I want to do? When you fall really in love, you'll feel the same way.' Then, 'I'm so sorry this had to happen, perhaps I always knew it would, perhaps I have behaved badly, but I should be behaving worse if now I tried to pretend that it was you.'

Luke drove away. She let her head fall on to his shoulder, and heard him murmuring to her.

She knew that she had made the right decision.

IV

She dried her tears before she got back.

'You're a brave girl, a wonderful girl,' whispered Luke. 'I'm so proud of you, and I love you so much.'

As they turned down the lane, the wind blew boisterously, surprising after the fineness of the morning. 'Why is it suddenly so noisy?' she asked.

'Maybe a storm is coming up. They can be quick in this part of the world, one never knows.' They turned in at the gate.

'Once I was afraid of this gate, now it is home to me,' she told him.

'Of course it is home. We are not through the wood yet, Crystal, my sweet, but we are coming out to something happier and better. Together we will find freedom.'

They put the car into the garage beside the big one, and came back across the drive. The freshening wind was tearing at the trees, and rippling over the grass. He has his arm round her, and she revelled in the sweetness of that embrace.

He opened the door into the hall; as he did so a violent gust of wind came racing down the lane, and rushed into the house before him. It ripped at a pile of newspapers lying on the table, and thrust them into a bundle on the floor. In a single instant they were blowing about the hall in a riot. But that was not the only thing. Mr. Tregarth stood there. He had drawn himself almost to his full height, a giant of a man, his grey hair brushed back and those eyes staring at them. Instantly Crystal knew that something was terribly wrong, and her mind went to Mrs. Tregarth.

'She—she isn't ill?'

'I don't know. I have not been there. I want a word with you. Somebody has been in my room.'

The absurd thing was that in the multitudinous events of the morning, she had forgotten it. She could feel the colour receding from her face, ebbing away, and she turned to Luke. But as she looked at him she realized that he also had changed. The other man with the unbelievable mood had taken possession of him. He released her arm.

She wanted to protest but there was no protestation that she could make. She stood there helplessly, then some automatic being within herself, a stranger to her (an unwelcome stranger), followed the beckoning finger of the old man, and went with him into his study. 'I should never have come back here,' she thought wildly, 'I should have refused,' and, even as she said it to herself, she knew that she had not been able to refuse. There was something about him that commanded, now something about her that obeyed.

'Sit down.' he told her.

She sat in the same chair, its rush seat sticking out with those crazy straw-like pieces. The window had been closed again, though the place smelt cleaner, and the lack of cobwebs on the smeary windows gave it a brighter appearance. But is was sinister, it still had him in it, and he was evil.

'Look at me!' he said.

She tried desperately not to look; she stared out of the window at the wind racing across the grass, and the trees bending in it; she tried to think of the storm that was coming, to think of anything save this man, but she was attempting the impossible. This was something that she could not do.

Slowly, and against her will, her eyes came round to his, and she saw his coming closer. The same thing was happening once more, the unforgettable and the unavoidable thing. He stared at her, and although he stayed in that chair, crouching there like some flesh-feeding bird, the eyes came towards her.

'You came into this room and this is something that you must not do. I forbid it. I enforce the laws in this house, and that which I forbid, is obeyed. You went into the cellar beyond. Answer me, you did go into the cellar?'

'Yes, I went into the cellar.'

'And there you saw—what?'

'A mangle, beautifully cleaned.'

'You saw a mangle! And a table?'

'Yes, I saw a table.'

'What was on the table?'

'I don't know. Paper, I believe, but I do not know, for I went no farther than the door.'

'You only saw a mangle?'

'Yes, I only saw a mangle,' she said slowly.

He stared at her. 'Listen to me. You will never cross this threshold again. If you attempt to cross it, you will hear my voice saying you are not to do so, because I forbid it. If you ever try to open the cellar door again you will find something terrible meeting you. Again I forbid it. This is something that you have got to remember, and for ever. It is something that will be with you as long as I live. Remember that. Whilst I live, you cannot come into this room or into the cellar. Do your understand?'

The mechanical person within her replied, 'Yes, I understand.'

She heard the sudden, sharp report of his hands clapping together. The noise was fantastic. It startled her so that she sprang up, dismayed. Now his eyes seemed to have retreated and gone far away. Now she knew that when she left this room she would never return to it again, not whilst he lived.

'You fainted,' he said. She knew this time that she had never fainted, but she said not a word for she dared not deny him. 'Better go and rest a little while, then you will feel better. Go! I have told you to go.'

She stumbled out of the room into the bleak hall beyond it, her heart making a strange noise, her whole being immensely disturbed. She could not believe that this was really herself. But never again! She would never go back into that study, she would never face those eyes, because she could not bear it.

Wretchedly she groped her way upstairs.

V

The storm was rising fast.

Obsessed with a violent headache, the result of that wretched interview in the study, Crystal had gone to lie down, and when it was time for lunch she found that she could not get up. She lay on bemused by the events of the day, agitated by the pain in her head, not knowing what would happen next. With the late afternoon she saw that thick clouds had blotted out the sunshine, and that sharp spurts of rain made a noise like gun-shot against the windows. She rose, knowing that she still felt desperately ill. She drank some water, washed her face, and hands, and made a tremendous effort to go downstairs.

She had heard the hall door slam some time before, caught by the wind in a violent burst, a strange event after the brilliance of the early

247

morning when the day had been sweet with the inspiration of summer. Now it was different.

She felt faint as she came down the stairs, and into the hall, to turn from the door of the study (now shut close) with a bitter feeling in her heart. She would never dare go into that room again. 'As long as I live,' he had said, and he had meant it. She prayed that she would never open that door again.

She went to the living-room, terrified that he would be there, for, utterly weak from the headache, she did not think that she could bear it. The light was dim but she saw Luke sitting there with his tea. The clouds had become so dense now that they made the room dark. He looked up.

'Crystal, you're not well?'

She felt her way to the table and sank exhausted into the chair at his side. 'I—I ought not to have done what I did. It has been a terrible morning.'

'But all right now. You're safe with me.'

'Is your father in his study?'

'No, for some reason or other he has gone out.'

'In this storm?'

Luke looked at her and she realized that his eyes were troubled. 'For some reason or other, he wanted to go out to the islands. I expect it was Dr. Fénon, and he would not let me accompany him, because he was in a dreadful temper. The weather is shocking. I asked him not to go because the motor-boat is unfit to make the passage when it is blowing up like this.'

He went over to the window, and stared out to a sea that had turned to lead; the waves were coming in, riding high, as though churned up by a master hand. The wind screamed as it blew across the cliff, shivering the grass, and at this moment Crystal thought of Mervyn's bungalow right down on the beach, wondering how he was faring. He always seemed entirely unaware of the viciousness of the waves, whilst here at the mill one was painfully conscious of them.

'I pray he does not bring the doctor here tonight,' she said.

Luke did not reply.

About the place and about him at the moment was the feeling that they were approaching a crisis. For some days now Crystal had known that matters could not continue as they were doing, the break must come. Could it be now? Luke turned away from the window, and came back to the table.

'It's shocking weather.'

'You think he'll be all right?'

'I don't know.'

She said, 'Why is it that he rides roughshod over this whole place? You dare not be natural with me, and I am rapidly getting scared of him myself. I always was in one way, but it's getting

249

worse. Couldn't you tell me anything? It might help so much.'

He sat down beside her, and putting out a hand gripped hers in his own. 'It isn't easy, you know. My father has one great god and that is money; I think there is nothing that he would not do for it. I never knew that money could drive a man so hard, but to him it is everything. He would never have gone out in this storm if it had not been for money.'

Crystal had always thought that the housekeeping bills were kept low because the family were not rich, but now suddenly her eyes were opened to a new aspect. Now she realized why the garden was tattered and dishevelled and so disturbingly untidy. Every pot-hole in the drive told her of this love of money which made old Mr. Tregarth so extraordinary.

'He pays me very well,' she said, 'he sent me a cheque to cover expenses in coming here that surprised me in its generosity.'

'I know, but then it was essential to get somebody here. The district nurse had said that unless we did get somebody more than Karin, she would have Mother moved. My—my father did not want my mother to be moved.'

'But if she would have got better attention, why not?'

His eyes avoided hers, purposely she felt. 'That is something that I cannot tell you, but my father wants her to give him the mill, just as he wants everything of monetary value for himself, and is determined to have it, no matter what the cost. I don't know. Like yourself, there are moments when I am bewildered. It seems that we are two people caught up in a titanic tidal wave. You ought to go away, Crystal, before this thing has power to hurt you more.'

'No, I'll stay. I want to be with you.'

His hand tightened on hers, and he drew her into his arms. His mouth was warm and tender, his arms caressing. There seemed to be peace when he kissed her, something alien to this house, where the wheel creaked, and where there always seemed to be the undercurrent which Crystal could not understand. Then they heard the sound of a rocket spitting up into the heavily overcast sky, and making the sharp noise of a saluting gun.

'What was that?' she asked.

'It was the call for the life-boat. They will be going out immediately. This is a dangerous coast, you never know what will happen next, and many lives are lost.'

She released herself and went to the window.

'A ship in distress,' she said, 'it means that somebody is in danger.'

'Very much so.'

She stood there staring out at the wind rippling the grass, and tearing at the trees. At this moment she did not feel herself, but someone quite unbelievable and different. She had a strong intuition that something was happening, and almost fainted, then she turned back into the room again and put her arms around Luke.

'It's your father. Somehow I know that it is your father and something horrible is happening to him. I—I am quite sure about this.' She paused a moment, her vision clearing, and the dizziness leaving her. 'Take my hand, Luke, and come with me. There is something that I want to try, it's a test, take my hand and do what I ask.'

Hand in hand they went out into the hall and to the door of the untidy little study. It offered no barricade, but now was just an ordinary room, and she opened the door as she would have opened any other, without fear, and with no danger of being forbidden. As they went inside the room it seemed to be darker than any other part of the house, for the north was completely overcast.

'Crystal, where are you going?'

She could only see the white blur of his face in the shadows, having lost definite outline, but she went across the room which seemed much sweeter now, almost as if the strong, foul tobacco scent had receded from it. She had the impression that the place was pleasanter, that something horrible had left it, as she crossed to the door of the cellar. It was then that she saw Luke putting out deprecating hands to stay her.

'Not there, Crystal, not there!'

But she did what she felt she must do. She lifted the latch, and although the door itself was fast locked and did not respond, she knew that by mere contact with the latch all her intuitions had been true. The old hypnotic spell was released. She was her own mistress, and Luke could be his own master. She wheeled round.

'Luke, your father said that whilst he was alive I should never be able to do this.'

'You must not go there, Crystal. Nobody goes there. Don't try the door, come back.'

A sense of triumph came to her as she turned and ran to his arms, feeling his warm body against her own and hearing his heart pounding. 'I cannot open the door, Luke, but only because it is locked, not because I have been forbidden. Don't you see that the power of evil has gone? Your father isn't alive any more. I don't know what has happened, but I am sure of one thing, he has gone for ever.'

If Luke believed her, he said nothing.

He lifted her like a child, and carried her out of the room, down the hall to the living-room where Pixie lay on the mat. The storm still raged beyond the window, but it was no longer important to them. Now she could talk to him.

'Luke, it was hypnotism, wasn't it? The village was right in everything they said about him. It *was* hypnotism.'

He nodded. 'Yes, I suppose so. The queer

253

thing is that I can talk about it now. I couldn't before, for always there was something that held me back. It was as though I was shut off from it, wrapped in a dark mist that I could not tear from me, something that although it was not part of me, entirely engulfed me. But now I can talk. It was hypnotism.'

'I feel that he has gone. I think you feel it, too. Luke, tell me the truth, what was it all about?'

He drew her down on to the old bent sofa, and they sat there, arms about each other. It might be insufferably dark, but for them the light was beginning.

'Dearest,' he said, 'I feel as if I had awakened from a bad dream, and something—I don't know what—has happened. My father has been the strangest man and, maybe, I have never understood him properly, I just don't know. As I said before, money was his god and he worshipped it. He wanted possessions, he loved money so much that,' his voice dropped to almost a whisper, 'he made money.'

'You mean he was rich?'

'I should think so, but he made money. He printed notes here, and when the press was working in the cellar it was the sound of the mill-wheel turning that drowned the noise. The mill-wheel was of vital importance to him. No wonder everyone thought that it was sinister, because there was something sinister about the whole proceeding, and after a time it has shown. The village realized it.'

'You mean he forged notes?'

'He made notes, and we took them out to the islands. He made me go and nothing could have stopped me. I had to go because he made me.'

'And it's over now. I'm sure it's over. Something has happened to change everything. It almost seems as though the house is free.'

'Yes, but we have got to destroy all signs of it. The press must be broken up and done away with. We must get rid of every trace, if what you say is true. We must never see that man Fénon again. He was in this, of course, and the extraordinary thing is that I can't believe it is over. I can't . . .'

The telephone rang.

He went over to it, and Crystal heard him speaking almost automatically at the little side-table in the hall. She sat there with the feeling that the storm was clearing completely, and that soon the sun would creep out and Smuggler's Mill would be a new house. She turned to the wall and saw hanging there the exquisite picture that the real Luke had painted, the picture of a Man in a garden. On the mat Pixie stared at her.

Then Luke returned.

'You were quite right. They have rung up from the life-boat station. My father was coming back in the motor-boat from the islands and there was another man with him. Fénon, I

255

suppose. Both were lost.' He was quite silent for a moment, almost as if he did not know what to say next. 'I ought to regret it, and I can't. I feel perhaps this is the cruellest part of all.'

'Let's go to your mother; after all she has a right to know.' And then, 'Those injections, those tablets you made her take, what was it all about?'

'My father wanted this house and never could get over the fact that it belonged to Mother. She would not give him possession, and had left it to me. He tried to dissuade her. The tablets were to weaken her resistance, but they had little effect. One day I knew, and she knew also, that worse would come. Then he could compel me to give him the mill, and I should have done so.' He paused, horrified. 'My mother was the one person he could not overcome, and that made him mad. She was terribly subservient to him, but she could not be hypnotized and he never quite managed her. She always said that the moment she parted with the deeds of the mill, she would die, and I believe that she was right.'

'Yet you gave her those tablets.'

'Yes, because it was not myself acting. Have you ever faced something that you had not the power to resist? Something wicked and cruel, and half of you knew that it was wicked and cruel whilst the other half just could not stop you doing the wrong thing?'

'Never quite, but I felt it coming.'

256

'I know. You were terribly brave and you stuck by me.' He put his arms round her. 'Kiss me once, sweetheart, just once before we go and see Mother. It's over now. The man who looked through the grille at you will never come again. He went down in the motor-boat with the other two. Tonight our lives change. Tomorrow I shall dismantle the press and get rid of it. We'll start all over afresh, and together.'

She kissed him again and again. She had the sudden sense of freedom, and now she could see Smuggler's Mill just as it had been in the old days and as it was going to be again, as their home. She saw happiness coming to them out of the mist, and her love for Luke going forward into the years with her.

'We'll start again, and together,' she whispered. 'Oh Luke, I do love you so much.'

Photoset, printed and bound in Great Britain by
REDWOOD BURN LIMITED, Trowbridge, Wiltshire

With warmest regards
to long time friends, Kathleen
& Kenneth Carter — who ♡
Truly live their faith. ♡ Col. 3:11

Russell Dretil

LIVE YOUR FAITH!

LIVE YOUR FAITH!

by

Russell M. McIntire

PELICAN PUBLISHING COMPANY

Gretna 1979

Library of Congress Cataloging in Publication Data

McIntire, Russell.
  Live your faith!

  1. Christian life—Baptist authors. I. Title.
BV4501.2.M236   248'.48'61   78-25579
ISBN 0–88289–217–7

Manufactured in the United States of America

Published by Pelican Publishing Company, Inc.
630 Burmaster Street, Gretna, Louisiana 70053

Designed by Mike Burton

DEDICATION
To Maellen,
a lovely and gracious listener
and a loyal helpmate

Contents

Preface

These essays were first published as articles for the weekly bulletins of the First Baptist Church of Clinton, Mississippi, where I was privileged to serve as pastor over a long span of years. At the insistence of good friends, I have gathered them together and prepared them for publication. It is my prayer that many will be strengthened, encouraged, and blessed in the reading of them.

I am indebted to many for these messages. They have come from many sources; some are my own. In reality, they are the overflow of more than thirty-seven years of ministry. Because of this, it is difficult to say from whence each has come. If any source has been quoted without giving proper credit, it is simply because the thought has become so completely my own that I failed to realize I was quoting.

As you see, these are more essays than sermons, although many of them have been preached. I share them with you in the hope that you will be strengthened through them in your pilgrimage as you daily seek to learn to live in your house of faith.

I am also indebted to Mrs. Cecil Brasell for the typing of this manuscript.

LIVE YOUR FAITH!

Attitudes

Facing Up to Life

My old college dean used to start every school year with a chapel talk entitled: "Altitude Depends on Attitude." He illustrated his point with a personal experience.

As a young man he had gone on a tour of the western states with a group of schoolteachers. On the return trip they came to Colorado and visited Pike's Peak. Part of the way to the top could be driven, but the last few hundred feet had to be walked. Two women in the tour complained all of the time about having to walk so far. The others encouraged them as best they could, saying that the sunset and view from that high peak were well worth the climb. The two women remained unconvinced, however, and finally stopped and sat down at a little resting place, and the others went on to the top without them. When the group returned from the peak, thrilled at what they had seen, the women were still complaining. When they heard how beautiful it was at the top and what they had missed, then they spent the rest of the trip bemoaning the fact that they had not gone to the top. Dean Pike would then lean over the speaker's stand and say, "Young people, your attitude determines your altitude in life!"

Think for a moment. Your attitude toward all of life is exceedingly important. Your attitude about your potential, your health, your family, your job, and your future will determine much of your success and happiness in life. Your attitude toward the setbacks, the rough times in life, is also important. So many things can and do happen to change plans and alter all of life. What then? Your attitude is the difference between bitterness and victory.

An attractive girl stopped beside the bed of a stone-deaf war victim. The youngster talked, and the visitor scribbled answers on the pad. Before the interview was over the young man, who was terribly discouraged, said, "Won't you come again to see me? It's awful not knowing what people around you are saying."

"Oh," wrote the girl on the pad, "I don't know that it is so awful. I'm as deaf as you are. Why don't you learn to read lips as I have been reading yours?"

Ships That Never Sail

King Solomon was not content with just the wealth and the power close at hand. He built a navy and it roamed afar seeking gold and treasure for the king. Later Jehoshaphat sat on Solomon's throne and he too longed for such treasures. He too built a navy, but for some reason the ships never sailed. The Bible simply says they were broken up by a storm while in the harbor. It may be that they never had a chance to set sail, but the inference is that the order for them to sail was not given. It seems to stand as a lesson to all of us of plans and intentions that are never realized or completed. Ships that never sail.

Most of us have an entire navy at harbor, unused, untried and unprofitable. It would be well to take inventory of the ships we have intended to launch but have never set loose: the habit we intended to conquer, the patience we intended to learn, the sweeter character we planned on developing, the regular prayer time we pledged ourselves to keep, the neighborliness we planned to show, the letter we intended to write, the good word we planned to speak. Or what about the book we planned to read, or the poem we intended to memorize, or the flower we intended to plant? Perhaps it is the unsaved person we planned to speak to, or the sick one we intended to visit, or the shut-in we promised to stop by and see. Your unsailed ship may be that talk with your son or daughter about life's deeper meaning or the word of love you planned to speak to your husband or wife.

What good are ships that never sail? They soon are broken up in the storms, and their purpose is never realized. One old sage wrote, "Good intentions are mortal and perishable things; like very mellow choice fruit they are difficult to keep." It's really sad to contemplate. One life to live, one act on the stage of life, yet so many of us spend so little time presenting a creative life to the world. We speak of large plans, of great hopes, of dreams to be realized, yet so many of these plans remain only plans.

It doesn't have to be this way—it shouldn't be this way! What if Christ had only intended to live a sinless life, but didn't make it? Or, if He had only thought of dying for the sins of the world? What if Paul had only planned to write his letter and what if John had never gotten around to writing down what God had revealed to him?

The widow coins are of much more value than the gifts the wealthy intended to give but never got around to giving. And it is, of course, much easier to intend to sing in the choir and even to criticize those who do, than to attend rehearsal and make a worthy contribution.

Max C. Otto, in his book entitled *William James, The Man*

and the Thinker, says: "Possibly the game of life cannot be won; if it can be won, it will be the players in the game who win it, not the superior people who pride themselves on not knowing the difference between a fair ball or a foul, to say nothing of those in the grandstand or the bleachers whose contribution is throwing pop bottles at the umpire."

You Are Your Decisions

Philosopher Karl Jaspers defines man as a "choosing creature." That man can choose among alternatives is his glory. There are forces that help shape him and his destiny, but man is a being created in the image of God with a capacity to choose and decide for himself.

What we often do not stop to realize is how important our decisions are. In a very real sense there are few large or great decisions. Some seem to be very significant—and they are—but they are not one decision but the accumulation of many smaller, almost forgotten decisions.

Consider the decision of the prodigal son to leave home. A tremendously significant and shattering decision. But was it one decision? Think of the many other decisions that resulted in the break. He had to decide that he knew as much as his parents—more actually. He had to decide that they didn't really have his best interests at heart and that he was getting a bad deal all around. He had to decide that they were rather old-fashioned and foolish people anyway. He had to decide that any place away from home would be better. He also had to take his stance toward money and decide that happiness came from wealth and freedom. All of these decisions and many more resulted in the real break with his family. How many times did he almost leave before he finally did? The actual decision to leave was almost anticlimactic for he had been bringing himself to it for many weeks and months. Even the cruel request concerning his inheritance, which inferred that his father was worth more to him dead than alive, was quite easily made. The break is made—not the one great decision but by an accumulation of many.

Interestingly enough, the boy's decision to return home was also an accumulation of many other decisions. He had to decide he was better off at home, that he was really hungry and wanted something to eat, that he was lonely and that the freedom and happiness he had sought had evaded him. He had to decide that his father would be gracious and wouldn't let him starve but allow him to become a servant in the household. He had to decide that he was wrong and had failed.

So you see, there are really no small decisions. Moses decided to turn aside and see a bush that was on fire, and a nation is delivered from slavery. A young man decides to ask a girl for a date and the two are soon married. A young person decides to attend a worship service and hears God's call to the mission field. We need to realize how important every decision is.

One other thing should be mentioned. This capacity to choose is one of the things that cannot be taken from us. Victor Frankl speaks from the concentration camp experience saying: "Every human freedom can be taken from a man but one—the last of the human freedoms— the freedom to choose one's attitude in any given set of circumstances, to choose one's own way."

Are You Alert?

Much emphasis is being placed today on the need for

people to be alert. "Get on the ball," we are told. For some of the sluggards there are even pep pills to quicken reflexes. The emphasis has been so constant and so intense that some have tried to keep themselves alert by the constant use of stimulants. All of us know, however, that artificially stimulated alertness will never take the true place of being alert and attentive.

The kind of alertness of which I speak in this little essay is that attentiveness that enables a person to receive the revelation he needs for great accomplishment. The great revelations of life come only to the attentive. Isaac Newton may have appeared to be napping under that apple tree; but when the apple hit him on the head, as the legend says, he was alert enough to realize that particles in the universe exert attraction on one another. His discovery of the laws of gravitation has been called one of the most important discoveries in the history of natural science. Archimedes may have appeared to be only taking a slow, restful bath, but he noticed that the level of water in the tub went up as his body entered the water. Because he was attentive to this commonplace occurrence, he discovered the secrets of specific gravity. In his joy over finding the answer to an assignment the king had given to him, he jumped from the tub and ran shouting, "Eureka! I've found it!"

Great revelations come only to the attentive. Moses was attentive enough to turn aside because a bush burned. Here he received his commission to deliver his people. In his cobbler's shop William Carey was attentive to his Bible and his leather homemade map of the world and went to India as a missionary. Elijah found out that God's voice was not in the whirlwind, the earthquake, or the fire, but in the still, small voice. We must still be attentive to hear His voice today. Isn't it the Psalmist who speaks for God when he says, "Study to be quiet so that you may know that I am God"?

Great revelations come only to the alert—to the truly attentive.

Mirrors and Windows

If you ever allow yourself to think about the final judgment of all men, what picture comes to your mind? A great white throne? A host of frightened people? A resplendent Judge on the throne attended by legions of angels? Our minds conjure some such scene from the picturesque language of the Scripture. Doubtless it really will be comparable to this. One element that will be present is generally missed in our thinking about it, however. It is the element of surprise.

Remember the "Inasmuch" parable of Matthew, chapter 25? Both of the groups of people share one thing: they are surprised! Surprised not only at the verdict, but at the menial tasks that were recorded as being done or left undone. Those who passed their final exam had not recorded any meritorious deeds apparently. They had simply fed the hungry, clothed the naked, and visited the sick and imprisoned. They were surprised that such menial service had been noticed. The others who were cast aside were also surprised that the failure to do these most ordinary tasks had been noted; they were surprised also to realize that they had not done them.

It reveals one important truth. The thing that God notices is not what we do so much as what we are! The doing of these menial tasks, or the failure to do them, is important primarily because it reveals the inner heart. Those who entered into God's presence were only doing what was the natural thing for a redeemed life to do. They were surprised that such ordinary things came up on the judgment day. The others were also doing what was natural for the unredeemed life to do, and they too were surprised that it was important on this final day.

The ones on the right hand were rewarded with a kingdom prepared for them; those on the left inherited the same darkness they had lived in on earth! The entire test was based on what each had seen or not seen. It was simply a matter of vision. One group saw those around them through windows; the other saw nothing for they looked into mirrors and saw only themselves.

Seeing and salvation go together. Jesus came to open blind eyes, so we could see Him, ourselves, and others. The redeemed of the world look through eyes opened by His reconciling love. The unredeemed see only as in a mirror—only reflections of themselves and their inner darkness.

What do you see?

On Spiritual Timidity

We just don't care enough. We would really rather not get involved! It is none of our business anyway, is it? So what happens? We go through life lukewarm—like Ephriam, a cake half-done. Our religion is a thing for the Sunday services, but not actually something to be lived day by day. That would be too costly. It would take involvement. It would take real moral courage and deep conviction, and these commodities seem to be in rather short supply today. We laugh at our warm-blooded South American neighbors, who seem to be constantly in revolution. But it re-

veals one thing: they can get excited about what they
believe and are willing to die for it!

Have you been in any fiery furnaces lately? Today, we
dismiss this Old Testament story by saying it was probably
just a story. No one could come out of that kind of fire and
not even have a smell of smoke! Why even a new toaster
will burn the morning bread occasionally. But the story of
Daniel and his three friends with the strange names details
a kind of moral courage and depth we see little of today.

It is doubtful if these fellows really wanted to be thrown
into that fiery furnace. They were not irrational. Few, if
any, men who show real moral courage have it in abundant supply, but it is there when it is needed. Most of them
would have preferred to take a safer way. And if the truth
were known, most of them had friends and loved ones
who begged them to take the easier, surer way. They never
set out to be martyrs, and all hoped they would not have
to be.

What happened then? Along the way somewhere they
came to a crossroad and they had to make a choice. In the
case of Shadrach, Meshach, and Abednego, it was a simple
refusal to bow the knee. The slightest little genuflection
would have saved their lives, but this would have meant
compromise. It would have been bowing to other gods.
Oh, but surely God would have understood. They would
be saving their lives by bowing. God would know that!
They would not be really worshipping.

There it is! That is where our logic breaks down! Whoever said we were to save our lives? Jesus said: "For whosoever will save his life shall lose it—and whosoever shall
lose his life for my sake shall find it. For what is a man
profited, if he shall gain the whole world (and physical life
also) if in the process he loses his soul?" The price of
spiritual timidity and cowardice? Your soul! And having

lost your soul, what medium of exchange will you be able to use to buy it back?

What does it mean? It means that living doesn't matter unless you have something worth living for, and the courage to live—or die—for it!

Stones or Prayers?

It is the same old struggle: the temporal versus the eternal, the physical versus the spiritual, outer brawn versus inner strength. Who will win ultimately? We say we believe that the eternal will be victorious, but when the crisis comes we like to have the power of the physical universe evident and behind us also. We speak of inner strength that has made our nation great, but we are depending upon our weapons and nuclear warheads to defend us and to keep us out of war. A few years ago the football coach at Notre Dame expressed our dilemma. Someone asked him if it helped to coach a team that many people prayed for daily. He said, "Yes, but it helps to have big boys, too!"

The Scripture tells of the stoning of Stephen with these words: "And they stoned Stephen while he was calling upon the Lord." There it is again—stones versus prayers. You answer: "Yes, but Stephen had no place to hide. He had only one alternative, to pray." True, but Stephen doesn't appear to be the hiding kind. His portrait is one of a man who had decided where the ultimate victory of life rested. He had made his choice. "Look!" he said, "I see heaven open, and the Son of Man standing at God's right hand." Stones may break and destroy the body of such a man, but a faith such as his is eternal. He had found the answer.

Who actually was victorious at Stephen's death? The men who stoned him and watched him die knew that they had won. But had they? Standing by, holding their coats, was another young man named Saul, who saw that day the gospel according to Stephen and never got away from the sight. The stones took the physical life of Stephen, but God took his soul to be with Him. The stones won the first round, but God spoke through the courage, faith, and death of one young man and spread the good news of salvation to the uttermost parts of the earth.

What Do You See?

One of the revealing things that has come from the study of psychology is the effect that a handicap has on the personality of the individual involved. All of us readily see how a complete loss of sight would affect a person in every way. We have seen some people so afflicted who at first gave up but then found themselves and actually profited from the experience. The valedictorian of my own college class was a totally blind boy. Undoubtedly he would have been a top student anyway, but he was motivated also to overcome his handicap. The psychologists have revealed, however, that the personality of a child is affected by other than total blindness. The near-sighted child is handicapped in sports and tends to take refuge in his own fancies. The far-sighted child is handicapped in school work and is often considered rather slow.

In the spiritual realm the reverse is true. Spiritually what we see is determined by what kind of person we are. The Scripture tells us that at Paul's conversion he was blinded and then that "there fell from his eyes as it were scales, and he received his sight." Truthfully, Paul received new eyes. Traditionally, it is believed that Paul's physical eyes were bad, but his spiritual blindness was cured at his conversion experience. The scales that fell from his eyes were those same scales that hang over many of our own eyes today—the scales of pride, ambition, prejudice, and nationalism. How our spiritual vision is dimmed by the kind of person we are. Paul may have been nearly blind physically, but he saw across continents and mountains and into the future with amazing insight and clarity when the eyes of his heart were opened.

In the Ephesian letter, Paul prays for the Christians at Ephesus and for all of us that our spiritual eyes might be opened that we might see the hope of our calling (or why God saved us), the splendor of our inheritance (or how much God through Christ has invested in us), and the power that is available to us in the task that is ours in telling the world of Him.

Let him that hath eyes to see, let him see.

Aspiring For the Heights

It's more than mere semantics. There is a great difference between ambition and aspiration. Many a Christian person, trying to live the Christian life, is desirous of increasing his influence and effectiveness, yet the Christian life is to be one of self-giving, not self-seeking. Where is the difference? To be ambitious is to be greedy for power and position.

Shakespeare had one of his characters say of Cassius, "Yon Cassius has a lean and hungry look, such men are dangerous." In the book *What Makes Sammy Run* we have a vivid example of how far ambition can drive a man. The end is desired so passionately that any means necessary is permissable to reach it. All of the energies of the ambitious life are directed toward a certain self-centered goal and everything, even life itself, is sacrificed to attain it. And, as is usually true, when the goal is reached, it does not satisfy, but turns to gall in the mouth. Ambitious souls, living for self alone, seek unworthy goals, and, amid apparent success, they fall.

Is the Christian then to sit back and not strive or reach upward? Not at all. The Christian word is aspiration. Where ambition is earthbound and its motives self-centered, aspiration is the reaching upward of life to lift mankind. The little life grasps an idea lower than itself and sacrifices honor, integrity, dignity, and any chance for real happiness to attain this unworthy goal. On the other hand, the noble life looks upward and grasps an idea above itself and reaches toward it, making every necessary sacrifice to attain it. In so doing he pleases God, lifts all mankind, and secures real happiness for self. Jesus said it quite simply and beautifully when he said: "Seek ye first the Kingdom of God and His righteousness; and all these things will be added unto you."

Aspire to please God and do His will and all else in life will take its proper place! This is the highest aspiration of noble hearts—to know God in that Divine-human encounter that lifts a man out of himself and places him on the high road of dedicated service to all mankind. To aspire to these heights is man at his best.

Covetous of Truth

In his *Essay Concerning Human Understanding*, John Locke

states: "It is a duty we owe to God to have our minds constantly disposed to entertain and receive truth wheresoever we meet it—our first great duty then is to bring to our studies and to our inquiries after knowledge a mind covetous of truth." How rare this is. Our minds are covetous of untruth, covetous of evil, covetous of gossip, and covetous of trash. But here it is suggested that we should be covetous of truth.

You remember what coveting is—to crave something, especially that which belongs to another person. Its synonyms are envy, greed, and avarice. We are warned in the Ten Commandments not to covet. I think, however, there is a sense in which we could and should covet the right things. We should not covet the knowledge or wisdom another has, that he might be lacking; but we should rather covet that knowledge and wisdom for ourselves. Coveting truth is not to desire something another has, but to desire truth rather than error. It means to be on the alert for truth wherever you find it. It means to be always conscious that you do not have all of the truth. It means to admit that there is more insight available. It also means a willingness to release that which you have believed if it can be proven untrue. Far too often we are ruled by our preconceived ideas.

The people at the turn of the century did not believe man could fly in a craft that was heavier than air. The Wright brothers heard frequently, "If God had wanted man to fly, He would have given him wings!" Twenty-one newspapers were given the story of the early flights of the Wright brothers, but only five printed any of the story at all and these with only a brief comment. Their first flight was made in December of 1903. On October 9, 1905, in reply to their request to sell the government some planes for scouting purposes, they received a reply stating that the United States Army "did not want to take any further action in the letter of the Wright brothers until a machine could be produced that would actually operate in horizontal flight." They had flown 104 flights the previous year.

We are not always covetous of truth. In the world in which we live today with so much change taking place on every level of life, it is mandatory that we become covetous after truth, for many of the folkways of our day are being proven completely untrue. Mr. Locke said: "We owe it to God—to bring to our inquiries after knowledge a mind covetous of truth."

On Large Subjects and Little Deeds

A young ministerial student some years ago came to my office for help in preparing his first sermon. "What direction are you planning to go in your message? Have you selected a text or a subject?" I asked. "Yes, my subject is 'Life'," was his reply. After a moment's recovery I said, "Well, you shouldn't have too much trouble speaking twenty minutes on that subject!" (That was what had been worrying him—how he could speak for twenty minutes.) The thing that I had to do was to let him down easily without robbing him of his enthusiasm. I said, "Well, what kind of life are you going to speak about? You realize life is a limitless subject. You announce that you are going to speak on 'Life,' and some may think you are selling a magazine to them. Are you going to talk about human life? Your life? The good life? Eternal life?" After about an hour he left. The next week he stopped by to tell me how he had gotten along during his solo flight in the pulpit. "What did you preach about?" I asked. "Sin," he said. I couldn't disagree with his choice because he, like all of us, probably knew more about that subject than the other one anyway.

What was his problem? He was looking at such wide areas to deal with that he forgot to notice the part of the subject with which he was acquainted. He was seeing the horizon and missing the flowers at hand. It is much easier to discuss in happy ignorance great wide problems than it is to roll up our sleeves and help solve everyday problems all around us. It is much easier to pray for the heathen in the foreign land than it is to drive across town and personally tell a lost person of your Christ. It seems more glamorous to give of our wealth to send missionaries than to give to heat the local building and pay the janitor's salary. Oh, we ought to have high vision and noble dreams and goals; but while we look at the far distance, let us not be guilty of stumbling over the one who needs us today. The words of Jesus when He said, "In as much as ye have done it unto the least of these . . ." should ring in our ears.

The Folly of Just Kicking

As a barefoot boy I fell into one of the oldest April Fool's tricks in existence. Some older boys placed a paper sack on the sidewalk. It literally invited a young boy to kick it. I did. The only trouble was that they had placed a brick in the sack! It reminds me of the army mule named Maggie, who died somewhere in France. Her grave is clearly marked with the following inscription: "In memory of Maggie, a mule, who in her lifetime kicked one colonel, one major, three lieutenants, eleven sergeants, twenty-seven privates, and one bomb!"

The lesson is obvious. Stop and think before you kick. There is probably more involved than meets the eye. When you kick against your neighbor, remember that he probably has troubles you know nothing about. When you kick because the patrolman gives you a ticket, remember what it would be like if there were no patrolmen at all. When you kick against taxes, remember how much you get in service, security, and well-being from being an American. When you kick against big government, remember you receive some of the benefits of subsidies so you can expect some of the controls.

In another realm we need to learn this lesson, too. There is evidence in the Acts that Paul was suffering pangs of conscience after consenting to Stephen's death. He was kicking against the goading of his conscience. When he finally surrendered in the Damascus Road experience, he found out that there was indeed more to it than met the eye—that in this, God had been reaching down for him for a special work. How many of us kick against that which down within us we know to be God's will? This often is the deeper reason for some of the visible kicking against others that we do.

Some even kick against the spirit of God as He convinces them of their need for salvation and seeks to turn them to Him. They suppose that they will lose something if they surrender to Him. How foolish. We lose nothing but our old sinful ways and gain all things, including life eternal.

The lesson? The next time you start to kick out at something, or someone, remember that there may be more involved than meets the eye. You might even be kicking out at the God who made you.

Preserving the Status Quo?

In the sixth chapter of the Acts of the Apostles there is a cry against Stephen. False witnesses are brought in to accuse him. What is their accusation? He is trying "to change the customs which Moses delivered unto us." They wanted to protect the status quo. This is not absent today. In the midst of great changes, there are many whose theme song is: "Come weal or come woe, my status is quo!"

How strange that this kind of thinking can be still present today. Our world has changed more in these past twenty years than in any other period of history. Every facet of life has altered. Much of the change has been for the better; some perhaps for the worse. But in the midst of this change, people who live in centrally heated and air-conditioned homes, things unthought of by their parents; who drive cars which can go farther in an hour than the people a few years ago could go in a day; who fly to faraway places in less time than it takes them to drive to the airport; who watch on television screens the happenings of history; who thaw out precooked meals, warm them in ovens that announce when dinner is ready, serving the food in dishes made of material that was unheard of a score of years ago—many of these same people, I say, accept these things but resist with passion any change in religious or social life. The idea still prevails that change and decay seem to go together in one phase of life, but changes in other realms are happily accepted. Some still cry for the "old-time religion that was good for Paul and Silas and is good enough for me." On the other hand, I haven't heard too much lately about "going back to the good old days of the kerosene lamp, the old cook stove, the mule-drawn plough, and the horse and buggy."

Change doesn't necessarily mean decay. When a sinful

man is born anew through the working of the Holy Spirit within his life, he is changed for eternity from decay and ruin. And because of this new truth, he is a new creature with all of the relationships of life changed. And, as he grows in grace, there will continue to be change, and he never more can or will be contented with things as they are. As Christians we cannot worship at the Shrine of the Status Quo for we are destined to be dissatisfied until we awaken in His likeness.

Have You Changed Your Mind Recently?

It is most interesting to study people wherever you are, but it is more interesting if you pick out a subject and study their attitude toward that one specific thing. Take the idea of change, of shifting mental, social, and spiritual gears. There are some who say that they will not change: "I like the way things are and I will not change."

There are some who want to change but who want, or say they do, the good old days. These seem to have the same idea as the writer of the great old hymn "Abide With Me" who wrote: "Change and decay in all around I see." Change doesn't necessarily mean decay. Just because we have electric light bulbs and modern plumbing does not mean that we have retrogressed mentally, socially, or spiritually. What these people usually have in mind is some one or two things that they recall were different a few years back, and they cherish them. What they do not realize is that those things they cherished were probably made up of human relationships—the large family, time to sit and visit, interest in what the neighbor was doing

on the acreage adjacent to theirs, and so on. We have
changed. We go so much more because our transportation
is much finer and faster. We do not talk about the neighbor
next door quite so much because we are concerned and
interested in our neighbors in South America and all over
the world. Times have changed and there has been some
decay, but not all change is bad. These people are resisting
a changing society. My concern in this little meditation is
the spiritual change, "the inner change" needed to face life
and its problems.

There are some who refuse this kind of change saying
that they cannot change. "I am what I am," they say, "and
nothing can be done about it!" What these fail to realize is
that they have changed even while they spoke the words
saying they could not change. Having said that they could
not change, they are different people for having said it.
They are more set in their fatalism than before they ut-
tered those dozen words.

Listen! What I am trying to say to each of us today is this:
You are going to change, you are even now changing. The
important thing is the "how" or the "what" of the change.
How are you changing? Into what are you being changed?

Bible

Bible Study–No Joke

This story appeared in the column of Adon Taft, religious editor of the *Miami Herald*:

A funny story with a moral found in the current issue of *Together*, the Methodist magazine, seems very appropriate for Miami right now.

According to the story, the minister entered a church-school class while the lesson was in progress and interrupted to ask one boy, "Who broke down the walls of Jericho?" "Not me, sir," piped the youngster.

The minister turned to the teacher. "Is this the usual behavior in the class?" The teacher answered, "This boy is honest and I believe him. I really don't think he did it."

Distressed, the minister sought out the chairman of the commission on education and explained what had happened. "Why, I've known both the teacher and the boy for years," the chairman said, "and neither would do such a thing."

By this the minister was heartsick, and reported his experiences to the official board. "We see no point in being disturbed," they replied. "Let's just pay for the damage and charge it to upkeep."

You say, "Well, of course this can't happen here." Perhaps not, but perhaps it could. Surely it should be a timely reminder for every Sunday school teacher, as well as for every parent. As Christians, we say the Bible is our sole authority. If this is so, and we believe it is, then it behooves us to revere it, to study it, and to hide its words in our hearts.

"In the Beginning God . . . "

Much has been said concerning the meaning of the early chapters of Genesis. Discussions of these chapters are not new. The meaning of these verses has been argued for years. Many publications have much in them that the conversative mind cannot accept.

There are two things brought out by these discussions that have concerned me. The first is the realization that there seems to be a fear of a critical analysis of the Bible. In these days when science is questioning every one of its theories and rewriting its own books, we who claim to have the truth should not be afraid of any searchlight.

My Bible stands on its own. I do not have to defend it. Through the years many have tried to hurt the cause of Christ by assailing the truth and inspiration of the Word. More often, however, the message of the Book nas been hindered by those who are its friends. Some who possess the Bible, but who do not let its message possess their hearts, have been its real enemies. Others who have tried to protect the Word by hiding it in some sacred ivory tower have also not been its true friends. "Thy word is truth," said Jesus. If it is truth, then it will stand against any of Satan's darts.

The second thing that has concerned me is that many a young mind has become disturbed and confused about what is really said in the Genesis account. Let me very simply and clearly say to every searching mind that the essence of the message of the opening chapters of Genesis can be stated in four beautiful words: "In the Beginning God!"

God did it! Let us give Him the glory.

Challenge

A Time to Stand Up

Almost daily we read about people not wanting to become involved. Recently the story was told of a man who was attacked in broad daylight on a busy city street by two hoodlums. They grabbed him, demanded his money, beat and stabbed him. At least a dozen people watched. Apparently no one even bothered to call the police. I can imagine a person not wanting to go up against two armed men who have attacked another. However, it is difficult to imagine people not wanting to become involved to the extent of calling the police.

On the other hand, what might have happened had one of those dozen people rallied to defend the man against those who were attacking him? With one to rise to his defense, perhaps the other eleven onlookers would have rallied to defend him also, and the hoodlums would have fled before superior forces.

Coincidentally, it was another group of twelve who one day stood before a host of people with a message that would change the course of history. One man by the name of Simon Peter stood up to address the crowd. Before the sun had set, over three thousand people had been changed eternally by the message they heard. But that is not the whole story at all. The Scripture tells us that when Peter stood the eleven stood with him! Without them standing with him, the story would have been different indeed. It was not one man the crowd saw and heard; they saw and heard the testimony of a dozen. To be sure, there would have been no Pentecost had that one not lifted his voice; but when he did, eleven others stood with him. One man may be called by God to do the speaking, but he is helpless without those who stand with him. That the Kingdom of God needs ministers, there is little doubt, but I feel the Lord will get enough of them. The real need is for men who will stand and be counted—who will become involved in Kingdom work. "Rise up, O men of God! The church for you doth wait, her strength unequal to her task; rise up, and make her great!"

Who Said It Would Be Easy?

On many college campuses today the buildings are built and only the very necessary sidewalks are poured. The administration waits until the students make the paths across the grass and then pours the sidewalks. It's easier to discover where people will walk than it is to keep them on the walks. There is a lesson here. We are a people who look for shortcuts. The "ten easy lessons" idea is not new. We look for the painless dentist and the easy chair. The get-rich-quick scheme always has its takers. This is not to speak against the expert dentist or the comfortable chair, but it does indicate something of the kind of people we are.

The idea is also evident in the realm of worship. The Far East has had its prayer wheel for years—spin the wheel and say fifty prayers. Jesus faced the same temptation in the garden: "Take the easy, crossless road," said Satan.

The "nevertheless" of Jesus settled the matter; He would not redeem a world with any shortcuts.

The history of Christianity could be written in man's attempt to find the easy way. The inventive genius of man has substituted rituals, creeds, and doctrines for inner transformation and moral righteousness. Much of our modern evangelism has been cheapened by making salvation so easy it has no meaning. Sometimes the lifting of the hand or the signing of a card or the mere saying of a certain prayer is substituted for a real transformation of all of life and a dedication to true discipleship.

Who said it would be easy? It isn't even easy to deny Christ and die in your sins! To do so you have to trample under foot every Bible published, every hymn written, every sermon preached, every building built, every righteous life, and every deed done in Christ's name. To deny and die means you have ignored the march of the church, the testimony of the Book, the cry of the martyrs, and the transformation of millions of lives. It isn't easy. It takes a special kind of hard, proud, egotistical person to deliberately go against the way of the cross.

Who said it would be easy? It wasn't easy for Christ to leave the glories of Heaven, to limit Himself in the flesh, to face the tempter's power and the thoughtless cruelty of mankind, and to carry His cross up Calvary's hill for your sins and mine.

Who said the Christian life was easy? It is easy to sign a card, join a church, disturb the baptismal waters, or attend the services; but to live for Christ is another matter. If He is your Saviour, He is also Lord of your life. It means you follow in His steps. He sets the standards, and He determines how and where you walk. If you truly follow Him, it may well be that a Calvary awaits you too!

Are we really challenged by the easy way? Down within us we don't really want it. Deep within, where it matters, we know we want the real challenge He offers. It takes real courage to live for Christ—and to die for Him. It isn't easy, but it's worth all that we have to give. And that's what it takes.

You Don't Have To Be That Way!

Man is the one who realizes that he can be better than he is. He is the one who reaches beyond his grasp. He is the part of creation who is ever discontented. He has sinned and is aware of it. He worships, but often his worship does not satisfy. He builds rituals and ceremonies, but still hungers for peace of heart. He wonders if he can really change; as he wonders, he knows he must. He convinces himself that he is hopeless and unable to change; then meets a friend who has been wondrously changed.

Nicodemus is the classic scriptural example. He was probably the best man his religion could produce, but he was still hungry and unsatisfied. Coming to Jesus at night, he hoped to find if this new young teacher could help him. The question he came to ask is never asked, but the answer to it is given. Jesus, seeing this hungry, seeking soul, answers his unasked question: "Yes, Nicodemus you can change, you must change, you must be born again!" With the divine "you must," the human "can I?" is answered.

What Nicodemus heard is what men and women everywhere long to hear: "you don't have to stay the way you are!" No matter how soiled you are, no matter how imprisoned by your sin habits, no matter how scarlet your record may be, you can be changed. No wonder the gospel is "Good News" to a sad, sick world.

Don't think for a moment that the unforgiven sinner

likes the way he is. He may put on a real front and build a house-of-lies, but underneath his rationalization and subterfuge is an unhappy man. The town drunk in one city once told me, "Preacher, don't think for a moment I like being this way!" But he did nothing about it.

Nicodemus wasn't the town drunk. He was a fellow with whom many of us could identify. He was respected by community and church, but he didn't like what he was. He felt the hollow hypocrisy of his life and longed for a change. "Is it possible for a man to be born anew and have a fresh start?" "Yes," says Jesus, "but you can't do it yourself; it must come from above." You cannot—God can!

How did it happen? Paul says, "Believe in the Lord Jesus Christ and thou shalt be saved. If any man be in Christ he is a new creature, old things are passed away, behold all things are become new." When divine grace and human faith meet, a new creature is formed and all is changed.

Carl Jung, the Swiss psychiatrist, says that "Christianity has added a new rung to the ladder of evolution—it has produced on the earth a new creature that lives in a new way to which the natural man can no more attain than a crawling thing can fly, a creature so radically different from what it has left behind that we can describe it by no other term than 'rebirth'!"

You don't have to stay the way you are!

Paying the Price

We live in an age where we look for every way we can to buy something for less. This is prudent and necessary. This has brought about the cut-rate store, where the marked-down merchandise is often inferior in quality, but many do not mind because it costs less. This philosophy, however, has moved into other realms of life where it is not a necessity nor is it prudent.

Some of us are going through life looking for bargains. We want success without paying the price for preparing. We are willing to cut any corners in order to reach our self-made goals faster. Holman Hunt, the great artist, has left for us the beautiful picture entitled, "The Light of the World." The picture, you recall, has Christ standing at the door. All of us know the story of the door having no latch on the outside. The artist explained it by saying the only latch is on the inside. The door is the heart of man and must be opened from within. But did you know that Holman Hunt spent three years painting that picture? He painted it out-of-doors at night by the light of a candle so he could get the proper lighting effect. Many times he had to wrap his feet in straw to keep warm as he painted.

There isn't any bargain basement entrance to greatness. We must be willing to pay the price. Some today in the realm of religion are looking for a bargain basement entrance too. Here of all places there are no shortcuts. The tempter tried to give Jesus a crossless road to take, but the Master refused. Dietrich Bonhoeffer in his book, *The Cost of Discipleship*, makes a stirring attack on what he calls the desire for "cheap grace." Those who seek this want the assurance of salvation without any responsibilities of discipleship. They think that they can claim Christ as Saviour without submitting to Him as Lord. How foolish! How impossible! How drab! The joy of the Christian faith is to rise from your knees and stand before your King, at whose feet you have bowed, and await your orders. The orders are clear and costly, but, oh, the joy and reward. "If any man would be my disciple let him deny himself, take up his cross daily and follow me." The rewards are equally clear: "Well done thou good and faithful servant. Thou has been faithful over little, I will make you ruler over much. Enter Thou into thy Master's Joy."

Everybody Isn't Doing It!

The chief rationale of many people, young and old, to justify their actions is to say, "Well, everybody's doing it."

Evelyn Mills Duvall in her little book for young people entitled, *Why Wait For Marriage?* speaks about this old excuse. She, of course, is speaking about promiscuity. She concludes from all her studies that everybody is not promiscuous. She states that not one of the studies made, including the famous Kinsey Report, reveals any universality of promiscuity in our country. The latest surveys of students in large eastern universities show that fully eighty percent of the girls were waiting for marriage and that only two percent could be classified as promiscuous. Of the men, more than fifty percent were of the same mind and were waiting for marriage. Everybody isn't doing it. The survey further shows that many men of the most flamboyant dress and style, and most open in their frankness, are also the most ignorant of sex and are still uninitiated. The facts reveal that there is a difference today from twenty years ago, but that the greatest difference is the openness in discussing the subject, and that we as a nation are better informed.

Carrying the thought into other realms, we can say also that everybody is not doing a lot of things people accuse "everybody" of doing. Everybody is not smoking marijuana, everybody is not taking pep pills, everybody is not cheating, everybody is not being unfaithful to marriage vows, everybody is not anti-American, everybody is not hating his brother, everybody is not despairing. Our problem is that we think in categories. We pigeon-hole people. The only mental activity some of us have is that of jumping to conclusions.

Granted that any immorality is wrong, there are still many fine, Christian young people who are waiting until marriage. Granted that one young person smoking marijuana or popping pills is too many, there are still multitudes of young people who have too fine an image of themselves to fall into this trap. Granted that one person cheating is too many, that one unfaithful husband or wife is too many, that one anti-American who tries to destroy the very basic tenets of our country is too many, that one hater is too many, we can still take hope in the fact that everybody is not guilty.

And even if the facts did substantiate the statement, would it justify anyone hiding behind it and seeking to excuse his own lack of discipline? After all, it isn't what everybody else does or does not do that each of us will be accountable for. It is what we ourselves are, or are not, that will be brought into the light on the day of judgment.

How Christian Are Your Reactions?

Any mature person who has accepted the Christian way of life as the way has made many and varied attempts to Christianize his actions. In every realm he has faced and made some decision about the proper Christian way.

Books have been written about "What Would Jesus Do?" We have struggled to try to make our actions, attitudes, and daily lives as Christian as possible. We are aware that we fall far short of the true Christian way, and we carefully rationalize to cover our un-Christian attitudes and deeds.

On the other hand, how many of us have given any thought to Christianizing our reactions? Isn't this where most of our problems are? If we meet a person who is in need, we will usually stop to help in whatever way we can. In the realm of our racial differences, we have tried to overcome our prejudices and look at people as one in God's sight. We have decided about most moral issues. We have tried at least to Christianize these actions. But what if the person we stop to help turns on us and tries to take advantage of us, or the person we are trying to treat as another made in God's image misunderstands and calls us vile names and spits at us? What is our reaction? How Christian is it? Or, in a much simpler vein, what if the waiter is slow bringing our food or the salesclerk is impolite, or the filling station attendant doesn't put the lid back on the gasoline tank and it is lost? What of our reaction? The reaction comes quickly, usually under stress, and our real un-Christian selves are unmasked and shine through for the moment.

It seems to me that this is what Jesus is trying to teach us when He speaks of going the second mile or turning the other cheek. He is saying that we are to be Christians all the way through. Not only are our studied actions to be Christianized, but our lives are to be so filled with Christ that we will be able to react as He would under the greatest stress.

Most of us need to dedicate our tempers and our tongues to the Lord, as well as our attitudes and overt actions. Actions do speak louder than words, and reactions speak louder than both.

What Can I Do?

Sometimes in our world of confusion and turmoil we get very discouraged and are tempted to shrug our shoulders and say, "Well, what can I do about it!" Frankly, I don't know what you or I can do about any of our problems, but I keep reminding myself of several things:

The people were in bondage in Egypt and all of them shrugged their shoulders and said, "What can I do?" But Moses saw a burning bush, turned aside to look, and heard God's voice telling him what to do about it, and a nation was delivered.

The people were hiding, waiting for the Midianites to come to steal their grain and animals. And God spoke to Gideon, and told him what he could do about it.

The giant walked up and down the valley floor and the soldiers of Saul shrugged and said, "What can we do?" God spoke to a young lad named David, who wasn't even in the army, and the nation was delivered.

The people were led into idolatry by an evil queen and a weak king. They said, "What can we do?" But God spoke to Elijah, and he stood before the people and said, "How long halt ye between two opinions; if God be God, then let us follow Him!"

I don't know what you can do. Confusion and uncertainty abound. Violence, senseless violence, is seen almost daily. I abhor it, and so do you. What can we do? We can express to one another our outrage over it. We can let our leaders know how we feel and commend those who take a public stand against such things, and demand that others do so. We can keep our own hearts in tune with God so we cannot be guilty of any un-Christian act. We can pray for the offended and the offender. We can help create an atmosphere of Christian love that cannot condone such evil acts. We can listen for God's voice that we might hear Him when He tells us what we are to do.

In the Second World War, the Germans were capturing a Polish town. One Polish woman ran into the streets waving her broom at the enemy. "You can't fight tanks and flame-throwers with a broom stick," her friends said. "True," she said, "but I can show which side I am on."

Christian Growth

What Kind of a Christian Are You?

You recall the old story of the tent revival meeting when the evangelist walked up the aisle asking people if they were Christians? One man proudly said; "Yes sir, I'm in the army of the Lord!" "What branch of the army?" asked the evangelist. "I'm a Baptist," was the reply. "Sir," said the evangelist, "you're not in the army; you are in the submarine corp."

Perhaps the most confusing thing about Christianity to the outsider is our various denominations. We all call ourselves Christians, yet we have such varied beliefs and practices.

Those of us within the faith have learned to live with the denominational differences, but we are fully aware of other kinds of differences. We see glowing Christians, growing Christians, creedal Christians, secret Christians, formal Christians, legal Christians, praying and nonpraying, paying and nonpaying, working and nonworking Christians, loving and nonloving Christians, witnessing and nonwitnessing Christians. The Bible tells of Nicodemus, who came to Jesus by night—the secret Christians; it tells of Lazarus, who had been given life by the Master but was still bound by the grave clothes. Couldn't that be a picture of many in the church today? It tells of Peter, the denying Christian, but also reveals him to be a truly penitent Christian, and it tells of Demas, who loved the world too much. We see fearful followers and faithless followers; we see arguing and ambitious followers.

All of these go under the banner of Christians. Whether they are or not is not ours to decide. God has delivered us from this decision. The Harvester will come and separate the wheat from the tares. In that day some may truly be revealed as "reasonable-facsimile Christians."

Paul mentions only two kinds of Christians—the spiritual and the carnal. The carnal Christian is that one who knows Christ as Saviour, but is still dominated by the flesh. The word for flesh in the Greek language is the word from which we get "carnal." In the Romans' letter Paul states clearly that to be carnally minded is to be the enemy of God. Those in the flesh cannot please God. In the first Corinthian letter he speaks of those in the church who are Christian but who live like the carnal-minded person. He calls them babies! They have to be nursed along, their feelings are always getting hurt, they are envious of others, and they cause division and strife. He concludes by saying, "They walk like mere men—not like redeemed men of God."

On the other hand Paul speaks of the spiritual Christians. These have the spirit of God within them, guiding their lives and conduct. These endure to the end, they love one another, they seek His face, they seek to follow His will, they overcome the world, and through these the blessings of God flow to bless and lift mankind.

What kind of a Christian are you? You don't know? Let me assure you that others do. Satan knows. He isn't blinded by our foolish statistics; he knows who are his. He knows that those who are not positively for Christ are on his side. The nonbelievers know, too! They may be poorly informed about what Christians believe, but they have definite opinions about how Christians should act and the kind of persons Christians should be! They may even hunger to find something in the Christian friend that will drive away their inner darkness, but they may not find it. Jesus also knows what kind of Christians we are. You can't fool Him! He sees us, sees our potential, and says, "Oh, what I could do with that person if he would let me, but he is so absorbed in other things!"

What kind of a Christian are you? It makes a great deal of difference to a whole world of people.

In the Spring . . .

Philosopher George Santayana, a professor at Harvard, came into a sizeable legacy and was able to relinquish his post on the faculty. Bennett Cerf in *The Saturday Review* tells of Santayana's last lecture. "The classroom was packed for his final appearance and he did himself proud. As he was about to conclude his remarks, he caught sight of a forsythia uncurling in a patch of muddy snow outside the window. He stopped abruptly, picked up his hat, gloves and walking stick, and made for the door. There he turned. 'Gentlemen,' he said softly, 'I shall not be able to finish that sentence. I have just discovered that I have an appointment with April.'"

With all of nature awakening around, which of us cannot feel an awakening within ourselves? The desire to get out into the outdoors pulls at us. The garden calls, or the yard, or the farm, or, as is true in my case, the golf course. The senses quicken, the sluggishness of winter is left behind, and we feel renewed physically.

Should it not be so spiritually? Let us look through

nature and see nature's God. Let us see that He quickens the life of the smallest creation when it surrenders itself to His will. So He will quicken the life of man, his highest creation, when that life is surrendered to His will.

As Christians we have an appointment with the God who gives us the beauty of spring.

How Big Do You Want to Be?

In this day when it seems that most of us are dieting, or should be, the question might seem to be a poor one. But bigness is relative, and we can wish to be larger or smaller. The television commercial asks the question to small children and they reply, "Big enough to ride my brother's bicycle" or "Big enough to see a parade," or "Bigger than my sister!"

The question has another side to it, however. The inner soul of man has a dimension, too. How "big" do you want to be in character, in service, in what really matters in life? The sad thing is that so many people seem to be on spiritual diets also. So many seem to be shrinking in the basic virtues of life, such as honesty, purity, loyalty, and dependability.

How big do you want to be? Big enough to make a living? Big enough to be a success? Big enough to own a fine home and two cars? Big enough to hold a position of power and authority? Big enough to have your name be a household word? Recently a young woman who had made it big in the rock music field was found dead from an overdose of drugs. She became a star, her name was a household word among the younger set, but how "big" was she? Her philosophy of life from her own lips was: "To stay stoned and have a big time!"

How big do you want to be? Big enough to bless your community? Big enough to contribute something significant to the world? Big enough to make the world a little better place when you have gone?

The Galilean carpenter said that real bigness is to be big enough to be servant of all. How big do you want to be?

A teacher anticipating a visit from the school board prepared the children to give a good account of themselves. She decided that one question an adult would ask would be, "What do you want to be when you grow up?" So she asked her class the question. One wanted to be a doctor, another a nurse, another a teacher. When the board arrived, she was only worried about one little boy's reply. He was slower than the other children, and she could never guess what he would say. Sure enough the questions were asked and the answers given. When the retarded boy's time to answer came, he put on his best smile and said brightly, "I want to lead a blind man!"

How big to you want to be?

Spiritual Calisthenics

There has been much said lately about how physically out of condition our people are. Many have made fifty-mile hikes to prove that they are not as out of shape as some would think. It is exceedingly necessary that we do keep ourselves physically fit. There is much danger amid all of our comforts of our not doing so. However, the greater danger is in our neglecting the spiritual. We are most certainly spiritually out of condition. Paul said: "Bodily exercise is profitable for a little, but Godliness is profitable for all things having promise of the life which now is and of that which is to come."

Paul was interested in the physical body. I'm sure he must have been vitally interested in athletics. Often he uses the terms of the sports' world. He speaks of fighting; of not shadowboxing; of fighting the good fight; of receiving the victor's crown. In II Timothy 2:5, he states: "No contestant in the games is crowned unless he competes according to the rules." In Colossians 3:15 he says: "Let the peace that Christ can give you keep on acting as umpires in your hearts, for you were called to this state as members of one body."

He would say today: "Get plenty of exercise, walk your fifty miles and more, keep trim, but don't neglect your soul!"

In the first letter to Timothy, the young minister, he gives some spiritual exercise to help develop Godliness. He mentions the Word of God, prayer, sound doctrine, and real faith. He goes on to stress the worth of Christian influence in words, conversation, in love, and purity. "Give attention to reading; to exhortation; to doctrine. Neglect not the gift that is in thee—meditate upon these things; give thyself wholly to them; that thy profiting may appear to all. Take heed unto thyself, and unto doctrine; continue in them; for in so doing this thou shalt both save thyself, and them that hear thee." (I Timothy 4:13–16)

"If You Are Waiting on Me . . . "

When does a person who is a Christian receive the Holy

Spirit within his life? Is it: (1) at conversion; (2) after conversion following a separate acceptance of the Holy Spirit much like the acceptance experience of receiving Christ in salvation; (3) at conversion but only in part—the receiving of the fullness of the Spirit comes later; (4) at baptism; (5) only by the laying on of hands by someone who stands in the apostolic succession?

Those who contend that a separate act of faith is necessary following the conversion are ignoring Paul's teaching in Romans, where he reminds us that "he who has not the Spirit of Christ does not belong to Christ." If you haven't received the Spirit, you haven't received Christ! Those who say that we receive only a part of the Spirit at conversion are making the Spirit less than a person. You do not hear any one say that a "portion" of Christ is received at conversion. How do you receive a part of a person? Those who say the Holy Spirit is received only at baptism or with the laying on of hands are forgetting Cornelius and his household and others who received the Spirit without either.

The emphasis has been on the wrong side. When we look at the Biblical teachings, it seems evident to me that God has in Christ done His part. The Holy Spirit comes at our expression of repentance and faith in Christ. The Spirit convicts, quickens, and indwells us. "Why then," you ask, "are there so many who give so little evidence of the presence and power of the Spirit in their lives?" If the life is a Christian life, it isn't that the Holy Spirit has not entered, but that the life has not been yielded to the Spirit's direction and control. The main difference in what many believe and what the Bible teaches is a matter of emphasis. The problem is not in God, but in us. It isn't that we must wait, pray, and hope that God will pour out His Spirit upon us. He has already done that! We must surrender our lives totally to Him.

Our hymn writers haven't helped us here. Nearly every hymn concerning the Holy Spirit implies that God must still do something—"Breathe On Me," "Spirit of God Descend," "Come Holy Spirit Heavenly Dove," "Holy Spirit From On High." All these are waiting on God to do what He has already done.

If we have repented and accepted Christ, His Spirit indwells us. Paul, I think, was surprised at the slowness of the people of his day to grasp this: "Know Ye not that the Spirit of God dwelleth in You?" If there is a second experience, it is on our part and not God's part. He waits on us. Our need is to surrender. But we want to put the burden on God! He says surrender; we say wait. He says surrender; we say pray. He says surrender; we say worship. He says surrender; we say tithe. He says surrender; we say prepare better sermons. He says surrender; we say come Holy Spirit.

If God should answer us in our own everyday language, He would say, I think, very quietly but positively: "Friend, if you are waiting on Me, you are wasting your time, and mine!"

Christian Living

True Goodness

Three crosses on a hill. Three men dying in perhaps the most excruciating way devised by men. Two of them died because they were too bad and one because he was too good. This is how it goes. We want everything leveled off at a comfortable mediocrity, so we crucify the two extremes. Why is it always like this? The answer is simple really. The extremes reveal too much. The one reveals to us how low we are capable of stooping, and the other how high we are created to reach. We rid ourselves of both, but there is another reaction to these extremes. We either rid ourselves of them or we are transformed by them. They have a strong magnetic pull attracting us their way.

The prodigal in every generation, when and if he comes to himself, is amazed at how deeply he has become involved in sin and how low he has allowed himself to stoop. On the other hand, the thief on the cross, who saw true goodness for the first time, was amazed that even though his hands were nailed to a cross, his soul could reach the very portals of Heaven. He was transformed by the sight. What do you conclude from this? Christian people are the good placed in the world. They have been here for nearly two thousand years. Few have been crucified and few have been successful in transforming lives. In fact, the other side seems to be having more success in its transforming work, doesn't it? Why is it so? Can it be that we are better at inventing ways to sin than at learning what true goodness is?

The goodness that transformed the repentant thief was not the mediocre nothingness of surface conformity. This repels rather than attracts. Jesus doesn't admonish us to seek first the half-conversion of conformity, but to seek first the Kingdom of God and His righteousness. When Christians do this, they will truly be filled with His goodness, and the transforming work we are commissioned to do will go forward. We can expect to be crucified for being too good, but in death we will bless the world by revealing again what true goodness is. Perhaps some dying sinner will see the goodness of God in us and be transformed by the sight.

Divinely Dissatisfied

Man is a restless being doomed never to be truly satisfied, yet ever striving and reaching for that which he hopes will satisfy. The advertisers help. One cigarette company claims that their brand satisfies; some soap companies guarantee satisfaction with their soap, and to be sure we are happy they throw in a glass or a towel. Everyone seems to be striving to satisfy us, but we are never truly filled. One milk company has maintained for years that the cows that give their milk are contented cows, so the milk will surely satisfy us, but every cow I've seen seems to be reasonably contented. Man, however, not being like the cow, always realizes that something is lacking and that he somehow should be more than he is. Henry George in his book *Progress and Poverty* says: "Man is the only animal whose desires increase as they are fed; the only animal that is never satisfied. The wants of every other living thing are uniform and fixed. The ox of today aspires to no more than did the ox when man first yoked him—all living things, save man, can take, and care for, only enough wants which are definite and fixed."

An old mountaineer came to town and saw a bunch of bananas for the first time. "Want to try one, Jake?" asked a friend. "No, I reckon not," he replied. "I've got so many tastes now I can't satisfy. I ain't aimin' to take on any more!"

The psalmist said: "I shall be satisfied when I awake in thy likeness." He knew what man was and that his fulfillment would not come on earth. Paul on the other hand said, "I have learned in whatsoever state I am, therewith to be content." Are the two contradicting one another? No, to be satisfied is to get all you want; to be content is to be happy with what you have. So we can learn to be content, but we should never expect to be satisfied.

Do you mean that a Christian will not be satisfied here on earth? True! Our ideal is beyond us. All of our spiritual growth comes as a result of this dissatisfaction. The Reformation grew out of a dissatisfaction with the church of the day. Every needed reform has come from dissatisfaction with the status quo.

We are doomed to be dissatisfied—with our own expression of the Christian life, with the expression of others of the life of Christ, with the organized institutions that struggle to do Christ's will on earth.

Can we be content? Yes. Satisfied? No. I shall be satisfied only when I awake in His likeness. Satisfied with Jesus? Yes. But is He satisfied with me? Until He is, I remain divinely dissatisfied!

The Pure in Heart

How wonderful to be pure in heart. Jesus established it as one of the steps to true happiness. Too often, however, as we read his words we do not complete his thought. Jesus links happiness and purity of heart to a third great truth—that of seeing God. This makes the idea more complex. All of us long for happiness and many long for purity of heart, but few of us really want to see God. Why? Because of another great truth we often miss: only the pure in heart want to see God! Only those who have complete and unmixed allegiance to God can stand in His presence unashamed. Only those who have received salvation and purity of heart by faith, through His grace and mercy, really want to see God.

Adam, with his innocence gone, felt embarrassed and fearful. He felt morally naked in God's sight, and so hid from His presence. "Where are you, Adam?" said God. "I'm here, hiding," Adam replied. "Why are you hiding, Adam? Have you eaten of the fruit of the forbidden tree? I didn't make you to hide from me. I made you to have fellowship with me that we might bring happiness to one another!"

Why was Adam hiding from God? For the same reason that all of the Adams of mankind have hidden from Him throughout the centuries. Only the pure in heart want to see God. The child who is disobedient hides when his father comes home. The guilty run and hide in their guilt. The cause of much of our frustration and insecurity is this guilt. Day by day we walk through life looking over our shoulders, fearful that we have been found out, fearful of the accusing finger that might be pointing at us. It is doubtful if David wrote any Psalms in the more than a year he was separated from God by his guilt. When Nathan said, "Thou are the man," David dropped to his knees in repentance and once again felt comfortable in God's presence.

The pure in heart not only will see God, they long to see Him. They wait anxiously for His return. Only the pure in heart can truly pray, "Even so, come quickly, Lord Jesus!"

The Christian's Credentials

Today is a day of credit cards, identification cards, and membership cards. On every side we are being told to identify ourselves. This is not new, although the modern credit card system is relatively new. The signet ring placed in the wax seal was for years the identification of a legal or royal decree.

On the day that Jesus walked the temple courts in Jerusalem, the Jews gathered around Him saying: "We have heard it said that Thou art the Messiah; how long must You keep us in suspense? If you are the Messiah, say so plainly." "Identify yourself," they are saying. Jesus answered: "I have told you, but you will not believe." (John 10:26, New English Bible)

Christianity is Christ becoming flesh and dwelling among us, and we are to behold His glory in the life He lived and the deeds He accomplished. His credentials were not creeds, but deeds. The only creed you really believe is that which you believe in enough to practice. Jesus said: "You say you want to know who I am, if I am really the Messiah. Then watch my life, watch my deeds. If the life and deeds are ordinary, then you will know that I am an ordinary man; but if the life and deeds are truly

Godly, you will know that I come from the Father." He concludes by saying, "I and the Father are one."

The men of that day watched Him and they saw the character of God in His life. Many of them believed. Others saw His deeds and became fearful. For if He was right, then they were wrong and because of their fear they crucified Him.

As Christians we have the same credentials. It isn't what we say we believe, but what we practice. The world is saying to the Christian today: "We have heard that you are a Christian, that you have found the meaning of life. Don't keep us in suspense any longer. Identify yourself."

It matters little what you say. The world is filled with creeds. The Christian's credentials are deeds! "My deeds done in the Father's name, these are my credentials!"

Identify yourself!

How Do You Draw a Circle?

"Johnny," said the teacher, "step to the blackboard please, and draw a circle." So Johnny goes to the board and takes chalk in hand. He starts a circular line which he finally made come out where it started, but it looks more like he has drawn an apple than a circle. He steps back and looks at his drawing and then very thoughtfully says: "Teacher, when you draw a circle you gotta have a center first!" How wonderfully profound. You do not start at the circumference; you start at the center.

Isn't this the cause of much of our stumbling and groping around?

Isn't there a parable here? Aren't we, too often, trying to live on the circumference without knowing or deciding where the center is to be? Perhaps the greatest problem in the world today is that of finding what the meaning of life really is—of finding out what is in life that will make a dependable center for life. With Johnny we can say: "To live a life that is meaningful you have to have a center!"

Within the circumference of life there are many points you could arbitrarily mark as the center, but there is only one center. Choose any of these other points and the wheel of life will still roll, but it will bounce and hobble along because the axle is off-center. Is it necessary to add that the farther away from the center you get, the rougher the bounce?

The message that the Christian has for the world is of supreme importance here. The Christian steps up to the world and asks for attention. The world has noticed him, for the life he lives is smoother and far more meaningful. So the world looks to the Christian for the secret. What is his reply? He says, "You may think me very narrow-minded, but life will prove me to be right. There is only one center of the circle of life. Like any true circle the center comes first. We do not arbitrarily choose it. It is already there! His name is Jesus. He is the way, the truth, and the life!" He is life's center. It isn't a matter of searching for the center of life until you find it. It is rather a matter of searching until you realize that in your own strength and wisdom you cannot find it! Then He finds you, and to your listening heart He says, "I am come that you might have life and that more abundantly. I am the resurrection and the life, he that believeth in me shall never die. I am come a light into the world that whosoever believeth in me should not abide in darkness. I am the way, the truth and the life, no man cometh unto the Father but by me."

How do you draw a circle?

The Angel in the Stone

Some years ago a popular magazine carried a cartoon that was amusing at first glance but which on closer thought contained great truth. It was a picture of a mother and her young son watching an artist at work. The artist, a sculptor, was busy chipping away at a large stone. He had started at the top and was working downward. He had already formed the head and upper portion of the body and wings of an angel. The little boy in amazement turned to his mother and said, "How did he know that angel was in that stone?"

Jesus looked upon Simon, Andrew's brother, and said, "Thou art Simon the son of Jonah: Thou shalt be called Cephas, which is by interpretation, a stone!" Jesus saw in the rough fisherman the man that he would become.

Every young woman must be able to see in the young man she is marrying the man he can become. She is literally betting her life on that young man, accepting his name, his reputation, his past and future. She had better be able to see the "angel in the stone."

In this day of tension, misunderstanding, fear, and emotion concerning human relationships, we as Christians know we are to love one another and are even to love our enemies. This is most difficult. We cannot be dishonest and say we love everything that another person does. But as Christians we are to love as Christ loves. He loves people, not for what they do, but for what they are—children of God created in His image—and for what they may become.

If we can learn to look at those around us through the eyes of Jesus, we will be surprised to find how often the roughest stone contains an angel.

Two Coins

Many of the truths of the Bible have been overlooked by well-meaning friends of the Bible because they have debated about whether or not the account is an actual occurrence. This is perhaps most true in the Genesis account of creation. In many instances, whether the account is an actual occurrence or not does not greatly alter its meanings. Jesus spoke in parables, and there is no valid reason why the writers of the Old Testament, inspired by the Holy Spirit, should be denied that privilege. Many actual incidents, when seen by the true prophet, have parabolic meaning. We must look always for these deeper truths.

One of the great lessons of the Genesis account of the creation of man is the lesson of the two coins. God made man in His own image, placed him in the garden, and figuratively gave him two coins, two mediums of exchange, each redeemable in its own realm. The one coin is obedience to God's commands. With it man is free to purchase all of the joys of the pure in heart. With it he can find happiness, peace, security, health, and length of days. This coin guarantees the presence of God and the assurance of His guiding hand day by day. With this coin man enjoys a happy home. With it he builds hospitals, schools, and children's homes. With it he erects altars and there learns what it means to love and sacrifice for the glory of God and the blessing of society.

The other coin is disobedience. With it man has purchased all of the sorrow, suffering, and strife that we see on every hand. Look around. Every broken life, every horror of war, every ravage of poverty, every alcoholic stupor—all these and much more have been purchased with the coin of disobedience to God's will. With it man has built a wall between himself and God; and try as he will, man cannot, in his own strength, get past this barrier back into the presence of God. Is it man's destiny to remain outside? Having disobeyed and turned away from God, is there no hope for him? In his own strength there is no hope, but what man could not do for himself, God has done for him. God, in Christ, has broken down the wall and has provided a way by which man can be reconciled to God and can have the peace and happiness he desires.

How is this accomplished? God, through His Spirit, comes once again to man convincing him of his unhappy emptiness, reminding him that he was made for fellowship with God. Suddenly, man, under the wooing influence of God, looks down and opens his hand and finds there, fearfully clutched and unused, the coin of obedience. With it he can, through Christ, enjoy fellowship with God. He realizes anew that true happiness comes only through obedience to God, and with this new-found insight he also realizes that this coin is the coin of the realm for which he was created.

A Good Name

Every right thinking person is horrified at the savagery that is apparently just under the surface in much of mankind today. It isn't a matter of race or creed; it is seen everywhere. There seems to be nothing sacred. Human life is not sacred; murder is done with little or no provocation. Truth is not sacred; a lie comes easily. Friendship is not sacred; to betray a confidence is common. The other person's property is not sacred; if it can be gotten, take it.

Place over against this the old virtues of integrity and honor, where a man's word was his bond, where a man died for what he believed was right, where he would be imprisoned rather than lie.

What is the difference? The person of honor and integrity has a high opinion of himself. He is a person made in the image of God and he cannot betray that image. He is a link in a chain of men and women of honor, and he cannot be the weak link. Spinoza did not approve of Louis XIV and refused pension and patronage by refusing to dedicate a book to the king. Dr. Harry E. Fosdick tells of a minister in New England who was told that if he persisted in the course he had taken they would cut his salary. The minister replied, "You can get very good fish in the bay and I know a place in the woods where you can dig roots that you can eat." He had a high opinion of his name.

As a boy I recall being overjoyed to see a field covered with unspoiled snow. It was life's greatest thrill to be the first to mark it. What would we do? We wrote our names in it in letters twenty feet tall. What do you do when someone asks you to try out a new pen? You write your name, don't you? A name is identity. It is something that is truly ours. We must be proud of it and think so highly of it that we cannot bemoan it in any way. The image of God within is far greater than the earthly name we bear. How important it is that we be true to the best within us.

At a recent encampment for a group of Christian young people, a young man ran breathlessly up to the camp director saying, "You can't guess what I've been doing!" "No, I can't. What have you been doing?" was the reply. "I've been out in the lake by myself in the rowboat and I've written my name across the water of the lake." Imagine the effort of such a task, and the futility of it. But the camp director said: "When we returned to the lakeshore a couple of hours later, that boy could still see his name written out there!" May he always be so proud of that name, and of the image of God within him!

Empty Amid Plenty

In Missouri years at a summer camp, Dr. R. G. Lee, the great preacher from Memphis, was the daily preacher. One day he mentioned how much it had rained in Memphis that year. Late that afternoon as the clouds gathered, someone told Dr. Lee that it looked like it was going to rain. He looked up and replied, "I don't think so; those are empties coming back from Memphis."

The word is used about people sometimes too. Jude in the Scriptures describes some people as "empty clouds." Nicodemus went to Jesus because he was empty—religious, but empty. Zaccheus climbed the tree to see Jesus because he too was empty—wealthy but empty. Jesus told of the prodigal boy who was free from his parents and out on his own, but empty inside.

A doctor went home from his work one day disturbed and discouraged wondering why he had ever thought he wanted to be a doctor. "Most of the people I treat aren't really sick; they just think they are," he exclaimed. "They just want to lean on me. And the crowd we run around with is a bunch of phonies, a bunch of empties—and I'm the emptiest of all." A man, trained and used in his profession—but empty.

The doctor and his wife decided to do something—at least to get away for awhile. They went to a distant city and through some casual friends were invited to a dinner party. The people were exuberant and attractive. They enjoyed the company of one another and were completely at ease. Just as easily the conversation turned to spiritual things, and the doctor and his wife found themselves in a deep discussion of eternal verities. "What is this?" he asked. "What kind of group is this?" His host replied: "We're just a group of Christian people who enjoy being together and sharing our experiences!" Needless to say, he and his wife found that which changed their lives completely. Through their influence many of the crowd of phonies at home became very real, and their lives became filled with meaning.

"In thy presence is fullness of joy" the Psalmist said. John writes, "And of his fullness we all have received one filling after another."

Lance Webb states: "Christ fills our emptiness with a satisfying friendship with God for which there is no substitute; with a deep satisfying purpose for living; and with a flood tide of new resources from which we draw sufficiently for every need."

The answer to your emptiness? "I will arise and go to my father. . . ."

Touchback or Touchdown?

You probably saw it happen. The Pittsburgh Steelers were playing the Kansas City Chiefs in a nationally televised football game. With the Steelers trailing and desperately needing points, Dave Smith, the wide receiver for the Steelers, caught a pass and was happily racing unmolested toward the goal line. As he crossed the five yard line he lifted the ball, one handed, over his head in a dramatic victory salute and dropped the ball! It promptly rolled into the end zone for a touchback instead of a touchdown. Instead of the six points and possible seven the Steelers anticipated, the Chiefs got the ball on the twenty yard line.

There must be some lessons in this for all of us. For the football players the lesson is plain: be sure you are across the goal line before you celebrate. For all of us in this old game of living the lessons should be equally plain: almost is not enough. You can almost succeed and still fail; you can almost graduate and still not have your diploma. You can almost not break the law and still break it. You can almost not get caught and still be caught. You can almost not become an alcoholic or drug addict and still be hooked for life.

Arnold Palmer's philosophy in putting the golf ball is very simple: "If you're not up, you're not in." He means simply that if you don't hit the ball far enough to get up to the hole it surely will not fall in the cup. Almost is not in.

The Scripture is filled with many famous "almosts." Lot's wife almost escaped the burning city. David almost got by with his sin and deceit. Demas almost made it, but loved this world too much. Agrippa almost was persuaded to enter the Kingdom but didn't.

The songwriter said, "Almost is but to fail!" There is no excuse for "almosts" in the spiritual realm. All has been provided for man's redemption; God has done His part. To almost decide to believe is to not believe at all.

How sad for a person to be able to score a touchdown and through carelessness score a touchback. Sadder still is to be able to live life abundantly here and throughout eternity and through carelessness or neglect miss all of life's richest blessings and rewards.

Whatsoever ye do

Do you know the difference between a religious film and a Christian film? Hollywood has produced many a religious film but few, if any, truly Christian films. Most people would make no distinction between the two, but there is an important difference. A religious film is one about some subject that has a religious connotation. Such a film could be about a man who is in search of a religion that will satisfy his soul's hunger, or it could only be a story about some shrine or building that has some religious significance. A religious film can treat a Biblical character in a very un-Christian way and still be called a religious film. A Christian film, on the other hand, is one where the entire film embodies Christian attitudes and lets the light of our knowledge of Christ and His teachings shine upon every relationship and life situation.

The same distinction can be made in the life of the religious person, the church member, and the true Christian. A person may be religious and have only a nodding acquaintance with Christianity. A person can, in fact, be considered a religious person and be only interested in studying or discussing any and all religious ideologies. The Christian, on the other hand, has an example to follow, a life to emulate, a cross to bear, a story to tell, and a mission to fulfill. He is aware of his Christian precepts and allows them to shine upon every relationship and circumstance of life. Every attitude and judgment is made in the light of Christ's teachings.

The truly Christian life, then, is one that accepts and follows Paul's admonition in I Corinthians, when he says, "Whether therefore ye eat or drink, or whatsoever ye do, do all to the glory of God."

Church

The Koinonia Meal and the Lord's Supper

Do you recall meeting a new friend when you were a child, and you just didn't want to stay away from one another? You would rush home to meals and then rush back as quickly as the family would release you from the table? You found in that new fellowship a real warmth that made you feel "good all over!"

Consider then the experience of the first Christians following Pentecost. Their newfound faith in Christ and the new friends that they had met because of Him pulled them closely together. Many, because of their conversion experience, were no longer welcome at home and had no home to go to; some were visiting in Jerusalem for the Passover and tarried longer to enjoy this new fellowship. Many were slaves who would hurry to the assemblage as soon as they could finish their work.

Out of this new "koinonia," this fellowship, grew several definite habits that most Christians follow today. These early Christians assembled together, they learned from the apostles, they fellowshipped, they broke bread together, and they prayed. The Scripture also indicates that this fellowship spilled over into the homes and that they went from house to house breaking bread and fellowshipping together.

We have very carefully kept the idea of assembling together, learning from the apostles, and praying. Often, however, we neglect the other things. Often the idea of fellowship is missed in busy church programming today. Often people feel unknown and outside of the group, but the true church makes every effort to include all in the koinonia relationship. Tied inseparably with the koinonia is the breaking of bread together. Indeed, Dr. Frank Stagg of the faculty of Southern Seminary, indicates that the evidence is strong that these are one and the same. He states, "The shared meal has been expressive of and an encouragement to, the ties which bind people into a fellowship of love, trust and mutual acceptance." Later in his *New Testament Theology*, he says, "Grammar favors the reference of 'the koinonia' and 'the breaking of bread' as being the same thing. The koinonia was undoubtedly a full meal, the Lord's Supper being so observed by the earliest Christians." Dr. William Barclay says: "The early church service as indicated in Acts 20:7 consisted of the Love Feast, which was a rich, full meal, probably the only real meal some had eaten since the last meeting. At the end of the meal they partook of the Lord's Supper. It was at this happy fellowship of Christian friends, after a fine meal, that they paused and remembered who had made it all possible and in whose name they had assembled. The Greek word for the Lord's Supper is 'eucharist' which simply means 'thank you'."

In a faceless world of IBM cards and numbers, surely one of the most important roles of the church of the Lord Jesus is to provide Christian fellowship for the church family, and there is no happier time in a family's life than when it sits down and breaks bread together.

Wanted: A Compass

A woman stepped into a variety store and asked the clerk for a compass. The clerk inquired concerning the kind of compass she desired. "We have compasses," the clerk replied, "that draw circles, but we do not have the kind that take you places!"

What a summing up this clerk unconsciously did of many of us today. We are running in circles when the world is wanting directions to a harbor of safety and security. The modern beatitude says: "Blessed is the man that runneth in circles for he shall be known as a wheel!"

One woman who was seeking spiritual guidance called a friend and asked her to recommend a preacher to help her. The friend said, "Do you want a 'go-getter' or a man of God?"

Oh, how false our values are! The world does not care for our frantic activity. They want direction in life's darkness. In the midst of conflicting ideologies, they listen for a clear voice saying, "This is the way; walk ye in it!"

We have the compass the world needs; it is The Book! It points unerringly, not to the north as an ordinary compass, but to a bleak knoll called Calvary. For here the eternal light of the world was shed abroad to illumine all seeking hearts.

Dry Land Swimming

There is a character in an old comedy by Thomas Shadwell called Sir Nicholas Gemcrack. Sir Nicholas had the habit of stretching out on a table and practicing swimming in the dry security of his own home. "I hate the water," he would say from his froglike position on the table. "I content myself with the speculative part of swimming; I care not for the practice of it."

When you stop to think about it, there seem to be a good many dry land Christians around.

They talk about their faith—
   They sing about it—
      They pretend to go through the motions of worship—
         They argue about what they do or do not believe—
           They want the church to prosper—
           They want the world to know Jesus—

But, what they actually do for Jesus is another thing. Ask them to teach a Sunday school class, and they are too busy with other things. Ask them to direct a group of young boys in the youth program or to serve on a church committee, and they have a thousand other things to take their time. Ask them to give their tithe, and they are immediately "under grace and not under law."

With a world in chaos and with trouble on every hand, the church of Jesus Christ needs people who are willing to "launch out into the deep!"

The Annual Call

A fine young ministerial student mentioned that he was on "annual call" in the church he pastored parttime. He did not know whether he would be called for another year or not. It seems that the last few pastors have lasted only a

year. If we believe the Lord calls pastor and church together, it seems to me that there can be no definite length
of time for them to work together. Some ministers contribute greatly just what a church needs in a given time and
need only to serve briefly; others spend a lifetime and
their contribution through the years cannot be measured.

One thought occurred to me as I talked with the young
minister. What if the church membership were on an
annual call? Suppose that each church member was voted
upon annually, and that reelection depended upon what
real contribution each person had made to the life of the
church. Would you be reelected? Certainly the contribu-
tions of church members cannot be measured. Some have
a stewardship expressed in activity, in filling places of
service, in taking places of leadership. Others, however, fill
just as valuable a place with their stewardship of follow-
ship, by faithfully being in their places of worship and
study. Still others, unable to attend at all because of ill
health or other legitimate reasons, contribute through
their stewardship of prayer.

All of us have something to give, something to do,
someone to help in some special way, and it is not on an
annual basis. We are saved for eternity.

"Who Is Sitting Beside You?"

Everyone is looking for a friendly church. Sometimes
people slip in late and leave early and then delight to say,
"No one spoke to me. That's not a friendly church!" The
idea of a church having to advertise that it is "friendly" is
quite amazing actually, for whatever else the church is

supposed to be, it is a fellowship. This implies friendliness, warmth, and mutual concern one for the other. That a true New Testament church would fail to recognize and reflect these qualities is unthinkable.

Implicit in such a fellowship is also an awareness of the worth and dignity of each individual. There cannot be anyone in a true fellowship who is merely a number. Even the smallest child stands as an individual to be made to feel the warmth of individual worth.

The rights of others are respected also. To disturb, when some are trying to meditate before a service begins, is to show a lack of respect for others. To leave before the service of worship ends, except in the rarest of instances, is to show an equal lack of respect for others.

In the book of James, in the New Testament, one of the earliest church fellowships was being upset by favors shown to some and a lack of respect for others. The well-dressed person enters and is given a fine seat. The poorly clad person is told to sit on the floor at the feet of others. Thoughts that produce such actions, within the fellowship of believers, are completely out of place. After all, the church is the body of Christ, and no one member of the body is to be favored over another.

So stop occasionally and think! We are the fellowship of believers in Jesus, the Christ. And for the fellowship to be effective, it must begin with you. How thoughtless we are when we sing "What a Friend We Have in Jesus," and do not even know the name of the one who worships beside us. Friendship with Him makes us automatically friends of those with whom we worship. A friendly church? How can a church be otherwise unless it forgets its true identity?

A friendly church? How can it be otherwise if you are friendly and meet and welcome those around you? By the way—who is that person sitting next to you?

Whom Do You Serve?

Much has been said recently about Christian responsibility to the church. I feel that a sense of caution should be injected against the constant reference to the church itself apart from the Christ we should serve in the church. Too often we speak of a duty that one of us has to the body of believers with whom we are joined in church membership, and we fail to realize that the responsibility is not to the church, but to Christ.

The acceptance of responsibility to the church is summed up in a little illustration about a bird who sounds strangely like many of our own church members. It seems that when this little bird built her nest she simply failed to put a bottom in it. When she was approached about a reason for such a strange nest she replied, "You see, I just love laying eggs, but I hate the responsibility." Many of us enjoy being professional pewsitters, but anything above and beyond that is simply out of the question. However, the emphasis is still not on our debt to the church. The stress should be placed on what we are compelled to do for Christ because of what He has done for us. The church as the instrument of service should not become more than this, nor should it become less. "For the love of Christ constraineth us."

The Measuring of a Church

Through the years many attempts have been made to measure the effectiveness of a local church. These attempts are still being made today.

From the value placed upon statistics today, many seem to believe that the local church can be measured by the number making up its membership. We speak with pride about the size of the membership of a church, but all the while we realize that twenty to thirty percent of the average church membership is made up of people who have long since moved away. There are others who measure a church by the size of its budget and financial program. The difficulty here is that the largest church budget represents only a relatively small portion of even the tithe of the membership of the church. The number baptized, even though above average, may not represent an effective program of witnessing, for there may be hundreds still untouched by the gospel message within the shadow of the church.

There are others, on the other hand, who seem to find virtue in lack of numbers. These often have a most critical spirit toward the numerically larger church. This kind of spirit indicates a low level of spiritual maturity.

The only measuring stick to the effectiveness of any local church's ministry is how much the Spirit of Christ has permeated the lives of the individual members of that church. Man, of course, cannot measure this.

Each of us can, however, search our own hearts and see what our attitudes really are. How much of the Spirit of Christ is reflected in my daily living? How much of His love do I put into practice in my life? How much of His humility and meekness is present with me? How much of His concern, His compassion, His willingness to sacrifice is present within me?

In other words, if the church is measured by the depth of the spiritual life of each of its members, since I am a member, the depth of my spiritual life is the measurement of the church.

It means then that we need to search our hearts as individuals and do some spiritual measuring. "If every church member were just like me, what kind of a church would my church be?"

Transferring Values

The old storytellers recognized it. They knew they could get people to see themselves or some great truth best in a simple story. whether the story was actually true or not didn't matter because its message could have been true hundreds of times over. One such story was of a handsome prince who fell in love with a very beautiful and lovely young princess. With joy the nations involved celebrated their marriage and rejoiced over their good fortune in having such a happy prince and princess. But the beautiful princess became sick and died. The prince's grief was terrible to see. But he eventually recovered. Then he built a memorial tomb for his beloved. He built using the best workmen and the finest materials. The tomb was beautiful, and the prince spent many of his waking hours at the tomb. There he decided that this wasn't enough. He built a great temple encircling the shell and tomb. That led to the construction of a tower with bells that rang out over the countryside. All of this took years and years, and millions of what we would call dollars today. Time and cost did not matter to the prince; he had to express properly his love for his beloved princess. Finally the tower and temple and shell and gardens were all finished. One day the prince, now an old man, looked down and saw the little tomb that held the body of his princess. It was now far overshadowed by the beauty of all the rest. In a moment's emotional outpouring, he turned to his servants and said, "Remove that thing!"

The lessons are clear aren't they? The end has been forgotten because he had been so occupied with the means. The goal had been lost in the achievement of it. Many a church loses sight of its goals in perfecting an organization. Many dreams of young parents are lost in the means of making enough money to make the dream come true. Many a young person's decision to do the Lord's will wherever He will lead has been lost during the time of preparing for such service. How many of us live on the outer edge and become so preoccupied that we scarcely realize that we have transferred our values and are now building around another center entirely.

Learn from the prince. Instead of removing the goal, let us point with conviction and courage at the lesser things that have distracted us and say, "Remove these things! I have but one life to live, and I want it centered in the eternal verities of life, not on the fringes."

The Church's Unemployed

Perhaps the greatest problem facing the church today is not the ecumenical movement or even making itself "relevant" to our day and times. It may well be that our greatest problem is within the ranks of the membership of the local church. Every church has the same problem. It is this: so many who are affiliated with the church are not truly affiliated with the principles of Christ's teachings. It is the same problem Amos and the other prophets faced in their day. So many people seem to think that God is fooled by our attention to the outward form and appearance of being religious. How can we be so blind? The God who created the heavens and the earth, who piled high the mountains and scooped out the valleys, who gave the bird its song and the flower its smell, surely must be able to know the heart of man. Jesus, even though limited by the flesh that clothed Him in His incarnation, often knew the hearts of the men with whom He talked.

And yet, there are on the membership rolls of most churches people who never participate in any of the activities of the church. The church could close its doors on Sunday and Wednesday nights, and it would be months before these knew, unless some of the faithful mentioned it to them. At the same time, if the church voted to remove them from the rolls, they would be disturbed beyond measure. God's unemployed! Perhaps it would be better to say the church's unemployed for they give little evidence of belonging to God at all. These know nothing of the joy of Christian living; they have no message to share with the world, so are not interested in witnessing; they feel no sense of God's ownership, so have no idea of Christian stewardship of life and possessions. Their only real thought of the church is that they expect the pastor to be attentive when they are in need of pastoral ministries, and they are quite critical if he delays or does not know of their need.

Harold Bosley states: "When I glance over the long catalogue of sins committed by church members and the church, I am convinced that the most effective argument for the claim that the church is a divine institution is that it has survived the sins of its members. Most human institutions crumble under this weight in a few years or decades, but not the church. Only an institution created and re-created by God could have not only survived, but flourished through two thousand years as has the church."

The Needed Revival

There were revivals before Pentecost. There were revivals under Samuel, David, Solomon, Asa, Jehoshaphat, Hezekiah, Josiah, Ezra, and others. There have been revivals in other religions also; the early history of India, China, and the Arab world reveal this. Science is in the midst of a great revival now; discovery had a revival in the fifteenth century. The Renaissance period was a revival of art and cultural life.

Revivals seem to be a part of history. Many in Christian circles seem to feel no need for a revival, perhaps because they have seen so many "revival meetings" and so few revivals! But true revivals are necessary because man cannot and will not run at peak endeavor all of the time. The human way seems to be the way of revival. As the springtime brings renewal of life to nature, so nature needs seasons of awakening and renewal. It is by the birth of revival fires that God keeps the human heart eager and fresh with hope. Indeed, the world is always in a state of revival; one part of human activity moves upward as another recedes, and in it all God is acting.

Pentecost was the first Christian revival. Although Jesus brought revival with Him, it could not be fully appreciated or realized until after His death, resurrection, and ascension. With the coming of the Holy Spirit at Pentecost there came an awakening, a revival in the Christian sense of the word, such as the world has never seen since. The Pentecost renewal still stands as our example, our model for true revival.

When Jesus ascended, He left His apostles without anything that looked as though it had a future. They had no organization, no army, no equipment, no money, no books, no university, no prestige, no political power or status. But He left them with a tremendous memory of all He said and did, and of His sacrificial death and glorious resurrection. He left them with the full assurance that He was with them and would return to be with them again in person. He also left them with the greatest commission that any group has ever been given: "Go witness to the World!"

When He left, the group decided to do two things—to stay together and to pray together. How wise they were! For ten days they prayed together, and the answer to their puzzled minds appeared majestically, mysteriously, and powerfully. The Spirit came upon them in power, and a revival broke out that changed the world's history, even giving it a new calendar.

What did Pentecost do for these people? It filled them. They had thought themselves empty and alone and helpless. They were filled with God's spirit, which gave them courage and conviction and power. Their eyes were opened! They were able to see that Christ was indeed the world's only hope! Their ears were opened! They could hear God's voice and the cry of a lost world. Their tongues were loosed and the Spirit gave them utterance! They amazed themselves, and amazed the world around them.

This is the revival we need. One that will do for us and our day what the Pentecost experience did for the early church and its day. And it can happen! God is still on His throne. He still works as He did then. He waits for us who are His church to pray for power and in that power to go witness to the world.

On Visiting Grandmother

One of the customs growing out of the day of automobiles and good highways is the custom of visiting grandmother on Sunday. Let it be clearly understood that visiting parents and loved ones is not only a joy but a duty. I wonder, however, if we think about what the Sabbath day's journey costs us and our children—if we make it regularly and at the price of attending the services of teaching, training, and worship on the Lord's Day? Suppose that you first journeyed to the House of the Lord. That Sabbath day's journey to worship and fellowship might be the journey that would change the life of all of the family. It could be far more important than even visiting grandmother. If the family journeyed first to God's house, it might mean that one or all of them would be caught up by the spirit of worship and find the way to heaven's portal. In that one Sabbath day's journey, the family might find new insight, new strength, new joy, new peace, and new oneness of spirit. It has happened before.

It was only a Sabbath day's journey from Olivet's Hill to Jerusalem, just a half mile or so, but the disciples tarried there in Jerusalem and were imbued with power that changed the world. These everyday people were enabled to do extraordinary things in the power they received. Lives were changed, a movement established, a commission accepted, a message proclaimed, and a world changed all from just a Sabbath day's journey.

Let us, therefore, first make our way to God's house for worship and Bible study and then visit grandmother. It would also be well to realize that the journey back from grandmother's should be in time for training and worship again. That part of the day is the Lord's also. The godly grandmothers, like Timothy's grandmother Lois, will understand and encourage such devotion to God and His Bride, the Church.

My Church

All of us realize that the church as an institution is much maligned today. Its death has been consistently predicted for centuries. Its faults have been glaringly displayed in magazine, book, newspaper, sermon, song and cinema. The favorite exercise of some little minds today is to put down the church.

We, who are within the church, are quick to admit that it is not what it should be. Perhaps we expect too much of a fellowship that advertises that its members are all sinners. No other large institution does that! No other organization invites people who are admitted sinners to join its ranks! It isn't surprising that such a fellowship will have problems. Even sinners "saved by grace" have enough of the "old man" within them to keep them from always being what they should be.

Our problem seems to be that we look at the church idealistically, in the light of its great potential and the dream of what it should be; when we see what it is in reality, we shudder at the comparison. This is not to excuse the church, but it is simply to remind each of us that the church is composed of an imperfect people who are on a pilgrimage toward perfection. It is not composed of a group of perfect people living perfect lives. Such a fellowship would appeal even less than the church does today to the man on the street.

To those of us who are members of a local fellowship of believers, there is a choice spot in our hearts for it. We speak of it lovingly as "my church!" Even the buildings take on a hallowed air, for within those walls so much of importance has occurred.

My church—here I accepted Christ as my Saviour and Lord of my life; here I followed His example in Christian baptism; here I sit with my fellow believers and partake of His supper. Here, within these sacred walls the decision concerning my vocational calling was verbalized; here we said our marriage vows; here we saw our children take their first initial steps of faith. Here the soloist sang his first solo; here the public prayer was first made; here the gift is offered. At this altar men have been chosen for the gospel ministry; here others have knelt for the laying on of hands to become deacons, servants of the Lord. Through the ministry of this church my loved one was buried, perhaps from this sacred place itself!

My church! It has not been what it could have been, and is not what it should be; but it is my church and holds a very dear place in my heart.

My church—scene of my decisions, altar of my devotions, hearth of my faith, center of my affections, and my foretaste of heaven.

It is my church because it is His Church, and I am His and He is mine!

A Distinguishing Characteristic

The disciples were first called Christians at Antioch, perhaps in derision, but in admiration and respect none-the-less. They acted like the Christ whom they followed. This distinguished them, set them apart.

Our day seems to be a day of sameness—of everything and everyone blending together into a unity of indistinguishableness. This is what some of our children are really rebelling against. We are a mimeographed replica of one another. We wear the same clothes, use the same soaps and colognes, watch the same programs on TV, and listen to the same music. We are even expected to like the same men and elect them to public office. The pressures are strong on all of us to conform, and most of us yield and are lost in the crowd of others just like us.

What distinguishes those of us who are Christians from the others? Nothing usually. It ought not to be so! Oh, it isn't that we should wear different clothes or live in different style houses, or that we should use a different soap or none at all. The difference is inward. It is in outlook and attitude and allegiance that we are to be different, and these things drastically affect our actions. People should know that we are Christians, not because they see us dressed in our Sunday best going to church, but because they see that we are the same kind of people day by day regardless of our clothing. They should see in us a desire to serve, to lift mankind, to point to our Christ from whom comes the peace that passes all understanding.

Paul says it another way in the first Corinthian letter. He calls Christians those who not only are called to be people of God but also are distinguished by another important thing: they call upon the name of our Lord Jesus Christ. Here is a distinguishing name, a descriptive phrase, a characteristic peculiar to Christian people. It stands alongside the word Christian or disciple or saint or believer or brother—those who call upon the name of Jesus Christ our Lord.

It means allegiance to the Lord Jesus. It means adoration and worship. Peter at Pentecost hinges his entire sermon on this phrase, "Whosoever shall call upon the name of the Lord Jesus Christ." When Paul is converted, Ananias is told to go to him. The objection that Ananias has is that "this Paul is the one who has been sent to bind all them that call upon the name of the Lord." So prayer in the name of Christ was and is the distinguishing characteristic of the Christian.

It is a calling that results from a feeling of need. It is a cry for help in distress, for victory when tempted, for forgiveness when conscience convicts, for direction in times of doubt, for composure in times of stress, for meaning when all seems void, and in gratitude when all is well. We call upon Him naturally, in full assurance and in every circumstance. If we ever find ourselves where we cannot call upon Him, then we are in the wrong place.

The privilege of this calling is open to all. Paul says in Romans 12:13, "For whosoever shall call upon the name of the Lord shall be saved." Our call to Him is in response to His call for us.

Altar Repairs Needed

Remember when Elijah challenged the king and queen to find out who really was God? They were to meet on the mountain, and he and the prophets of Baal would have a contest. An altar was to be built and a sacrifice placed on it, and then the gods of Baal and the God of Elijah were to be asked to send fire from heaven to consume the sacrifice. The arrangements were made. The king and queen and their attendants were there. In my mind I can see the royal tent pitched on the mountaintop. The slaves fan the royal subjects and serve them the niceties for such a gala occasion. The Battle of the Gods was taking place. What could be more spectacular?

The prophets of Baal erect their altar and place the sacrifice on it. All day long they pray and dance and cry out to their god. Elijah grows a bit weary of it after awhile and taunts them suggesting that their god may be on a vacation or hard of hearing and they should shout louder.

Finally Elijah's time comes, and the first thing he does is to repair the altar that had been broken down. Then he built an altar in the name of the Lord. You know the result. In response to Elijah's prayer fire came from heaven and consumed the sacrifice completely.

What is an altar anyway? Ideally it is a place where we meet God. For this purpose it is built. It follows then that any effort to repair an altar is a striving to reestablish a vital relationship with God. It occurs to me that this is symbolic of what most of us need to do in our own personal lives—to repair some altars.

The altar of our initial experience with God in Christ might well need some attention. We made our vows to God. We accepted His offered salvation, but what have we done with the new life He has given? Have we grown and developed spiritually? We offered Him our very selves, our time, energy, thoughts and capacities, but have we really given them to Him? We should reexamine that experience and test its validity.

The altar where we established our home in His name

may need some repair work, too. Under God we promised to raise our children in the admonition of the Lord and to dedicate our home as a place of devotion and prayer. Has it been so in your home?

There are so many altars that may need some repairing: the altar of praise and witness, the altar of service, the altar of private prayer, the altar of stewardship and generosity. All of these are likely to need attention. So many sacrifices have been made on these to false gods that they are probably in a sad state of repair. In the name of the Lord we should repair and reestablish these symbols of a personal desire for a vital relationship with our God.

When we do this, we can be sure that heaven's fire will come down upon us, and the offering we make will be received. We can be assured that others will notice and shout as they did in Elijah's day, "The Lord He is God, the Lord He is God."

God is not reluctant. We are rebellious. Repairing the altars of God is the first step of renewal.

The Little Things That Discourage

The pastor is not supposed to be discouraged. He is supposed to have the latest word from the Lord, the extra portion of faith and the reserve of power from which to draw. It is true that the experienced pastor has found these resources or he would not have survived, but even these extras do not keep him from being discouraged, sometimes wondering if it is all worthwhile.

Strangely enough it is not the great crises and problems that discourage, for he gets ready for these and is able to accept the outcome. The real problems that drain his spiritual resources are little things. On Sunday morning when Sunday school ends, he heads for the pulpit to direct the congregation in worship, and must fight his way through an exodus that is taking place in the corridors. If physical facilities are limited and he has two morning worship services, he knows that some have already worshipped at "early" church, but many have not. The steady stream of children of church members who come to the office to call mother or daddy away from the morning paper to come and pick them up or, as sometimes happens, to beg the parents to allow them to remain for the worship hour—these are the little things that can drain and discourage. There are many other little things—Sunday night worship service neglected or ignored by many, children who sing faithfully in the choirs, but whose parents never hear them.

Little things—like empty pews or unused offering envelopes left unclaimed in the Sunday school room. Little things—like Bibles left at the church, unmissed and unopened for weeks at a time. Little things like those who name the Lord as Saviour but make no contribution of time, energy, or money to His Kingdom's work. Little things like teachers, trained and experienced, who will not teach a Sunday school class. Little things—like children who never hear their daddies pray; like the child who is convicted of sin and wants to publicly claim Jesus as Saviour and Lord, but whose parents hold him back until the convicting power of the Holy Spirit ceases to burn his heart and the desire leaves.

Just little things, but the discouragement is often bigger than life. Little things like nails on the cross that crucify our Saviour all over again.

The Little Things That Encourage

Great victories come all too rarely. When they do come, the momentum they bring keeps the song in the heart for days and weeks. One cannot live on the momentum of great victories; the gaps between them are too far apart. We are sustained in life by the little things that lift and encourage us. The pastor grasps these little things as a drowning man grasps a log that floats by. These little things keep the fire burning and the soul aflame.

Little things like the tears that he sometimes sees in the eyes of the congregation as he speaks, tears of concern and conviction, which reveal that some are listening to what he is saying after all. Little things like genuine affection in a child's voice as he greets his pastor. Little things like the Bible in the hand of the star athlete, or the genuine expression of appreciation for a message as the worshipper leaves church. Little things like the faithful people who have been present for all the services of the church for years upon years, and who will be present as long as there is breath in the body and alertness in the mind.

Little things like the concern of a parent for the spiritual growth of the child in the home. Little things like the forgiving spirit, the widow's mite, the willingness to serve in any possible way, the faithful completion of the task accepted, or any little evidence of spiritual maturity and growth. Little things like the young people who, with tremendous potential, come forward to say, "I do not know what God would have me to do, but, whatever it is, I'm ready,"

Little things like a child's prayer, a warm handclasp, a friendly smile, a rosebud for the pastor's lapel every Sunday morning. Just little things—like the child who comes forward before all the congregation to publicly profess faith in the Lord Jesus—little things like these that have eternal significance.

Just little things, like the college young people who sing in a volunteer choir, and during their busy schedule, take time to practice to bless us in our services. Little things, like a dedicated, trained church staff working together as a team to the glory of the Lord. Little things that make you feel all over again the nail-scarred hand resting on your head commissioning you to service in His Kingdom.

Little things that make it all worthwhile—like a letter from a missionary couple who say, "Thank you again for what you and your church have done for our lives. We're here because you're there." Little things_____

The Rhythm of the Church

Like all else in God's creation there is a rhythm in the church. Bonhoeffer brings it to light when he speaks of the church gathering together and then scattering abroad. He speaks of the priceless privilege granted the Christian community in gathering together. He scarcely realized how precious the gathering together was until the concentration camp experience denied him the privilege.

However, he realized, too, that often the church uses the gathering together as an end within itself and fails to catch the real rhythm of the church. Theodore O. Wedel, in his book entitled *The Gospel in a Strange New World*, reminds us that we as Christians were first called to be disciples or learners, and we are then called to be apostles, messengers, or sent ones. Christ invites us to "come and see" and then to "go and tell!" This is the rhythm of the church.

We gather together to find strength in the fellowship of the redeemed. We praise and pray and seek to understand His holy purposes. We teach and train and prepare. We give and undergird our planning with our material support. But this is not the gospel; it is only a portion of it. This is not what Christ came and died to establish—a group of people gathering together and then going out forgetting who and what they are. What happens to the church when the church building is locked up on Sunday night? Does the church go out of business for the week? Is this all there is?

We must realize that if we are the church of the Lord Jesus Christ on Sunday, we are still the church on Monday. What then happens to the church on Monday? It is scattered abroad into the offices, stores, schools, and campuses. It is in the board meetings of the business executives. It is in the classroom, the dormitory, the playground, and golf course. It hits the road with the salesman and finds itself in neighboring cities still in business for the Lord. We are the church, and we need to realize it! On Monday we scatter into the suburban areas and the inner city. Wherever Christians go there is the church. Every Christian is a minister of the church, and they go into areas their pastor cannot possibly go. Christians need to realize this and truly be about their Father's business.

This is the rhythm of the church. Some would have only the gathering; some would prefer only the scattering. Both are a necessary and integral part of the whole. We need the strength that only the gathering can give. We need the scattering to accomplish His purpose.

A coastal rescue unit once became famous for its rescuing operations, saving people who were shipwrecked. The people were so appreciative they built them a building to help in their work. The building became the center of their activity and they became so important that they soon hired others to do the rescuing and forgot who and what they really were. It must not be so. The church gathers and scatters. It must or it is not the true church.

Supposing Him to Be in the Crowd

The story of Jesus confounding the leaders in the Temple when He was but twelve years of age is ever familiar. There is one phrase, however, that the Biblical account contains, which is often overlooked. Luke says: "And when they had fulfilled the days, as they returned, the child Jesus tarried behind in Jerusalem; and His mother knew not of it. But they, supposing Him to have been in the company, went a day's journey."

How often do we, of His spiritual family, the church, fall into this same error. We make our plans, promote our programs, project our goals, always supposing Him to be in our midst.

Often we wonder why our so carefully laid plans do not work out as we think they should. We wonder why the revival, so fully planned and publicized, never really revived anyone. We are distressed because that building was never built, or the budget was never pledged, or the goal was never reached. Could it not well be that we have made so many plans "supposing Him to be in our midst"?

How often worship services are ineffectual because the people have come unprepared for worship; the choir has come to sing, but not to worship; the organist and music director have come to lead, but not to worship; and even the pastor has entered to preach, but not to worship.

Christmas Evans, the great preacher, was once late entering the pulpit for the worship hour. A deacon went back to tell him the service had started. The door of the study was ajar. The deacon heard the pastor speaking and realized that he was praying. The pastor was saying: "Lord, I've gone into the pulpit the last time without you. If you do not go with me, I'll not go!"

Let us not be guilty of "supposing He is in our midst." Let us invite Him in, and let us pray, expecting His presence in response to our heartfelt prayers.

Submission

Through the years, God's people have been very stubborn. God has been very patient.

To Adam and Eve He said: "All is yours except this." But they said, "We want this too!" To Lot God said: "Don't look back." Lot's wife said, "No, I want to see what's happening." To the chosen people God said: "Thou shalt have no other gods." But God's people shouted, "No!" and brought earrings and precious metals and made a calf. To Jonah God said: "Go to Nineveh, that great city," But Jonah said, "No!" and headed for Joppa. To the Jewish people God said: "This is my beloved Son in whom I am well pleased." But they shouted, "Crucify, crucify!" Jesus said: "No man can serve two masters." But God's people said, "Yes, we can. We love you, Lord, but we love the world, too." The Bible says: "The earth is the Lord's and the fullness thereof." God's people say, "No, this is mine!"

We have been very selective. We have selected what we want to believe and have ignored, or tried to explain away, that which we do not want to accept. We accept the grace

He gives, the salvation He offers, the escape from damnation that is assured, and the glories of heaven that are promised. But, we have refused to let Him be Lord of all our lives.

As a result of this, the world dies in sin, the church struggles along, the Christian life is not joyous, and the presence of the Holy Spirit is often far removed.

When will we learn the answer to all of life's problems, to all the church's problems, and that the road to the happiness we desire is found in complete submission to Jesus Christ our Lord. "If any man will come after me, let him deny himself and take up his cross and follow me."

Revival—Do We Really Want It?

Many of us, indeed most of us as Christians, faced with the godlessness and immorality that is prevalent today, have been praying for revival. If we are honest, we will admit that we have at times doubted if it would come—if even God Himself could stop the floodtide of indifference and evil. Our efforts have seemed to be so futile and ineffective. Our prayers have seemed to go unanswered or, if answered, the answer was, "Not now!"

I am convinced, however, that our prayers are being answered and the answer is a resounding "Yes!" God hears and answers our prayers if they are within the framework of His will, and it is truly His will that "none should perish!" If you are desirous of revival, how much more does the Holy Creator, God of the Universe, desire it?

And it is coming. It may very well be upon us. You say, "I don't know what you're speaking about. I don't see any evidence of revival." But it is much nearer than you know! The problem is that it is taking a different form that we expected. In a national magazine there was a lengthy article about the young people today who are turning from drugs to Jesus the Christ.

These young people have cut loose from all of the things that have formerly held meaning for them. In their searching and despair they have sought escape in drugs. Now they are realizing how futile and tragic this is and are seeking help. And help is available. It is coming from Spirit-filled Christian young people, many of whom have found that faith in Jesus the Christ is the best way to kick the drug habit, and that they can really be "turned on" by a real heartfelt expression of salvation and of new life in Christ. They unashamedly are calling themselves Christians. Rather than the peace symbol of the hippy, they are giving the lifted index finger sign that points to one Saviour for all.

Your reaction may be negative at first: "This isn't what I've been praying for. This isn't apparently within the framework of the established church." But before you cast it aside, remember two things: God works in mysterious ways; His ways are not our ways. Remember, also, that the revival Jesus brought was not what the people of His day were expecting either.

When we pray, we must say—and mean it—"Thy will be done!" and then rejoice and praise His name for every manifestation of His loving grace.

The Atmosphere of a Church

Have you ever visited a strange city and felt the atmosphere of the place? There is a certain distinctive air that is present. Great art galleries have an air about them as do many other such places. Driving into a parking lot by a great football stadium, your heart quickens and you begin to feel a lift as you anticipate the thrill of thousands of people enjoying a great sports event. The air of excitement and anticipation is present.

The church building has an atmosphere about it also, but the distinctive atmosphere of a church radiates from the people who make up that church family. Those who enter as visitors soon catch the spirit of the regular worshippers there. Since this is so, what should the atmosphere of our church be?

First, it should radiate, by the relaxed peace and harmony of the congregation, the warmth of their fellowship. The way a visitor is greeted and made to feel at home indicates that the fellowship is Christian.

The atmosphere of a church should also reveal a spirit of anticipation. "We are in this sacred place to bring our empty lives into fellowship with our God; because of this anything can happen. I should leave this service heartened, or forgiven, or strengthened, or encouraged, or lifted, or redeemed if that is my deepest need." This is the kind of spirit that should be present in every worship experience.

A spirit of reverence should also be evident. "The Lord is in His Holy Temple; let all the earth keep silent before Him." Without this spirit, worship would be mockery.

Needless to say, this kind of an atmosphere will be contagious. The most casual visitor will feel the warmth of the fellowship, the spirit of anticipation, and the reverent awe that is manifested and will want to share in this experience and become part of such a congregation.

Let one other suggestion be made. The atmosphere of a

church is nothing more than the spirit of the individuals who make up that church family. If, then, each of us as individuals enters with the spirit that has been suggested, then our church will be fulfilling its true destiny under God.

Unity of the Faith

Much is being said today about uniting as many churches as possible into one church. The ecumenical movement has been going on for years directing its attention toward a better working together of the different denominational groups and a resulting unity of some of them. Some congregations of different historical and doctrinal backgrounds have already united; others are still trying to work out the details. In Kansas City, Missouri, three or four churches of one area, all of different denominations, each unable to afford a new church building, have gone together and have built a church plant with one of the pastors named as senior pastor and the other pastors as co-ministers. The interesting and confusing thing is that each of these groups will retain its own identity and denominational beliefs, but they will be called one church and will have the same building. One New York Protestant Church lists in its bulletin each Sunday the five different denominational groups it cooperates with and helps to support with its gifts. The form of baptism the candidate desires will be administered by one of the several pastors.

To those of us raised in a strict denominational environment, where the lines are drawn quite clearly, this seems strange. But before we become too critical, let us realize that the differences are not God's differences. The Church of the Lord Jesus Christ is not divided. In Harsanyi's book entitled *The Star Gazer* Galileo says to John Melton, "Real faith never divides men. Divisions are created by men themselves; they speak of dogmas—and then at once talk of heretics. They watch each other, instead of watching God."

The old joke tells of the pastors of churches of different faiths debating about what church the Lord Jesus would join if He returned to earth at this time. Each expressed his belief that He would unite with his group. The Baptist pastor waited until all had spoken and then said, "Gentlemen, I don't believe He'd be interested in making any change at this time."

The truth of the matter is that when Jesus does come He will not join any group. He will come and gather up all the groups, those who are truly His, and He will, with them, have his truly redeemed church. The only unity we have is in Him; man being the way he is, there is little chance nor any real purpose served in uniting all into one group.

If we are not His in the first place, the rest is of little importance anyway.

Left With No Choice

Things are not as they should be in many realms; in one particular realm they are most certainly not. A study of the early church finds a spirit of urgency and fervor that is lacking today. These early Christians, surrounded by the world that opposed them at every hand, were not daunted. Often outsiders thought they were beside themselves. Paul was reported to be out of his mind by some of the Corinthians. Most of the time it is a waste to try to explain your motives. Someone has said: "Never explain; your friends do not need it and your enemies will not believe it anyway." But motives not for his own popularity but for the sake of the message. The minister and his message are so entwined that if there is doubt as to the minister's motive, then his message is not heeded. So Paul says, as translated in the New English Bible, "It may be we are beside ourselves, but it is for God, if we are in our right mind, it is for you. For the love of God leaves us no choice—from first to last this has been the work of God. He has reconciled us men to himself through Christ, and he has enlisted us in this service of reconciliation—we come therefore as Christ's ambassadors. It is as if God were appealing to you through us, in Christ's name, we implore you, be reconciled to God."

Here is our motive. It is clear. We have no choice. His love leaves us no choice. If we are His, then we are to be busy living and testifying with life and lips that He is our Saviour and Lord and that He died for all men everywhere. But where is the fervor of Paul and of the early church today? How long has it been since you were, as a Christian, accused of being out of your mind?

Years ago Kipling was on board a ship going to Europe. Boarding the same ship was General Booth, of the Salvation Army. A large group of his people were on hand with their tamborines to see him off. Kipling later told the general how he disapproved of all this clamor. General Booth said, "Young man, if I thought I could win one more soul for Christ by standing on my head and beating a tamborine with my feet, I'd learn to do it."

The love of Christ leaves us no choice!

Is There a Steeple on Your House?

A few years ago a local church publicized its spring revival by asking each member to place in the front yard an announcement about the revival. The signs looked exactly like real estate signs announcing that the house was for sale. Suddenly on one day, a weekend prior to the revival, four hundred or so houses "went up for sale," or so it seemed. The signs read, "Attend Our Revival" and then told of the place and time of the services.

The interesting thing about this kind of advertising was an unanticipated plus. As a person would drive through the communities of the town, the homes of those members of the church were revealed by the signs. In one block there would be signs in each yard, but a few blocks away there might be several blocks with only a few signs.

The thought came through clearly. What if there could be such an indication in front of every Christian's home? In this very un-Christian land of ours wouldn't it be exciting if you could drive down the street and know if the people in those houses were professing Christians? What if an unbeliever in real personal crises could know that the second house from the corner houses a Christian family who would be able and willing to help in time of need?

Paul in the verse in Philemon salutes the church in your house. It's a beautiful thought.

As a member of the Christian family, each of us is the church. When we are attending services at the church building, we are the gathered church. When we leave to go about our business, we are still the church—the scattered church. When we are at home, we are in every sense the church. Let the church then be the church.

In the Christian home the attributes of the church should be present. There should be the same atmosphere of worship—respect for one another, reverence for parents and children alike, where it is perfectly normal and easy to stop and pray together. There should be the same obedience to Christ in the home as is in the church. Who is Lord at your house? If it isn't the Lord Himself, then the family needs to re-examine its profession. The same fellowship of love should be present in the home and in the church. "By this shall all men know you are my disciples in that you have love one for another," said Jesus. The same sense of mission should be evident in the home as is evident in the church. One unbelieving neighbor said to his Christian friend who had just moved next door: "Now, don't work for my salvation. Show me yours. Let me see that the Christian life is possible, and that it works, and I'll talk to you about it!"

Is there a steeple on your house? Oh, I'm not suggesting that we literally build steeples for our homes, but the idea is sound and good. There should be some indication to the most casual observer that those who live in this house profess to be Christian. Perhaps a beautiful metal fish on the door would be sufficient.

But remember—when you put up an outward advertisement, the product must measure up to it. So the question of the steeple on your house isn't properly put. The real question must be, is Christ really present in your home?

Faith

You Must Believe

There are some things you don't have to make up your mind about; some things can wait. What you believe about the real meaning of God and the ultimate realities of life, however, cannot be delayed. You believe something about these things, and your life will reveal your beliefs. As you drive down a freeway you may be trying to decide whether you will turn off at the next exit or the one following, but while you are deciding, you are speeding down the road at fifty miles an hour. At that speed you cannot delay your decision very long.

Sometimes we would like to hide behind a little convenient agnosticism and say we just do not know—and there are some details we do not know—but what we really believe about the realities of life and its ultimate meaning are being revealed in our lives. One great preacher called them, "life's forced decisions!"

What do you believe about God? Belief in God is not so much faith as fact. There is a creative power behind this universe that started it, sustains it, and orders it. We know some things about this created world: it is law-abiding; it is predictable; it builds mountains and daisies, men, mentalities, and personalities; it produces mothers, sunsets, and a man named Jesus. These things are fact!

You may believe it is all merely physical, that atoms and

electrons by mere chance brought something out of nothing and order out of chaos. Or you may believe that this creative power is God who made the heavens and earth and sent His son Jesus to reveal what He is really like. But you can't remain neutral. You are living life one way or the other. Your concept of love, work, respect for human life, right or wrong, suffering and death are shaped by what you believe. Philosophically you may doubt God, but psychologically you have a god and what you believe is revealed by your life.

You may be one of those whose life is better than your creed. You live better than you profess. Your life reveals a deeper understanding of ultimate realities than you are ready to admit. If this is your condition, you should examine your honesty and enlarge your creed.

On the other hand, your creed may be better than your life. You may profess to believe noble things and to have a personal relationship with God revealed in Christ, but your life does not truly reflect your creedal stance. If this is your condition, you should examine your life and its commitment to see where you have failed.

You do believe something, and what that something is will become more evident the longer you live.

The Unnecessary Burden of Complexity

We seem to work very hard at making things different and complex. Dr. E. Stanley Jones says, "If there is any one thing that we need to grasp it is this: The Christian way is the way of simplicity."

We are to turn from evil to Christ and His goodness. Evil

is by nature complex and devious. Lies are complex and tangled. If you lie, you have to remember everything you say, and you have to tell other lies to protect yourself for telling the first one. Truth is simple and straightforward. Tell the truth and you need nothing to prop it up. Often people prop up every statement by assuring others they speak truth, usually by adding an oath to the statement to make it really strong. The man who speaks truth does not need extra words, nor does he need to resort to swearing. The truth stands on its own merit.

The Christian life is also the life of simplicity. It is based on one simple decision: accepting Christ as Saviour and Lord of life. If this decision is made, then all of life falls in to support it. "Seek ye first the kingdom of God and His righteousness," and all other things will take their proper place. This decision is the engine of the train of life. God's will is the track on which it runs. Life like this is beautifully simple and secure. Jesus lived by one simple rule: "I do always those things that please Him." How beautiful! What else does a person need than that for motive and goal?

The simple life like this, however, is not understood. It stands as a threat to devious and complicated men. They will attack it and will probably crucify it. Men have a tendency to destroy what they cannot emulate or understand. But even under attack the Christian life is simple. Jesus before his accusors answered not at all. Then finally they said, "Are you the Christ?" He replied, "Even so." Then the Roman governor said, "Are you the King of the Jews?" He replied, "Thou has said!" The beauty of the Christian life is that the life itself is its own defense. You do not have to defend yourself. Live it and time will validate it! And if evil men crucify you, you know you will live again. It's as simple as that.

A prominent writer tells of visiting a village where a

missionary named Murray had been laboring for years. The visitor asked one of the people in the village, "What is it to be a Christian?" The reply came very simply: "To live like Mr. Murray!"

Give me the simple life!

Reaching For God With Our Fingers Crossed

The god most people worship may really be dead. Some seem to think so. If he is dead though, he is the god that man has made in his own image. Such a god would be inadequate anyway, and the idea of an inadequate god is contradictory. What is the problem revealed in all of this discussion about God anyway? Isn't it that our humanism is catching up with us? We seem to think that man must be able to understand everything he remakes into something he can explain, or he dismisses it with some intellectual gymnastics. This is not new. The only new problem today is that some of these gymnastics are being done by those who should know better.

Any thinking person has doubts. Doubts give bones to faith. Facing them honestly and seeking answers is as God would have us do. The man in the Scriptures who brought his son to Jesus cried, "Lord, I believe, help thou mine unbelief!" This earnest seeker admitted his doubts, and his searching was rewarded. The honest doubter will find God far more eager to reveal Himself to man than man is to know Him. Doubts, like the seventh chord in a major scale, are made to be resolved. The seventh note pulls toward the tonic demanding to be completed. In this same way, honest doubt pulls the seeker toward truth.

Our problem seems to be one of holding back; a fear of

what we might find. The prevalent attitude seems to be one of entering into all of life's experiences and relationships on a wait-and-see basis—a finger crossed concept. The child will wait with fingers crossed, hoping that what he wants will come true. Half-heartedly many attend school, fearful that they won't make it—and they don't. Many even enter marriage with this finger-crossed attitude. No wonder one of three marriages ends disastrously.

Why should the realm of religion be different? If a person seeks truth with his fingers crossed, he is not really seeking at all. Such a half-committed life can expect no real assurance.

The reality of God, like every other experience in life, is an individual matter anyway. God may be dead to some, for they have closed themselves up so that even His grace and love cannot reach them; but it must ever be an individual matter. If a vote were taken and men voted that God was indeed dead—if all the Bibles were confiscated and the churches closed—somewhere a man named Abraham would uncross his fingers and reach out a hand of faith and find that hand firmly grasped by the unmistakable hand of the Living God.

Live in Your House of Faith

At the heart of our Christian profession is the fact that as Christians we have accepted a point of view, an ordering of life, an interpretation of the meaning of life, a conviction of how life is to be lived and of its true destiny. This ordering and understanding of life, which we have accepted, is distinctively different from the outlook of the non-Christian. As Christians we have assumed definite obligations. We have accepted a way of life lived by another and provided for us by His atoning death. We have been transformed by His presence and enabled by His indwelling Spirit. He has made us different. If He hasn't, why bother with it?

What is our problem then? It seems to be one very simple truth. We have difficulty living in the house our faith has accepted. We seem determined to live for today only, not to act like transformed people, but to be as unloving as those who do not know our Christ. What I am saying is simply this: "If we are Christians, let us live in our house of faith, happily and in full accord!"

We say proudly we believe in the Bible. "Yes sir, every jot and title!" But many who shout the loudest perform the least! The Bible says: "Thou shall have no other gods before me." "The Sabbath is holy." "Love thy neighbor as thyself." "Seek first the Kingdom." "Bring you all the tithes!" Live in your house of faith!

We say we believe people are lost, but how many have you visited and witnessed to this week? Live in your house of faith! We say we believe in the church. Happily we sing, "I love thy church, O God." But the church must often take the leftover energy, time, and thought from civic and social organizations, if it gets any of our time and thought at all. We are proud that the pulpit is the center of our worship, but what happens? The pastor preaches his heart out, and many are not there to listen and many who are present do not hear. He who is commissioned of God to proclaim a message that will transform lives usually gets to proclaim it only to those who have heard the old story so often. Live in your house of faith! If you say you love the church, then give it first place. Let others know of your love and concern by your actions and service. Great churches are built by great people. Great preaching is caused by great listeners. To serve in God's house is a privilege. To teach a Sunday school class is a privilege beyond measure. To usher in God's house should be counted as a high honor. To participate in a worldwide program for God is the privilege of every Christian. Live in your house of faith!

The problem too often is that many are living in a house of their own making or are trying to live in someone else's house of faith. These houses are built on the sand and will not withstand the storms of life.

Are you a Christian? If you are, then live in your house of faith. It is built upon the Rock of Ages and will not fail. Christian living really works. Try it!

The Singing Teakettle

Much around us is disturbing. The news is filled daily with rapes, beatings, and killings. Our policemen daily risk their lives in the streets of our cities. It is most distressing.

The tendency of many of us is to let this kind of news color all of our thinking. We see our own problems and the problems that are immediately around us. We add to these the unrest of all the world and find ourselves disturbed and depressed. Some are more prone to do this than others, but even the most optimistic of us tend to see only the shadows and valleys.

Is there anything that we can do to keep our spirits bright? Can we learn the lesson of the singing teakettle that "sings even when it is up to its neck in hot water?"

Certainly I am not advocating a blind whistling in the

dark, but rather a realistic renewal of faith. We can look with eyes of faith at all around us. Has everything fallen apart? Of course not! There are relatively few people involved in the instances that make the headlines, and they are disturbed by unhealthy social conditions and are often excited by professional agitators. Read the rest of your morning paper. Babies are being born into Christian homes, fine young people are standing before God in Christian marriage, many young people are investing their summer in missionary activities, and churches are proclaiming God's love, mercy, and grace. Look around! The sun is still shining, the flowers are still blooming, friends are still concerned, and love is still love. In short, God is still on His throne!

In the midst of adverse circumstances, the Psalmist said, "Why art thou cast down, O my soul, and why art thou disquieted within me? Hope thou in God!" The man of faith believes in God regardless of outward circumstances. He believes in the right, in his fellow men, and in himself. He lives to serve others and continues to believe that the same righteous forces that have prevailed in the past will win today. He is keenly aware of the need around him and daily strives to lift another's burden, but he refuses to let his faith wane or his eyes be distracted from his vision of God.

Our nation has survived and has become a great nation because of this optimism and faith, and this same spirit will continue to make it so.

Slightly Out of Focus

Many a photograph has been ruined because the camera

was not properly adjusted. The picture is blurred and not clearly defined, because the camera lens and the subject were not properly related one to the other. This is a picture of much of life. Many an employer and employee do not properly relate one to the other, because they are slightly out of focus with each other. Many homes have this difficulty. Far too many parents and their teenagers have a relationship that is blurred and fuzzy, because they are slightly out of focus.

On the college campus of today there is occasionally held a week of religious emphasis. Often it is called a Focus Week. It means that as human beings we are not properly related to our heavenly Father. Our relationship to Him may be completely out of focus, or perhaps just slightly out of focus.

Another analogy is the magnifying lens and the rays of the sun. Every young man has experimented at times and found that a magnifying glass, held properly exposed to the sun, can focus the rays of the sun on a newspaper, and the paper will catch fire and burn. But, if the lens and sun are not properly related to each other, the rays are powerless.

The inherent tendency with all mankind is to get life out of focus with the God who made us. Call it what you will, it still exists. We have a prodigal's nature within us, and we seek any far-off land where we can have a try at being our own gods. To the prodigals, life is out of focus. There are among us also, however, some lives that appear to be only slightly out of focus—not prodigals, but elder brothers. These lives are not lived in a far-off land, but they are as powerless as the rays of the sun when the magnifying glass is not properly related to the sun.

Let this remind us that all of life is designed around sun centers. Each galaxy has its sun center. Each family has its sun center, and each life must have its sun center. If the sun around which your life revolves is the Son of the Living God, then your life will be a power-filled, light-giving, ennobling influence for righteousness. But the secret is in the focus, in the relationship of your life to the Son, who is the only center of real living.

Graduates

Bring Out the Best Within You

Two things are often overlooked as we see the world situation around us. One of these is that there is no such thing as a social wrong, but rather individuals within a society who are wrong. The society takes on the mood or character of those who make it up, but it is still in reality an individual matter. Any solutions that come must come through the repentance and redemption of individuals within the group. There can be no group repentance except as individuals within the group repent. The second truth is this: that any change that occurs in us as individuals must come from within us. Repentance is not a gift-wrapped package that God places on the altar for us to pick up at our earliest convenience. Whatever the qualities of character we desire, they must be mined from the inherent gold within us. Let us, then, bring out the best within us.

How can it be done? Let me suggest six things which will help us do this:

1. *Decide for Christ.* Paul says that God has given us the knowledge of His glory in the face of Jesus Christ. He came as God Incarnate to show us how to live, and to die for us that we might live as He would have us live.

114

2. *Determine priorities.* What are you going to give yourself to? Things temporal that will vanish away or
things eternal that will never die? You must decide.
Jesus drastically reminded us of the necessity of this
choice when He told of the rich man whose barns fell
on him: "Thou fool, this night thy soul is required of
thee." Too many of us have lives like a doll, stuffed
with sawdust. Recently a painting was sold for
sixty-thousand dollars. It was a painting of a can of
Campbell's Tomato Soup! Sometimes you will have
to decide what is best from among all that is good, for
there are many good things clamoring for our time
and attention. Life is like a bus. You can only put so
many on board. If you fill the bus and the Lord
Himself stands on the next corner, you can't stop to
let Him on for you are already filled! If you read this
book, you can't read that one. If you listen to this
music, you can't listen to that. Determine priorities.
3. *Dedicate all to Him.* All of us have talents, some one,
some ten. All came from Him. Dedicate them to His
service and glory. He has given us time also. This too
must be dedicated to Him. Take time for meditation.
Like an iceberg, life is ninety percent unseen. Too
many people live in the past; many others say,
"Someday I'll do this and so!" "Carpe Diem" says the
Latin—"Seize the day." It's all you have.
4. *Discipline desires.* This is what Jesus meant when He
said, "Deny yourself." He meant that we must make a
choice. Here are those priorities again. You can't
serve God and mammon. The artist said, "Art begins
where freedom ends." It is so. Only as the artist
dedicates himself to his work and disciplines himself
to his creating can he build the masterpiece.

5. *Dodge detours.* There are no shortcuts, no get-rich-quick schemes. There are no "ten easy lessons for happiness" or success, either.

6. *Desire to please only Him.* The secret of Jesus's life is spelled out very clearly on one statement recorded by John. Jesus said, "I do always the things that please Him!" We won't be able to do that, but we can try!

God has placed us here for a reason. Each of us has much more within us than we realize. Find out why He put you here! Bring out the best, the gold, that is within you.

The Formula for Tomorrow's Miracles

A miracle is "an event or effect in the physical world deviating from the known laws of nature, or transcending our knowledge of these laws." It happens, but is something we cannot explain with our meager knowledge. We live in an age filled with yesterday's miracles. Much that we accept today was unknown or even unthought of fifty years ago. We use, daily, things that would have been called miraculous by our grandparents. What made these past miracles possible will make the miracles of tomorrow possible.

Never think for a moment that all of the miracles have already occurred. The realities of today were the visions and dreams of yesterday. Dream your dreams without fear and hesitation. You will see greater advancements in every realm than any generation in history. Let not yourself say: "There is nothing left for me to do!" Listen! All of the textbooks haven't yet been written. All of the sonatas and concertos have not been composed. All of the poems have not been written. All of the mathematical problems have not been solved. There are still plenty of x's in the realm of science that are unknown. All of the orations have not been delivered. All of the sermons have not been preached. All of the advancements in commerce and industry have not been made. All of the problems of social relationships have not been solved.

Dream on, look ahead, see your visions, and hold them to your heart. One little girl was awakened by her father early in the morning so the family could get an early start on a vacation trip. The girl looked up, saw her daddy, and said: "Oh, daddy, you made me lose my place in my dream!" Don't ever let it happen, young people! Don't lose your place in your dreams. Miracles are all around us. They are the visions and dreams of men and women with courage and dedication and purpose in life.

Let me give you a formula then to help turn these visions, these miracles into realities. Here it is: YM + V + PT + GW equals TM. Your Mind, plus Visions, plus Proper Training, plus God's Will, equals Tomorrow's Miracles. With Robert Service we say:

> Carry On! Carry On!
> Fight the good fight and true;
> Believe in your mission, greet life with a cheer
> There's big work to do, and that's why you're
>   here.

> Carry On! Carry On!
> Let the world be better for you;
> And at last when you die,
> Let this be your cry;
> Carry on, My Lord! Carry On!

A Student's Prayer

Oh, Lord of all life,
   even this life of mine,
   grant me foresight to know where I'm going
   grant me insight to know where I am
   grant me faith to know who Thou art
   grant me wisdom to know who I am

      teach me patience so I may learn
      teach me courage so I may grow
      teach me humility so I may serve
      teach me Thy love so I may love

        help me bear this day
          the cross that I must bear,
        help me walk reverently
          on my daily pilgrimage,
        help me seek diligently
          to know Thy will for me,
        help me die this day
          so you might live in me.

Oh, Lord,
   my prayer is not for a lighter load
      but for a stronger back
         to live each day, this day, for Thee.
Amen.

                        By Russell M. McIntire, Jr.

More Mountains to Climb

Recently a young friend who had graduated from college three or four years ago was speaking with me. He was in a reflective mood. "The thing that troubles me is that I have graduated from college and have taught school a couple of years, but I don't know anything. I'm not an educated person." His problem is a common one, but he is far better off than he knows. Few are as candid as he. Few will admit their lack of knowledge. On the other hand, he is far more educated than he knows.

The essence of education is not the compilation of a large number of facts carefully catalogued in one's mind so that they are readily available. That is the realm of the encyclopedia or the computer. An educated man is the one who is acquainted with great ideas and who sees the ideas and principles working in his own life and in the lives of those around him. One of the greatest lessons he has learned is how little he really knows. He has, however, also learned what he needs to know and where to go to find it.

In his book, *The Years of Our Lord*, Charles Crowe tells of a young doctor who talked with John Dewey just prior to the great philosopher's ninetieth birthday. The skeptical young medico blurted out his low opinion of philosophy. "What's the use of such clap-trap?" he asked. "Where does it get you?" To which Mr. Dewey replied: "The good of it is that you climb mountains." The young doctor was unimpressed. "Climb mountains! And what is the use of that?" Mr. Dewey answered, "You see other mountains to climb. You come down, climb the next mountain, and see still others to climb. When you are no longer interested in climbing mountains to see other mountains to climb, life is over."

A Challenge to Graduates

Graduation speakers everywhere will be reminding you that you must profit from the past, serve in the present, and anticipate and provide for the future. Nothing can be done about the past; it is gone. Today is to be lived to the very fullest, but what should effect our living today most dramatically is the challenge of tomorrow!

What was it that opened the eyes of a man tending his flocks on the plains of Midian centuries ago? He saw a bush that burned but was not consumed and heard a voice, the voice of God, speaking from out of the bush. God spoke, and Moses listened. He was told that he had been selected as the earthly leader who with God's help would lead his people out of bondage. What really stirred the heart of Moses? The voice of God? Surely. The promise of God to be with him? Most surely. But the vision God gave him of a great tomorrow must have been the greatest challenge. A land of promise, a goodly land where the people would live at peace with God and man. Surely this must have sustained Moses through all of the experiences of his life. When standing before Pharoah, when at the Red Sea, when the people murmured, the vision of tomorrow must have been the constant dream in the heart of Moses.

This challenge has lifted many a heart and life. Paul's vision of a world where pagan gods and formal meaningless religions were replaced by the King of Kings reigning in the hearts of all mankind moved him forward against all opposition. The challenge of a world lighted by brilliant electric lights pushed Edison onward. The vision of travel by air, swiftly across the face of the earth, challenged the Wright brothers day by day.

Look at Moses and the challenge of tomorrow. What did it do for him? It made him realize that the present would soon pass, and it made him dissatisfied with the way things were. Every great movement in history has been made because someone was dissatisfied with the status quo. The challenge of the future made him realize that there was no time to delay. It made him aware that there would be obstacles in the way and opposition to the cause, and that the challenge would require personal sacrifice.

It was apparent to Moses that he was inadequate to face alone the challenges that were ahead, so he was made to realize they must be met by faith in God and by daily prayer. His assurance, however, was that if he followed God's leadership the challenge of tomorrow would be met and he would be victorious. "If God be for us who can be against us?"

A world is at your feet, my young friends, whether you graduate from high school or college. This year, the future is in your hands. You can lean back on whatever your small victories have been and try to go through life coasting, or you can, with humble faith, realize that perhaps "Thou art come into the Kingdom for such a time as this." The challenge of tomorrow is before you—a world with opportunities unthought of a few years ago, a world in need of leadership, a world of people hungry and searching, but not knowing for what they hunger and search. You as Christian young people have the answer. His name is Christ. Lift Him up before the world, and they will be drawn to Him: "Say unto the cities of Judah, Behold your God!" "And I, if I be lifted up from the earth will draw all men unto me!"

A Word to Graduates: Enjoy Yourself–Wisely

It is so easy for an older person to tell today's youth what he would do if he were young again. We do not know what we would do. My personal conviction is, however, that youth is the time for enjoying life. Everything is new; every day is so unused. Wide-eyed, uncynical, uncomplicated young people are joys to behold. They are like blotters that soak up all they experience, but like used blotters they often have the words reversed and the values wrong.

Too many young people today think that their problems will be solved when they are out on their own and making their own way. Success is measured by owning a car and having a big wedding. Most young people realize the value of a good education, but it is measured in an enlarged earning power rather than in acquiring wisdom.

Wisdom is the right use of knowledge. Simply to know is not wisdom. There are many educated fools, and no fool is as great as a learned one. To have knowledge and know how to use it is true wisdom, and true wisdom and spiritual enlightenment go hand in hand. You may not believe it, but in your faith in God you will find the two things for which all mankind searches—wisdom and pleasure. And, whether you believe it or not, the quickest way to both of these is through a vital religious experience. The greatest man who ever lived, the Incarnate Christ, gave us the formula for happiness: "Seek ye first the Kingdom of God and His righteousness and all these things shall be added unto you." Here is faith, wisdom, and happiness.

When you start to draw a circle, you do not start at a point on the circumference and draw a line back around to that point. You first establish the center, and from that center you draw the circumference. So in life. True wisdom is to know where that center is. True pleasure is to live life around that center, knowing that with that stake driven down, you are then free to do what you like and will like what you do, for the center is God.

Enjoy yourself—wisely!

Judging Others

The Deceitfulness of Outward Appearances

Perhaps our most common sin is that of judging someone by mere outward appearances. In our minds we create an image, and if we see someone who fits that image, we like him at once. But if for some reason he does not fit our pattern, there is immediate tension. How often have you heard it said: "I just don't like his looks!"

We know better than this! Pass by two young people walking down the sidewalk and from the back you can seldom, in this day and time, tell if they are two boys or two girls, or one of each. With so many "beauty-parlor miracles" around, you may not even recognize your wife when you come home from work.

In Will Durant's *The Story of Civilization* the author says of Xerxes I of Persia: "He was every inch a king—externally; tall and vigorous. He was by royal consent the handsomest man in his empire—but he was only great in his love for magnitude, not in his capacity to rise to meet crises or to be in fact or deed a king." Of the death of Xerxes Mr. Durant writes: "After twenty years of sexual intrigue and administrative indolence he was murdered by a courtier and was buried with regal pomp and general satisfaction!"

The Bible often warns us about judging anyone in any way at all, because we are so easily deceived by externals. Only God can look within, where the real man abides, and tell what manner of man he really is. Paul in defending himself against those who so misjudged him said: "Once convinced of this—that Christ died for all and rose again that men might no longer live for themselves but for Him—then I estimate no one by external apperances." Then Paul adds somewhat sadly, "I once even judged Christ by what was external."

How harsh and unfair we are! Quickly we judge one another by a moment's impression, and in our haste and blindness we are probably more often wrong than right. The frown may be from an inner burden and not indicate a surly spirit; that swagger may be covering for an inadequate spirit and a need for understanding; that short temper may be because of heavy burdens about to crush a strong spirit; the young man's beard or long hair may be a struggle for identity in a faceless world; and even some of the questionable things we hear that others have done were perhaps done with motives behind them that might explain and even justify them.

We are not in the judging business. How grateful we should be to be freed from such heavy responsibility. Paul said: "I do not even judge myself for although I am not aware of any wrong within me, that does not clear me—it is the Lord who judges me."

"Our Father . . ."

As the pastor of many students in the past dozen years, I have developed a habit that may be good or may be bad, but which is inevitable, I believe. Not knowing the parents of most of the students and knowing little or nothing of their home background, I have found myself judging the parents by the child. Sometimes this can be completely wrong and misleading, I am sure. Most of the time, however, it is an adequate measure, I believe. In either event, it always happens. Parents are judged by the children that come from their homes.

This means, then, to all of us as children, that we should strive to give the people the right impression of our parents and our home life. If that home life wasn't all that it should have been, there is still the obligation on our part to reveal the best of it.

In another realm this stands true, also. As Christians we have been enabled to become the "sons of God" because we have believed in the name of Jesus the Christ. As sons and daughters of our Heavenly Father, we must realize that just as human parents are judged by the actions of their children, so the Heavenly Father is judged by the actions of His children. In this light let us examine our lives and see what impression we are leaving with the unbeliever who is our neighbor. If he has shown little interest in accepting our faith, could it be that what he sees in your life and mine is not attractive and winsome? Is it possible that the Creator God of the Universe is being judged falsely and harshly because of our inconsistent lives as His "children"?

Think on these things the next time you bow your head to pray and say, "Our Father. . . ."

The Leaven of the Pharisee

The Hebrew sect called the Pharisees started out very

nobly. These were dedicated men who sought to live their faith in God. Somewhere down the way, however, they took a wrong turn and became self-righteous men instead of Godlike men. Their approach to godly living became a negative thing. Their virtue was in the many things they did not do that set them apart from lesser men who did these questionable things.

The result was that they believed it was their duty to pass moral judgment on all others. They sought to make men good by pointing out their sins, by criticizing them. This provided two kinds of satisfaction to the Pharisees: it helped the one criticized since it was done for his good, and it helped the Pharisee for he found satisfaction in being superior to the one he criticized.

This spirit is too frequently evident today in the Christian fellowship. Many within the fellowship of believers fall into this trap. These people have taken a negative road and have built themselves up by tearing down their Christian brothers. These feel called of God to pronounce judgment on others. Frequently they center their attention on one poor soul and voice their criticism openly and without even being honest enough to investigate and see if the person they criticize is in any way really guilty of any wrong deed. Needless to say these Pharisee Christians (if there can be such) are not happy people. They miss the real essence of the Christian faith. The center of our faith is a cross, not a judgment seat. A cross is where men are died for, not criticized. Jesus said, "Father forgive. . . ." He also said, "Judge not that ye be not judged!" He judged the world from the cross and in the process drew all men unto Himself, but He was Jesus the Christ. Only He could do both.

Our business as Christians is not as complex or difficult as some of us think. We are not saved to straighten everyone else out by picking the motes out of their eyes. Thank goodness that's not our responsibility. The Christian way is to "take the mote out of your own eye first," and then you will see your brother as someone to love, lift strengthen, and minister unto.

Dr. E. Stanley Jones was speaking in Malaya through a Chinese interpreter. He used the word Pharisee. The interpreter stopped him and said, "What sea was that?" Dr. Jones said, "The Dead Sea." Jesus said, "Beware of the leaven of the Pharisee."

Identity

My Cup Runneth Over

The psalmist sings of his cup running over. We agree that it is a beautiful psalm and a beautiful thought, but I wonder if we really believe it. Do you really feel that the cup of your life is running over? Deep down most of us are dissatisfied and feel that our cup is only half filled. We look at the fellow next to us, however, and conclude that he has everything going for him. His cup does indeed run over, it seems.

What is the problem? Isn't it that we have not decided what it takes to fill the cup? In our materialistic world and with our secular orientation, we have concluded that life's cup must be filled with the things of this world! Ask the average person what would make his life complete, and he will begin to list things—a new car, a bigger house, a boat and motor, and on and on! This is one of Satan's oldest traps. If he can get our eyes filled with this world's goods and our ears filled with the raucous voices of this temporal world, he has us where we are doomed to live ineffective lives. As long as we crave "things," we will think that our cup is only half filled. In reality it will be bottomless and can never be filled!

The psalmist has something completely different in mind. He is thinking of the strong Shepherd arms that lift him, the assurance of every need being met, the quietness

129

of green pastures and still waters, the refreshing renewal of strength, the confidence of a guide along the way, the comforting presence in sorrow and protection from evil! He sings of a table in the presence of enemies and of the healing oil upon his head. It is from all of this that he concludes that his cup is running over! His cup overflows, not with material blessings, but with the goodness and mercy of Almighty God.

If we have life, health, food, and lodging, our cup overflows! If we have been found of God and have been redeemed by His grace, no cup in the world can contain our blessings. In truth, as Christians, our cups are not cups at all but artesian wells!

The Path Through the Water

There are four occasions in the Scriptures where the waters miraculously part and a path appears in the sea for God's people to walk through. You quickly recall the children of Israel at the Red Sea, and if you are a student of the Bible at all you are familiar with the crossing of the Jordan by God's people into the promised land. The other instances, however, are not so well-known.

Elijah, God's prophet, is about to retire from his work and, indeed, from this earth. The Scripture doesn't make it clear how everyone knew this, but apparently the ones who were his followers knew. Elijah with Elisha, his assistant pastor, leaves Gilgal for the other side of the Jordan. He suggests that Elisha might wish to remain behind, but Elisha makes it very clear that he is staying close at hand. The young ministerial students in Elijah's seminaries meet them in Bethel and Jericho and they warn Elisha and try to get him to stay behind, but he continues with his teacher. Three times Elijah suggests that Elisha remain behind and three times he refuses. So they arrive at the shores of the Jordan River. There are no bridges; there are no boats at hand; there is no crossing place. Elijah takes his robe, rolls it up, and slaps the waters of the Jordan. The waters part. God's prophets walk across the dry river bottom between the waters piled up on each side.

Elijah turns to Elisha and asks him what he wants from him before he leaves. "Let me have the power that you have, doubled dipped" says Elisha. Elijah then promises that it will be his if he will watch and see what is to happen. You recall the story. The chariot and horses of fire come down out of the sky, Elijah is ushered on board, and the chariot disappears like a comet in the Judean skies. Elisha stands determined and courageous, seeing it all. When the smoke clears, at his feet is the robe of Elijah.

Here is the moment of decision. The robe of Elijah is symbolic of Elijah's office, his awful responsibility as God's prophet. To Elisha, it is a challenge, a new opportunity, a door to service, the entrance into new life; but also it stands for the awful responsibilities of the prophetic office.

My son asked me one night as we talked of this, "What alternatives did Elisha have?" Then he answered his own question: "Elisha could sit before the mantle of Elijah and think; he could weep; he could run in fear; he could delay; he could refuse to have anything to do with it; he could pick it up and carry it back to Jordan in his arms and find a way across the river and enshrine and worship it. Or, he could reach down a trembling hand of faith and pick it up and walk to the Jordan, roll the robe up, and slap the waters and shout, 'Where is the Lord God of Elijah?' and quietly walk through the waters on dry ground." And so Elisha did!

The challenge of this day is before you. The robes of multitudes of God's servants who have gone before are at your feet. The same alternatives are yours. But the waters part only for those who accept and walk by faith!

The Cure for Crossed Eyes

Sometimes a child is born with crossed eyes. The two delicate organs of sight are not aligned properly, so the vision is impaired by objects seen as overlapping one another. A trained physician, who specializes in this realm of medicine, will sever the muscles that turn the eye and will align the eye with the other and carefully sew the muscle back to the eye. Often the glasses that were formerly needed are needed no longer after such surgery.

Dr. Emil Brunner, the great European theologian, speaks of the fact that sin has made us cross-eyed. We look through eyes that do not focus properly. "The scandal of Christianity," he says, "exists as a scandal only so long as we are full of ourselves. To believe in the cross of Christ is no scandal for those who have seen how perverted is their own wisdom, the wisdom of natural man. The foolishness of the gospel is divine wisdom to all those who have been healed of the perversion that consists of making man's reason and goodness the judge of all truth; the perversion that places men, instead of God, in the center of the universe."

This is our problem. With the crossed eyes of sin, we have placed ourselves at the center and have made ourselves to be God. Our values, therefore, are perverted and our wills selfish. The only answer is the transforming power of God's grace. When we have consulted the Great Physician and have had the eyes of our hearts properly aligned with His, then we are able to see things as they truly are. And then, like the blind man healed by the Master, we shout, "All that I know is that once I was blind, but now I see!" This is the only thing that will make lost mankind see straight.

Whose Fault Is It Really?

A few years ago a little boy was sent to me who had driven his Sunday school teacher almost out of her mind by his antics. When I questioned him about why he acted like this, he said, "Well, I don't really know; you see the old devil gets in me and just does these things." It wasn't really his fault, he was saying, it was another something inside that did it and used his body. It is true to a certain extent. Satanic forces are in the world. The devil, whoever or whatever he be, does not have a body of his own; he must use ours. But the point is that he doesn't just use our bodies, but our minds and wills also. What we know to be true is that, in the final analysis, we must admit that we are the ones who act wrongly, and we are the ones who are really at fault.

Don't smugly laugh at the boy. We do the same thing. We excuse ourselves many ways. The Greeks blamed their wrong actions on the gods. Adam said, "The woman thou gavest me, she gave me of the tree and I did eat." The Moslem blames his "kismet," his fate. The Hindu or

Buddha says that his "karma" is bad, the results of the deeds of a previous life are catching up with him. A surprising number of people blame it on the stars. Some of us blame it on our subconscious minds, but we make the subconscious largely what it is. The most prevalent evasion is to blame it on the crowd or on the environment: "I did only what anyone else in my circumstance would do." "Everyone's doing it!" How often have you said these things?

All of these devices are evasions. We know this deep within us. Oh, to be sure, we are influenced by many of these outside forces. But still, we are responsible people and are then responsible for the kind of person we are. And, interestingly enough, we cannot be changed, even by the transforming power of God Himself, until we face up to the responsibility. Only when we admit that we are the ones responsible can the transforming power of God make us into what we long to be. The old Negro spiritual said it so well: "It's me, it's me, oh Lord, standing in the need of prayer."

What Is Your Life?

Kierkegaard, the Danish philosopher, divided men into two groups, the drivers and the drifters. He said that he was tempted to run after every man in the street and ask him: "Are you alert or inert? Master or slave? Creator or creature? Lifter or leaner?" It would be well for us to examine ourselves and try to decide who and what we are. A photographer classified all of his customers as publicans or pharisees after the Biblical story of the Master. He said that the publicans accepted their proofs for what they were and made their choice, but the Pharisees would want more sittings and more proofs and then want the negative retouched extensively. These, he said, refuse to accept themselves for what they are. A golfing friend used to classify preachers according to a golf drive. "That one," he would say, "is a short drive down the middle." Another would be a long drive in the rough, etc. I carefully kept him from classifying me, at least while I was with him, and I noted that he carefully avoided classifying himself.

Why is it that we so carefully wear masks as though we could conceal ourselves from ourselves, or even from God? Adam started the pattern, and we all have followed. The Scriptures tell how God's voice walked in the garden and said, "Adam where are you?" Adam admitted he was hiding. "Why?" asked God. "Because we are naked!" he replied. "Who told you you were naked? Have you disobeyed?"

Could this be the lesson we need to learn? That the basis of sin is that we first think we are more than we are and try to be God? Then, failing in our attempts at Godhood, we become less than we are and try to hide? All the while we are refusing to be what we are! Wasn't this the lesson the prodigal son had to learn—that he wasn't God, able to make up his own rules and control his own destiny; that he was not an animal in a pen, content in the mud; nor was he a servant in his father's household, but a son! Until he recognized this, he never really knew who he was.

So, we must learn. Our identity is not in the outward appearance but in the inner man. A state governor had a famous evangelist in his home for dinner. He had never met or even seen him. When they met, the governor was amazed that the man was very small and almost unattractive. The evangelist noticed the governor's reaction to his appearance and said, "Governor, isn't it wonderful what God can use!"

A violinist owned a rare and expensive Stradivarius violin. Many of the news articles made much of the instrument. During one concert he played the first half and in the midst of one selection raised the violin and crashed it to the floor. The crowd was aghast. He said quietly: "Don't be alarmed. I bought that violin today for a few dollars in a department store. Now I'll get my Stradivarius and finish the concert." His lesson was plain. The music was not in the instrument, but in the man, made in God's image, who played upon it.

You are you because God made you that way. He put you here for this day and hour. What you do with his gift of life is entirely up to you!

On Building Pyramids

One of the great wonders of the ancient world was the great pyramid of Egypt. Its base would cover eight football fields. Over a hundred thousand slaves labored for more than twenty years placing two million limestone blocks into place. Each block weighed two and a half tons. When I stood at its base a few years ago, two college boys with me decided they wanted to climb to its peak. Although, at the time, I wasn't much older than they, I was old enough to know I didn't want to climb forty stories of pyramid with each step three feet or more high when all I could see upon arriving at the peak (assuming I did) would be the sands of the desert. The boys made it with a guide showing them how and were soon waving at us from its peak.

Often since then I have seen in this picture a truth that has helped me understand myself and other people better. You see, we spend much of our time unconsciously building pyramids in our minds and placing ourselves at their peak. The young person who seems to be the nonconformist, the off-beat, is most likely struggling to find his identity; he is building his own personal mental pyramid.

What it means to me is this: if a boy cannot be the smartest and make the best grades, then he may try to be the best athlete or the best musician, or the most popular, or the best dressed. Somewhere he will discover a pyramid where he can stand alone at the peak. If he fails at being outstanding in one of these realms, then he will seek unconsciously to be distinguished in some other way. It may be that he will be the sloppiest, or the worst dressed. It may be that he will have longer hair than others, or a beard. It may be that he will be the loudest, the most vulgar, or the one who is "anti" everything. For the girl, it may be that she will be the dumbest, the wackiest, the wildest, wear the tightest dresses or be the loner. It takes as many forms as there are people, and some of the pyramids can be good as well as bad. The point is that we are competing to be noticed by our peers.

As in everything else, Jesus anticipated us here. He gives us a lesson in true pyramid building, which will solve all of our mental gymnastics. He says to build your pyramid, but place at the apex of it, not yourself or some earthly goal, but place God and being right with Him at the very top. What is He saying? "Seek ye first the Kingdom of God and His righteousness and everything else will take its proper place." He is saying that we will never know who we really are, or be properly related to those around us, until we have properly related ourselves to the God who made us.

Who Am I?

In the story of the prodigal, told so beautifully by the Master, He is sharing with us a glowing picture of every life. We are that prodigal. We are the ones who seek to get away. Many a prodigal has moved into that far distant land, although his feet have never left the father's threshold. Prodigality is an attitude more than an activity. The pigpen can be in a man's heart and mind. Many of us have mentally and morally been a long way from our earthly fathers although we see them daily.

The prodigal in the story did leave home. He spent all of his father's goods in wasted living. And he woke up in the pigpen he had made of his life. Man is a responsible being. He must live in the world he makes for himself. He can't blame another.

When the prodigal came to himself, he looked around and for the first time realized what had happened and who was at fault. He said: "I don't know who I am, but I'm not made for this pigpen life!" Until now, he had thought he was the center of the world. Until now, he had thought himself to be God. It was not until he failed in his attempt at godhood that he came to himself, and when he did, he was willing for the first time to ask the basic question of the universe, "Who am I anyway?" He thought until now he had all the answers, but he finally realized that he didn't even know, had not even asked the right questions. "I don't know who I am, but I am made for finer things than this. My father has slaves that are far better off than I. I will arise and go to my father!"

The beautiful and wonderful truth of it all is this—it wasn't until he got home that his question was answered. When he saw his father running to meet him, when he saw the joy in his father's face, it all became meaningful to the boy: "Why now I know who I am! I am my father's son! This is where I belong! For this I was made." And the father's response? "Kill the fatted calf. My son has found out who he is. He has found himself; he has realized that he is his father's son!"

The true joy of life is living in proper relationship to your Father, and only as we understand and accept our relationship to Him can we have the proper relationship with ourselves and with our brothers.

Who are you? Or rather, whose are you?

Special Days

CHRISTMAS

Some Uses of Christmas

It is evident that many are "using" Christmas for various reasons, mostly for material gain. Its symbols are used to sell every conceivable thing, both good and bad. Christmas does have some very important and valuable "uses," however, and should be used accordingly to serve noble ends. Let me quickly suggest six ennobling uses of this holy season.

Let me suggest, first, that it be used as a season of healthful relaxation and recreation. This may seem to be a strange suggestion to some, but many of our spiritual problems stem from the rushing, frantic pace of everyday living, which allows little time for real relaxation and a proper change of pace. Doesn't it do your heart good to see the usually busy father on Christmas Day tossing the new football with his sons?

Secondly, it should be used for renewing the ties of home. If the coming of Christ into the lowly home of Joseph and Mary suggests anything at all, it stresses the importance, in God's eyes, of a good home. Families should be closer together at Christmastime than at any other time.

My third suggestion is that it be used to patch up some strained relationships. It's really hard to dislike anyone at Christmas. We send a cheery greeting even to those we feel have treated us unkindly. You can't have any real hatred in your heart when you sing, "Peace on earth, good will to men."

Again, it should be a season of remembering the less fortunate. The baby in the manger calls attention to the fact that not all of life's necessities are available to all, so out of our abundance we share.

It is also a season for a return to sentimentality. We grow so burdened and sophisticated, we scarcely realize we have emotions. Everything about Christmas has a soul-stirring quality about it. Nothing stirs the heart like the sight of a newborn babe. Add to this the fact that this Babe is the world's redeemer, and the coldest heart is moved.

And, of course, the Christmas season is a time of drawing near to God through the birth of His Son. Isn't this what God has in mind all of the time? Isn't this perhaps the reason He, the Father, drew near to us in the Son so that we might be drawn closer to one another as His children? This, it seems to me, is the real use of Christmas.

Where Is He?

Almost every phrase of the Christmas story in the Scripture has some message in it, and almost every phrase has been captured in poem, sermon, or song. One question always reaches out and grabs my heartstrings as I read the account of Christ's birth, and it is extremely relevant today. The wise men stop to ask directions. Their question is, "Where is He that is born King of the Jews?"

We have no record as to whom they questioned. If they asked the shepherds on the hillside, the answer would probably have been: "Well, I've heard all my life that the Messiah would come, but I don't expect Him in my lifetime, so I've really paid no attention." If they asked the Pharisee, he probably would have said: "Oh, but this isn't the time for the Messiah. There are yet many things to happen before he comes. I'm in the Sanhedrin, and I'm sure if he were coming, we would be the first to know!" If they had asked at the inn, amid the laughing men, the reply would have been: "A King in this place and in Bethlehem? What fools would ask such a question here?"

Lift the question into the hungry hearts of men the world over and they ask it longingly, hopefully. Job cried out, "O that I knew where I might find him!" The cry echoes around the world as men search for that which alone can satisfy the hunger of their souls.

Lift the question into the arena of today's America and you have an entirely different insight. When Christian people look at all of the decorations, the advertisements, and the exploitation of the Christian season, they say in questioning amazement, "Where is He in all of this?"

Dr. Leonard Griffith tells of a school Christmas drama. The pupils did it themselves. The stable, the manger, the figures of Mary, Joseph, the shepherds, the wise men, the animals were all there, as well as a doll for the baby Jesus. One little fellow kept coming back around looking at the scene in wonder. Finally his puzzled expression attracted the teacher's eye. "Do you have a question, Johnny?" "Yes," he replied. "What I'd like to know is—where does God fit into all of this?"

In the *Saturday Review of Literature* a few years ago this article appeared: "Last night John Elzy, watchman at the Grand Eagle Department Store, while making his rounds of the bargain basement, found the body of a man lying under a counter. He was thin to the point of emaciation, apparently in his middle thirties, and was shabbily dressed. His pockets were empty and there were no marks of identification upon his person. Store officials believe that he was trampled to death in the Christmas rush and crawled under the counter for shelter. But they are unable to account for what appears to be nail wounds in his hands! The police are investigating."

Where is He?

A Christmas Meditation

What do you want for Christmas? We hear it over and over. The children make out long lists. One boy, a few years ago, wanted "his two front teeth." A young man may want nothing more than a portable radio with white sidewalls and power steering. A young woman may want only a small diamond with the right young man attached to it.

We might really be surprised at what some people would like to have for Christmas . . . or for anytime for that matter. A kindly word, a friendly smile, or a warm handclasp might do wonders to many a heart. What should we really want for Christmas? Knowing the day, the season, the meaning of it all . . . what should we really want and expect from it?

Let me share with you a few of the things I personally would like to have that are suggested from the season and its meaning.

I wish for all a real spirit of joy. The angels told of glad tidings for all people—not just for family and friends, not just for neighbors and close associates, but for all mankind. If there is any meaning at all in Christmas it is its universal meaning. Not a particular group or a particular nationality, or a particular race or a particular social level, but all are to hear and rejoice over the good news, the glad tidings. Our faith is to be a joyous one because we share it with all the world.

A second thing I wish for is an understanding heart. God's way is the way of concern, of truly caring, of trying to understand all people and their needs. One Polish refugee mother brought her sons to our land. They got caught up in the American way of celebrating Christmas: Santa Claus became a reality to them. She knew her limited funds and tried to discourage them, but they were not to be held back. They insisted on going into one of the large stores to see Santa.

They approached him in reverence and awe. He took them upon his knee, and excitedly, they began to speak to him in their own tongue. That special Santa happened to be a Polish man who answered them in their language. Their faces lighted up, and they shouted to their mother, "He understands us, he understands us." Perhaps the world's greatest need is for an understanding heart.

I wish too for the spirit of a child. I grow weary of the pseudointellectualism that looks down in cynicism at the beautiful simplicity of this season. It was a Babe that started it all, you know. And this One said, "Except ye become as this child. . . ." If we could have a childlike faith, a childlike openness, a childlike honesty, and a childlike expressiveness, our joy would be as boundless as theirs.

I wish further that we could get the spirit of giving that is truly Christian. "Thanks be to God for His unspeakable gift. . . ." What was that gift? It was the best that God could give—Himself! That is what Christmas giving is all about. Your friends will appreciate your gift, but, more than all else, they will appreciate the fact that you remembered to give. If your parents are still around, they will appreciate more than all else your giving of yourself. This is true of all of us, but particularly to those who are home for Christmas, or who are going home. It's nice to see old friends, to rest awhile, to relax a bit, but the best gift to your parents is yourself. Stop a little, sit and visit, share experiences, and give yourself to those you love.

The same thing is true in your relationship to Christ Himself. The best you have to offer to Him is yourself.

EASTER

What a Difference a Day Makes

You've thought about it, haven't you? One special day can made a great deal of difference to you. Sometimes it makes a great deal of difference because things are much brighter; sometimes things are darker. The change can be for good or ill. One day does make a difference though.

Thomas Edison was one day a discouraged tinkerer on the verge of a great discovery that eluded him. The next day the experiment succeeded and he had an incandescent bulb that worked! One day William Carey was a shoe cobbler, the next day a foreign missionary. One day Gerald Ford was a frustrated vice-president of the United States, the next day, president. What a difference a day can make.

Of all the lessons Easter teaches, this one is the most clearly defined. One day made all the difference in the world.

One day the followers of Jesus were a discouraged, puzzled, confused people. Their leader, whom they had believed was indeed the Messiah promised of God, had been slain in the most disgraceful way. He had been buried and the tomb sealed. Their world had collapsed. Then suddenly, at the next day's dawning He had risen from the grave. He appeared before them; He broke bread and blessed it; He thrust Thomas's hand in His pierced side. It was indeed true. He lives!! He lives!! What a difference a day makes.

What a difference this day would make if you would let the risen Christ become your Saviour and the Lord of your life. What a difference this day would make if we as Christians would really take Christ at His word. What a difference it would make if we would really accept the fact that it is more blessed to give than to receive, that we should love our neighbors as ourselves, that we can only live by dying to self, that the pure in heart see God and the meek inherit the earth. We, as Christians, accept these things as being true, but what a difference it would make if we really lived them.

Easter Sunday is the day that makes all the difference in the world. It stands as living proof that Jesus of Nazareth is indeed the Christ of God. He lives, and "because He lives, I too, I too shall live."

The Song of Easter

Maybe your mind does not work like this, but mine does.

When I read, my mind visualizes and my ears hear music. The problem is that I am not an artist, nor am I truly a musician, so these sights and sounds cannot be given proper expression.

What do you see and hear when you read the Easter story? Let me share with you the things I hear, and perhaps you can put it to music and share it with the world.

The Song of Easter is a song
  filled with minor chords and solemn words
    the "lento" movements of a Man
      carrying a cross—a heavy
        cross—and a heavier heart.
A man bruised and beaten
  sinless, but dying for sinners.

It is a song filled with the "agitato" movements of the
  jeering throng—
    the priests with dignity and calling forgotten
      the soldiers trying to do their duty
        the screaming mob who only a
          week before had cried "Hosanna."

It is a story filled with the "affettuso" moods of
  a weeping mother
    and weeping friends
      and heartbroken fearful disciples.

It has the "dirge" movements of death—of the clanging—
  of hammer on nail
    of the whistling deadly spear.

But—through it all are the pastorale strains of love
  and tenderness, grace and mercy.

In it—this Song of Easter—is the militant march of the
King.
    "Who is the King of Glory?
      The Lord Strong and Mighty
        He is the King of Glory!"

It is the song filled with the "brilliantes" and "allegros"
    of victory
      of triumph over sin
        over death
          and the grave.

It is the song only understood by sinners who know their
need
    and who turn penitent heads
      to call Him Lord.

And all who turn to Him will live—
    because He lives!

Messages From an Empty Tomb

A newspaper report about an Easter Sunrise Service
stated: "It began at five-thirty and was over just after the
dawn!" Far too often this is true. Far too many of us have
just such a narrow understanding of the resurrection. We
tie it in with Easter Sunday and give little, if any, thought to
it at other times. This is, of course, to miss the lessons of
the event. The stone wasn't rolled away from the tomb to
let the Christ out but to let us in that we might learn the
lessons the empty tomb has for us.

If the empty tomb does anything, it shouts outward through the opened door that new life is possible because of the Risen Lord. The Light shining forth from this "one-of-a-kind" burial place illumines all of life and reveals its meaning and deathlessness.

Too often we think of the resurrection only in the realm of the ultimate resurrection of the soul. We separate man into soul and body like the ancient Greeks. Man is not a dichotomy, however. He is one. When we speak of the resurrection, we speak of the resurrected man, of his personhood raised to new dimensions of living, not only ultimately in the final resurrection, but here and now! The resurrection does, of course, light up the mysteries of death, but it also teaches us that man's life in Christ is raised to new vistas of service and meaningfulness. Its immediate message is that we do not have to stay the way we are.

The resurrection validated all of the claims of Jesus concerning Himself, as well as the claims His disciples made concerning Him. It also, however, put God's eternal stamp upon the Christlike life. Why is it that when we are made for this kind of life, we so rarely live it or see it in others? Why when we are created for meaningful, authentic existence do we spend so much of our time in meaningless, inauthentic living? The answer can only be that we have missed the message of the resurrection. The Light from the tomb bursts forth to reveal to us that in the Resurrected One is Life, here and now. Real life that can only be claimed and lived by faith! Real life that has a deathlessness in it simply because God thinks it is worthy of being continued endlessly—that it is His idea of what life really is! The resurrection is trying to shout something to us through all the clamour and noise of this world. Its message is that we are to live the resurrected life now!

That our minds, attitudes, relationships, goals, and motives are to be resurrected and made new. It is telling us that we are to walk away from every visit with the Resurrected One, renewed to walk in newness of life.

Why did the custom of wearing new clothes on Easter Sunday originate? Because it was spring? No. It came from a theological understanding of the resurrection: resurrected people have to have some clothes to wear, and a resurrected person is indeed a new person, so new clothes are needed! Isn't this what Paul is saying: "For God who commanded the light to shine out of darkness, hath shined in our hearts, to give the light of the knowledge of God in the face of Jesus Christ—if any man be in Christ he is a new creature: old things are passed away; behold, all things are new."

This is resurrected living! This is real living!

THANKSGIVING

Recapturing the Pilgrim Faith

The year has gone by so swiftly in this good day in which we live. I wonder if that first year went swiftly for the Pilgrims? I doubt it. It was a difficult year. Many of the group of settlers died from sickness; many were slain by hostile Indians; few had enough to eat; all were lonely, insecure and uncertain. Yet after that first year, after the first small harvest, Governor Bradford called for a day of thanksgiving. Their first holiday did not celebrate the anniversary of a conqueror, the birthday of a statesman, the end of a war, or even a military victory. It simply was the expression of thanks by a humble people to their God for His protection and leadership. The holiday is distinctively ours as Americans, proclaimed by our president each year. We are not ordered to give thanks, but we are reminded of the blessings we enjoy as a nation and are asked to recall that "our help cometh from the Lord who made heaven and earth." Since this is our holiday, we would do well to stop this week and try to recapture some of the spirit of our founding fathers. Let me then suggest that we seek to recapture:

I. A Simple Faith in God

There are several kinds of atheists in our world. Some are academic atheists who say there is no God because they cannot comprehend Him. There are also militant atheists who disbelieve that there is a God and who want to make all believe as they do. On the other hand, and there are many, many more of these, there are practical atheists. These say that there is a God and then live as though He does not exist. Many of us fit into this category, don't we? We say we believe in Him, yet we do not pray, we do not meditate, we do not contribute to His work, we attend worship services almost casually, and we do not live as He has commanded us to live. How hypocritical we are. We say we love our neighbors, yet we do not know their names. We say we want peace, yet insist that our government be armed to the teeth. We say we want less central government, yet we want more subsidies for our own special interests. We say we love, but our attitudes often prove differently. We lie and call it expediency. We cheat and call it good business. We say we love God, but many of us spend more money on one football weekend than we give to God in a year.

Our Pilgrim fathers had a simple faith in God. Whatever their faults and their inconsistencies, they believed quite simply in Almighty God, and this faith shaped their thinking and their lives.

II. A Strong Dependence Upon God

They recognized that God was under all that they did. What blessings they had they knew came from Him. We need to recapture this sense of God's ownership of all things. "The earth is the Lord's and the fulness thereof," the Scripture says. It is He who has given us all things, even our ability to gain wealth.

When will we learn? Under everything that we have is God. We are using His laws, His materials, His air, and His life principles. Under all of our achievements as men is the sustaining hand of our creator. Faithful stewards recognize this truth. They know that all things are God's, and they return to Him that which He requires of us as His stewards. We need to recapture this sense of real stewardship of all of life if we are to be truly Christian.

III. A Sense of Mission Under God

Although the historians do not agree on just how spiritual all of these Pilgrim fathers really were, many do agree that these people came seeking a new place to live, a new opportunity; and many came seeking a place to worship God as they saw fit. These felt that God had indeed brought them to the good land.

Through the years there has been this underlying spirit running through our nation. We are "one nation under God!" Our coins say, "In God we trust." Although we fall far short of these noble ideals, they should undergird all of our thoughts and actions.

The city of Damascus is one of the oldest cities in the world. The reason it has survived, they tell us, is that there runs through its gutters and sewers a stream of fresh water that flows from a spring rising in Mt. Herman. This fresh water daily washes the city and keeps it surprisingly clean and fresh. Such has been the undercurrent of Christian faith and mission throughout this land of ours.

IV. A Sincere Gratitude Toward God

Shakespeare said: "God's goodness hath been great to thee—let not day nor night pass but still remember what the Lord hath done!" We are to know that all things come from Him and must learn to be grateful and to express our gratitude in true thanksgiving. Let us thank Him day by day, in public and in private, in song and in the life we live. Let us thank Him at all times, under all circumstances. Joyce Kilmer said, "Thank God for God!"

Let us then strive to recapture these four simple but profound thoughts that symbolize the spirit of the founders of our nation: a simple faith in God, a strong dependence upon God, a sense of mission under God, and a sincere gratitude for and to God.

A Thanksgiving Prayer

O Lord, Our God . . .

So often we come rushing into Thy presence as a child rushes in to ask his earthly father for a dime to buy a trinket.

So often our prayers are so rushed we end them having never really prayed at all.

Often we are so filled with our own desires and imagined needs that we have no thought or feeling of gratitude.

So at this time of thanksgiving give us the gift of Thy quietness that we might be still and know that Thou art

God and that all things come from Thee. Give us Thy calmness so that we may linger in Thy presence. Grant us the gift of Thy Spirit that He might help us give utterance to the gratitude we know we feel.

Now, Lord, having already received the answer to our prayer we become aware of all that Thou hast done for us. We see the scales, the balances of life before us. On one side we see those many calamities, worries, trials, and fears, imagined or real, from which Thou hast delivered us. On the other side we see the many obvious evidences of Thy love and care. With the help of the Spirit we are enabled to see the many additional blessings Thou poured upon us, unmerited and often unobserved.

For all these we simply thank you, Lord.

But most of all we thank You that we have Someone to thank—how empty life would be without this. In Jesus name. Amen.

PATRIOTIC

Experiencing Democracy

A person living in a land of totalitarianism experiences democracy for a brief moment when he sees a citizen of our land. One minister visiting in a Polish village only a few weeks after the hostilities ceased in Europe, picked his way with his interpreter through the debris. As he passed the town hall, a group of men seemed unusually interested in the American and watched his every movement. After they had passed by, the interpreter turned to the minister and asked: "Would you like to know what they said as you passed by?" "What did they say?" he asked. "They said, 'there goes democracy'!" In the fleeting moment, they had experienced democracy because they had seen an American.

Imagine what it is to such a person to receive a visa allowing him to come to our country, and imagine his shock and disappointment upon living here awhile and finding out that so many Americans never really participate in keeping the democracy they enjoy. So many receive so much and do so very little and seem to appreciate not at all the blessings they have.

What a shock it must be to the immigrant who has never had a chance to vote as a free man to find that almost half of our American citizens never bother to vote. When we vote, we have the opportunity in a very real way to experience democracy. Harold Blake Walker in the *Presbyterian Tribune* says: "A man should not say, 'I live in a democracy,' but rather, 'I experienced democracy last Tuesday when I entered the voting booth and cast my vote for it'!"

How sad that so many privileged people, citizens of a free land, never really do anything but live in a democracy, as though that were their inalienable right. Unless we all experience democracy, it may well be that one day not one of us will even live in one!

"Let Freedom Ring"

On this July Fourth we are thinking about the freedom that we enjoy as American citizens. In 1776 our struggling little nation cast off the shackles of the old world and became a free nation. Our Fathers built this nation on a dream, on an idea. They believed that man could rule himself—that men could bind themselves together voluntarily as free men and could govern themselves. Throughout these years we as Americans have kept this dream and have struggled with it and watched it grow. It has not been an automatic thing, for there have always been those who would try to take it from us or demand that some at least not be free. It has perhaps suffered most from its friends who have taken it for granted and who have not realized that freedom must be nurtured and cared for and carefully protected and earned by each succeeding generation. But today we are free and we "praise the Power that hath made and preserved us a nation!"

There is another kind of freedom that many here and around the world have not discovered and do not enjoy. It is the freedom that can only come through Jesus the Christ. "If the Son therefore shall make you free, you shall be free indeed!" It would be well to look briefly at this freedom while we rejoice in the freedom we enjoy as Americans. This freedom can be appreciated by even the slave in chains, for he can, although enslaved, be free indeed.

What did Jesus mean about being free indeed? He did not mean freedom from hardship, suffering, and trials. In His own life He did not experience such freedom. He was not speaking about freedom from trials, testings, or temptations. What would life be like if we had no challenges like these to face, to meet and conquer? He did not mean freedom from the natural physical laws of the universe, for we all live within these day by day.

What did He mean then by being free indeed. He meant freedom from sin, from the guilt of past sins, from anxieties about tomorrow and its sins and temptations, and concern over today and what it has to offer.

Free indeed! This is the greatest freedom of all. It is more distressing to realize that some who profess to know the Christ of the Cross are burdened with guilt and besetting sins. Jesus said it clearly: "If you obey my teaching you are really my disciples; you will know the truth, and the truth shall make you free. If the Son makes you free, then you are really free!"

Let freedom ring—freedom from anything that enslaves the minds, bodies, and souls of men!

"Unity in Diversity"

No one ever thought it could happen! The very idea of a people as different from one another as those who peopled the American colonies ever uniting and living at peace with one another was preposterous. Thomas Paine in his *Rights of Man* said it this way: "If there is a country in the world where concord, according to common calculation would be least expected, it is America. Made up, as it is of people from different nations, accustomed to different forms and habits of government, speaking different languages, and more different in their modes of worship, it would appear that the union of such a people was impracticable. But by the simple operation of constructing government on the principles of society and the rights of man, every difficulty retires, and the parts are brought into cordial unison."

This doesn't mean Americans have always agreed! This is where we are misled today, I think. We have gotten the idea that a unified people need be of one mind on all issues, but it is not so. Presidents have been elected by only a vote or two; never has one been voted in unanimously. Many, many people didn't really desire to declare independence from Britain. Indeed the signers were persecuted, and many did ultimately sacrifice all properties but never their "sacred honor."

A great nation can be unified on the dream of free responsible men and women governing themselves while still differing widely on how this can best be accomplished. The mark of a true freedom-loving citizen is the ability to disagree and still be agreeable.

Perhaps the greatest diversity of thought in early America was between John Adams and Thomas Jefferson. They started out together in their desire for freedom, and for a free nation, and both played key roles in establishing our nation. But they soon parted, each joining opposing parties. When Jefferson was elected president, Adams refused to attend the Inauguration, and for years they ignored each other. Finally a friend intervened, and Adams broke down and wrote Jefferson. From that letter followed a stream of correspondence that continued through the years. They differed on many things, but they united in their love for our country and their deep regard for each other.

On July 4, 1826, Adams lay dying. His family heard him say, "Thomas Jefferson still lives!" But he was wrong. That same day in Virginia, Thomas Jefferson had already died.

On many things they were poles apart in their thinking, but in their desire to establish a great nation, "Under God, indivisible, with liberty and justice for all," they were in complete unity.

This dream, yet unrealized in many ways, still unites the hearts of loyal Americans. May it one day come true!

Young People

How Can You Know That You're in Love?

Through the years, this question has been asked literally hundreds of times. Perhaps the following test will help you if you find yourself seeking the Lord's will in this most important decision of finding life's partner.

Let me begin by saying that love is basically a committal of life to another, and I believe therefore that you can fall in love with whomever you want to fall in love. The songwriters and motion picture writers do not agree. To them love is some sort of reaction that cannot be controlled or directed. It is my conviction that you should fall in love with your head as well as your heart. How sad it is that too often young people become physically attracted to one another, and even physically involved, before they ever put their brains into gear to think about what kind of husband or wife, or father or mother, either of them would be.

One other thing—just because two people are in love doesn't mean that they should marry. One of them might already be married to someone else; or one might be a lazy individual with low ideals and no goals in life; or one might even be approaching alcoholism. No, just because you are in love doesn't mean you should marry. You might be too young to be ready for marriage, or perhaps need to finish your education first.

159

How can you tell if you are in love? Answer correctly and sincerely the following questions. They are not as simple as they appear. Study them carefully. Each question is loaded with meaning and implication.

1. Does he (or she) offer me the kind of life I want? (Socially, morally, economically, vocationally, religiously.)
2. Would I be proud to introduce him (or her) as my mate? (After the glow of the honeymoon, marriage is a mutual admiration society.)
3. Would I want my children to call him daddy (or her, mother)? (Your children will be just like him or her.)
4. Do we share the same spiritual goals and ideals? (Your faith is needed most in crisis times. It is important for you to be together here.)
5. Would I want to look at him (or her) across the breakfast table for the rest of my life? (Have your pictures taken when you first get up in the morning and exchange them. Put the picture on the other side of the breakfast table. If a month later you can still swallow, you may have the real thing.)

Are you really in love? Remember, puppy love leads to a dog's life. Love at first sight may simply mean that he's in love and she's a sight.

This is one of the greatest decisions of your life. Seek God's leadership earnestly. Conduct yourself during your courtship in such a way that you can honestly kneel before the Lord on your wedding night to thank God for leading you together and to ask His blessings on the home you have established in His name.

Worrying About the Wrong Generation

Everyone shares a deep concern about the youth of our day. Some are quick to pigeonhole all young people as "wild" or "bad," or "hopeless." Others are honestly concerned, striving to find ways to help the young meet life's problems and not be downed by them. Some want to be overprotective and want to deny the young person the right to make his own mistakes. Some wish to be too permissive and not give proper guidance and light. There must always be a balance between the extremes, but whatever is done must be done in love and because of love.

Actually, I think the emphasis is wrong. A New York columnist told that on New Year's Eve his high-school-age son asked for the car. All that night the parents stayed home, turning down invitations, because they were worried about the boy and wanted to be home should he need them and call. About midnight, the phone rang. "There has been an automobile accident," the girl at the desk of the local hospital said. "One of the persons involved wanted me to tell you not to worry. He is going to be all right!" "Thank God!" sighed the columnist. Then the girl continued, "It is your father!" Later the writer telling about it said: "I guess we had been worrying about the wrong generation."

That is our trouble, isn't it? We should be more concerned about the fathers than we are about the sons. Particularly is this true if the boys are in church. The modern day church, with its varied programs, offers the youth of today experiences and training that many of the parents have not been privileged to have. The youth are faithful to the church and its program. It is the father who brings the child and goes back home to read his newspaper or go to the golf course. The boy learns what it is to witness; the father never does. The boy learns what a true steward of all God's blessings really must do; the father never is exposed to this training.

The youth of today are led astray by adults. They purchase the marijuana and the benzedrine pills from adults. They are exposed to obscenity by adults and purchase their pornography from adults.

We've been worrying about the wrong generation! Our thrust as a church should be, must be, to witness to and win the parents. To train the child and not to train the parent is to add confusion to confusion.

Listen fathers—this is for you. Search your hearts; you are the ones who can do so much. For you, the church and community wait. For you, your son and daughter wait. What kind of example are you setting in morality, faithfulness to God and His church, Christian stewardship, and basic honesty?

"Until a boy is fourteen he does what his father says," stated Dr. Pierce Harris. "After fourteen, he does what the father does."

Miscellaneous

How Do You Think of God?

In our rushing, busy, noisy world, we need to stop from time to time and regroup our forces. "In quietness and in confidence shall be your strength," says the prophet Isaiah. Dr. James Reid in his book, *The Springs of Life*, states that "the key to the discovery of God is in listening, trusting, obeying. As we think of Him and are still, there comes a voice, and a road opens. It may be a hard road, a shadowed way. But as we step out on it, light breaks and into the heart comes a peace that makes us sure that we are one with him." Dr. R. L. Middleton in his wonderful book entitled, *Thinking About God*, suggests that there is nothing more exciting for a Christian to do than to think of the compassion of God, the gentleness of God, the mercy of God, the solicitude of God, and the grace of God.

Let me share a little guideline to thinking about God. God deals with individual men and women. He has chosen to work in and through them to accomplish His holy purposes. Try this mental exercise then:

Remember Adam and think of Him as Creator
Remember Noah and recall His Righteousness
Remember the Ark and think of Redemption
Remember Abraham and know He calls men
Remember Lot's wife and know He hates sin
Remember Sinai and keep His Commandments

Remember the Cloud and the Fiery Pillar and follow
   his leading
Remember Elijah and stand tall before kings
Remember David, repent and receive a new heart
Remember Esther and know that you have come for
   such a time as this
Remember Isaiah and volunteer for service
Remember the prophets and weep for man's foolish-
   ness and sin
Remember Bethlehem and kneel to adore
Remember John the Baptist and behold the Lamb of
   God
Remember Jesus and hear his parables, see his gen-
   tleness, feel his love and concern
Remember Calvary and cry for forgiveness
Remember the empty tomb and know you too shall
   live
Remember Thomas and cry, "My Lord and My God"
Remember Olivet and seek a lost world
Remember Pentecost and let the Spirit control
Remember Paul and know nothing but Jesus Christ
   our crucified, risen Lord

You see how it works? When you stop and get quiet
and let your mind take a walk with God, there is no
stopping place nor limit to your wanderings.

Dr. Reid is right! He concludes, "The root of our problem is the neglect of thinking about God. But when we
really think about Him, we have our hand on a door that
will lead us out into a new world.

How Do You Spell Tomorrow?

In graduation season, from kindergarten to college, we

honor our graduates. In all of this, much will be said about tomorrow—about the graduate facing tomorrow. This is important, of course. Attitude toward life and its meaning determines the kind of meaning we put into life. Or, to put it another way, how you spell "tomorrow" means much. Some spell it "t-o-y!" Some spell it "d-u-t-y!" Others spell it "t-r-u-s-t" or "c-h-a-l-l-e-n-g-e." A few spell it "w-o-r-k." Some spell it "w-e-a-l-t-h," some "m-i-s-s-i-o-n;" others spell it "f-r-e-e f-r-o-m a-u-t-h-o-r-i-t-y!" The cynic spells it "n-o-t-h-i-n-g!" How do you spell it? As you can see, it makes a great difference. Some of these spellings would be more than adequate. Perhaps one of the clearest spellings, and one of the most meaningful, would be "o-p-p-o-r-t-u-n-i-t-y." This would say much.

To the thoughtful person, however, there is only one way to spell tomorrow. It is spelled "t-o-d-a-y." There can be no other spelling, really. One of the illusions of life is that this present hour is not the critical, decisive hour. The great delusion of man is that he will get everything done tomorrow. This is your day! Seneca said: "The greatest loss of time is delay and expectation, which depend upon the future. We let go of the present, which we have in our power, and look forward to that which depends on chance—and so relinquish certainty for uncertainty."

This is your day. Live it well. How many foolish acts of today will cloud all of our tomorrows. How many things unsaid today will haunt us tomorrow. How many neglected opportunities today will leave us empty tomorrow.

On the other hand, how many victories will be won tomorrow because of proper decisions made today. How many rough places in the road of life will be smoother because the student has learned his lessons well today. How many precious memories will enhance tomorrow because today has been filled with joy and good living.

So the question is wrongly put! It isn't so important how you spell tomorrow! It is rather, how do you spell today?

We Need Each Other

It is really strange. In this day of technology and men walking on the moon, we are still centuries behind in the most fundamental, yet most important, relationship in life. Like Cain and Abel we have still not learned to live together as brothers. The question, "Who is my neighbor?" directed toward the master Teacher is still being asked today.

It is time we learned the answer. As God told Cain, this kind of sin is like a wild beast ready to pounce on us and devour us. If we do not learn it soon, it will be too late.

We have stressed differences between people. What we need to emphasize is that we are more alike than different. Paul reminded his readers very clearly that from the basic standpoint of our relationship to God, we are all the same: "There is no difference—all have sinned and come short of God's glory!" All of us need a Saviour. All of us hunger and thirst; all of us suffer pain and anguish; all of us cry more frequently than we admit; all of us know that we are more than clay, that we have a desire to reach beyond our grasp. We all know that the true way of happiness is to live peaceably together, each trying to make some contribution that will benefit all.

In this day when news is bounced via satellite from continent to continent, when jet planes tie nations together daily, when international trade is the only means of survival for all of us, we need to realize that this is one world and that we need each other.

A Rockefeller Foundation report said it this way: "An American soldier wounded on a battlefield in the Far East owes his life to the Japanese scientist Kitasato, who isolated the bacillus of tetanus. A Russian soldier saved by a blood transfusion is indebted to Landsteiner, an Austrian. A German is shielded from typhoid fever with the help of a Russian, Metchnikoff. A Dutch marine in the East Indies is protected from malaria because of the experiments of an Italian, Grassi; while a British aviator in North Africa escapes death from surgical infection because a Frenchman, Pasteur, and a German, Koch, elaborated a new technique.

In peace as in war we are beneficiaries of knowledge contributed by every nation in the world. Our children are protected from diphtheria by what a Japanese and a German did; they are protected from smallpox by the work of an Englishman; they are saved from rabies because of a Frenchman; they are cured of pellagra through the researches of an Austrian. From birth to death they are surrounded by an invisible host—the spirits of men who never thought in terms of flags or boundary lines and who never served a lesser loyalty than the welfare of mankind."